MW00655627

MUTUAL INTEREST

Glassworks

MUTUAL INTEREST

A NOVEL

OLIVIA
WOLFGANG-SMITH

BLOOMSBURY PUBLISHING

NEW YORK • LONDON • OXFORD • NEW DELHI • SYDNEY

BLOOMSBURY PUBLISHING
Bloomsbury Publishing Inc.
1385 Broadway, New York, NY 10018, USA

BLOOMSBURY, BLOOMSBURY PUBLISHING, and the Diana logo
are trademarks of Bloomsbury Publishing Plc

First published in the United States 2025

ISBN: HB: 978-1-63973-332-3; EBOOK: 978-1-63973-333-0

LIBRARY OF CONGRESS CATALOGING-IN-PUBLICATION DATA IS AVAILABLE

2 4 6 8 10 9 7 5 3 1

Typeset by Westchester Publishing Services
Printed and bound in the U.S.A.

To find out more about our authors and books visit www.bloomsbury.com and
sign up for our newsletters.

Bloomsbury books may be purchased for business or promotional use. For information
on bulk purchases please contact Macmillan Corporate and Premium Sales Department at
specialmarkets@macmillan.com.

After many
Toward more

Marriage . . . should not be based, as it so often is, upon mere physical attraction, but upon the higher plane of mind and character. Marriage is a partnership, in which each partner has equal duties and equal rights.

—FRANCES WILLARD, *OCCUPATIONS FOR WOMEN*, 1897

Who invented all these improvements? . . . The answer is always the same; everybody and nobody, a will always under control, an ever-watchful eye, an intrepid search for novelty, and an insatiable longing for improvement, which, so far, seems to me the most marked feature of American civilization.

—PAUL BOURGET, *OUTRE-MER: IMPRESSIONS OF AMERICA*, 1895

> *Essential Oils—are wrung—*
> *The Attar from the Rose*
> *Be not expressed by Suns—alone—*
> *It is the gift of Screws—*

—EMILY DICKINSON, CA. 1862–64

MUTUAL INTEREST

PRELUDE

They called 1816 the Year Without a Summer.
Mount Tambora, acting on a timeline much too profound in scale to note that it was then part of the Dutch East Indies, erupted in the largest volcanic event in recorded history. The explosion took thousands of local lives and one third of the mountain itself, leaving a crater half a mile deep and four across. Tsunamis, monsoons, epidemics swept the world. In Ireland, there was typhus. In Bengal, cholera. In New England, snow in July. Tephra in the atmosphere deflected solar radiation, causing crop failures across the Northern Hemisphere. The price of anything edible rose faster than the flooding rivers. Livestock starved. A national emergency was declared in Switzerland, where the food riots were the worst. For months ash billowed and married itself to water vapor—brown snow in Hungary; red in Italy.

The sunsets were unusually spectacular.

In fact, the volcano erupted a year before the stolen season. It was April 1815: three weeks into Napoleon's Hundred Days, two months before Waterloo. The world was otherwise occupied. An entire summer, its weather largely unremarked upon, fell between the eruption and the Year Without a Summer.

But we are all familiar, aren't we, with the universe's peculiar sense of timing. The pause between the flash of light and the sonic boom. The freeze under the touch of an unwelcome hand. The stalled moment preceding fight or flight, resistance or capitulation.

First, before panic or pain: delay. Why should Earth be any different from the rest of us?

The Year Without a Summer is neither the beginning nor the end of this story, but time and cause unravel in all directions, and we find a hollow, simplifying comfort in Capital Letters. The Dutch East Indies. The Hundred Days. A pin in the map, legitimizing both the pin and the map itself. It is a false ease, but the world is too complicated to look straight in the eye, and we require a starting point—even an invented one.

More besides death and despair came out of the Year Without a Summer. (This tension, too, is a universal constant.) Turner painted the ash-veiled sunsets. The unseasonable weather trapped Mary Shelley's party in their Swiss vacation villa, where they shared a challenge to pass the time: write something to frighten us.

And the sudden expiration of so many of the world's horses, whether by starvation or by merciful bullet, created a transportation gap.

Enter the dandy horse. Picture a bicycle with wooden carriage wheels and no pedals, a balance board for the wrists in the place of handlebars. To steer, the hands are held close to the chest—as if the rider were either anxious about something they cannot articulate or mimicking a Tyrannosaurus rex. The vehicle is propelled by pushing the feet along the ground, paddling like a terrestrial duck. A ridiculous, unsettling contraption—slow-motion, yet hyperspeed; playful, yet inspired by global catastrophe.

From the dandy horse—banned from New York to Calcutta, for pedestrian collisions and for calling attention to the vulnerability and silliness and improbable shape of the human body—decades later, of course, came the bicycle.

PART I

ONE

A pin in our map: Vivian Lesperance of Utica, New York, rode her
first safety bicycle on her seventeenth birthday. It was April 10, 1898.
Ten thousand miles away, Mount Tambora observed with geological
indifference the eighty-third anniversary of its new shape. (Vivian had
never heard of the Year Without a Summer. Do we begrudge her this?
Or is the natural lifespan of a memory something less than fourscore
years?)

Vivian wasn't pedaling. She was cupped in the handlebars like an off-
kilter figurehead, stomach swooping and feet splayed, skirt knotted at the
knee and fluttering. Leaning back against the braced forearms of Patience
Stone, whom Vivian's parents called a tomboy but who wasn't, because
despite cropping her hair like Joan of Arc she'd won Queen of the Snow
Ball two years running. Patience Stone, Vivian thought, simply knew how
to do more than one thing. This talent the Lesperances, small-minded
and suspicious, could not name—and so she was a tomboy, because that
at least was something they could sneer at.

"Hold still," Patience said, and Vivian tried. She was drunk: a birthday
slug of whiskey from Ruf Thomas, her father's underpaid apprentice at
Lesperance Carpentry. Tipsy, Vivian found it was thrillingly easy to lean
into each bend in the road, but difficult to stop once she'd begun. Patience
nudged her to the center. "No such thing as tomboy," Vivian gasped, as

if continuing a conversation—then they crested the next hill, and the ecstatic wind stole her next words from her throat.

Truth be told, Vivian hadn't needed the whiskey to wax bitter toward her parents. All afternoon she'd been favoring her own battered ego like a wounded limb—ever since, rather than wishing her many happy returns, her mother and father had observed the anniversary of her birth with another improvised speech, another collaborative catalog of the certain suffering that awaited her in adulthood. (If necessary, they always seemed to imply, by their own hands.)

The morning's thesis had been a familiar one: Vivian was developing; soon, she would have to marry. There was not, after all, enough money in the household to indulge an old maid.

Inevitably (Vivian's mother had amended) she would choose poorly—she had, in the neighborhood, only poor choices.

For instance (Vivian's father had interjected), did she think they hadn't noticed her spending time with the Thomas boy?

Mrs. Lesperance's rejoinder could not quite be called a defense of her daughter: the girl might as well, she'd said; she stood little chance to do better. But she should remember, they'd not take her back at the first sign of trouble.

From there things had devolved into a typical patchwork of barbed asides, comments that skewered Vivian's composure without ever being precisely directed at her. Perhaps, her parents mused, she *would* end up an old maid, and they could all starve to death on sawdust together.

Or else she'd find work—something poorly paid, or dangerous, or ill-reputed.

Or else, more likely, she would fail to do so.

Or else, or else, or else.

It was typical, this muddied litany of future sins and punishments. Today, as on many days, it had driven Vivian stubbornly out of the house in search of whatever her parents would disapprove of most.

First there had been Ruf and his flask. And then Patience Stone had arrived, as if special-ordered for Vivian's purposes—even delivering herself by bicycle.

Gravel skidded beneath their wheels; Patience ducked low and rested her chin, just for a moment, on Vivian's shoulder. The other girl's hair was damp against Vivian's cheek—whether with sweat or Oriskany creek-water or lavender eau de toilette, Vivian couldn't have said. Patience was well-groomed, as adventuresses went. Vivian shivered.

Really, she was certain, her parents hated Patience not because she was a tomboy but because Vivian liked her. As with Ruf Thomas; as with anything at all, really. This spiteful push and pull, Vivian thought, was the simple formula that kept their household spinning. They were a family of polemicists: her parents' opinions, and her own actions, were chosen only in opposition to one another.

Someday—the thought was vapor amid the whiskey fumes—this philosophy would rip her to shreds.

The accuracy of this prediction will perhaps be assessed in future chapters. And of the Lesperances' strange attitude toward their only living child, we will have more to say, presently. But before we leave the subject of Patience, we are compelled to correct Vivian's self-centered explanation of her parents' disdain for her friend: in fact, the Lesperances had held a grudge against the Stones and their set dating back to the excavation of the Erie Canal (from which Patience's grandfather had profited handsomely). The details of this one-sided feud are, frankly, too tedious and manufactured to divert us. Suffice it to say that Patience's forebears had seemed to prosper wherever Vivian's had struggled, and the Lesperances had consolidated their sense of disappointment until they found it possible to blame the Stones for complaints ranging from the failure of the Lesperances' ancestors to purchase land in what was now the city center, to the failure of any of Vivian's four older siblings to live past infancy. (Vivian's anomalous survival had been difficult, for many years, to trust. Prophylactically, and with unfortunate success, her parents had restrained themselves from forming any excessive attachment to her.) To Mr. and Mrs. Lesperance, devoted curators of vast and inarticulate pain, the Stones were convenient, unwitting enemies. Any other well-heeled family might have served them just as well.

Alas, Vivian was not privy to all this context—only its visible symptoms. And though she would not have admitted it, her parents' disapproval of Patience Stone *did* lend her a certain allure as a companion. To say nothing of the girl's access to such luxuries as Florida oranges and safety bicycles.

"Quit wiggling," Patience said now. Her laughter hitched with each stroke of the pedals. Ditch lilies and newly seeded fields smeared, pale green and muddy brown, at the edges of Vivian's vision. They were moving fast enough, she thought, to render Ruf's whiskey redundant.

Vivian liked liquor, so far. Well—she liked what it did for her, its muffling haze. She'd been weaving down the carriage road in a half-pleasant fog when she'd heard something she liked even better: a two-fingered whistle and the whir of spokes. "Lesperance!" Patience had barked, and spat with precision. "Many happy returns. Climb aboard." (Patience Stone remembered birthdays. All her life, she would keep an excellent social calendar.)

At seventeen Vivian was already a woman on the edge, with a general interest in blurring the world into something the eye could skip past. But she was not partisan, yet: a bicycle might do it as well as liquor. She'd climbed aboard.

Whence this frustration, this drive for escape? If asked, Vivian could not have articulated it. It felt less a decision than a compulsion, an elemental law. She was observant enough to see that her parents and neighbors did not share her particular itch of discontentment, the perpetual urge for distraction. But she did not question this discrepancy—their situations, she reasoned, were entirely different. What, after all, did Patience Stone have to hate? And Mr. and Mrs. Lesperance thrived on misery. If given satisfaction, Vivian was sure, her parents would not have known what to do with it—except, perhaps, to pick it apart and suffocate it, to discover whether it harbored any secret flaws.

With the benefit of our perspective, we can report one more crucial piece of information to which Vivian was not privy. Call it her first, or most foundational, misunderstanding.

In Vivian's early childhood her father had volunteered for the fire brigade—a popular method, among dissatisfied local men, of attempting to establish a reputation for gallantry, competence, and physical prowess. For the lucky few, promotion to fire warden carried enviable additional benefits: a leather hat, a speaking trumpet. Perhaps even (or so dreamed those bitter volunteers denied the responsibility of the position) a sense of confidence and peaceful self-regard. Many rank-and-file firefighters dreamed of the opportunity to distinguish themselves on a call, to earn the warden's hat and an honorary ovation at the Firemen's Ball. (A morally slippery wish at best, since such opportunities could only be occasioned by disaster.)

Inevitably, some hook-and-ladder men set about staging the scenes of their own heroism—setting empty buildings ablaze, all but guaranteed to be the first valiant (if mysteriously prepared) volunteer on the scene.

Arson was a hanging crime, in those years; at the least, it warranted life in prison. These sentences had been carried out locally in Utica, and in recent memory—in fact, it was one such case that gave Vivian's father the idea. (He was confident, sparking flint to tinder in an abandoned farmhouse, that he had learned from his predecessors' mistakes.)

Mr. Lesperance had not been caught. But later that night, after he and his ingenuous fellow volunteers had extinguished the blaze, Vivian—nine years old, toothy and slightly knock-kneed—had wandered into the kitchen doorway just as her father finished gleefully confessing the act to his wife.

Vivian had not overheard the story—told by her father with uncharacteristic flair, received by her mother with uncharacteristic enthusiasm—of Mr. Lesperance struggling to kindle a spark in damp straw, watching flames begin to lick the derelict house's faded walls and sagging rafters. The heart-pounding minutes spent crouching in a copse of birches a quarter mile up the road, letting the fire's smoke and crackle build and crest and consume the building. Timing his entrance so that he could be believably first on the scene. Then: beating back his own inferno; hauling water and clearing cindered beams; screaming himself hoarse at his civic-minded neighbors, when at last they arrived, for their tardiness.

"It was beautiful," Mr. Lesperance had said in the kitchen—joy shining beneath the soot blackening his face; pride cutting through the smells of grease and smoke. His wife felt it, too, this sense of near-intoxication. It was the thrill of unfamiliar, unlikely success; of escaping dangers physical and judicial. It was the sense of superiority in having tricked their fellow citizens, the hope of soon being literally crowned their warden. And—why deny it?—it was the bitter release of sending some small part of this ungrateful world up in flames. (Perhaps, by this measure, the

Lesperances' marriage was a happy one: they bared the worst of their characters to each other, without reservation or judgment.)

"It was beautiful," Mr. Lesperance had said again, a little-used laugh rumbling in his chest. "And everyone saw me."

"But not the setting of it," Mrs. Lesperance had cut in sharply, her eyebrows demanding confirmation. (The couple had disagreed, early on, about whether to engage an accomplice.)

It was at this point that Vivian had yawned in the doorway. "I heard voices," she'd lisped, rubbing sleepily at one eye.

Under the circumstances—reeking with evidence, having just confessed to a hanging crime—her parents had heard her announcement as a threat.

Had she overheard them, she might have been inducted into their conspiracy. She might have grown into her inheritance, a paradoxically satisfied junior curator of the family's museum of grievances. But as it was: shaken until her teeth rattled, asked again and again what she had heard (truthfully, nothing), Vivian had—not for the first time, or the last, but perhaps the most fundamentally—been unable to give her parents the answer they wanted.

If only each of us could replay the scene of our deepest misunderstanding, to see the thing from all angles and with clear eyes! But in such a world, our lives might unspool so differently we would not recognize ourselves. And would our paths be straighter, for the knowledge? Would our endings be happier? Or is it in pain and confusion that we reach for—and in so doing, name—what we love most?

Vivian was, so far, reaching blindly. Unbeknownst to her, throughout her adolescence (even long after the material threat was softened by time), Mr. and Mrs. Lesperance had nursed the quiet fear that she might betray them to the authorities—and an accompanying resentful sense that she was willfully holding the possibility over their heads. (Her father never did receive the promotion, the fire warden's leather hat and speaking trumpet. This, too, was added to the general familial stew of disappointment.)

The reasoning behind such a complex aversion cannot be communicated to a child, but neither can the general atmosphere be hidden from her. Vivian knew with absolute clarity that her parents disliked her. In this she was correct. She was less aware—for the emotion itself was less legible, including to Mr. and Mrs. Lesperance themselves—that they *feared* her. But some part of her must have known it, depended on it, or else she would never have lived so boldly (if through her pain).

This much was certainly true: of her limited retaliatory options Vivian preferred open conflict to suffocation, and so she aimed to disappoint.

In this Ruf Thomas was, at first, an end in himself. Vivian's parents complained in violent agreement that Ruf was lazy, that he turned up to work barely sober, that he had no respect for authority. And yet, each week he collected their money. This arrangement, in its microscopic humiliation of her parents, piqued Vivian's interest.

Though Ruf was neither an intelligent nor a handsome man, his body and his nervous habits collaborated in doing him one great favor: he had twin gaps between his canines and bicuspids where no adult teeth had ever grown in, and he unceasingly explored the spaces between these obstinate baby teeth with the tip of his tongue. It gave him a thoughtful look; introspective. Only by such misdirection—and by having first attracted her parents' disdain—could a man like Ruf have earned a lingering glance from a woman like Vivian.

He did drink. At twenty-three he was young, she thought, for the *way* he drank. Not the amount of liquor—which she underestimated, having only the novice habit he was encouraging in her from which to extrapolate—but the way it affected him. There should be too much snap still in his elastic, she thought, for the groaning, green-gilled shuffle that possessed him most days until midafternoon.

Ruf was an interesting puzzle, at first. An old man in a young man's body, who both infuriated and lived off her parents despite having yesterday's oatmeal for brains. Then he kissed her, on the woodpile—a cord newly stacked for the *house*, not the shop. Domestic and intimate, as forbidden as she could get with a man who was around so much he might have been furniture. The kiss was tolerable. Then he got her drunk, and that was phenomenal. At last, the world blurred to nothing and she could think.

Patience Stone's bicycle ride had interrupted Vivian's fourth try at drunkenness. The moldy metallic flavor of the flask; the brush of Ruf's furred knuckles—she was acquiring a knack for whiskey. She was teetering on the edge of love with it.

But it was souring, already. In the way her parents, without *liking* Ruf any more than they ever had, had begun to speak of him as a natural and inevitable destiny for Vivian. As good an idea as any, if their goal (as Vivian knew it was) was to get rid of her. A perfectly serviceable snare, set in their own backyard—and the stupid girl (for so Vivian saw herself, suddenly) had spared them the trouble of arranging the thing.

Now, speeding downhill, Vivian leaned shrieking into each turn until capsize felt inevitable—yet it never came. Patience bent forward and fitted her collarbone to Vivian's shoulders. She pushed, steering with her passenger like a rudder.

Slung over Patience's handlebars, Vivian saw a world transfigured by momentum—from a desolate plain to a passage leading somewhere, her old neighborhood reduced to smears of color on the walls. She moved fast enough to have a vision of the future—no specifics, just a faith in its existence. Vivian's head cleared. Her vision sharpened. Tears streamed.

She reached escape velocity.

OUR SUBJECT IS change. Some change is so gradual it cannot be tracked with the human eye; some is cataclysmic. The development of the bicycle was the first sort. Like the spread of ash in the atmosphere, the build of pressure beneath Mount Tambora. Vivian's first ride was the second. An eruption. (The two types of change are always entangled this way, like lovers slumbering in a train compartment. Unconscious and always moving forward, the quick and the slow are mutually interested.)

Vivian taught herself to ride Patience's bicycle over the course of a dozen scrapes and one sprained wrist. Even after she saved the pocket money—money that in another life would have drained to whiskey—to buy her own, the women sometimes still rode doubled. For the thrill of it, the exponential miracle of two bodies balanced on one unlikely contraption. Pressed flush, sternum to scapula, using one another to steer.

Vivian saw Ruf less, somehow, though he was still around as much as ever. Even the least athletic of us will vault unthinking over furniture, if sufficiently excited. We may even fail to notice when we bark our shins crossing the room. Absorbed in something more interesting.

Alas for Ruf Thomas. But glory and trumpets to the invention of the bicycle. Is there a more beautiful sight than a woman going fast enough under her own power to escape her demons?

And how do you weigh the sight of it, the rushing whooping gorgeous cold wind in her hair, against the thousands dead in pyroclastic blast and subsequent famine?

Any attempt to keep a ledger is hopeless; yet, to abandon the task is to abandon each other. But quick, catch a glimpse of her as she passes: Vivian Lesperance is riding out of Utica.

PATIENCE, ONCE AGAIN, was the bridge out. When both girls were eighteen, Patience was sent to spend a season with her aunt in New York—for cultural development and for cotillion. The tacit expectation was that she would find a husband by the end of the year, a prospect she looked forward to with the same benign interest as she did the museums and theatrical revues. As the only sister marooned among five brothers, Patience lobbied successfully for the right to invite Vivian along to the city as her companion. Vivian's parents were only too willing to send her, seeing the venture as another kind of opportunity to consolidate their antagonists. (And whether pawning their daughter in matrimony to Ruf Thomas or sending her to Manhattan to live off the Stones for a while, one method of escape was as good as another to the Lesperances—however differently the options might strike Vivian herself.) But if Vivian was careless enough to develop champagne tastes, they told her, that would be her affair and her disappointment upon her return.

(Privately, though still unclear on logistics, Vivian had already decided there would be no return.)

A FEW HUNDRED miles by train, to reach a city like nothing Vivian had ever seen. Patience was much preoccupied with the interminable preparations for her debut—having her wingspan measured in satin, learning to fold herself in thirds from the waist—and so Vivian had ample time to herself. She spent it observing tourists and locals with an equal, almost extraterrestrial interest—and she learned fast, keeping quiet in tearooms and theater lobbies until she'd mapped the faux pas that would mark her as a bumpkin, aping society mannerisms by the end of her first week. After a look at her wardrobe, Patience's aunt Daphne had some of her niece's old clothes altered to fit Vivian. The silhouettes were outdated, but Vivian wore them with a kind of ethereal confidence (born of ignorance) that disarmed any notice of their flaws. In fact Aunt Daphne's set was rather taken with her—hardly surprising, as she was reflecting back to the women their most flattering portraits, focusing all her considerable survivor's faculties on courting an invitation to remain in New York beyond the summer.

Aunt Daphne nearly broached the subject, during an afternoon card game. "You're a dear," she said dreamily, as Vivian refilled her bridge party's glasses of lemon squash. "How lovely it would be if you could come out this season, with the other girls."

Vivian moved carefully, topping off a glass. She smiled at the women, waiting for the implied offer to bubble to the surface.

Perhaps we can forgive Aunt Daphne, for letting the invitation lie unexpressed. It would have been an astronomical act of generosity, to sponsor an unconnected provincial girl through the enormous expense of a debut and to chaperone her through a social season. In raising the subject at all, Daphne had simply yielded to a moment's impractical daydreaming. Her cheeks were flush with sugared lemon and heat and good conversation; she was partnered in the card game with Emily Drexel, who was wearing a bracelet that Daphne had given her twenty years before, and together they had taken the last three tricks running. The window was open, letting in fresh air and the familiar sounds of the neighborhood. Her rheumatism wasn't bothering her. The glass at her elbow was full again. Patience's little friend Vivian was here, and she was responsible for some portion of this happiness—for a moment, Aunt Daphne gave her credit for all of it.

Vivian didn't resent her for dealing out the temptation of a society debut and then shuffling it back into the deck without a second thought. But Vivian did take a lesson from the experience: to seek out and control her own opportunities, rather than waiting for an unlikely jolt of charity from the powerful. To find back entrances to those rooms and minds and checkbooks to which she wanted access.

Not everyone has the talent for adapting such lessons for immediate use. In another life, Vivian might have had a career as a battlefield general.

As it happened, there was a back entrance to the debutante ball itself. The organizers sought to convey prestige with a crowded call sheet— besides the debs and their escorts there were flower girls, pages, ushers, "princesses" (an awkward title, as at least one member of a genuine monarchy was in attendance), and junior debutantes, girls of fourteen and fifteen watching the whole circus in queasy anticipation. Vivian had a nominal position as Patience's attendant—a role that demanded exactly nothing of her, to the satisfaction of both young women. She blended in seamlessly, fascinated by the pageantry of glittering nonsense. The St. James bows and booming announcement of each white-gowned ingenue; the pimply escorts sneaking swigs of gin between laps of the ball- room; the furtive cockroach skittering across the gold-leaf wainscoting— Vivian loved it all.

We can spare a moment to watch Patience's presentation, after all she has done for us. She carried herself well: charmed in the receiving line, curtsied without a wobble, came away without smudges on her kid gloves. Her escort, though not the boy she would eventually marry, was a perfectly nice young man—whenever they crossed paths over the ensuing years, they would always remember to ask after each other's dogs by name. Patience had a fine time at cotillion and then set off into her own story, seeing Vivian less and less as their calendars diverged. She would marry for love; keep a house in Paris upholstered in pink brocade; mother bright and ambitious children. She would also join the first Sherlock Holmes fan society and make a pilgrimage to Baker Street so excellently costumed as Dr. Watson that she would be served in a gentlemen's club. (Patience had a lifelong fondness for supporting roles, and so we hope we have engaged her with her blessing. For our purposes, we will leave her here. We wish her well.)

As the party wore on, gaslights flickering and punch sloshing onto silk slippers, Vivian found herself drawn to a drab, nervous figure on the fringe—the only other woman in the ballroom in a dress simple and shabby enough that Vivian would have known how to remove it.

Electra Blake was a society reporter for the *Metropolitan News*. This was the first cotillion she had covered for the paper's gossip column, written under the pseudonym of the Midtown Tattler. Turnover on the society desk had been astounding, with one male Tattler after another bullied into quitting by his fellow reporters doctoring his byline to read "Miss Nancy" and asking him for the trick to a perfect soufflé. Electra's uncle, an assistant editor at the paper, had sacrificed her to the position and called it doing her a favor. (Electra, who harbored only an average interest in high-society gossip and no journalistic ambition whatsoever, wondered privately what favor this was meant to bestow.) On the night of the ball, Vivian happened upon Electra doubly burdened—professional anxiety over being the only female journalist she had ever heard of, compounding with the personal embarrassment of being a cheaply dressed observer among some of the city's richest debutantes.

"Here," Vivian said by way of introduction, pressing a slice of cake and cup of punch into Electra's hands. "You haven't eaten all night. Let me hold that." She reached for Electra's pencil and calfskin notebook. Electra, startled, gave them up.

The cake was of almond sponge and a sugared glaze flavored with lime juice. There were sliced berries floating in the punch, which fizzed against the back of her throat.

"You're right," Electra said, swallowing. "I'd forgotten." More bracing than the refreshments was the thought that someone—not only *someone*, but this striking stranger in a uniquely unintimidating costume—had thought to bring them to her.

"Your necklace is lovely," Vivian said, tapping her own collarbone.

Electra blushed. She was wearing her mother's costume jewelry, under protest. It sat heavy on her chest, a tender spot for her all evening. "I—well, thank you. Miss . . . ?"

"Vivian Lesperance," Vivian said, enunciating each syllable. She passed back the notebook. "Have you been through to the veranda?"

The two young women spent the remainder of the evening together, middle-class ballast enabling each other to enjoy the luxury without capsizing in it. They giggled and snarked and accompanied each other to the washroom; fetched each other cup after cup of punch, even after someone spiked it with gin. And in the *News* on Monday, in enumerating the charms and scandals of the cotillion, the Midtown Tattler devoted a full paragraph to the "charming new arrival, Miss Vivian

Lesperance, who drew her own attention even amidst the glittering firmament of these last debuts of the century."

In this way Vivian was able to enter society without ever precisely coming out. She simply *appeared* in fashionable rooms, a striking girl with a brightly painted smirk. The skills she had developed to survive as the feared and fearful child of a dismal home served her well in her new environs: a studied silence kept her from embarrassment while she learned the customs of her new world, and had the happy side effect of making her a cipher in a society that craved mystery. Her talent for remembering—and repeating—the names and accomplishments of others made her popular with the vain; her sobriety without shaming revelers gave her a friendly reputation among the respectable and the debauched alike. Vivian was popular. She had a knack for deducing the most interesting guest or conversation at any party—and before long, the very fact of her attention was enough to convey the status.

Electra was her first real friend in the city—a complicated label, to say the least. The friendship was real, but it was also useful. Vivian quickly made habits of charging meals to the *Metropolitan News*; staying most nights in the Blakes' guest suite (creeping back to Electra's room after the house was asleep); and, most significantly, copyediting the Tattler's columns before Electra filed them.

Through this last pattern of journalistic sleight of hand, Vivian never attended a salon or concert without the event being noted in ink, with particular mention of her presence—and soon, in a twist of high-society flimflam, she developed a reputation as an arbiter of taste. Invitations mounted. She was still considered mysterious. Nobody could determine where she came from—new money, certainly, but from no clear industry or part of the world. But besides the Tattler, she had the whisper-network endorsement of Patience's aunt Daphne—and there were New People cropping up everywhere in the city in those days. Indeed, the function of the gossip columns was in large part to chortle at the embarrassments and errors of the nouveau riche. Vivian benefited from this tradition as well: New Yorkers depended on the society pages to assign them their targets of mockery as well as their idols, and on the subject of Vivian's flaws the Tattler was remarkably silent.

She lived by a decadent shoestring, filling the gaps between luncheons and four-course dinner parties with stolen rolls and wax-wrapped caramels. She never quite confessed to being homeless—she wrote to her parents only that she was staying on in New York; told Aunt Daphne only that she'd made other arrangements; told Electra only that no gala or dance was as comforting as the spare daybed in the corner of her boudoir. Most nights the two young women eventually slept tangled in Electra's sheets, hair mussed and faces shining. But whenever the Blakes were traveling or entertaining a full house and Electra asked her regretfully to stay "at home" for an evening, Vivian lingered late at parties, or dipped into dance halls (she learned quickly which venues did not charge women admission), or wandered wrapped in a borrowed greatcoat and a fog of tipsy delight until sunrise.

This improvised and dishonest arrangement lasted, improbably, through the fall and into the winter. Of course it could not have lasted forever. Eventually Vivian's ruse must have crumbled. She and Electra were not much more than girls, after all, playing with Electra's youthful freedom and her parents' money—and there was not enough of either remaining to sustain the game for long. Without some intervening circumstance Vivian would eventually have been mistaken for a prostitute or frozen on a park bench or at least publicly embarrassed and sent back to Utica more or less disgraced, a foolish young woman reaping the consequences of her foolishness, saving as much face as she could in the return to anonymity—and to whatever quotidian punishments her parents, and societal expectations, could devise.

Instead, she met Sofia.

ON THE LAST night of 1899 Vivian and Electra rang in the New Year together—though the party was so raucous and crowded, they were as intimate with any number of strangers as with each other. Electra was also working, her notebook holstered at her hip, and so she recorded it all: the pink fizzing pyramids of coupe glasses; the sparklers and cigarettes dropping indistinguishable ash onto the carpets; the peals of intemperate laughter and tears of intemperate jealousy. The parade describing a deafening circle through the halls of the building, after it was declared too cold for brass instruments in the streets. The operatic recital that had to be cut short when one of the singers fainted from the heat. The sounds of church bells, bugles, shrieking whistles, and salutes or attacks from all manner of firearms echoing in and out the open windows, mixed with gusts of snow.

And one performance among many, cutting straight to Vivian's heart.

Sofia Bianchi was an independently wealthy Venetian chanteuse with a widow's peak like a diadem and a voice like one of her native city's *acqua altae*—a natural phenomenon that hit everyone the same, but still left you with the urge to mark its height on your own doorjamb. To keep a personal record, a combination souvenir and explanation, showing when you'd been flooded and how high.

This was Vivian's high-water mark: well past midnight at the dawn of a new century, Sofia in champagne-colored silk and seed pearls, slowing "The Sidewalks of New York" to a velvet, Italian-accented ballad. The months since the debutante ball had been transformative: Vivian was no longer the girl who had scanned the crowd for the least intimidating figure. Now she was drawn to whoever glowed most brightly.

Sofia's supposed escort that evening was her drunk accompanist. When Vivian approached, he slid chivalrously aside to make room for her— straight off the edge of the piano bench and onto the floor. The women left him there, snoring gently, while they made their introductions.

"That was beautiful," Vivian said. Sofia's long fingers still rested on the keyboard, miming the waltz's last chord. With apparent nonchalance Vivian pressed the key beside her hand, the ivory warm to the touch. Somewhere deep within the instrument, a hidden hammer struck a hidden string—a single note rang, so softly that only the two of them were close enough to hear it. More vibration than sound.

"It's a strange lyric," Sofia said. "To *trip the light fantastic*. But,"—she gestured to the bacchanal variously whirling around them, hanging from the open windows, lying unconscious at their feet—"I thought perhaps this is what it means."

Vivian smiled.

Electra watched it happen. She even reported on it—a mention by the Tattler made tickets to Sofia's concert series among the most sought-after of the new year. But she didn't realize what precisely she had seen, until

Vivian (with rather less tact than she might have employed, given her new understanding of how it felt to be the lover rather than the beloved) broke off their association in order to move into Sofia's suite at the Fifth Avenue Hotel.

Electra tried to avenge her wounded pride in the press, but by this time it was too late to stop the juggernaut she'd created—particularly with the sudden loss of Vivian's editorial eye. In fact, Electra's column began to suffer against its competitors in other papers largely *because* of her failure to breathlessly cover (and compound) Vivian's continued rise among the Four Hundred. Eventually Electra gave up her experiments with society and the society pages alike, relinquishing the Tattler's byline and marrying one of the city's first traffic cops—a welcome yielding to convention, directions clear as a whistle and a waving hand. Her aberrant months with Vivian became a youthful embarrassment she recovered from as well as she could in introversion, maintaining a studious ignorance of each day's news.

LIFE WITH SOFIA burned bright. They ate all their meals in restaurants, spent their early evenings seeing and being seen in hotel bars and lounges. Sofia did most of the being seen: her beauty was architectural, load bearing. An entourage of artists and entertainers orbited her, considering her all the more fashionable for being foreign—imagine such a chanteuse keeping house in New York, rather than one of the capitals of Europe!

Vivian was one spangle in Sofia's constellation, among Sicilian Shakespeareans and Muscovite muralists—never so exposed as to draw gossip about their particular association. But Vivian had a front table in every nightclub, a box in every music hall—and a moment at the end of every performance to take Sofia in her arms in the dressing room, congratulatory bouquets heaped around them like snowdrifts. "Viva," Sofia called her, a linguistic joke that migrated from public to private rooms: an exclamation over toasting glasses; a cheer at the apex of a party; a murmur from one plush mouth into another. It needn't have been witty in order to cast a hook into Vivian's stomach: it was the first time she had ever experienced affectionate abbreviation.

Pet names aside, Sofia was a performer, not a conversationalist. She did not ask questions, which suited Vivian. Likewise with their bohemian set in general—though Vivian was not a poet or an actress or an anarchist, and though she found they often tended too far either in the direction of blood-and-thunder or whimsy for her tastes (and sometimes simultaneously), she appreciated this set's commitment to living in a perpetual present, their insistence on remaking their own destinies (and performing them as loudly as possible). This philosophy enabled Vivian to keep her origins and her heart to herself, and absorb what she wished from Sofia—whether given consciously, like jewelry and flowers and charming anecdotes, or unconsciously, like the regal posture Vivian learned to copy; the taste for caviar; the silver cigarette case (a forgotten gift from Sofia's American manager) she pocketed against future financial hardship.

There was no end to the things Vivian learned from Sofia: piano scales and arpeggios. Basic Italian—first the vocabulary necessary to argue and to make love, then filling in the gaps. She learned to blow smoke rings; to bring a woman to paroxysm in the space of three kisses; to mix a perfect Brandy Crusta. (Vivian rarely drank anymore, but Sofia ended each evening with at least two cocktails.) Vivian learned to spend money, and to manage it wisely. (Remarkable in itself, as the two skills rarely coexist.)

And finally, after better than three years of this arrangement, Vivian learned that she did not have the constitution to be an applauding audience of a partner. Things could not last forever, especially once Sofia grew bored with New York and began to seriously review offers of engagement in Paris. Vivian felt now that she could not bear to live life according to another person's itinerary, even if it would let her cross the Atlantic on a luxury liner and see the great cities of the world. By the waning days of their association, Vivian was approaching fluency in New York's native tongues—wealth, influence, fashion. She no longer required an interpreter.

She still harbored her provincial origins like a shameful secret—sending polite, vague letters to her parents just often enough to keep them quiet; receiving their even less frequent replies via post office box. (Mr. and Mrs. Lesperance did not ask how she filled her days, or whom she saw in the city, or when she might to return to Utica—they would never have stooped to showing interest. But they repeated frequently both the misanthropic dread that in her next letter she would ask them for money, and the arch comment that the longer she lingered in the metropolis, the fewer suitors she would have to choose from—and the older she would be, attempting to lure them—when the city grew tired of her.)

Meanwhile, Vivian kept up a careful study of aspirational New Yorkers—old money, captains of industry, the artist set—and aped their mannerisms and their opinions until they came naturally. Her camouflage was, like so much about her, atypical. She could spot other newly monied bumpkins at a thousand paces—by their poor taste, their confusion, or their insecurity. They tended to be defensive when insulted, where the "right" sort of people simply froze in steely silence.

During one visit at a socialite's country house, Sofia and Vivian made a new acquaintance.

It had, thus far, been an ill-favored morning: Sofia was bored by the party, which was of a less artistic mien than their usual set; Vivian was torn between her old longing to spurn the group and draw out Sofia's feline affection, and her new inclination to practice her own charm and influence on the bores.

It was in this tense atmosphere that they were introduced to the unfortunate Oscar Schmidt. A "soap man," their host said, though Schmidt clarified stuffily that his business was "Personal Care."

He was from the Midwest somewhere, that much was obvious almost before he spoke. It was hard to guess his age—he had an incongruous appearance, mutton-chop whiskers on what otherwise looked like a boy's face. Professional-grade moisturization, Vivian supposed. He looked like a person in disguise. She felt almost involuntarily compelled to tease him—to show the other natives that she was of their tribe, not this Schmidt's; to reignite some spirit of play between herself and Sofia, and clear the morning of its fog of tension.

"I wondered which lady's new perfume we were smelling," she said. "Now I see it must be yours."

Mr. Schmidt's face fell. She watched him shoulder the mantle of offended gentility—a clumsy transition, as it always was when feigned. "It's not," he said coldly, but with the telltale heartland in his vowels.

22

Vivian almost shook her head at him. Had her interest lain elsewhere, she could have coached him: the proper response, if any, was "I'm sure I don't know what you mean."

As it was, the interaction did what each of Vivian's interactions was calculated to do: propelled her farther in the direction she wanted to go, and away from what she wanted to escape. "Now *that* man," Vivian whispered to Sofia, crossing the lawn, "was a yokel."

Sofia muffled a musical laugh. "*Viva,*" she said, half-scolding, and laid a hand on her arm.

CURIOUS, ISN'T IT, how profoundly inconsistently we identify on first meeting the people who will change our lives. Vivian had been able to hear herself chime against Sofia from across a raucous ballroom, though they would ultimately spend only a few decadent years together. But upon meeting Oscar Schmidt—the man whom, over the coming decade and beyond, she would make puppet-king of an industrial empire and punch in the eye at his secret mother-in-law's Christmas party—Vivian felt only mildly derisive amusement at Oscar's accent and the length of his sideburns at their first hello.

Our subject is change—inevitable, relentless. There is nothing to do but turn the page.

TWO

Oscar Schmidt was born twenty years before Vivian on a wheezing ghost of a farm in central Ohio, and he spent the balance of those two extra decades worrying.

Oscar knew too well the lessons of the Year Without a Summer, though not by that (or any) name. His grandmother remembered it—his mother's mother, Hester, the Midwestern laundress; his paternal grandmother did not survive to meet him, and judging by family lore would not have found doing so sufficient motivation to make the crossing from Germany anyway. But Grandmother Hester, as a girl, had built an uncanny Fourth of July snowman with her sisters—and then, less cheerfully, had weathered a summer of die-offs. Blight and barren earth and pigs butchered half-grown lest they eat each other alive. Hester's parents, desperate, had fallen in with religious revivalism. (There was a lot of it going around at the time—unseasonable weather reacting all over against shame and fear and hope of salvation. Who, testing summer ice on the millpond, was thinking about a pyroclastic eruption in the East Indies the year before? Easier to believe that Someone was sending you a message, withering the earth wherever you touched it.)

Whatever messages Oscar's great-grandfather heard that summer, in prayer meetings and surveys of lost crops, he finally acted on them by shooting himself with his hunting rifle—rigging a foot-operated contraption to pull the trigger, a final testament to his resourcefulness in extremis. Hester had discovered her father's body. And whatever sorrows this passed to her in turn, she swallowed for the rest of her life. But the swallowing made her over, rearranged her posture and her personality—and particularly, as she became a mother and later a grandmother, her determination not to allow other children the luxury of contentment. Though it trickled to him slow and indirect as meltwater, Oscar was raised by that unseasonable millpond ice. Raised by the eruption, half a world away, that crystallized it with blind dispassion.

What did it mean, to be descended from catastrophe? It meant a general familial disapproval whenever he appeared to lack employment, even momentarily. It meant vacillating continuously between thrift and poverty, with Oscar never completely certain whether a given act of deprivation was by choice or by necessity. Was there no money for shoes in a larger size? Or would crimping his toes build character, by some ambiguous means? Were there really war shortages, or were other children in friendlier houses getting butter and meat? Was it random tragedy that killed both of his parents (one kicked by a horse; the other felled by influenza) before he was ten? Or had some divine authority judged Oscar undeserving of them?

This last suspicion was encouraged by his grandmother's oft-repeated cautionary tale about that unseasonably cold summer of 1816, a fairy story worthy of the Brothers Grimm. Though Hester cut her father out of the account entirely, something grisly and horrible stalked her reminiscence all the same. That topsy-turvy summer, she made clear, hadn't been a playful anomaly. Not snow angels and skating on the millpond. People had suffered. There were consequences to upsetting the natural way of things. And in every telling she made sure to allege that the disruption had been caused by some naughty girl or—much more likely—boy, whom God had been obliged to teach a lesson. Someone shirking his chores, Oscar's grandmother speculated; kicking the back of the pew in church; indulging in impure thoughts. (The probable offenses shifted as Oscar aged; shame, he learned early, grew with you.)

Hester's intentions were to develop an industrious character in her grandson and, less consciously, to exact a jealous revenge for her own unhappy childhood. She achieved both, for all the relief it brought her. But she produced also an unanticipated result: a boy prone to the constant cataloging and augury of his own flaws. A nervous mystic, always reading the sky and earth and the moods of others for signs of divine reprimand. Where he could not find satisfyingly damning omens, he settled for anticipating them. Oscar saw himself at the center of a grand pagan cosmology, cause and repository of countless disappointments.

And yet, the revelation of his own queerness clocked him like a sucker punch.

IT BEGAN—OR RATHER erupted—in Oscar's fourteenth summer, when a new clerk sprang up like jimsonweed behind the counter at the general store.

In addition to a uniform that fit him so awkwardly it seemed perpetually caught in an embarrassed struggle to hide his body, Hiram Ainsley wore lifts to even out a limp—which made him appear to lean in with rapt interest whenever he was addressed. Oscar came in for a box of clothespins for his grandmother and was so flustered it took him three attempts to complete the transaction. Hiram had eyelashes substantial enough to cast a shadow and hair so thick he forgot pencils in it. Oscar, he imagined, could have lost his fingers in it up to the third knuckle.

Oscar caught Hiram once, sorting mail, holding someone's unopened letter up to a lamp like he was candling an egg. It took the edge off, knowing he was nosy. Otherwise it would have hurt to look at him. (In which case, Oscar would insist to himself for long years afterward, he might have been fine.)

He was practiced enough in self-denial to school himself insensate by day. But Hiram began to twine through his dreams, and there was no act of will or anesthesia that would eradicate him. It was hard to judge the greater torture—the endless shameful recurrence of the dreams, or the moment they ended, when Oscar was ripped from ecstatic phantasmagoria to reality.

For months Oscar was tormented, unsure if his affliction was a punishment for something he'd done, or the crime itself—and if the latter, what greater punishment awaited. He hid his soiled linens (an intimidating challenge, with his warden an expert laundress); he scratched and slapped at himself, gnawed at his fingernails until they bled. He stopped going to the general store entirely. Then, disaster: Hiram appeared at a church picnic, sudden and sinuous as a snake in Eden, and took over serving lemonade just as Oscar and his grandmother approached the head of the line. In a collar and jacket, he was, if anything, more formally attired than ever—but without his familiar green-striped uniform he looked undressed to Oscar. Hiram's own clothes! This was more intimate, in its way, than anything Oscar's subconscious had dared conjure. His cut-glass cup trembled in his hand. Then Hiram—in front of everyone; in front of God; in front of Grandmother Hester—reached out to steady Oscar's wrist as he poured, and Oscar came so close to fainting he wished he'd died instead. Hiram offered him a polite, maybe even a pitying smile. In a fit of shame and desire Oscar's body rebelled—there was nothing to cover himself—he cascaded lemonade down his shirt-front to excuse his escape. "Well," his grandmother said as he fled, and he lacked the courage to look back.

Never previously ambitious in study or trade, Oscar became overnight a model applicant, feverish in his zeal, for any occupation that would take him out of town. He stalked the mail for answers—making sure to always retrieve it, of course, when Hiram was not on duty. Still, it was unavoidably and exquisitely painful to imagine him sorting the envelopes into Oscar's pigeonhole—square-fingered hands shuffling and slotting card-stock, long-lashed eyes peeking at a return address, squinting to read through the onionskin. Would Hiram know before Oscar did that he was leaving? Would Hiram care?

Of Oscar's many attempted escapes, fate delivered him two options: a scholarship to the college in Gambier, and an apprenticeship with a soap-maker in Cincinnati. Only the latter was far enough from home to necessitate relocating, and so Oscar's choice was made for him. He took a southbound train and, inexorably, became an entrepreneur in the business of Personal Care. Whether this was punishment or reward he would debate with himself for decades to come. Our object here, perhaps, is to settle the litigation.

IT BEGAN WITH soap—salt and soda ash and pork fat from the city's many meatpacking plants, which, in his first months of probationary employment, Oscar picked his way through a slush of blood and offal to collect. Each day he used the refined end product of his industry to scrub the intestinal grease of its raw stages from beneath his fingernails; each week he sent his surplus wages back home to Grandmother Hester. Presently, he expanded his repertoire from soap alone to include all manner of unguents and perfumes. Among the Civil War's many rippling effects had been the parallel popularizations of hygiene (as necessity) and cosmetics (as distraction). Oscar learned the business of both, from errand boy to amanuensis to office clerk. The advertising copy came naturally—it was easy for Oscar to draft paragraphs on the fear of embarrassment or offense, the shame of never being *entirely sure* one was doing enough to scrub oneself clean of one's filth.

For alongside all this success, to Oscar's horror, his perverse nature resurged. Hiram had been a symptom, not a cause: the first snowflake falling on a summer meadow. Here Oscar was on the other side of the world (or at least of Ohio), his bedrock still quaking. The urges bloomed stronger as he grew into manhood, and in the multivalent chaos of urban upward mobility he was often able to lose himself—dodging down alleys, or into anonymous saloon backrooms—for long enough to indulge.

Long enough, even, to enjoy himself.

It was easy enough to spot the fairies, rouged and tweezed and swishing for trade—but Oscar wasn't trade, or didn't want to be. He didn't want to be anything. And yet he wanted everything, everyone—and for the most part, he got it. On a few occasions he even joined those who sat for company in the city's seedier slides, staining and powdering himself with the wares he peddled to women in his daylit life. (The Vaseline was a competitor's product—but quality came first.)

Always, afterward, he collared himself again and shame cascaded until he struggled for breath. But now, at least, he was not trapped in these feelings at a church picnic, like a butterfly pinned to a piece of felt. Now, at least, he had business to absorb him.

BY OSCAR'S EARLY twenties he had a permanent position at the soap company. He distinguished himself: his strict obedience and diligent work ethic the twin legacies of Grandmother Hester's command; his enthusiasm and talent for the business of perfumes and powders his own. He was a model protégé—never questioning, never innovating, expertly memorizing the norms of an industry settling into tradition after a wartime boom. Alongside his wages he mailed home cakes of laundry soap and cashmere-scented bath bars to replace the volcanic kettles of ash and fat that bubbled in his childhood memories. When he visited, he found his grandmother had been bathing with the laundry soap as well as washing linens in it, and had stacked his toilet bars in the woodshed where their "pansy smell" wouldn't pollute the house. Oscar's visits themselves created the distinct and increasing impression that she would prefer to stack him in the woodshed for similar reasons.

Oscar tried desperately to appease her—he left his odalisque's cabinet of scents and tinctures behind in his Cincinnati washroom; he returned his voice to the Teutonic-inflected breadbasket twang of his youth. He asked after nobody, to avoid asking after Hiram the general-store clerk. This practice gained him nothing but a local reputation as a snob, and ignorance of the fact that Hiram had married a third cousin and moved to Danville.

At home, Oscar could not conclusively decide whether he was a bare-faced sissy pervert or merely a paranoiac whose family did not love him. Caught between these possibilities, the result was the same: he began to dread his visits north, then to avoid them entirely.

He got a lot of work done, between his bouts of recreation and recovery.

Within a few years he was offered a promotion, the youngest junior partner in the company's short history. The position came with the opportunity to manage a satellite office. Just a few weeks later—almost simultaneously, as if orchestrated, though whether by a divine hand or a satanic one would occupy Oscar for many sleepless nights—two things occurred. First: Grandmother Hester died, characteristically without fuss or ceremony, severing Oscar's last tie to the heartland. And second: a sensationalist rag from New York published a breathless exposé of the city's disgusting underbelly. Oscar read all about it on the train back to Cincinnati from the funeral. Fairy dives and bathhouses in the Bowery; cruising on the waterfront; pansy brothels.

Oscar was developing a perverted claustrophobia in his current city. He'd sinned in too many dark corners, become a familiar face in too many bars where survival depended on anonymity. And he'd climbed into a new social class, the change vertiginous and strange—lunch counters he'd once scrimped all week to patronize now laughed at him when he approached, wearing suits ordered from shops he'd once assumed served only royalty. He was caught between his old life and his new, his farm boy accent and his fourteen-step toilette. He had too much money to continue living the life he knew, but not enough—or not the right kind—to dissolve into the upper echelon of society. He was a precipitate suspended in solution, like a botched formula in one of his office's basement laboratories.

In short, Ohio and Oscar no longer knew what to do with one another—especially after the loss of, and liberation from, Grandmother Hester. By contrast, New York was a world away, enormous, its population continually refreshed by sailors ("sea food," the tabloid reported the queers called them) and immigrants. No one would know him; no one would care to know him. *Everyone* would be new in town. Oscar even convinced himself that in a new city, he might outrun his sexual affliction. A common enough mistake: the hope that a change of scenery will produce a change of metaphysics.

At the next board meeting Oscar made the argument for the company's expansion, and for his own escape.

It worked in his favor that the request came at a moment of uncertainty in geographic hierarchy—telegraphy had by this point divorced information from its flesh-and-blood couriers, and money was pooling on the Eastern seaboard like water running downhill. But bricks and mortar (to say nothing of aging executives' custom) lagged behind—Cincinnati was still Headquarters, and as an industrial engine New York's reputation still trailed that of Baltimore or Pittsburgh. Thus, in his bid for a leap in status that he had not precisely earned, Oscar was able to take advantage of the general confusion (not excepting his own) as to whether New York City constituted a center or a periphery.

In the end, this was the deciding metric his superiors used in granting him oversight of the Manhattan office: New York's meatpacking industry was smaller than Cincinnati's. An inevitable circumstance, perhaps, in an island city trapped between two rivers. But there were always by-products, and Oscar had motivation enough to corner the market.

OSCAR TOOK TO New York like a fish to bouillabaisse. By day he contracted with meatpacking plants for their by-products and consolidated small-time vendors of starch and scent extracts and tooth powder. He replicated his company's systems at boutique scale, becoming known in the region for the quality and consistency of his simple signature products. New York society allowed him into its ranks (though relegating him, of course, to the second-class status of an arriviste). Soon he moved from his initial set of furnished bachelor rooms to a spacious apartment with its own kitchen—and a housekeeper who went home each night at seven, leaving his evenings his own business. He mixed at social clubs with bankers and lawyers and railroaders and advised them, when requested, on which cosmetics their wives might prefer as presents. He laughed at the crude jokes the husbands made in reply to his suggestions, affecting an understanding of female anatomy he did not possess. He did not mix with the wives themselves, beyond the bare minimum of social politeness—in fact he gained a mild reputation for discourtesy with ladies, which gossips attributed to his provincial origins. (Grandmother Hester would have been aghast at the insinuation of bad breeding.) In truth, Oscar kept his distance from the women of his set lest they recognize a kindred spark in him.

For he lived a double life, like a dyspeptic vigilante, arranging his business and social calendars uptown between anonymous encounters with men on the Bowery. He went by Hester in the clubs, a choice he did not examine, and visited each establishment on a six-month rotation to ensure the turnover of all but the most wolfish clientele. He lived in fear of, among much else, confusing his signals—of mincing or rouging his neck or sporting a red tie at the Astor; of handing out his business card (Oscar Schmidt, Personal Care) to one of the anonymous fags at the Slide. There were queers uptown, too, of course—Oscar occasionally drifted in morbid reverie in his social club's smoking lounge, wondering which of his fellows fondling their Rubenesque brandy snifters would end the evening on his knees before which of the others. But Oscar couldn't bear the risk—and he was new money, still feeling like an uninvited guest in his own palatial apartment. For accuracy we are bound to call it slumming, but he was more at ease—or as close as he ever got—among the out-of-work porters and merchant marines of the Bowery than among the robber barons of Fifth Avenue.

And Oscar was popular, in the clubs. He was a rare cocktail: winsome yet broad-shouldered; retiring yet rapacious; receptive in bed—or rented closet, or shadowed balcony corner—yet strong enough to lift a partner off his feet.

Within reason—within the confines of absolute anonymity—Oscar enjoyed the attention. Indeed, some days it felt like all he lived for. He did wish, occasionally, for conversation. Sometimes he even felt a paradoxical yearning for the repressed days of Hiram's invasions of privacy—the way the clerk had leaned into discussions or peered at other people's letters. The alluring impression of rapt interest, even if it was a fiction born of nosiness and orthopedic shoes.

Oscar, both assessed by and assessing men like livestock and parting in most cases without a handshake, watched with some envy as less nervous revelers made friends, took repeated lovers, even shared their real names. But the risks were not worth the rewards. Besides, as a cosmetics empresario, there was always the dormant threat of celebrity among even the working-class fairies. (On one particularly nightmarish occasion, on the "legitimate" side of a bar with a seedy backroom, he was recognized and congratulated on the popularity of a new cologne even as he drew breath for an anonymous proposition.) And even yielding to temptation without incident still sent him vibrating with shame until the world blurred around him; in this way he lost many a fortnight. His one consolation was that the terror and revulsion, the cycle of disgust and desperate yield, ensured that there was no danger of attachment to any single "husband." Oscar had seen men and fairies alike made doubly vulnerable by love—to blackmail; to attack; to ruin. There were always, eventually, consequences.

AS HE ENTERED his thirties, and the ranks of bachelors in his society cohort began to thin, Oscar felt the looming threat of exposure and tried to broaden his repertoire. He made a single visit to a "sporting house" for normal men. Sometimes mentioned sotto voce in his club uptown, the establishment rather disappointed in its promise as a squalid underbelly. A piano player in the parlor serenaded Oscar as he purchased overpriced champagne on ice; the washroom dustbins were cleaner than the drinking glasses in any of the fairy dives he frequented.

Still, he managed to have one of the more embarrassing experiences of his life there—twenty wilting minutes of panic and confusion, until the pitying over-rouged girl from Weehawken finally flexed the cramp from her hand and said, "Sometimes it's nice just to talk."

Considering himself thus doomed to bachelordom until either the world or womankind contrived to change themselves entirely, Oscar resigned himself to cultivating a vague reputation for virility in his public life. Demonstrating his manliness was an ongoing project, Oscar found; once achieved, it could be lost again, especially with the professional handicap of an industry that seemed to surround him in a cloud of lavender-smelling talcum. (This, of course, was the reason behind his coldness when introduced to Vivian at the socialite's garden party—her joke about his "perfume," born of her own insecurity and intended only to distance him as a new-money outsider, struck Oscar rather closer to the bone than Vivian could have foreseen. We ply dangerous waters, whenever we tease new acquaintances.)

Oscar's performance was made harder still by his social origins: most assertions of masculinity that his body had memorized (cutting ice, pitching hay, spreading pine tar) were now beneath him. Instead he learned to golf, to smoke cigars, to hunt canvasback for sport. He learned the art of country-house sloth, or at least of affecting it. He trained his laugh deeper, his stance wider, his manners more boorish. He switched from sandalwood to musk. There were still jokes and insinuations, especially as his business continued to improve—When would he settle down? Make some girl the envy of all her friends, with a bottomless vanity and a life-time's access to next season's perfume?—but at least the teasing and gossip always made the foundational error of presuming him normal.

Whenever he could, he lost himself in industry to avoid losing himself (for so he termed it) in sin. When the clock struck midnight at the dawn of the twentieth century—when all the city was lost in revelry, when across town Vivian was approaching Sofia and her liquid voice at the piano—Oscar was burning oil at his desk, reviewing paraffin contracts, the only human occupant of his office building. (He did encounter stray vermin, on these nocturnal shifts, but they didn't interfere with one another's business.) There were queer celebrations he might have attended, but in fact they were *too* significant for his taste. Two "balls" at separate dance halls on the Bowery had been advertised so heavily that Oscar was unwilling to risk exposing himself to conversation, to lamplight, to identification as anything more than an anonymous and disassociated anatomy.

Business was good, the better for being his frantic distraction from his vices. And so, despite all adversity, despite the pathological nervousness that sometimes burned his stomach lining as if he'd swallowed lye, for nearly two decades Oscar enjoyed—if that is the word—that kind of coldly increasing success that describes almost perfectly the hollow shape of happiness.

And then a child (in fact he was twenty-seven) arrived out of nowhere (in fact from Ronkonkoma) and tore the protective shell of Oscar's business to shreds.

THREE

S quire Clancey—the third and final pin in our map—did not set out
to ruin Oscar's career. It was done accidentally, without need or
malice, and with the wholly inadvertent assistance of his parents, who
had come to the very ends of their ropes.

On both sides—the Squire-Sacerdotes and the Clanceys—Squire was
descended from as close to real aristocracy as New York could boast
(having been a commercial rather than a courtly center from what our
self-absorbed subjects considered the beginning). Owing to textile money
on one side and dry goods on the other (and profiting from the slave trade
on both), it had been many generations since members of either clan had
worked for a living. (Though the global depression following Mount
Tambora's eruption did leave a legible scar in the ancestral balance sheets,
the families' fortunes had already been too well established to succumb to
a single summerless year.)

Squire's parents spent the early years of their marriage enjoying popularity as well as wealth, with a reputation for being good-looking, well-
dressed, and generous with their wine cellar. Neither of their families, in
New York's collective memory (which trended long on such matters), had
produced a scandal.

This happy situation left them totally unprepared for the challenge of
raising their son.

As soon as he was old enough to have a personality, Squire exhibited a strange one. He had almost a scientific mind (this alone would have been concerning enough), but applied it seemingly at random—and with a fanatical, sometimes even destructive, fixation. In an inexplicable—or at least unexplained—effort to learn knotwork, he braided all the tassels on an heirloom Persian rug in the drawing room, a job it took the servants the better part of an afternoon to unravel. He ruined an intricate fire screen of taxidermy hummingbirds, writing the Latin name of each species directly onto the linen backdrop. (He made several mistakes, which he corrected by smearing ink over the errors with his bare fingers. He was an enthusiast, not an aesthete.) He drew elaborate maps on drafting paper—first of New York, its familiar main stems and numbered cross streets; then of Spain and Africa; then (most unsettling to his parents) a land of no physical reality, with frothing pink waterfalls cascading from lime-green Himalayas. He had a constant yet mutable fascination with atlases in general—in various phases he charted the depths of the world's largest lakes, the lengths of its rivers, the heights of its mountains. (During a fixation on volcanoes, he noted with a pleased asterisk the two recorded heights of Mount Tambora in separate editions of his atlas. His constitution did not prompt him to research the eruption or its worldwide effects. Interest in human context came late to Squire, when it came at all.)

To his parents, who might at least have understood—indeed, who pressured him fruitlessly toward—the sporting ambition of tourism, Squire's interest in geography seemed so purely mathematical as to be nonsense. But in his own mind, Squire was building a catalog of the universe. He could *feel*, flipping the pages, that the Nile ran north but the Mississippi south. He could trace ancient glaciers in the lakebeds left by their clawing fingers. How did the world work? *Why* did it work? He was instinctively devoted to mapping the invisible. In time, this instinct expanded from geography to metaphysics.

Closed-doors eccentricity his parents might have managed—this was high society, after all—but as Squire aged, he began to involve their guests. Before one luncheon, he snuck into the butler's pantry and mixed two decanters of separate vintage wines into a punch, then stood dramatically in the middle of the sherbet course to reveal the undetected experiment—wasting a great deal of money and, even worse, embarrassing four of New York's best families.

Attempts to send the boy away to school were, perhaps predictably, abortive. (Mr. Clancey drew the line after two shamefaced expulsion interviews in two over-upholstered headmasters' offices, though for her part Mrs. Clancey would have tried a third.) Despite this persistent failure to be formally educated, Squire read too much—indeed, they could not keep him from it—and absorbed only the strangest ideas. Not the society mores of the novels of manners, nor the clear and picturesque narratives of adventure stories. From *The Adventures of Tom Sawyer*, for instance, he retained only a loud and insistent fascination with caves—often expressed (in mixed company!) by macabre questions about how long one might survive in various systems, or whether human beings thus trapped might eventually adapt beyond the need for eyes, like certain fish he'd read about. At age sixteen, the last straw: Squire, in an illegal exploration of the construction site of a new-money monstrosity, broke his arm and had to be rescued by a bricklayer—at the height of the shopping hour, with multiple important witnesses. When questioned, he explained that he'd been hunting for *Iguanodon* bones in the slag piles.

A family of the Clanceys' standing could afford one curious subspecies of domestic harmony: they had the resources to avoid each other. Considering Squire too dangerous a liability to allow in town, his parents scaled back to opening their house on Madison Avenue only a few times a year. Thereafter Squire lived most of the time with his mother (who had marginally more patience for him) in their summer place on Lake Ronkonkoma. His father kept a lonely watch over the Hudson and palisades, in the "winter" country estate that Squire and his mother visited principally for the family's storied annual Christmas party.

Squire had more success among the tourists at the Ronkonkoma resorts, if only because the population was refreshed so often that he lacked the chance to make a particular impression on any single cohort. His parents considered this rootless existence a success, in their son's case. Still, as the other young men of the Clanceys' set began to ascend (largely regardless of intelligence or talent) to paths of higher education, business, and influence, Squire's parents were increasingly frustrated by his persistent "oddness." (In fact he was bored, and lonely, and smarter than either of them. But these facts were not expressed in forms the Clanceys recognized, and Squire did not—could not have—prioritized their meager understanding.)

He had a preoccupation with the local legend of Lake Ronkonkoma, that it was so deep as to be bottomless—connected to other bodies of water, or possibly to the ocean itself, through an uncharted system of subaquatic caverns. Squire sometimes lost full afternoons standing knee-deep in the lake, studying the surface as though calculating whether he could dive in and surface in Long Island Sound. In the off-season he repeatedly attempted to enter the closed resorts—his only explanation, each time he was apprehended jiggling the handle at a servants' entrance, that he had never been inside an abandoned hotel and found the prospect interesting.

His parents worried—in their separate thoughts, and collaboratively via letter and telegram—first that Squire would fall in with the wrong people, then (more disappointing still) that he would fall in with no one at all. How would it end? Mr. and Mrs. Clancey wondered. What would become of them all?

They began to think with a rancid fondness of the early, childless days of their marriage.

It was during this same period that Squire became, without the benefit of forewarning or advice, a man. He was being more quarantined than raised, but still—in this as in all things, progress is inevitable.

Squire's body was an instrument he learned to use in secret and isolation, as he experienced most pleasures; he was in time an autodidact virtuoso. He understood—based on the baffling decisions of characters in novels, and on the slippery ellipses implied in etiquette guides, and on the anthropological observation of his supposed peers—that intimacy was something normally experienced as a connection between multiple people. In his own experience, it was simply one more valence of solitary exploration.

As if he did not have obstacles enough to normality, shortly after his twentieth birthday Squire's hair turned almost uniformly moon-gray. It even shone. His brows, however, remained black and thick. The contrast made him look like the victim of a prank—or, given the circumstances, like some kind of fairy-tale creature kept locked in a castle. At first, his parents consulted specialists on potential dye solutions—but such personal deceits depend on rigorous maintenance, and with Squire himself an unwilling partner in the conspiracy, the results were shocking and quickly abandoned. Indeed, he developed an almost mean-spirited pride in his hair. One of his few fastidious bows to conventionality was parting it each morning and evening with a handsome set of silver brushes. This uncharacteristic attention belied his claim that he simply didn't care about the defect enough to . . . Enough to *what*? he might have challenged his parents. This was how it grew. What, after all, was there to *do* about it?

Still, some days he pulled at his hair in the looking glass. Some days he wished himself unremarkable.

Things came to a head at the turn of the century, when Squire was twenty-five. He spent much of that year in deep passion over Victor Hugo's *Les Misérables*—though in his typical fashion he bypassed the novel's cast of heroes and villains, lovers and monks, tragedians and clowns and had eyes only for the chapters meticulously detailing the history and layout of the Parisian sewer system. Indeed, Squire had almost never felt a stronger connection to another human being than the one he felt to Hugo on his first reading—the novelist interrupting his action at its very apex, the doomed revolutionaries' last stand, to run to thousands of words on the subject of fetid municipal infrastructure. Squire cut the pages with trembling hands. He wrote a letter of appreciation that bordered on a declaration of love, but did not know how to address it. (Had he looked into the matter seriously he would have been further stymied by the fact that Hugo had died fourteen years earlier.) In the end he dropped the letter, earnestly and with private ceremony, into a storm drain.

Squire was particularly interested in sewers in the months thereafter—learning as much as he could (which was not much; he envied Hugo his archival resources) about different systems across the world. He had a local's bias, of course, for the history of New York's sewers—from the first covered troughs of the Dutch colonial era to the battle against cholera and the explosion of pipes and tunnels over the course of the century then drawing to a close. It was by Squire's present day a hidden network, a human-made natural wonder branching beneath the city like an inverted tree flowering in filth and slime.

By December 1899 it took only the slightest conversational opening—and sometimes not even that—to set Squire loose on the topic of the sewer system like a whirling natural wonder himself, a cyclone of enthusiasm that tore through general conversation, lifting trees by their roots. When Squire held forth his cheeks flushed; his silver hair stood on end where he worked his fingers through it. He fluttered his hands, squinting at the ceiling to summon a number or fact, leading himself down a winding tunnel into the noxious dark—speaking with breathless fervor of forgotten systems of ancient pipes and the bodies of victims of terrible crimes and rats as big as dogs, rats that had never seen the sun.

If Squire's parents had thought things could not possibly get worse, this latest fad disabused them of the notion. Sewers, filth, disease; effluent pipes and secret passageways—whatever society took pains to avoid, it was impossible to keep him silent on. If was as if, his parents felt, he were trying to undo all the millennial work of civilization, one conversation at a time.

Plans for the family's Christmas party on the Hudson were especially grand that year, if the guest list remained as exclusive as ever. The last Christmas of the century had the Clanceys' set feeling grandiose and important, as if they were the culmination of all human history. There was to be a costume parade and a charades tournament, both with fabulous prizes. A qualified expert would give a lecture predicting life in the year 1999. (Not too seriously, of course—he was the entertainment, not a professor.) A few days before the party, three towering fir trees were brought in to scrape the ballroom's ceiling, trimmed with tinsel. From one of them the groundskeeper had to evict a family of affronted squirrels—the peak of Squire's interest in the preparations. But he did find himself caught up in the spirit. Besides the excitement of the holiday there was the rare ease of seeing his parents happy together, and with Squire feeling at least a participant in their happiness, if not the cause.

On the day of the party, Squire had just dressed and finished arranging his thatch of tinsel hair when his parents descended on him in a pincer formation. (A rare collaborative effort, from two people who had not cooperated on anything more involved than delegating a task to a servant in some years.)

"This is an important evening," his father began. A hothouse gardenia was already stationed as his boutonniere; he looked stylishly out of season. "There are going to be a lot of people here, and they're not coming to be upset."

"No," Squire agreed, uncertainly.

"We need you to be careful tonight," his mother said. Her hair had been fixed in a pompadour rising to a pearled aigrette, the feathers telegraphing each nervous tremble of her head. "Try not to say anything about . . . well—"

"The damn sewer," his father supplied.

"Well," his mother said. "Yes."

Squire had not been planning to—he never *planned* to—but he had been himself long enough to know his limitations, and he knew he was being given an impossible mandate. He was about to navigate fifty conversations with people he hadn't seen in a year—all of them wolfish gossips full of false sympathy, with normal sons who had spent their first years of adulthood at Harvard or Yale or carousing abroad instead of invalided halfway out Long Island. He was about to weather fifty polite, pitying inquiries as to *how he had been amusing himself lately.* "What . . . what am I to say?" he asked in a weak voice.

"Just nothing disgusting."

"Or outrageous."

"Or memorable," his mother added—then, perhaps realizing she had gone too far—"Just please no sewers. Just for tonight. You can't bring them up with these people."

"Why not?" Squire asked.

Something his parents never realized: if they could only have given him a reason that made any sense to him, he would have been perfectly willing to comply. But always they heard the question as obstinacy, or antagonism, or stupidity—and they had ice sculptures arriving in half an hour, and their first eager guests shortly thereafter.

"Because of course you can't," his mother said, her egret feathers performing an exasperated semaphore.

"Because if you do, you'll regret it," his father added.

Squire and Mr. Clancey hadn't spent enough time together for this threat to have any clear meaning, but that made it all the more ominous.

Squire tried. He did try. But all evening he felt the mounting pressure of his unvoiced enthusiasm, which the empty chat of the other guests tacitly labeled monstrous. Listening to them, parroting their clichés with difficulty and stopping his mouth with champagne every time a tray floated by, Squire began to reach the limit of his endurance.

He was going to do it, he realized, as a brace of spinster cousins approached him with wassail-flushed cheeks and compliments on the party. He was going to talk to them about sewers.

How might history be different, if Mount Tambora had had the ability to flee the scene before its eruption? To spare Earth's inhabitants the inconveniences of its nature and its power, by removing itself to the planet's core or the void of outer space? Would it have saved lives? Or would its sudden absence have had larger consequences than its outburst?

Squire's case, though less fantastic, was ultimately no less explosive. He fled the party without notice. (Indeed, no one missed him until much later, the cousins who triggered his flight being easily distracted by subsequent amusements.)

Outside, the frigid air and twinkle of stars and gaslights raised tears in Squire's eyes. He was panting as if the sprint down the house's staircase had been a marathon. His breath clouded.

"Fuck," he said into the darkness.

Hansom cabs and vis-à-vis sleighs were milling in the driveway as guests arrived in a steady trickle and, less reliably, departed. Furtively, impulsively, Squire joined the less reliable.

Over packed snow to Yonkers, by the late train into the city—its avenues and cross streets variously raucous and pious in observation of the holiday. Squire's patent-leather oxfords slid and slipped over the slushy pavement. In minutes they were ruined, his toes numb.

Squire's mind was curiously blank that evening, at least when it came to the real world and its consequences—he was no more conscious of his freezing feet than of the dismay his absence would cause, when it was discovered. The party felt impossibly distant, a phantom gathering—something that had happened years before, on the other side of the world, rather than an ongoing bacchanal fourteen miles north.

Despite this detachment, Squire's stride was purposeful. He scanned the cobblestones, kicked at clods of gritty ice in mounting urgency—until at last, having traveled half a mile south in fits and starts, he found what he was looking for.

In *Les Misérables*, Jean Valjean clears loose paving stones and an iron grille from the entrance to the sewer "like what is done in delirium, with the strength of a giant and the rapidity of an eagle." In the space of a moment he finds himself in a long tunnel, a place of "deep peace" and "absolute silence," safe from the desperate clash of weapons above.

Squire had the delirium, and the wish for deliverance from chaos. But either Valjean had been rather stronger than Squire had understood, or Parisian sewer grates were no match for New York's cast-iron manhole covers. Squire struggled with his for long minutes—finding nothing nearby to press-gang into service as a lever, he scrabbled with his fingers, shredding his nails, reaching into the ventilation holes and pulling hard enough to dislocate one of his knuckles. His trousers were soon soaked through with grimy slush from knees to hem. In the frigid air no smell came up from the vents—it seemed almost antiseptic. Squire had a desperate vision of subterranean, luminescent frozen lakes, the buried springs of Manhattan's rural past still running their course through humanity's lost treasures and secret fears.

His skin stuck and pulled against the cold metal, as if the sewer were doing its best to accept him. But their efforts were in vain.

If gaining entry to the city's network of pipes had truly been Squire's practical goal, he could more efficiently have stayed in Yonkers. He could have found one of the fast-flowing streams—partially iced over, at that time of year—that disappeared into a brick culvert, and followed it into the dark. (And to his almost certain doom, washed out into the Hudson long before the outflow joined up with the city's warren of vitrified clay and cement-mortar pipework.)

As it was, a passing policeman found Squire locked in battle with the manhole cover and asked—not unkindly—what the hell was the matter with him.

THERE WAS CONFUSION and delay, as ever, in the challenge of sorting the world's expectations of Squire from the reality of him. There was medical attention and a suit of dry clothes, to start—but having traded his ruined tailcoat for a jacket of reach-me-down cut and a shirt several inches too long in the sleeves, a nurse's gauze making mittens of his hands, his hair cowlicked into conceptual art by a hot towel rough as burlap, Squire found the policemen even less apt to take him seriously. They thought, at first, that they'd apprehended him attempting some kind of vaudevillian crime—perhaps returning to the scene of a hobo squat. "No, no," Squire explained. "We have a house on Madison Avenue." He had to say it several times before they even believed he meant it, and several more before anyone agreed to waste time looking into the story. "But it isn't open," Squire said. And then, remembering, ice in his stomach—"everyone's in Yonkers."

SQUIRE SPENT THAT New Year's Eve—while Vivian duetted with Sofia; while Oscar burned the midnight oil at his office—in a sanatorium in St. Augustine.

His parents tried at first to admit him to an asylum, but he was declared not sufficiently insane or violent. Recovering from this disappointment, he spent two confusing if peaceful months reading in a low canvas chair on the sandy crabgrass lawn, breathing the purportedly healing atmosphere of Florida. It was unclear—to everyone concerned—what precisely he was meant to be healed *of*, and when actual tubercular patients began to queue for his bed, Squire returned to New York for March's leonine entrance—repentant in spirit, almost unable to remember his fit on the evening of the Christmas party, but stubbornly unpathologized and therefore incurable.

His parents, having been given a break in which to recover from their own nervous upsets, were at last ready with a plan of action that—for good or ill—suited all parties. Upon reflection, they found that in isolating Squire out of town, they had been going about things all wrong—making him their particular responsibility, and limiting his stimulation until he felt forced to invent his own. In the metropolis, they realized now, Squire would be most occupied and least conspicuous—and, policed by the public eye, no longer under their sole jurisdiction.

Of course, in point of fact they were giving up—attempting to slip the Sisyphean burden of repressing their irrepressible son.

They intended Squire's new situation as a punishment, but—Is this love? Do we measure such things by intent, or result?—from rarified enough guardians, estrangement looks like freedom, and a pittance like more than resources enough to live eccentrically. To give him the run of the ancestral townhouse was out of the question. (The desecration of the hummingbird fire screen was still fresh in his mother's mind, even over a decade later.) Instead, they leased him a French flat in a bachelors' district—shelving him, they thought, like a pair of ready-made shoes in a department store—with a doorman to act as warden. This accomplice they compensated handsomely in return for information on Squire's movements and any worrying trends. (Alas for the Clanceys, they overestimated the doorman's devotion to the project: besides having a laissez-faire philosophy generally, he took a liking to Squire, who reminded him of a favorite stage comedian of his boyhood.) Squire's parents granted him the smallest monthly allowance they thought decently livable—in fact a princely sum for almost anyone, but particularly so for a man who found most luxuries pointless and nearly all social mores to be unnecessary inconveniences.

This is not to say Squire found nothing to spend money on. During his questionable convalescence, he had transferred his affections from Victor Hugo and the phantom streets of the sewer system to a new fascination du jour. The sanatorium library had a handsome copy of Faraday's six-part set of scientific lectures for young people, *The Chemical History of a Candle.*

In Faraday's obsessive yet conversational tone, his meandering deep into the minutiae of an object prized by most citizens of the world precisely for its thoughtless simplicity, he might have been speaking directly for Squire's ears. "There is no more open door by which you can enter into the study of natural philosophy," Faraday wrote, "than by considering the physical phenomena of a candle."

Squire relished metaphors, often appreciating them literally. This one enthralled him: *no more open door than a candle.* He returned to the city in a new fit of interest—unseasonably freckled and with hair rendered almost bioluminescent by the Florida sun, having absorbed the science and manufacture of candles and in the spirit to talk of little else.

New York's resources for an interested, enthusiastic young man were almost infinitely more thorough and varied than Lake Ronkonkoma's.

With the conspiratorial silence of his doorman-warden, Squire met with C. K. Lawrence, the bemused owner of a candle manufactory in Lower Manhattan. The accommodating merchant—slightly eccentric himself, in his fidelity to his business past the flicked switch of the electric century, and with a healthy, intimidated respect for the Clancey name—gave Squire a tour of the premises, and a historical lecture on the field as he'd seen it change over the course of his career. Cotton wicks dipped into layer upon layer of rendered tallow for cheap, greasy tapers; the process of purifying the same tallow into clean-burning stearin by boiling it with quicklime, decomposing it with sulfuric acid, and pressing out glycerin. His new water-cooled machines, hand-operated to cast perfect molds in almost odorless paraffin wax with tightly braided wicks. The new fashions—as, Lawrence admitted with wounded but honest pride, candles moved from necessity to ornament—for chemically colored waxes in mauve and magenta.

Squire was rapt. He wanted to participate. "I have some money," he said.

"Oh," Lawrence blinked. Squire, familiar with the expression on his face, knew the man was trying to decide whether he was joking.

"I'd like to be in business," Squire said. "If I find someone to make it alright with the money, the paperwork, would you help me spend it?"

How many millions of struggling laborers have lain awake over how many centuries, fantasizing about receiving such a proposition?

"It's a bad business," Lawrence choked finally, moved to mirror Squire's frankness.

"Why?"

In answer Lawrence pointed overhead, to the buzzing yellow sun of an electric light bulb. Squire made a dismissive gesture. "And the supplies," Lawrence said. "Lime, tallow, the oils and dyes. Those contracts go to soap companies now. Especially the local shipments."

"Oh," Squire said. "I'm sure we can change their minds."

FOUR

Squire—or more accurately his money—did change things. Not enough to upset the shipping lanes of economic and technological progress, of course. But quite enough to nearly scuttle the latest Midwestern arrival in New York harbor.

In service of his new hobby, Squire—acting under the advice and partnership of Mr. Lawrence, when not represented by him directly—chanced to make inquiries with nearly all of Oscar Schmidt's suppliers. And the Clancey name, to say nothing of the implied fortune standing behind it, was an almost mystically powerful local motivator. Squire could pay top dollar for his materials; he could also (though he was insensible of this fact, still it served him) threaten to ruin the reputation of anyone who refused to do business with him. A good relationship with his family was considered almost a more valuable investment than anything on Wall Street. And so Squire's name and his money tripped happily around the city's slaughterhouses and chemical plants and shipping yards, everywhere scooping up the raw materials of Oscar's livelihood.

Why, Squire wondered, did the world reward some impractical fixations with prestige and fortune, and sneer at others as disgusting or deranged? Why was it insane for him to love the sewer culvert, which carried away disease and secreted ancient springs, but charming of him to love the candle, which melted animal fat onto socialites' best linens and rimed their windows with smoke? What made one a better "open door" into science and society than the other?

This is not to say Squire was successful, by strict definitions. He did have an undeniable intuition for certain creative aspects of the business— but Mr. Lawrence was correct that electricity was squeezing their entire industry into obscurity. Moreover, Squire's fascination ran to bespoke products and an artisanal, almost literally molecular interest in the chemistry of the venture—the very nemesis of efficiency and entrepreneurial spirit. He was impractically partial to brightly colored wax and strangely shaped molds. And, reasoning there was no need to halt progress at removing the *un*pleasant odors from burning tallow, he began odd experiments with scented oils and absolutes. (More finite resources divided between our protagonists! Bergamot, lavender, rose—these essential tinctures, too, began to be snatched from Oscar's waiting hands before they were even unloaded from cargo holds.)

But these scented candles, which tended toward eye-watering potency, were a novelty product at best—or would have been, had Mr. Lawrence believed in them enough to advertise them—and increased overheard costs still more.

Over time, this peculiar cycle of mercantile capitalism eddied itself into a Charybdis: Squire leeched away more and more of Oscar's lifeblood, without ever himself turning a profit. The fact was that, operating from the twin bottomless coffers of his allowance and his family's reputation, Squire was disinterested in success.

AS FOR OSCAR, there was no great mystery as to the cause of his misfortune. His vendors, with impersonal shrugs and hollow regrets, made no secret of the cause of their diverted business. Oscar learned the name *Squire Clancey* within a month—and learned to hate it almost as quickly. There followed several years for him to nurse the feeling, letting it take root in the compost of his decaying career and reputation.

The failures came in a cascade of delayed and cumulative consequences— into 1902, then 1903, then looking ahead to 1904, Oscar was given plenty of time to cringe in anticipation of each blow. The great labor of his career thus far had been the development and coordination of a complex and many-dimensional set of schedules: harvest, processing, delivery, production. Tallow churned from the city's slaughterhouses in a ceaseless bloody mass, a paradoxically limited yet overwhelming supply that, as the by-product of another industry, would wait for no man. Oscar's near-miraculous administrative triumph had been to marry this rough, frantic, mercilessly efficient cadence to the delicate and far-flung production of his cosmetics' other ingredients. For instance: his rose oil and water came from Bulgaria, where blossoms were picked and processed still rimed with morning dew. Each ton of rose petals (a jarring concept, perhaps—but any substance can become a crushing weight, when sufficiently accumulated) yielded half a pound of distilled oil. Jasmine was even worse: it had to be picked by specialists, workers trained not to bruise the petals and thus mar the scent that was finally extracted. Eight million jasmine flowers yielded two pounds of liquid absolute.

Each of these harvests had to be timed and calculated to match the availability of local distillers, and their requirements in turn: wood and water; bottles and corks. Only so many flowers could be grown and processed in a season. Now Oscar learned of cascading shortages and conflicting orders and lagging chains of supply; now he learned that troublingly significant percentages of next year's crop, next year's oil, next year's deliveries were promised elsewhere. (Were promised to *Squire Clancey*.)

Oscar's production schedule was so complex and fine-tuned, it was possible for Squire to ruin it with relatively little effort, and even less awareness—a kind of accidental guerrilla warfare. The long lead times also gave Squire the opportunity (if that is the word) to inflict twelve or eighteen months' misery with a passing interest (What *was* a tuberose, anyway? he asked Mr. Lawrence) that he'd have long since forgotten by the time the order was filled.

The meatpackers and their tallow defected to Squire, too, though for unrelated reasons: as locals they knew the name "Clancey," and they had no time to hold their supply while Oscar sought Cincinnati's approval for an emergency adjustment of the New York office's production flow. Even now, the next herd was marching into the abattoir.

Oscar Schmidt and Squire Clancey were, of course, far from the first ridiculous and privileged men to wage a proxy battle over tallow and fragrance. Personal Care had for centuries been a brutal industry of warring empires. Capital Letters, pins in the map: the Silk Road, the Incense Road, the crazed and bloody European lust for oil and spice. The Catholic Church had long since sourced its frankincense tears from the Horn of Africa. The Dutch East India Company, stamping its name on Mount Tambora and designating its entire neighboring archipelago the "Spice Islands," had used genocide and slavery to harvest nutmeg and cloves. (The eruption of 1815 did little to interrupt this process.) Flowers had long been conquered and conquering, too—gardenia, orchid, jasmine. Invading Romans brought "English" lavender to England. In turn, English naturalists named for themselves Chinese rose varietals that had already been cultivated for millennia. And turpentine camps, which razed virgin pine forests to harvest fragrant resin, had been among European settlers' first contributions to their American colonies.

And sandalwood: an animal, almost buttery scent, like living skin. Native to India, the Hawaiian Islands, Australia. Made from the very heartwood of the tree, not its resin, the oil grows more potent and abundant with the age of the specimen. Sandalwood is sacred to at least three religions, officially declared a royal tree in multiple sultanates and provinces. And there is no way to harvest and distill the oil but to destroy the heartwood, grinding trees—the older the better—into fine powder. Now Oscar and his clerks, Squire and Mr. Lawrence, fell over themselves in a race to order it done.

Two small men scrap over resources, feeling what they know as desperation, insistent that "everything" is at risk. A fault line trembles, and on the other side of the world it snows in July. There are no stakes but the global; there is no timeline but the infinite.

FOR HIS PART, Squire sought no rivalry—but of course, the universe does not distribute antagonism according to intention. And no conflict remains one-sided for long; every animal instinct demands that we defend ourselves when cornered.

The escalation in the press was Oscar's own fault—even by his own design, however poorly it served him. The threat of failure raised a doubled panic in him—as a self-made man with no safety net and a social reputation that depended on performing nouveau-riche largesse, he could not afford the kind of financial collapse now darkening the horizon. But worse, almost, was the blow to his foundation as an industrious, productive, *normal* man—in his own eyes as in others'. Any successful businessman, in a commercial capital such as New York, could not properly be sneered at no matter his business. But each drop in Oscar's profits seemed to bring a reciprocally greater public notice to his strange fields of expertise, his powder-puff industry, his confirmed bachelordom.

He was his own worst critic. Oscar had never had a consciously transactional deal with himself, never claimed that his professional success earned him the right to—or atoned for the sins of—his sexual life. But when things changed, he felt the loss of the unspoken arrangement like the plunge from a breathable atmosphere into deep water.

Desperately he tried—officially, in firms and offices; casually, at his club and in his associates' walnut-and-malachite smoking rooms; insidiously, in rumors muttered near infamous gossips and society columnists—to discredit Squire. After all, Oscar was an experienced career man in his forties, having risen through the ranks of Personal Care at an honorably modest pace and painstakingly made a name for himself in the metropolis. Who was this razzle-dazzle princeling, jeopardizing New York's most reliable local source of bath soaps and eau de toilette?

But in this offensive Oscar overestimated his own cachet, as a still-new face in an old city, feuding with a scion of one of its oldest families (albeit a crackpot recluse raised in the outer lands). If he brought attention to their rivalry, it was to his own detriment. Gossip columns (even the *Metropolitan News*'s "Midtown Tattler," no longer under Electra Blake's reign but still thriving) began to gloat over his financial upset, and to poke fun at him for his very efforts to turn the tide through social opinion. And anyway, wasn't there a certain . . . *old-fashioned* character to his products? Bland cakes of grandmother-scented laundry soap; perfumes marketed to be cringingly sprayed on a handkerchief, as if too embarrassed by bare skin? Rumors began to circulate casting Oscar as a denizen of the century just gone, and Squire as one of the future's many competing heralds—albeit, for now, generating more noise than power.

Squire himself resented the coverage, if only because it drew the attention of his parents. After each evening edition that mentioned Squire's name in combat with Oscar Schmidt's came a familial telegram cautioning

Squire to act respectably, even threatening to return to town to police his artistic experiments. Who, Squire wondered, was this man of whom he had never heard, this stuffy middle-aged farmer-clerk from *Ohio*, imperiling his fragile and hard-won happiness? (Squire's own peculiarity did not, of course, disqualify him from his birthright as a snob of the first order.)

By the dawn of 1904, the two men still had not met—a combination of Oscar's wounded avoidance, Squire's delegation of his day-to-day "business" to Mr. Lawrence, and a shared healthy disdain for animosity— but they had weathered a few close calls, having through accident and obligation been present at several of the same large society functions. There was much general, amused speculation as to whether and when they would accost each other at last—and many low-stakes bets were made on the outcome of any resultant fisticuffs. (Oscar was the brawnier of the two, but older, and—this had begun to be discussed, in whispers and in printed innuendo—there was something almost delicate in his carriage.)

Things came to a head when a reporter—Squire, giving a ham-handed but earnest answer to the man's question, had not even realized he worked for the press—quoted him out of context, daubing a libelous sneer over Squire's already cringingly patrician statement that he "didn't mean any harm in succeeding, and hoped he'd left [Schmidt] something to live on." The quote ran as part of a gossip column that referred to Oscar as a "horti-cultural gent"—stopping so short of the accusation of queerness, the words seemed to teeter for balance even as he read.

Oscar felt caught in quicksand, lashed to railroad tracks. Disgrace was coming at last, he knew. And he could do nothing to stave off this long-dreaded breakdown—for decades, his only cultivated skills had been avoidance, self-deceit, and disassociation.

He was, miserably, practicing each as well as he could on the night everything changed.

OUR THREE PLAYERS at last drew nigh at an illegal but fashionable gambling palace for machine politicians and mock-aristocrats—the party held at a luxurious social hall located four blocks, traversed often (but never on foot), from the Fifth Avenue Hotel. Plush wallpaper and dim lights and *baccarat* pronounced reverently, not like French but like its own language. A language only partly of words, more the shush of cards and the tap on a tabletop and the decorous, fetishized offer of a change in one's luck. A game won not by being dealt the better hand but by guessing correctly who had been. A game that let you bet on the likelihood of a draw, turning even parity into something the player won or lost.

Squire was in attendance at the invitation—more accurately the insistence—of Mr. Lawrence the candlemaker, who maintained that his business partner should show his face now and again in order to supplement his finances with the mystique of social collateral. Squire traveled a mathematically precise and nearly silent circuit over the burgundy carpet, keeping his smiles polite and his feet moving to minimize the danger of being trapped in conversation and (inevitably) behaving outrageously.

Oscar entered the casino night in hollow observance of what he still, nervously, counted as his set's standard behavior—and in a private, self-loathing mourning over an event held in the same social hall a few evenings before, an open drag ball associated with one of the dives in his rotation. What separated Oscar, he wondered miserably, from the men who had cavorted here openly and with city permits? What tacit decree ensured that Oscar was damned, by himself and others, for the same proclivities?

The two men avoided each other as enemies. But a third and more powerful attendee, they did not countenance at all.

(Have you also forgotten Vivian, in the distracting tableau vivant of our peacocking male rivals? Careful: this weakness is among her most easily manipulated.)

Vivian and Sofia were late in their association, the night they came to the gambling palace. Reduced, or heightened, to stoking excitement via games of chance. Their very entrance to the clubhouse was one such game—Sofia carrying an eagle-feather fan, in a satin dress that seemed to glow under its own power; Vivian in a black tulle tucker that lent her, rather than modesty, an androgynously intimidating sensuality.

They had argued over trifles, preparing to leave for the evening. They arrived in a tense, glittering silence.

The attendants at the door had been charged with stroking male egos, with collecting tickets and dues and bribes, and with turning away gentlemen with insufficient credit (whether on Wall Street or Fifth Avenue). They had not, however, been briefed on the proper procedure if a pair of rogue women were to challenge their post.

"Antonio has asked me to play cards for him," Sofia said—handing over the invitation addressed to a Sicilian actor who had been courting her (and, out of necessity, Vivian) with seemingly infinite patience. He was playing Shylock even as they spoke, in a production that saw him dodging roses by the dozen at each curtain call. "And this," Sofia said, pressing Vivian's hand, "is my good luck charm."

Vivian could feel the shifting tides in the touch, the glance, the play of power across this well-guarded threshold. Her lover's attention was drifting—to Antonio and his roses; to Paris and points beyond; to her career. Though still beloved, it was undeniable: Vivian's stock had fallen; she had been demoted from partner to "good luck charm."

Vivian had resolved to let the singer take her leave without grudge or regret, winning by yielding to the player with the better hand. The resolve was wavering: Vivian was only human. She felt an anxious pressure to make other arrangements while it was still possible—before the ties were fully loosed. She dreaded the thought of being filed away in a boarding-house, or the hunt for employment trimming hats or washing laundry, thirteen hours a day in steam and hot starch, or—worst of all—a defeated return to Utica.

With initial relief, in the first blush of life with Sofia, Vivian had let her duty-bound letters to her parents lapse—and Mr. and Mrs. Lesperance had reciprocated, the whole family giving up the pretense of filial piety by correspondence course. But ever since, Vivian had suffered a growing sense of guilty paranoia, the uneasy feeling that she was neglecting something critically important. And a few months ago, just as Sofia's devotion had begun to wane, Vivian had received a letter in her post office box: a clipping from the *Herald-Dispatch* (it had only been the *Herald*, the last time Vivian had seen a copy in person), announcing Ruf Thomas's marriage to Honoria O'Shea. "Provided our daughter is still alive," Mrs. Lesperance had written—her taste for melodrama undiluted by her own participation in the preceding silence—"let her take updated stock of her prospects."

Vivian had counted on her fingers: Honoria O'Shea could not have been more than seventeen years old. Vivian was on the wrong side of twenty-three, with four gray hairs (of which she was aware). Sofia was looking elsewhere, and now the closest thing Vivian had ever had to a "real"—male—suitor had married a girl the same age she'd been when she spurned him, six years before. As though opening an old book to the same page.

Girls, Vivian knew, could not circle back six or seven or ten years older and pick up where they had left off.

But oh, why would she want to? Utica, her parents, her prospects—she had cast them all aside for a reason, and the very thought of a return trapped her breath in her throat.

But what if no heads turned her way again, after Sofia? What if she were to run out of road?

Back on the threshold of the gambling palace, the attendant holding Sofia's repurposed invitation paused, stammering. He turned to his colleague, who was busy with another guest.

At a loss for proper procedure, the man pivoted—as they often did—to Vivian.

Middlemen were so willing, Vivian had found, to yield their authority at the first sign of conflict. When push came to shove, it seemed, most people—even the powerful—only wanted to be told what to do and find comfort in the execution of their orders. When struck at the right angle, and with confidence, such people split like logs.

Through her secretly mounting alarm at the precarity of her situation, through the echo of Sofia calling her a "good luck charm," Vivian tried to soothe herself with this thought.

She arched an eyebrow, gave the panicking attendant a permissive nod.

"This way, ladies," he said gratefully, and parted the portieres with a smile.

Once they had entered, Vivian and Sofia were tolerated in the club-house. And as the night wore on more women would appear, scattered among the card players or nursing cocktails on plush settees—some shocking young people in short hair and waistcoats; others ancestresses old and important enough to disregard propriety. As Vivian had already found, the very ability to bribe or charm or strong-arm their way into the room burnished these few aberrations with a kind of mystique, credentials assumed by all without ever being exactly granted. It was an uncertain position, but a tenable one.

Until—the thought erupted—one's luck ran out.

Sofia pressed Vivian's hand again and disappeared in the direction of the bar, her dress trailing light. Vivian—who had not been calmed by liquor in long years—circled the floor, fighting an uncharacteristic lack of certainty.

As she anticipated her looming break with Sofia, Vivian's own fragility menaced her, like a pulse beating quick in a thimble-less hand. She felt transitional as a ghost. She had never been truly alone in the city, and the prospect frightened her. (Though Vivian had a genius for improvisation and exploitation, we cannot call either a synonym for independence.) And she was tired. Even success—finding another star to hitch her wagon to, for as long as their paths ran parallel—was an exhausting prospect. Vivian wanted to be in charge of her life—and, if at all possible, of someone else's. She wanted to extend the flashes of power she felt over door attendants and maître d's into permanence.

She took a seat at a bridge table, smiling enigmatically. Transmuting, she hoped, her own insecurity into outward-facing inscrutability. She played once and won—felt herself an invulnerable sphinx, a warrior-goddess who would make a private estate of Central Park. She played again and lost, all the previous hand's winnings and two dollars more—and was shriven to pieces on the disappointment. Someday soon, she thought, when Sofia had withdrawn across the Atlantic with her burbling laugh and her warm hands and her pearl-clasped purse, Vivian would be unable to cover her own debts.

For now, she gave her lover's name to the dealer tracking wins and losses and gave up her seat at the table.

The stupid loss of the two dollars smarted doubly because Vivian had been saving where she could in the margins of her and Sofia's largesse, cultivating a secret economy—not so different from her early days in the city, between stints at Electra's, stealing rolls and passing slowly past lamplit gallery windows to disguise her lack of a place to sleep. But having survived such a bluff once did not make her eager to repeat the trial, particularly not when she had such a richly feathered nest from which to fall.

A new thought flickered, spectral in the anxious whirl: perhaps *this* was why women married. Perhaps it all came down to a disturbing letter and an empty purse and four gray hairs. Perhaps the Honoria O'Sheas of the world simply ran out of road closer to their front doors.

IT WAS ON her second, unsettled lap of the room that she recognized Oscar. The soap man, she thought; the yokel she'd teased at that garden party in Westhampton, or Tuxedo, or wherever it had been. The Midwesterner with mutton-chop whiskers and a muse's complexion. At last the name sprang to her mind: Oscar Schmidt. The society pages had been using it for target practice in recent months, as his business and his social reputation circled the drain.

Perhaps, Vivian reasoned (and correctly), it was in an attempt to salve his wounds that Oscar was visibly drunk at the baccarat table—albeit in an inward-facing way, a politely dismayed sloppiness. (Eventually Vivian would learn that Oscar was a man with a shallow draft; very little liquor was needed to float him.) He clung to the table as if he had brought it to a party where it had no other acquaintances, and now worried whether it would enjoy itself without him.

Vivian felt an almost-tenderness for the man—and an almost-regret for sneering at him the previous summer, even in jest. She saw in Oscar, after all, her saddest potential future: a rejected transplant, a nouveau-riche aspirant given the humiliatingly slow-motion bum's rush back to Peoria.

Or, she thought, wherever.

Vivian would never be able to muster a strong compassion that did not begin in some form of self-interest. But such beginnings can develop in unexpected directions.

She watched for a moment longer as Oscar stared at his cards and muttered to himself—reprimands, encouragement, consolation. Besides her guilt and her pity and her fear-tinged sympathy, this charmed her: Oscar wanted to solve his problems without involving others. Vivian decided, at least for an evening's schadenfreudian distraction, to get involved.

"Mr. Schmidt," she greeted him.

Oscar startled, slopping half his glass of wine onto the carpet. He blinked at her, fright without recognition. He did not remember her.

In Oscar's defense, we will note that he had had more to worry about lately than one feminine insult at a garden party: he had received notice via the afternoon mail that his superior at the soap company would inspect the New York office in three weeks' time. Traveling, Oscar anticipated with dread, all the way from Cincinnati specifically to berate or even fire him for letting Squire Clancey skewer their business.

Vivian, of course, was not privy to these specifics. But she recognized at a glance, if vaguely, the prey instinct planted in Oscar by his Grandmother Hester; cultivated in a lifetime of illicit desires meticulously obscured; and teetering now on the edge of nervous collapse. "Vivian Lesperance," she said. And, to manifest the possibility in his wine-saturated mind: "I'm a friend of yours."

"Oh?" Oscar said, pathetically hopeful.

"Your glass is empty," she observed, and led him to the refreshment table.

Gentling a gun-shy ruminant with a proffered treat—but for the breadth of Oscar's shoulders and the sway in his step, Vivian could have been feeding Electra Blake on the night of the debutante ball. In this case, she plied Oscar with more of the vintageless but free-flowing wine. She kept a careful distance during their conversation, as he seemed as likely to tip each glass over onto the bunting-swagged bar as into his own mouth.

Oscar had by this point drunk enough to have acquired mystical powers, a blessed freedom from the constraints of time and space. Yes, he was in this chintz-and-damask social hall, shuffling cards and losing money to people who were laughing at him whenever he turned his back and who would sneer about him in print in the morning editions. But he was also a time-traveling resident of three weeks hence, rising to receive his disapproving manager in his office.

Oscar dreaded losing his position at the company—in many ways, employment there had saved his life. But there was also an illicit thrill in the prospect of being ruined, and free to wallow in everything he'd taken such desperate, unsuccessful pains to deny himself.

For besides all this computation of present and future conversations—and in a way most vividly, for it was the one vision in all the dreamscape that comforted him—Oscar was taking involuntary, hallucinatory refuge in memories of his favorite slides downtown. The raucous floor shows; the highball glasses still smudged from the last man's mouth; the constant vigilance for knockout drops in one's scotch and soda. The silent understandings reached over the offer of a cigarette; the sickly-sweet release in the darkness of the balcony tier. Most of all, the cacophonous arch banter across tables crowded with rouged, svelte-cut, muscled, raucous, blessed anonymity.

Now here was Vivian, an ambiguously sexed pillar of straight-backed black wool and tulle and attentive concern, refilling his glass and asking him questions that seemed to cut through the whole stream at once. A society lady, making small talk; his boss, asking him to account for himself; a fellow fag on the Bowery, inviting him to dish.

Oscar, fiddling amid the flames, let himself go. Was he having a pleasant time? he repeated. No, Miss Lesperance, he was not. He was not having much of a time at all. He had lost fourteen dollars at a game he had never heard of, and nobody could explain how in a way that satisfied him. He was drinking boiler-room vinegar without a year and had lost one of his gloves. (He flexed his hand to show her.) For almost an hour now he had been trying to find the door, but every time he stepped he ran into a gaming table and lost money at it, so he'd reached the point where to move in any direction seemed more dangerous than to sit and wait for death. Was this considered an amusing way to pass an evening on Fifth Avenue?

Oscar delivered this diatribe in a toothless, sadly entertaining anger that tilted more than a few times into camp. Though Vivian didn't know the particular secret version of Oscar erupting through his uptown facade, the hidden Bowery fairy who so feared exposure he'd accidentally drunk himself visible in the very lion's den, she had run long enough with Sofia's artist set and seen enough of the long-haired Village scene to recognize the queer language Oscar was speaking—and had read enough of the barbed, barely anonymous pseudo-libel circling him to know he was flirting with his own doom.

She felt a flare of intoxicating power over Oscar, an awareness that she held him in the palm of her hand. She could protect him, keeping him in unintelligible conversation with a lady on the room's periphery until she poured him into a cab. Or she could top off his glass and spin him back into the fray, let him swish directly into the last society reporter he would ever meet. The sense of power warmed her center, dissolving some of her general fear for the future. She wanted to hold on to the sensation.

No one would have mistaken such a feeling for affection, but the end result was the same: Vivian decided for the moment that she would keep Oscar occupied, help him keep his hair pinned up.

Oscar, of course, was insensate of this kindness.

"Perhaps a casino night chafes in its honesty," she said, "but isn't the great project of most parties to make debtors of one's friends?"

"*Friends!*" Oscar protested, as if disagreeing with the very concept.

"Oh—are we among enemies?" Vivian asked, mock-conspiratorially.

Just as she asked, the crowd eddied so that Sofia was momentarily visible across the room, her swan's neck bent to attend to an heiress's anecdote. Vivian faltered, her smile wavering.

But Oscar, too far gone to notice, was already unburdening himself like a burst dam. With painful relief he abandoned the subtle cunning with which he'd attempted to discredit his rival in months past, and simply complained. His *nemesis*, he explained in a slushy voice, was haunting the gambling hall this evening. Stalking him. Squire Clancey—the man's given name was Squire!—Oscar composed himself and began again. Squire Clancey was a candlemaker, *obviously* doomed by incandescence, now trying to cut into the perfume business with no experience. A newcomer affecting old-fashioned manners, he called himself a "chandler"—as though, Oscar sneered, they were living in either the distant past or the country of France.

Vivian, bolstered by her foreknowledge of the gossip in the social news, deduced at once the truth beneath his bluster: that paraffin wax and animal fat and scented oils were limited resources, especially in an island city, and even a "doomed" man could be a competitor.

And now Squire the chandler was *here*, Oscar cried! He'd decided ruining Oscar's business was not enough, and had had the gall to invade his social circle!

Vivian was further touched, that Oscar objected to any man's presence in his sanctum over her own. Perhaps, she thought with a twist of
polluting fear, there was some uninvited solidarity that bound all outsiders
and arrivistes. Perhaps all her self-invention had come to nothing. Perhaps
this stranger could see Utica written across her face, the same way she
read his own origins in his mien.

Or, she hoped, not. Maybe Oscar couldn't see her at all, through his
haze of bad wine and his endless list of grievances against his ghostly
adversary. Maybe he'd forgotten about her entirely.

As if in answer, Oscar rested a hand on her forearm and scanned the
crowd. "Wait," he said, interrupting his own diatribe. "He was just there."
As if Vivian would understand everything, if only she got a look at this
Squire Clancey.

And she did see him, for a moment, after Oscar pointed: awkward,
excellently dressed, slightly older than Vivian. Pacing with a deliberate
step, as though measuring the room for new carpets. The silver flare of
his hair like a struck match.

But behind him, blazing brighter still in Vivian's vision, was Sofia:
lingering over her third cocktail, smiling lips still bent to the heiress's
jeweled ear.

Sofia caught Vivian's eye and pantomimed surprise, her gaze flicking
pointedly to Oscar's proprietary hand on Vivian's arm.

Vivian might have laughed, extracted her arm, and ordered Oscar a
cup of strong coffee. She might have followed the glow of Sofia's dress
out of the gambling palace and learned to applaud, to be patient and dutiful
as Antonio the actor or delicate and coy as the bejeweled heiress. She
might have devoted herself to extending their arrangement as long as she
could, wringing it for the last desperate drops of sustenance.

Instead, she made a gesture of shrugging dismissal to Sofia and spoke
aloud the obvious solution to Oscar's problem. "You should go into business with him," she said.

Oscar pretended to retch and almost fulfilled it as prophecy; he wiped
his mouth on his sleeve. "Hideous notion," he said.

Vivian managed a polite laugh, quieting her pounding heart. She was
desperately glad he hadn't warmed at once to the idea, which she felt
herself a fool for voicing aloud. What good was it to her, if she gave Oscar

Schmidt the very key to driving Clancey out of competition, but left herself a disinterested bystander?

From across the room Sofia smiled, not quite kindly, and toasted Vivian and Oscar with her near-empty coupe. The last sip of champagne as radiant as Oscar's skin.

LATE IN THE evening, when Vivian had seen Oscar depart (stumbling into a hansom) and knew he wouldn't witness her betrayal, she sounded Squire out.

"Mr. Clancey," she said, stepping bodily into his path as he paced. He was a small man, she noticed; in her party shoes, she looked him squarely in the eye. "Vivian Lesperance. How goes the fight? I hear you're battling incandescence."

She could tell at once that approaching the subject so directly had been an error—Squire's expression knocked itself flat, into a kind of blank panic. (Vivian was in fact the fourth person to attempt a joking congratulation on Squire's business acumen over the course of the evening; Squire was uncomfortable with both business and jokes.)

"You were talking to Schmidt, before," he said. "Are you a reporter?"

"No, no," Vivian said. This would require, she saw, an even slower simmer than she had foreseen. She only hoped she had the time. "Not a reporter," she said again. "Only making conversation."

At this Squire blanched still further. "I never meant . . ." he began. "I haven't . . ." He made a helpless gesture. "I'm interested in candles," he said.

Unlike his other would-be conspirators, so ready to congratulate him on his success not in the business of chandlery but in the more entertaining and useful arena of humiliating an outsider, Vivian had brains (and interest) enough to course-correct. "Have you had any luck this evening?" she asked.

He brightened. "Oh, rather," he said. And with no further warning Vivian found herself plunged into the report, studded with casually profound oxbows of historical and scientific context, of a complete mastodon skeleton—local to the Hudson Valley!—that Squire had stumbled upon in an oddities museum not ten blocks from Washington Square. (In fact, the beast and its patchily educational placards had been on view since well before the Civil War—but Squire was still acquainting himself with his native city after his long and formative exile.)

For the second time in one evening Vivian observed an open floodgate, a self usually carefully repressed and now sent rushing forward to meet her unbridled. For the second time she was touched, charmed, by an odd and honest soul.

And for the second time, she noted the vulnerability of such eruptive personalities to a firm guiding hand.

She would have to marry one of them, she thought. It couldn't be helped.

She considered her options for a moment. Even as she nodded and encouraged Squire's deluge of information on ancient herbivorous molars; even as Sofia's laugh rang out from the back of the hall like a timer counting down her last moments of protection, Vivian stalled—as if deciding whether to bet her last dollar on red or black.

Squire was younger, and richer, and of better standing. His unconventionality amused her. But it was old money, old pedigree, his breeding and privilege inescapable. (Vivian watched him, even as he made a prehensile trunk of his arm to demonstrate a point, effortlessly signal a waiter and obtain an off-menu cocktail garnished with—incredibly—spiced walnuts.)

Vivian did not often acknowledge her limits—if she had, she would by this point have been raising Ruf Thomas's children in Utica—but she doubted she could carry off such a match. She could not afford an upperten gentleman. She would have to bargain for a new-money companion, imitation astrachan rather than Alaska sable. A marriage was a business transaction, with permanent consequences—not like the love affairs she'd been living on like rental properties. (This was the natural tone of Vivian's worldview, and her experience of New York had not motivated her to adjust it.)

It was one thing, she thought, to spend a few years riding into glittering parties on the train of Sofia's gown. But for a marriage, she needed someone she could trick. A fellow yokel.

Besides which, Squire was a sexual cipher—if there were hidden signals in the mastodon story, Vivian thought, they had been beyond her—but after listening to Oscar rattle on for half the evening, she was fairly confident in his queerness. (How heartbroken he would have been, to know how easily she saw his secret soul!) With such a man there would be, Vivian reasoned, no need to bother each other.

FIVE

Once Vivian had identified her quarry, all the rest was triangulation.

From Oscar's perspective, it was a remarkable yet believable coincidence: a chance encounter on the pavement outside his office, his name called in a tone of such joyful surprise that he stopped midstride, eyes pricking.

In fact, Vivian had lain in wait for over an hour, circling the block until her heels blistered.

She'd meant at first to let herself and Oscar drift together naturally, at a geologic pace, over the course of a season. But there was no longer any question of leaving things to chance: Sofia had been offended by Vivian's straying attention at the casino night, and it had finally severed whatever had been fraying between them. Sofia had given in to Antonio (or would let him think so for long enough to amuse herself). She sailed in two weeks for Europe, and had asked Vivian preemptively to turn in her key to the suite on Fifth Avenue.

Vivian had used practicality to tamp her grief at the parting. After all, she told herself, she'd known this was coming. (Vivian's constitution, like Oscar's, was one of those that insists anticipated hardships are easier to bear.) Rather than book a train to Utica, she'd sold her secreted cigarette case and taken a room in a shabby hotel on Eleventh Street, paper cringing from its damp plaster walls. She had enough for a month, if she scrimped. But she'd had to move up her timeline.

"Imagine, meeting you again," she said, and took Oscar's arm. "Vivian Lesperance."

"I remember you, of course," Oscar stammered.

In truth, he retained from the casino night only a vague sense of embarrassed obligation to her. Under normal circumstances, back when the wheel of fortune had hoisted him high above his fellow men (whatever he did in the alley shadows at night), Oscar might have spurned Vivian's friendship lest it threaten his spun-sugar cloud of virile bachelordom. But it was 1904, and Oscar was tired, and near despair. (All morning he had been rehearsing, for an audience of the ticking clock and the scuttling rats in the woodwork, the speech he would make to account for his dismal performance when his supervisor arrived from Cincinnati.) Vivian's hand was confident and possessive on his sleeve, and—impossible to silence this voice—this was what he was *supposed* to be doing: escorting a beautiful (he was fairly sure? Certainly she was at least striking) young woman down a sunny city block.

Thrown off balance, depleted of the strength to resist conventionality, Oscar was suggestible.

Vivian suggested they get something to eat.

A FRONT TABLE at a sunlit tearoom, with all of Park Row as chaperone—respectable, but intimate in the crowd. Vivian led their performance as a comfortable twosome, and Oscar was borne along on the strength of that performance, a leaf on the foaming tide.

He took his tea with lemon, she with milk. Both unsweet. They ate finger sandwiches and currant-studded cakes with a flavorless, cloying scrim of icing. They were both good eaters, and fair—silently apportioning the tiered tray into equal halves, neither of them adjusting the balance to account for sex. Vivian noted with approval that Oscar neither wallowed in chivalric self-denial nor expected a delicate appetite from her. This, she thought, she could work with.

By the same token, in avoiding both gendered posturing and prandial jealousy, Oscar began to relax—more than he had, perhaps, in months.

Vivian plied him with questions about his apartment, his haberdasher, his favorite escapes from the city. She asked about Ohio without mockery. She stayed away from innuendo, from questions about his industry and his nightlife.

Oscar felt the conversation lift like an ascending kite, and gave himself credit for it. He was amazed to find himself talking with, getting to *know*, a woman. (For he thought he *was* getting to know her—this obfuscation was another of Vivian's gifts.) The novelty of the exchange made him even more suggestible.

Vivian suggested he tell her how business was going. (She had her wits about her and her object in view, now, enough to keep from mentioning Squire yet.)

She listened with interest to Oscar's sober, brave-faced summary of his local division's prospects—baldly spun toward optimism, so unconvincing one could hardly even call it disingenuous. "Sales may rise and fall, but hygiene is a constant necessity," he finished, wooden and overworked.

Vivian twisted to look over one shoulder. "Why do I feel as if I've been invited to a dress rehearsal?"

Oscar blushed and occupied himself with a cucumber sandwich for as long as possible.

She extracted the truth with only modest difficulty: that Oscar's mentor would be making a special visit to the New York office, particularly to address the dismal hash he had made of local affairs. The meeting was four days hence.

Vivian pushed her cup and saucer aside and, jabbing at the tablecloth, *suggested* how Oscar might better handle such a meeting than in feeble self-defense.

Vivian did not yet understand the specific chemistry of Personal Care—lye and offal, oils and unguents, concretes and absolutes, by-products sourced from near and far to be endlessly recycled, repurposed, reevaporated. Her expertise would come with time, and quicker than to many an industry man. But, more crucially, she had already mastered the basic physical laws of negotiation and human vanity. "Listen, it's no good to say hygiene's a risk-proof venture when you're losing money," she said. "That just makes it sound as if you're finding a way to go under on a sure thing."

Oscar changed color, his weeks of anxious planning sieving through his fingers. "Then what do I do?" he asked, finally.

Hunkering over the table, Vivian swallowed a petit four and laid out his strategy for him like a boxing coach between rounds. "The problem is that there are no raw materials to be had, yes?" Careful, careful—she skirted an abyss in the shape of the name *Clancey*.

Oscar nodded.

"Then why take responsibility for that, as if you're in meatpacking and, and"—Vivian waved her hands, unversed in the jargon—"and floristry and what-all as well as soap? What fault of it is yours?"

Oscar blinked at her. It was as if, after months trapped at the bottom of a very dark well, he saw a thin, miraculous rope descending toward him from the surface. "That's true," he managed.

"It's like you said," Vivian said. "People need soap. They're not going without, they're just going without *yours*. And we know they're not buying a local competitor"—again she skated a figure eight around the two-ton elephant of Squire Clancey, melting all Oscar's ingredients into his candles—"they're shipping your own company's out from Ohio." She rubbed two fingers against her thumb. "*That's* waste, coming and going—not manufacturing here, then paying to transport product halfway across the country."

"Well," Oscar said, "you're partly right. There are other factors." (There weren't, not many, but she'd wounded his professional pride.)

"You let your manager know you need more resources," Vivian said. "Expand to New Jersey, upstate. Or get competitive with"—she pursed her lips—"folks in the city. You figure out the particulars. But don't stand there and try to tell him everything's dandy, because he wouldn't be coming out if it was."

Oscar let out a sound that was not quite a laugh. "You want me to ask for *more* money," he said.

"It's what you need, and they've got it," Vivian said simply. "Tell them they've got to give you some straw to spin into gold." She picked up her teacup again. "They'll find it for you, unless they're fools. They know as well as I do what you're capable of."

Oscar was dismayed to find his returning smile watery. Years of desperate, tightening spiral had left him honeycombed beneath his surface, vulnerable to the smallest flattery. "I'll have to think about what you've said, Miss Lesperance," he said. His voice was thick; he folded and unfolded his napkin as if to cover it.

Vivian, of course, had seen this at the casino night, as clearly as if he'd been spotlit. (Drunkenness cast such things into relief; as an observer, Vivian appreciated it as a time-saver.) Oscar was a fragile man, adrift with a broken rudder. He only wanted one good shove to set him on a new tack—at the shover's discretion.

Vivian signaled for the check. "My treat," she said. It would nearly clean her out, but if she'd calculated correctly, it would be worth it. "You can thank me by inviting me to dinner," she said, and smiled at him. "After your triumph."

FROM THERE IT was as easy, if as perilous, as coasting downhill. Vivian could almost feel the wind in her hair. And this time she was steering, with her own feet on the pedals.

Oscar emerged from the interview with his manager, dazed and blinking, with his position intact and the promise of an increased budget for the New York manufactory in the next fiscal year. He was on probation, granted—but after spending so long (at least weeks; more precisely a lifetime) anticipating execution, Oscar felt like he'd been blessed by the very hand of God. His senses were sharpened: colors brighter, scents richer, all sounds melodious.

He even dared, for the first time in many frustrated months, to indulge in a visit to the clubs. This once-habitual activity had an unprecedented result: the morning after, Oscar recalled without shame the anonymous young man who had moved against him, his lavender enamel cufflinks like a cardsharp's hidden aces. This time, this adventure seemed to Oscar less a sin and more an earned reward—perhaps even made sweeter by the preceding self-denial.

The two victories became entwined in his mind: he had received a vote of cautious confidence in his professional judgment; he had let a man fuck him without wishing afterward for annihilation. Flimsy spoils, to be sure—and Oscar's circumstances were still tenuous, his general attitude still self-loathing. But dim lights burn brighter in a wasteland. Oscar found quite enough in his situation to rocket him to euphoria. And he credited it, with bewildering gratitude, to the girl who had stepped sideways into his life out of the ether.

VIVIAN PARLAYED THIS into a proposal over the course of two and a half conversations, spanning the first half of the summer.

In the meantime she kept up appearances, tipping the servants at dinners and parties and lawn tournaments. Things would have been easier if she could have accepted an invitation to a country house, and lived off an acquaintance for a week or two—but Oscar would not leave his office, and so Vivian, too, had business in town. To finance her plan, she whittled herself down to a pauper's life: reusing coffee grounds, taking three cigarettes whenever she was offered one, drying her stockings on her bedpost. (Her one window faced south and would have made quicker work of the task—but passersby might have noticed the hose, and craned to see what unlucky girl moved in the room behind.)

In this phase of insecure economy and strategic hunger, Vivian found herself thinking of Electra Blake. (She refused, with insistence but limited success, to think of Sofia. Vivian's glance skipped over breathless reviews of Sofia's concert series abroad, as a flat stone skips once, twice, thrice over the surface of a lake—before, inevitably, sinking.) On one of her rambling walks, attempting to subdue her appetite through the jostle of exercise, she made a looping circle past the Blakes' townhouse. But there was, of course, no sign of Electra.

Vivian shook herself, sloughing off the ghosts of past acquaintance. She, no less than Electra with her traffic-cop husband and her set of tidy rooms in the Bronx, had new business to attend to.

First came dinner at a mutual acquaintance's, a socially magnanimous man from Oscar's set (from, that is, the set Oscar still clung to by his fingertips) and his ebullient new bride from Spuyten Duyvil. Oscar suggested Vivian's addition to the party, then paid shy, proprietary, grateful attention to her throughout the evening. It might not even have been called flirting, but for how Vivian received it—in the cadence of her answering laughs, and the angles her body made with Oscar's, she transmuted general conversation into courtship.

Gossip bloomed even before coffee was served—encouraged principally by the hostess, who had thrived at such whisper-filled parties in her girlhood and was overjoyed at the chance to concoct one herself as mistress of her own house. Smiles were poorly concealed behind lace-gloved hands; stage murmurs circulated: Oscar Schmidt, of all people, had finally set his cap at someone.

Oscar heard the rumors, and they buoyed him like a life preserver. Gone were the monikers like "horticultural gent" and "Mr. Washed-Out"; silenced were the rumblings that he was a queer and a failure and a hopeless hayseed. Everything was drowned out by the possibility of a romance, the drama of an unexpected match between unconventional— though still acceptably compatible, of course—partners.

Oscar was shocked, pleasantly so, to find himself enjoying the gossip. There was still physical terror to combat—the inevitable expectation, now shrouded in whalebone and petticoats and the suggestive pealing of feminine laughter; the memory of his failure with the whore from Weehawken. But there were other factors, now: Oscar's increasing age; his declining fortune; his boundless desperation for security.

And so, he resolved to try again: to let a woman (he coughed) lay hands upon his person. And to . . . and to reciprocate.

And there were always, Oscar thanked God, the comforts of chauvinism—for, beyond perhaps the obligatory unpleasantness of the wedding night, a wife could always be refused. How many men did he know who regularly visited their wives' bedrooms? Were there *any*, above the age of forty-five? Oscar had almost reached the all-purpose excuse of middle age! He could be busy; he could be tired; he could be gouty or rheumatic or uninspired. And a wife who failed to stoke excitement was always the guilty party. How much less embarrassing, how much *nobler*, Oscar thought, to refuse a wife than a prostitute.

Yes: marriage, at this point, made sense.

WHEN HE SAW Vivian again, seeking her out deliberately at an archery tournament in Great Neck, he leaned into the performance of the courtship. He escorted her over the uneven lawn, held her parasol while she shot—tactfully refraining from remarking on its worn handle, the tear in one of its panels. (Vivian's situation was showing first in her seasonal accessories). He praised her form, and her sportsmanship after a close loss.

In fact, Vivian's disappointment was rather less casual than she pretended—the prize, a golden paperweight in the figure of a huntress, would have bought her another month in her current limbo. Though why she would choose to prolong the situation was becoming a more difficult question for her to answer by the day: she was foggy with fatigue and uncertainty, weak and dyspeptic from the unpredictable diet of stale soda crackers one night and five-course dinners the next. She was, literally, losing her aim—her last arrow had flown wide of the mark thanks to a spasm of her exhausted muscles, a blurred drift of focus.

This is how quickly desperate circumstances crowd out one's dreams, personal and professional: Vivian's very notion of "success" was foggier than it had been even a few weeks before. What was her plan, she wondered, wandering in one of the dehydrated dazes that pricked at her behind the eyes and sometimes siphoned away entire afternoons by the clock. Did any of it even make sense? Why court Oscar Schmidt? Why merge his business with Squire Clancey's? Why do *anything*, really, but lie down in a dark room until she felt less dizzy?

She might have already given up, had it not been for her motivation— bedrock-strong—not to strive *for* anything, but to *avoid* a return to Utica.

Her parents had written again, the letter amounting to four pages of complaints about everything in their line of sight—from their neighbors to their employees to the weather; from Vivian's penmanship to the way Mrs. Stone asked after her (as if they were her social secretaries) to the memory of a plate she'd broken in adolescence. According to local gossip, the Lesperances insinuated, Vivian was not merely forgotten but infamous. In their home, they seemed to imply, she would find herself every bit as adrift and unprotected as if she were wandering friendless on the streets of New York.

Even on her wooziest, weepiest days, Vivian was sure of this much: she could not reappear on the scene in Utica; she could not put herself close enough at hand again for her parents to pinch and shake and criticize in person. After five years' independent adventure in New York, however mixed, she was not confident she would survive the disappointment of a return.

Besides, Vivian had invested too much to back out. She had anted her entire summer. To pursue Oscar, and to await him, was her only viable option.

Oscar—privy, of course, to none of this line of thinking—fetched her a glass of sparkling lemonade. He felt an effervescent frisson as he passed her the cup: the church picnic with Hiram Ainsley, all those years ago; the ladle of lemonade and touch of his forbidden hand, steadying yet unbalancing; the eruption and spill and the shamed flight across the town green that had still, somehow, not ended, though Oscar was a man of forty-three and had put so much distance behind him he could go no farther without wading into the sea.

Like lye and animal fat, the remembered and the present party churned together in Oscar's mind and reacted against each other to produce something entirely new, something not caustic or greasy but beautiful and enticingly perfumed and, above all, useful.

Vivian sipped her lemonade and thanked him, smiling. If her exhaustion, her precarity, her uncertainty of her own future showed in her face, they served to sharpen her into a being Oscar recognized, if vaguely, as kindred. Her suffering made her trustworthy.

OSCAR, FLUSTERED AND overdressed in a dove-gray coat and hat—as if already prepared for the wedding itself—called on Vivian at her hotel. Rather than inviting him up, she received him in a cramped sitting room off the lobby, which was uncomfortable enough to be private and allowed her to keep her mildewed, empty room a secret.

The proposal itself was awkward, rote—too formal yet too effusive. The acceptance matched it. Both parties were performing roles they had seen onstage and read about in novels but never truly understood. Still, the relief, the joy, the hope after long uncertainty for a happier, more stable tomorrow—these emotions were real enough on both sides, if only indirectly related to the matter at hand.

Neither Oscar nor Vivian was entirely sure whether at this step in the proceedings a kiss was appropriate, or indeed expected. After a moment's hesitation, each waiting for a cue from the other, Oscar spread his arms. His hat dangled from one hand. "Should—may I?" he asked. The tinge of fear, the lack of authority, would characterize every time he touched her for the rest of his life.

Vivian shrugged, laughing. Tears stung her eyes. The relief of having a plan in motion, secure footing and the surety of her next meal while she gamed to capture Squire's business and arranged for her own fortune, was nearly as heady as genuine infatuation. "I guess you'd better," she said.

Their kiss was chaste, overly symmetrical, so mechanically precise a matching of lips that their noses interfered as if they'd been faultily configured. Though both Vivian and Oscar had many times gasped and clutched and lost themselves to others' bodies, there had always been desire to gild the action—without it, they were grossly aware of the facts of flesh and breath and spittle, and the quick peck felt somehow more intimate, almost disgustingly so, than nearly anything in either of their pasts. (Nearly, nearly. Twin faint echoes, melancholy twinges that kept them grateful for the comparatively fulfilling, at minimum lucrative, present: Ruf Thomas on the woodpile; the Weehawken whore.)

Having thus christened their arrangement, the would-be lovers broke apart. Vivian gummed her lips, self-conscious of her chapped skin after feeling Oscar's. "Well," she said. "Thank you."

She was so ready to dive into her new life, her new management of their shared enterprise. So ready to plan—not wedding breakfasts and trousseaus, but a campaign to rescue Oscar's business. (Hereafter, according to Vivian's internal law, *her* business.)

But Oscar's own wheels were turning; he had his own preoccupying practicalities. "And of course," he said, with a confidence she had not seen from him in all their previous acquaintance, "of course I'll ask for your family's blessing. Provided—forgive me"—the thought almost a concussion, as he brained himself on the immediate monolith of his fiancée's mysterious origins—"provided your parents are still living?"

For Oscar had never quite been cured of the desperate drive to please his elders, neurotically instilled in him by Grandmother Hester. Her death, and his own parents', had merely orphaned and frustrated the urge. Here, perhaps, was a way to graft himself onto a new family tree, to please a new set of ancestors with his fealty to convention and authority. A chance to prove himself normal, regular; a chance to receive a validating handshake from the establishment in the person of Vivian's father.

Vivian herself, who lived so far from this mindset that its possibility had not even occurred to her, was horrified. "That won't be necessary; they'd never expect you to," she said hastily—missing, she realized too late, her one chance to put the matter to rest by orphaning herself with a lie.

Oscar insisted, pig-headed first in chivalry, then—when pressed—in chauvinism and patriarchy. It was tradition. It was only proper. It was, when push came to shove, his decision.

Thus Vivian had her first encounter with the defining frustration of a strategic alliance with a gentleman (however disgraced): there was no possibility of direct refusal.

And so she found herself, after all her tactics and persuasion and daring leaps to avoid exactly this result, on a train to Utica.

SIX

Oscar was, at first, oblivious. Bumping over suburban tracks from Utica's train station to Lesperance Carpentry, he felt himself cushioned by the sense of calm security that Vivian had introduced to his life. With mild interest he compared this landscape with his own native country: he was a stranger to the particular pine-scented chill and inhospitable boulder-studded soil of the Adirondack foothills, but deeply accustomed to the sound of wind filtering through cornstalks, and the labored creak of laden wagons, and the ubiquitous vegetal funk of manure. If Vivian was unusually tense and quiet beside him—if she cringed at the too-familiar shops and offices, the streets crowded with phantom acquaintances— Oscar did not notice. The scene was recognizable enough to settle his own spirit, but too new to harbor any unpleasant memories. None of the local ghosts had any business with him. Indeed, his confidence was bolstered as they traveled farther and farther from the city center and he realized Vivian was like him—a farm girl! His pulse quickened. He had chosen his bride, he thought, better than he had even known. He would be able to charm her parents—he had the language of such outskirts, dormant but still fluent in his subconscious.

As they arrived, however, even Oscar began to perceive that something was wrong.

Vivian's parents received them in near silence, filing onto the porch at their approach like skeptical spectators at a poorly attended parade. "Well," her mother said, as her father accepted Oscar's handshake. "It's true after all."

Without precisely inviting them in, the Lesperances retreated, letting the out-of-season storm door swing shut behind them—then propped it open again accusingly when Vivian and Oscar were too occupied with unloading their luggage and paying their driver to follow immediately.

Inside, they'd moved two ladderback chairs in from the kitchen to accommodate the whole party. The Lesperances took these seats, out of either politeness or intimidation, towering over Vivian and Oscar on the low horsehair couch.

Vivian swallowed against the crush of the room: the same furniture, the same paths worn even deeper into the floorboards, the same faded bouquets of desiccated strawflower hanging from the rafters. An unfamiliar crocheted blanket crouched menacingly on the arm of the sofa, as a warning that new devils might lie in wait among old enemies.

They ignored Oscar completely at first—even Vivian, who almost forgot him in her peripheral vision. It was as if the meeting had an agenda, and it was not yet time for new business.

"You're thinner," Vivian's father observed, after a silence. Vivian allowed that it was true. (Her fortunes had too recently improved for her to thrive again, physically.)

"Doris Stone says you've been making a spectacle of yourself," her mother said mildly, as if commenting on the weather.

This simple statement went through Vivian like a hot knife. What had Patience's mother (who had only ever been kind to Vivian's face) told her own—and when? The two women hardly spoke; they were, depending on whom one asked, enemies. Was this gossip from last week, or from the nineteenth century? And what was the "spectacle"—Vivian's cavorting in New York society? Her itinerant penny-pinching between successes? Her tumbling affairs with Sofia or Electra Blake? It was a venom-tipped weapon of a sentence: insulting Vivian, and frightening her, but almost perversely compelling her to ask for more detail.

"I haven't had the pleasure of seeing Mrs. Stone, lately," Vivian said, attempting a breezy tone.

Her mother smirked at the affectation, and this silent expression did more to capsize Vivian than any remark could have. This, she understood now, was what their purely epistolary relationship had kept at bay: the fact that her parents were the only two people who would never be fooled by her reinvention. The Astors and Rockefellers were nothing to the Lesperances, and the figment of their own Manhattanite daughter was less than nothing. They had wiped Vivian clean as a child; had watched her fail at her first attempts to walk, to talk, to lie and reason; for eighteen years they had seen her (and when necessary, imagined her) at her small and spiteful worst. They knew her too well, or else had leveled too many allegations against her, to credit her newfound success.

Vivian was, as she often did, giving her parents both too much credit and not enough. Behind their resentment and disapproval hid the same selfish fears and confusions they had always harbored where their daughter was concerned. It was unsettling, seeing her return after years away, and with someone new. So many unknown variables. They felt the eternal villagers' distrust of a stranger arriving in town. Was the stranger Oscar, or Vivian? The Lesperances could not have said. In place of articulate grievance they could only rewarm old fears, old rancors, old resentments.

"Mrs. Stone sent a clipping," her father took up the line. "About you and that *actress*." Otherwise telegraph-brusque, he enunciated both syllables of the final word, as if each held its own accusation.

Vivian swallowed the urge to correct him that Sofia had been—was still, somewhere on the other side of the Atlantic, where Vivian momentarily wished she could join her—a *singer*, not an actress. "I've been lucky enough to meet lots of interesting people," she said.

"Sounded pretty snug." Her mother raised a doubtful brow—and at last, horribly, turned her attention to Oscar. Opening their acquaintance, and the negotiation over Vivian's hand in marriage, on the veiled accusation of her Sapphic affairs. "You met the girl?" she asked.

"I'm . . . not entirely certain?" Oscar, who had been introduced to Sofia twice but retained no memory of either meeting, and who had no idea what his prospective in-laws were talking about, looked to Vivian for a cue.

Mrs. Lesperance sucked her teeth. "So that's how this'll be," she said, gesturing between the fiancées.

"Clipping sure made it sound," said Mr. Lesperance, "like you'd know it if you saw it."

Somewhere behind Oscar's eyes, a penny dropped.

"Oscar is a regional manager," Vivian said abruptly. "In—he works with the meatpackers."

This attempt to paint Personal Care with a more masculine brush, to arrange herself and Oscar like paper dolls of Husband and Wife, surprised her even as it left her mouth. She was newly humiliated by her own fear, the cringing urge to bend to her parents' judgment. In New York she didn't mind unconventionality, danger, living as she chose; even in precarious or lean eras, the future there seemed nothing but a stairway to the sky, the steps hers to nail in place and mount with pleasure. But that vision was stripped away here, and it was like waking up sober after a night of raucous misbehavior.

"You make a good salary?" Vivian's father asked, looking over Oscar doubtfully.

"She's got nothing," her mother said. "I don't know what she told you."

"It's—a good business," Oscar said after a stammering moment's embarrassment. The pleasant evocation of the Ohio countryside had turned on him; echoes of Grandmother Hester's disapproval had so filled the room that he was having difficulty focusing on the conversation at hand. "I've had luck. But," and he gave a nudging nod at Vivian, as though trying to present her for reassessment or parole, "already, your daughter has shown she has a better head for the business than most of my clerks. You should be—"

"*Hah*," Mr. Lesperance said, as if he'd seen laughter in books but only learned to pronounce it phonetically.

"I'll start supper," Mrs. Lesperance said, standing.

Vivian tried to gloat: Well, Mr. Schmidt, did you get what you wanted? Aren't we a cozy group? But it brought only fresh misery. Her plan was a failure. This, she thought, would be the pattern of her remaining days: ricocheting between these hateful, long-established tortures, her family of origin and the institution of marriage. Until one day, there would be nothing left of her to bounce back.

$\sim$

VIVIAN SPENT THAT night in her childhood bedroom, now crowded with bundles of fabric scraps and unsold furniture. Oscar was exiled to the loft over the woodshop, where the Lesperances bunked a hired hand (Ruf's successor) in busy months—and, though Vivian was not privy to this knowledge, where Mr. Lesperance himself now slept when things were especially unharmonious in the main house.

Vivian stared at dust caught in a moonbeam, too far from sleep to even talk herself into it. Despite the blunt conversation on their arrival, Oscar had not yet actually asked her father—or, now that he saw the lay of the land, her mother—to bless their marriage. Their return train was not for three days. Two more sleepless nights, if Vivian could survive them; the final, formal, soul-crushing request for approval; its inevitably awful, even if affirmative, response. (Indeed, she thought, it might tarnish all her plans simply to know her parents approved of them.)

And then . . . ?

The thought thudded ruinous and sickly with each heartbeat: all this—her father's rusting needle-toothed saws and the kitchen scraps' fetid rot by the washbasin and the snakes in the woodpile where Ruf Thomas had done his best to sedate her into submission—all of it had all been here the whole time, waiting to gloat over her return. It would always be here. No matter how long she stayed away, no matter how far she traveled.

And she would marry, she had no better choice but to marry, a man who pledged fealty to this world. Who wanted to ask its permission to continue living. She could play out whatever games of independence and rebellion she wished, but in the end she was doomed to be crushed between—

Interrupting her litany came a tap at the door, furtive but insistent.

She opened it to find Oscar, hair disheveled and sawdusty, legs bare below the hem of his nightshirt. He stood contrapposto—at first glance a relaxed posture, though in fact he was wound to a manic frenzy, and merely favoring the foot he'd injured by stepping on a pine splinter in his pitch-dark creep across the yard from the woodshop.

Vivian tensed, as if in anticipation of a blow. Her braid hung thick over her shoulder. A draft from the depths of the house raised the hair on her arms. Had she so badly misjudged the temperature of Oscar's blood? (Where did her greater obligation lie, she wondered, if he made a premature demand of wifely duty, here, under her parents' roof?)

"Hello," Oscar said, after a moment. The volume of his own voice seemed to startle him.

In spite of everything, Vivian had to bite back a laugh. "Hello," she said. Oscar stood silent another moment, tugging self-consciously at the sleeves of his nightshirt. "Did you need something?" Vivian asked, and braced her knuckles on the lintel.

Oscar leaned toward her, until she smelled the cedar planks he'd been bunked among and the last traces of his tooth powder and the rank, insistent odor of midnight anxiety. "I think," he said in an almost breathless whisper, "we should leave."

Now Vivian did laugh, a surprised outburst she stopped with her palm. "Whatever for?" she asked.

Oscar performed a burlesque of pleading exasperation—bugging his eyes, sinking at the knees, sweeping a long arm toward the sitting room where they'd been held hostage on arrival.

Though he'd never taken part in the floor shows at the Slide, Oscar had seen enough of them to be a more than competent vaudevillian. After Vivian's horrible afternoon and sleepless night, such clownish validation from such an unexpected source was a powerful relief. She collapsed forward onto his chest, shaking in silent mirth until tears streamed.

Oscar, unprepared for this reaction, enfolded her in an awkward half-embrace. "I'm sorry," he said.

"Oh *don't*," Vivian said vehemently, wiping at her cheeks. "But we can't leave," she said. "You haven't asked them yet."

Oscar simply shook his head. Such a small gesture, to mark such a glaring break with propriety.

In her gratitude, Vivian let herself embrace him as she would a real lover: one hand cupping his elbow, the other laid against his chest. It was not the same as it had been with Sofia, or even with Electra—but it wasn't nothing. "There's no train until tomorrow," she said. "I mean, this afternoon."

"Then we'll get a room in town," Oscar said.

"My father would have to drive us in the morning."

Oscar's eyes shone. Of course, he thought—she didn't know where he came from. He hadn't told her. "I can rig a cart," he said. "If you can show me where they keep it." He lifted one foot, hopping slightly. "And if you can dig out a splinter."

KNOWING THE ROADS better, Vivian drove on the foggy, midnight ride to the station—though the reins were largely ceremonial, the horse being the most expert of the party.

"My family—" Oscar had to pause to clear his throat, not having spoken in some time. "My family didn't approve of me," he said.

Vivian nodded, her eyes on the swaying road where it vanished into the mist.

Oscar had intended there to be more to say—that a disapproving family wouldn't always have such power; that their opinions didn't matter, once a person found better-suited society. But of course he was permanently hobbled by his origins; of course his very life had been defined by the bottomless shame Grandmother Hester had instilled in him.

"An *actress*, though," he said—overpronouncing the word, in a stagey echo of Mr. Lesperance's comment the previous afternoon. Oscar swept a hand over his forehead, arranging a phantom coiffure with Byronic disdain.

Vivian's chest collapsed—a laugh, a sigh, a sob. "She was a *singer*," she said—correcting now what she had been powerless to correct in the room.

Oscar sucked his teeth.

They did not, either of them, say the words for what they were—did not evoke ancient Greeks or modern dens of sin, did not confess or share the unspoken centers of their secret hearts. Still, for a quivering, witching-hour moment, Vivian and Oscar each glimpsed the vague shape of something new between them.

They sent the cart back with the innkeeper's son, who loaded his bicycle for the return journey. Oscar rented two rooms, and they did their best to sleep the rest of the night—but their pulses beat high in their temples at the melodrama of the sudden flight; the fear that Vivian's parents would come after them like an avenging mob of two; the unexpected thrill of collaborative connection in a relationship they'd each, separately, considered a false front. They slept fitfully, rose late, ate a hurried breakfast punctuated by nervous glances at the doorway. (Of course, no one came to fetch them. If Vivian's parents had cared enough to police her, they would have long since begun.) Finally the pair boarded the train back to their disreputable, adopted cosmopolis, the many overlapping cities called New York. Safe in the upholstered lacuna of their shared compartment, the possessing thrill that had animated their bodies for long, traumatic, transgressive hours left them suddenly. They dozed, spent—lulled by the clatter of the tracks, fingers brushing on the seat between them.

SEVEN

As our newly bonded quasi-lovers rocked somnambulantly into Grand Central Station, Squire Clancey, too, was experimenting with both train travel and new frontiers—though his own journey, as was so often his experience, was more solitary and circuitous.

The Interborough Rapid Transit Subway was christened a few days before Halloween 1904, with an opening line from City Hall to Harlem. Squire was among the breathless, intoxicated mob crowding the platform when it opened for paying fares. He waited hours to buy his ticket; tripped underground with a lightheaded ease that his younger self—scrabbling broken-fingered at a manhole cover uptown—could hardly have imagined. He craned to stare at the nesting domes of the Guastavino ceiling, a tiled cavern somehow more expansive than the vault of heaven. He let the crowd carry him, shoved and swept and herded into the clattering wooden train cars. He stood flush with innumerable other New Yorkers, from Brooklynites wearing made-up ties on elastic (if they wore them at all) to society scions in evening wear. Squire himself lost a pearl cuff-link—a sacrifice he was happy to make to the subterranean gods, even in the person of a light-fingered neighbor.

He rode the train from the tip of Manhattan to the end of the line at 145th Street. His car lurched in uneven bursts of speed—here motoring at an express clip ("Fifteen Minutes to Harlem!" A group of boozy youths took up the chant popularized by the city's pasteboard advertisements); there slamming to a crawl, as suddenly as though they'd struck some fantastical tunnel-dwelling livestock. Squire did not care. Again and again the thought intruded, both scientific and sublime, that he was *underground*— like Jean Valjean, like Jules Verne, like every fricative Frenchman real and imagined whose deep-tunneling exploits he'd ever read with envy. Mapping the invisible. He scanned the clattering shadows for hidden messages, peered out at each station into the impossible lamplit caverns like goblin cities—kiosks selling tickets; unlicensed vendors already surreptitiously distributing packets of nuts; comfort stations with subdivided toilet stalls and cakes of soap rough as sandpaper.

One need never leave, Squire thought.

Perhaps even more notably: for the first time in Squire's life, others shared his passion. At each of these station stops more people pushed into the cars—men in straw boaters and bowlers and Brilliantine; ladies whalebone-stiff above the waist and sweeping full-skirted below, like mythical chimeras impossible to avoid. Squire found himself crushed in a welcome press of impersonal joy, as chaotic as it was general, and seeing reflected in each intoxicated eye—glassy with the recycled air of so many lungs—active enthusiasm for the very thing that had set his own blood pounding. They were *underground*—five hundred millennia of bedrock accumulating overhead like a heavy blanket, granite and schist and gneiss and the comforting weight of the city itself. A community of like-minded fellows; a cozy den that traveled at miraculous speeds. The train yawed on the tracks, and Squire jolted—one way, then the other; watered silk and brushed wool and even the incongruous satin-lined wing of an opera cape; the warm press of all the bolstering bodies behind the fabric, eccentric and accepting and flush with mutual excitement. He stumbled—someone caught him before he hit the floor, the heat of a supporting palm slipping beneath his jacket. (Had he ever been touched just there?) "On your feet, soldier," someone else laughed, lifting him by the elbow, and—or was it yet a third person?— rubbing encouragement between his shoulders.

At 125th Street the train burst suddenly from underground onto an elevated line, and Squire's stomach swooped as if he were flying.

He bought another ticket, and another. By dawn he was one of New York City's first and most dedicated subway commuters, despite his independent wealth and his habit of traveling by foot or hansom for his (only middlingly frequent) appearances at the offices he shared with Mr. Lawrence. It became for him an almost daily exercise: at least one circuit of the island.

The breathless crowds of opening day thinned, of course, and Squire was left to tamp himself down again as best he could—riding in repressed silence, schooling his expression to reflect the businesslike blankness of his fellow riders'. Still, it was a settling ritual, and one he missed dearly whenever unforeseen circumstance or obligation upset his plans.

The subway carried Squire through much, that first season. After four years bankrolling his collaboration with Mr. Lawrence, Squire had not lost interest in chandlery—indeed, some of his most inspired innovations came to him in the rush and rumble of the train. But his reputation had suffered in his colleague's eyes, largely from his commitment to scented tapers. His prototypes for these novelties remained almost sickeningly potent, and Mr. Lawrence could see neither a need nor an appetite for them—a prophecy fulfilled by his own refusal to market or improve upon them. Thus Squire was becoming a sort of lucrative mascot of the partnership, his ideas taken less and less seriously until Mr. Lawrence allowed him to contribute little beyond his allowance.

This lack of encouragement had rather the opposite of its intended affect: thus stifled, Squire's ideas mutated into the truly experimental. As time went on, his creative proposals were rarely actionable—sometimes not only because of the bottom line but also for existential, even thermodynamic reasons. For instance: his daydream of a candle mansion, with real wicks sprouting from wax-molded furnishings, designed to melt into new architectural configurations around its inhabitants. A brightly luminescent home, shelter and light and warmth at once, ever shifting its shape to the owners' specifications.

But Squire had to admit, when Mr. Lawrence diplomatically raised the point, that even his idealized conceptual sketches had the appearance of a catastrophic conflagration.

Other times, his innovations were rejected purely for business reasons—at once simpler and more complex than the laws of physics. This was the case, for instance, with his plan for an apparently colorless candle that would melt to reveal a vibrant core of dyed wax and the fizzing sparkler of a "firework" wick. It was possible enough to create a prototype, but at prohibitive expense—and the effect was grotesque, with a high, smoking flame and gory red wax bleeding from the candle's center as it burned. Squire's dream of blind surprise at the color of each product's hidden center even extended, fantastically, to himself and Mr. Lawrence and any concerned employees—he envisioned the technician blindfolded, the colored waxes poured and molded and concealed in total secrecy.

"Why would that matter?" Mr. Lawrence asked, nervously. Squire could not answer; such questions did not rear their heads in the safety of the subway car.

HE RECEIVED, ONE morning over breakfast, a beautiful copperplate invitation to the wedding of Miss Vivian Lesperance to Mr. Oscar Schmidt.

Squire was unsettled by this—a social gesture he understood even less than most, given that the bridegroom had smeared him in the press and taken pains to cut him in every room they'd ever shared. (In fact, of course, Vivian had snuck Squire onto the guest list for the reception, hoping to accustom Oscar to the sight of him.) Beyond a general mistrust of an invitation from a man he had ample evidence despised him, Squire had a poor track record as a wedding guest—we trust you, by now, to imagine for yourself a few illustrative examples—and as a general rule did not consider himself fit for the purpose. Thus self-disqualified, he made his excuses via a hastily returned card. (Vivian, who left no loose ends, would destroy his false regrets before Oscar could receive them.)

Squire rode the train an extra circuit that day, exorcising all the anxiety of the unusual social hurdle.

THE DAY OF the Schmidt wedding itself passed unmarked in Squire's datebook, but it was later that same uncanny spring that he strode into the office—fresh from his morning subway ride, though he'd had to double back in a cab—to find his father's hat and stick in the cloakroom, and the man himself in conference with Squire's own business partner.

He surprised them midmeeting, their heads bent close over Mr. Lawrence's ink-stained blotter.

Squire, unaccustomed to encountering his father on public property, at first assumed that there was some familial emergency. But in fact the elder Mr. Clancey was performing simple reconnaissance, he and his wife having found in Mr. Lawrence a more reliable informant than Squire's doorman.

Spread on the desk between them were balance sheets of the candle business's quarterly figures, with a column in bottle-green ink showing Squire's contributions offsetting the partnership's losses—a near perfect match for his allowance from his parents, minus only the bare minimum he needed to feed and clothe himself and to ride the subway.

Included alongside this feat of accounting, neatly arranged like evidence in a criminal investigation, were Squire's conceptual sketches for his increasingly eccentric candles and accessories. Eerily reminiscent, Squire saw now (straining to adjudicate the designs through his father's eyes), of the worst of his adolescent fantasy cartography.

As the surveilled party, Squire can perhaps be forgiven any lack of sympathy for his betrayers. But Mr. Clancey found plenty of pity for himself: he chafed in the role of investigating his son's habits. He resented his having been dispatched on the errand at all—it was his wife who usually handled these things—and only the prison of his sex, the obvious impropriety of Mrs. Clancey (née Squire-Sacerdote) visiting a suite of offices with a tessellated lobby floor, like some victim of foul play appealing to a private detective, had induced him to set the meeting. It raised for Mr. Clancey unpleasant memories of his humiliating interviews in head-masters' offices, after each of Squire's boarding-school expulsions—the way, Mr. Clancey had been convinced, the tweedy deans had blamed *him* somehow for his son's failures to conform. Even now, as the man who had set the meeting, Mr. Clancey was having difficulty shaking off the sense of having been called on the carpet.

And now his cover was blown—with more than a little thanks to Mr. Lawrence himself, who startled and blushed at Squire's sudden entrance and so seemed to confirm their conspiracy as something illicit.

Mr. Lawrence, for his part, didn't relish the betrayal of his young partner—truthfully, his benefactor. Beyond a practical personal interest in the continuation of their financial arrangement, he *liked* Squire, and real affection gilded his gratitude. In his conversation with Mr. Clancey, he'd underlined the harmlessness (even, sometimes, the almost profitability) of their business venture, making the best case he could for its continuation. The outfit's staple products—Mr. Lawrence had the tact not to say *his* products, his sensical, *normal* products—nearly always broke even. To balance their books depended on the infusions of Clancey capital, yes, but it wasn't an *entirely* bottomless money pit. The plain tapers still sold very nearly well enough to offset Squire's . . . experiments.

In this argument Mr. Lawrence had been compelling enough to confuse Mr. Clancey, if not to convince him—and at some considerable cost to his own dignity, since the business plan amounted to an appeal for charity.

But the simple fact remained that Squire was odd—both as an individual and (almost more unsettlingly to Mr. Lawrence) as a typical representation of his class, with a head for neither business nor profession nor manual labor. It had been with an almost paternal relief of his own that Mr. Lawrence had learned there were concerned guardians monitoring the situation, interested in any intelligence he had to report concerning, if not Squire's welfare, then at least his public habits. And so he had indeed reported in full—an unburdening of his conscience that he traded for an equal and opposite affliction of guilt, at Squire's interruption of his betrayal.

These were the hues that shaded Mr. Lawrence's blush.

Squire smiled through the interaction, bearing stoically his own embarrassment and disappointment. If pressed, he likely couldn't have identified his emotional response as sadness, let alone explained its cause. Squire was more intelligent than either of the men seated before him; already, at the age of thirty, he had contributed more creativity, curiosity, and earnest effort to the world. Beyond this, he was an independent enough thinker to see—to feel—the cruelty inherent in their conservative "concern."

But the conspirators had all the force of convention on their side, and Squire had no one in his corner.

Ever since his parents had released him into Manhattan as though into a wildlife refuge for fragile, charismatic megafauna, Squire had been creating a kind of bubble world—occupied by himself and Mr. Lawrence and his doorman and the quotidian adventures of his imagination; occasionally menaced by shadowy, confusing figures like Oscar Schmidt; kept spinning by his unmonitored allowance and the centering centrifugal force of the subway's daily circuit and, most important, by his own priceless freedom.

And now, at the sight of his father—appraising, disapproving, recalculating—that bubble world had been punctured. Already, it was losing atmosphere. He could feel the air thinning in his lungs.

"I've—excuse me," Squire managed. And, bowing to his father as to an aristocratic stranger, he fled for the nearest subway station.

He rode the train for the rest of the afternoon. The service was delayed, sluggish—as if it, too, were falling victim to the entropy of Squire's private universe. Its power over him was diminished—he had barely to feign the ennui of his fellow passengers. He tried to dream up a new idea for a candle and found his passion cooled there too—it was as though he had sprung a general leak.

Everything in his life, he reflected, was on just the same circular track. As with Madison Avenue, then Ronkonkoma, Yonkers, St. Augustine, now his independent days and his candle business—every Eden fell; every seeming escape from his parents' rapt disapproval became in hindsight a prelapsarian fantasy. Every fixation that felt so promising, so freeing, eventually led back to the same starting point.

Squire had bought himself a last chance, perhaps—by staying within the limits of his allowance; by keeping his eccentricity relatively private, compared with his past scandals; by lucking into a sympathetic informant in Mr. Lawrence. But his parents would run out of patience—if not today, then someday soon—and recall him like a damaged appliance.

And who knew what, then? They were running out of places to keep him.

When he returned at last to his apartment, the doorman reported that his father had waited two hours and left a card. Squire took it with trepidation. *Careful*, read the single word on its reverse.

EIGHT

The return to the city had given Oscar and Vivian structure again, and though after their trip to Utica it took longer than either would have liked for the ghosts of their private pasts to entirely dissipate, gradually they each came back to themselves, returned to their present cares and purposes. The shared trial of the interview with the Lesperances was a bond, if not a wholly pleasant one. As the daily and nightly rhythms of "real" life were reestablished, the trip to Utica took on the unreality of an embarrassing nightmare. Had they really been chided like schoolchildren on a horsehair sofa? Had Oscar really snuck across a woodlot in his nightshirt, and Vivian really tweezed a splinter from the sole of his foot, with nothing but moonlight to see by?

Had they really held hands on the train home?

At least they had a mutual interest in letting the memory fade. It was one of many mutual interests, all of them principally controlled by Vivian.

Oscar returned to his office and its unforgiving balance sheets, Vivian to the post-Sofia evolution of her artistic social circle. (About this we will have much more to say, presently.) In the short term Oscar and Vivian planned their wedding breakfast, chose witnesses and linens, shuffled and reshuffled the order of melon and consommé on the menu. After the dust settled, the newlyweds found a set of rooms they could nearly afford—depending, Vivian calculated, on the success of her plan and the speed with which she could implement it. They were a thrifty distance west and north of the pearly string of Fifth Avenue mansions, but still closer to the city's spine than to its seedy shoreline. They economized by retaining Oscar's bachelor furniture—Vivian took particularly to a pair of dark leather armchairs, large enough she could almost use one as a sofa.

On their wedding night they managed, mercifully briefly and with bated breath, to christen their union.

Does this surprise you, given what you know of them, given what they by this point knew of each other? Consider, then, the solemn, holy, suffocating weight of institutions. Consider the confusions of youth on Vivian's side and shame on Oscar's and matrimonial amateurism on both. Just as there are some arts that can be learned only by the physical attempt—such as, notably, riding a bicycle—there are certain societal and native prejudices that can be lost only through misguided experience, never through the theoretical workings of even the most brilliant mind. Tell us—tell Vivian and Oscar!—what is a wedding?

Now, examine: Does every part of you understand every part of your answer?

The consummation of their marriage felt no less optional to Vivian and Oscar than had the consommé at the wedding breakfast, or indeed the signing of the license. Nevertheless: this duty discharged (with some mutual insult but no lasting injury), they returned to other pursuits.

Both husband and wife, when body and mind demanded, dabbled in amorous encounters. Oscar fought against some considerable new shame to do so—despite Vivian's tacit approval and his sense (albeit vague) of his wife's own tendencies, he struggled against a general principle that with his bachelor days behind him he should make a clean pivot to celibacy. (As in other seasons of his life, his convictions on the subject of sexual abstinence took him only so far.)

With their move north making the Bowery inconvenient, Oscar began venturing west into that brackish, shadowy periphery along the river. Most evenings he went out in what he fancied a convincing maritime disguise: a Guernsey sweater hugging his Adam's apple, oilskin trousers (suspiciously unweathered), and thick-soled boots. Indeed, Oscar developed a fondness for this ensemble—and a pride in the figure he cut when wearing it—that in another man we might have simply called a defect. But given Oscar's past attitude toward his own physical needs, his attempts to deny (and, where that failed, to punish) the very fact of his body's existence, it is tempting to read the capacity for petty vanity as a rehabilitative step.

Vivian saw to the laundering of this nautical costume without comment. She even considered the purchase of a sheepskin vest to complete the ensemble, but thought better of it. She was learning the contours of Oscar's small but bigoted pride—which of his insecurities she could safely manipulate; which others, when prodded, would cause a defensive eruption. Her husband had real secrets, or secrets he fancied real—and though slow to anger, when roused he had all the power of patriarchal civilization with its finger on the scale.

And besides, money was tight.

VIVIAN HID HER own affections in plain sight. She fell in with a cluster of Tiffany Girls, the anonymous technicians who cut and assembled lozenges of opalescent glass under the studio's name. The girls drank chianti and strong coffee well into the evening in an open studio near Cooper Union, breaking into pairs and trios to discuss art and anarchy; they were young, conservatory-trained, and barred from working as soon as they married. (This ensured a brisk turnover of anyone ill-suited to Vivian's purposes.) They smoked more than any women Vivian had ever known, and soon had indoctrinated her into the habit. At first, Vivian knew them only as a revolving, indistinguishable whirlwind of bohemian sensibilities and calloused hands—until she met Margaret Booth, Meg to her friends, originally of Fall River.

Meg was bright and brassy as sunset, with strong prejudices about the quality of postimpressionist art and none whatsoever as to the quality of wine. She believed in free love and coral lipstick—and the latter had, at their first meeting, been more stubbornly stamped onto Vivian's collar than the woman's name had been into her memory. But soon they had arranged a second encounter, then a third, then a tenth—always in Meg's rooms, a boardinghouse suite not unlike the one Vivian had just escaped by lassoing Oscar, with the elevated train rumbling by the third-story window often enough that liaisons had to be carefully timed.

Meg was consistent in her principles, sometimes annoyingly so. The qualities Vivian admired in her (or at least found useful—she would never learn to reliably distinguish between these sensations) came as part of a logically consistent yet frustrating whole. For instance: Meg did not care that Vivian was married, nor that she saw other women—both eminently convenient traits. But she also stepped out herself in turn. At many a dusky Greenwich Village kaffeeklatsch Vivian glimpsed Meg in the lap of one ink-stained girl or another—laughing, barraging each other with opinions on literature or fashion or universal suffrage—and was forced to tamp the jealous instinct of a woman accustomed (even among Sofia's crowd of admirers!) to sexual monopoly.

Or this: Meg practiced free love, and practice makes perfect. Vivian appreciated this, ardently. But Meg's sense of anarchy extended almost indiscriminately across traditional institutions: she was vociferous on the side of any labor union in any argument; eager to boozily rake the coals of the Pullman Strike or stand interminably at memorials to the Haymarket Martyrs; ecstatic on the subject of Emma Goldman dashing a glass of water into an investigating detective's face. Early in her acquaintance with Meg, between puffs of a postcoital cigarette, Vivian was subjected to a campaign stump speech for Eugene V. Debs as the Socialist candidate for the presidency—peppered with barbed asides that a bomb in Washington might do the job just as well.

Privately, Vivian found this simultaneous call for rigid reorganization and explosive anarchy stupid to the point of inanity. The only people who decry the system as it is, Vivian thought, are those who lack the skills to manipulate it to their advantage. (A common enough failing, to misidentify one's own individual benefit from an institution as its heroic disruption.) Though she'd dreaded the hazards of factory life so much that she'd starved herself and seduced Oscar to avoid them, Vivian could not muster a corresponding sympathy for the abstract "worker." And by Vivian's calculations, Meg had barely been ten years old during the Pullman Strike. Vivian doubted, smirking, that she had followed it in the papers with the devotion she now claimed.

But Vivian had been raised in an atmosphere of caustic resignation, her parents spitting bile at the state of the world (and, especially, the state of Vivian) but rejecting out of hand any attempted improvements. So there was something heady, at least for an evening hour or two at a time, about a girl convinced she could change the world forever with 3 percent of the popular vote and a lit match.

Furthermore, after the blazing affair (and blazing loss) of Sofia, and as Vivian began to juggle the mille-feuille business of being a wife, she needed something simple—and with someone she found just foolish enough to take her leave without regret at the end of each visit.

Besides, in the end, there was relatively little conversation involved.

Meg even met Oscar, once, when the two women's paths ran parallel for some blocks after a liaison and happened to terminate in Vivian's appointment with her husband before Meg's with a streetcar. Vivian watched as her partners made a few minutes' polite, flaccid conversation, as though they had nothing in common (or in dispute) beyond a square of pavement. It was a source of some private amusement for Vivian, who knew them well enough to see both the boldness being repressed on Meg's side and the anxiety on Oscar's. She might have played the placating hostess, had she not been sure that the encounter would have no sequel. As it was, she was content to let the connection fizzle—and neither Meg nor Oscar ever mentioned the episode again. Oscar had strong personal motives for maintaining an atmosphere of sexual privacy. And though Meg was against marriage on principle, she did not evangelize; she was only politely uninterested in hearing anything about Vivian's.

AND WHAT WOULD there have been to tell? Vivian and Oscar were discreet; they were independent; they were even affectionate with each other. They kept separate rooms but always breakfasted together, trading the morning papers in companionable silence. When Oscar discovered an involuntary tendency to remove his wedding band in his sleep and fling it into his bedclothes—it was perhaps sized incorrectly; at any rate it chafed—he took to placing it carefully in a dedicated porcelain dish on his nightstand.

As a married man, Oscar also found he had the freedom—and the assistance of a live-in expert—to explore those dimensions of ladies' fashion that had previously been prohibited by his performance of manly indifference. He was occasionally drafted to assist Vivian in dressing—there was no question of hiring a maid, not with the Schmidts' finances as they were—and thus he was able to satisfy a lifelong professional, artistic, and architectural curiosity about the proper rigging of feminine undergarments. Corsets and laces and garters, petticoats and tuckers and chemises, every inch of the human body armored and padded and cinched and draped.

And, of course, accessorized.

Oscar developed a particular fondness for Vivian's hatpins—these items having been especially difficult to examine unobtrusively in social settings, positioned as they were so close to ladies' faces. Vivian's pins were mostly plain enamel, given her humble circumstances, but she had one intimidatingly handsome specimen (loaned by, and never returned to, Patience Stone's aunt Daphne): a seven-inch shaft of gold with a razor point, it dissolved at the head to a filigreed mist cupping a teardrop lobe of pearl and nephrite jade. (Had it been sentimental and guilty attachment to the pin's origins that had prevented Vivian from pawning it during her summer's hardship? Or the consciousness that it telegraphed wealth and status from the very crown of her head, at a moment when appearances mattered most?)

Oscar regarded Aunt Daphne's hatpin with such naked admiration, Vivian let him keep it in a bud vase on his desk when it was not in use. He was interested in collecting more—would ideally have procured an entire bouquet of pins in a similar style, and contrived an appropriately fetching method of display—but he was startled in his early research to discover the value of the piece, and had to table the nascent hobby in hopes of a happier financial day to come.

Indeed, though the newly established Schmidt household enjoyed an odd and fragile harmony, even their modest expenses were beyond their means. And Vivian soon felt the confident itch that she was too ambitious, too intelligent, too impatient to economize her tastes and simper before bill collectors when she could see the path to fortune lying at her very feet. It was, after all, the reason she had married Oscar: her vision for his industrial future, and her own by proxy.

IT WAS ALWAYS, she reflected after her first attempt, going to be a hard sell.

Marrying Oscar had secured her a captive audience: she could suggest that he merge his business with Squire Clancey's and retain the right to speak to Oscar again, however offended he might be. He could storm into the next room, he could sulk for a week, but the suggestion was hardly grounds for divorce.

But a marriage certificate did *not* guarantee that Oscar would warm to the idea once he had heard it—not in one conversation; not in ten; not ever.

And the cardinal insult of womanhood was the fact that she would *have* to convince him. There was no metric to bypass even the most idiotic of husbands.

Vivian erred, perhaps, in jumping straight to the suggestion of collaboration with Squire. But she had been obliged to choose between beef and sugar to meet their weekly bills, and she had already spent two decades of her life among people who relished wallowing. Her patience was exhausted.

"Clancey has connections that would be useful," she said. (How was this a controversial statement, she thought, when Oscar was slogging through his fourth fiscal year at a loss to the man?) "Join forces with him and you'll gain those connections, and every vendor you lost, and the right to market Clancey's product—" She bit off the thought, remembering too late that it was taken as gospel in the Schmidt house that Squire Clancey had no good ideas, no useful products. Only luck and malice.

"He has no idea what he's doing," Oscar maintained. "He doesn't know the first thing about his own business."

There were endless variations of this claim, its supporting evidence voluminous (if repetitive and incomplete): Squire's anachronistic investment in candlemaking in the first place, of course; the fact that he bought up only sweet-smelling essential oils and solvent extracts, ignoring the neutral and even unpleasant notes that made a good scent into a complex olfactory accord; or that he (famously!) could not tour a slaughterhouse without a handkerchief (scented with a perfume *of Oscar's own design!*) pressed to his nose. Every time Vivian raised the topic—more obliquely with each attempt—Oscar responded with insults and rumors, some, indeed, *of his own design.*

Weeks lengthened to months of gentle nudges, invisible suggestions, feigned ignorance (increasingly so, as Vivian familiarized herself with the workings of Oscar's company), and leading questions, using Oscar's junior clerks (befriended for this purpose) as unwitting mouthpieces and informants.

Finally, Vivian achieved a bit of wholly undesired progress: though no more receptive than ever to the idea of a merger, Oscar convinced himself to attempt to run Squire out of business.

Vivian's campaign had succeeded, if in nothing else, in keeping Squire Clancey and his damnable outfit in the front of Oscar's mind—and in his state of wounded pride, revenge was a more palatable goal than collaboration. After all, he pointed out, he'd won his New York office its increased budget for the new fiscal year. Why not use it to torpedo the competition? Wouldn't this be more direct than painstakingly luring back each individual supplier?

Oscar had his secretary set a preliminary meeting with Squire and his partner, Mr. Lawrence; he prepared for it in eccentric, largely illogical brainstorming sessions, putting more care into the gloating speech he dreamed of making after negotiating Squire out of his business than he did into any actual proposals or plans. He performed these draft tirades for Vivian, graciously soliciting her feedback on phrasing (was "ungentlemanly" better, or "amateurish?") and on his posture (feet firmly planted, one hand on his lapel, as if declaiming a sonnet)—but ignoring her general suggestion that perhaps the whole hubristic venture was doomed.

She'd created a crackpot Rockefeller, Vivian thought with exasperation and—it must be said—some measure of affectionate amusement. A captain of industry's garbage scow.

"We'll ruin him," Oscar said, recalling his improbable success the last time Vivian had counseled him to bluster and bluff his way through a business meeting.

But Vivian knew the difference. His meeting with his employer had been about salesmanship, self-defense via the flash and bang of desperate charm. Now, on the contrary, was the moment to balance the ledger; to bury pride under the simple facts of supply and demand and the clear-eyed calculation of another man's advantages, many of them innate societal privileges that could not be wrested in a single transaction like a pirate's booty. (Put simply: Squire was no good to them dead.) She knew Oscar's confidence was misplaced, would scuttle him totally—even if he somehow succeeded in buying Squire out, it would be a ham-fisted victory, the ruthless acquisition alienating the suppliers and contractors who would fear execution by the same scimitar. Oscar would end up with a fraction of the vendors and deals he should, venting arterial gouts of profit into New York Harbor for the sake of his pride.

Of course, there was no possibility of Vivian attending next month's ill-fated meeting with Squire and Mr. Lawrence. (Sex was, on this matter, an equalizer, more powerful even than social class: the unrecognized female by-products of suburban Utica were no more welcome in downtown offices than ladies boasting the signature of Mrs. Clancey, née Squire-Sacerdote.)

And anyway, Vivian reasoned, by the day of the meeting it would already be too late.

Time to counter Oscar's self-sabotage was short—but the city, as it always did, provided a solution for those who knew how to look.

Vivian entertained and rejected several potential snares: a play or opera would make it too easy for the men to ignore each other by feigning pointed attention toward the stage; a restaurant encounter could be rushed through, or tables taken on opposite sides of the dining room.

Finally she settled on her best option, discovered via pasteboard notice in Herald Square: the New York Aquarium in Battery Park would fete the opening of a new exhibit (a pair of Atlantic walruses) on the following Monday, admitting in preview only members in good standing of the Zoological Society and their guests.

The first step, of course, was registering a membership on Oscar's behalf.

Tickets secured, she wrote a brief, quasi-friendly note of invitation to Squire Clancey, impersonating her husband. It was an affectionate forgery, as she carefully traced the slender loops and floating serifs of his penman-ship. *Recalling your interest in the natural sciences*, she wrote, *I thought you might find this event diverting.* A fussy, old-fashioned turn of phrase, Vivian thought with a smile—she could hear it as if from Oscar's own lips. *I extend the invitation from one amateur zoologist to another*, she continued. *I look forward to our next meeting, whenever your schedule permits. Yours, &c., Oscar Schmidt.*

NINE

Buildings, no less than landmasses, accrue and shed history in layers of sediment and slow erosion—or, less often, in pyrotechnic blasts. In the unusual case of the New York Aquarium, the building was paradoxically older than the ground one crossed to reach it. Before landfill connected it to the southern tip of Manhattan, the Southwest Battery—a circular sandstone military fort—stood for decades on a mound of rocks one hundred yards offshore. A teardrop pendant bristling with cannons. More than a pin in the map: a new island added to the world atlas.

For the first phase of its life, a drawbridge connected the Battery to the main island and Broadway's taproot. Built in a fervor of simmering tension, it was garrisoned with troops during the War of 1812 but never saw action—briefly packed with munitions and frightened young men, then turned over to seabirds and administrative offices. Fisherman, in turn, began colonizing the drawbridge and dropping their lines into the choppy, unclaimed waves between the city proper and the citadel—as if it were not a military fortification but an amusement park.

Such, perhaps, is the power of suggestion: the army and city collaborated to make it one. The fort became Castle Garden and Battery Park—a promenade, a raucous beer garden. Saltwater bathhouses purported to heal everything from rheumatism to tuberculosis. The old fort, now roofed and sporting a decorative cupola (like a picnic bonnet on a bareknuckle boxer), became a concert hall—packed for performances by touring orchestras and dance companies, operas tragic and comic. It moonlighted as an exhibition venue, for decades hosting demonstrations of telegraphs, fire engines, and all manner of spectacular technology and exotic artifacts. Eventually the city filled in the shoreline, extending itself with landfill. New York's appetite for recreation subdued the ocean itself and claimed the space around the fort as parkland, as if winning it from the harbor in a game of cards.

In 1855, another sea change: Castle Garden was repurposed as the nation's first commissioned immigrant receiving station. Over three decades, upward of eight million people—two-thirds of new arrivals to the United States—passed through the building's chaos and confusion to be registered; guarding their meager luggage in the old soldiers' barracks; waiting for processing in the darkened opera hall; dodging corrupt officials and small-time scammers and the quotidian, above-board horrors of the system as it was intended to function in order to emerge from the military fort–cum–amusement park as newly minted Americans.

Finally (nothing is ever final; still, let us mark another pin in our map), the federal government took over immigration control and moved operations to Ellis Island. Once again, the building had a vacancy. And this time, perhaps strangest of all, it became a museum of fish.

Backed by the dark waters of New York Harbor, which it collected daily to process for its denizens, the fort—still recognizable in shape and structure, with the legend AQUARIUM tacked over its paramilitary entrance—now held a semicircle of seven shallow, indoor, open-air pools with waist-high railings (the better to observe marine mammals and other superficially visible creatures), plus huge tanks set into the walls full of deeper-sea fish both exotic and local. The mosaic tile floors were dotted with potted palms and pillars thick as smokestacks; between dark wood paneling, dim lighting (for the health of those animals accustomed to turbid waters), and the brackish splashing smell of the pools, it felt like a cross between a hotel lobby and a fecund swamp. And if the disparate ghosts of soldiers, bureaucrats, operatic clowns, inventors, and polyglot immigrants rubbed shoulders with the captive fish and scuttling bottom-feeders, it was no handicap to the tourist atmosphere—New Yorkers, after all, being accustomed to a crowd.

SQUIRE APPROACHED THE aquarium in a state of nervous agitation, repeatedly adjusting the brim of his hat. He could not, even after days of calculation, account for Oscar Schmidt's inviting him to the exhibition opening. It was by some measures an even stranger offer than the seat at his wedding breakfast—at least a marriage was a standardized and semi-public ritual, with the necessary trial of spectators and with some invitations penned with gritted teeth in the name of propriety. But who had ever heard of asking a personal enemy to an *aquarium*?

For years Oscar had snubbed and smeared Squire at every opportunity; had done his best to sabotage his business (if largely unsuccessfully); had—most grievous of all—drawn the negative attention of Squire's parents. And then with no forewarning, and so close together the messages seemed almost to come by the same day's post, Oscar had arranged both a business meeting for the following week (Mr. Lawrence had had it marked on Squire's calendar, suggesting pointedly that Squire let him do the talking)—and this, a personal affair.

A man more accustomed to social fluency might have feared a trap of some kind. But Squire was painfully well acquainted with the feeling of interpersonal confusion, the disconnect between what made sense to him and what the rest of society considered typical behavior.

Perhaps, he thought cautiously, a normal man would recognize this as an olive branch. Perhaps it was an opportunity for Squire to acquit himself of any conflict with Oscar and his business.

Perhaps if he conducted himself correctly—if he expressed the expected level of interest in the aquarium exhibits; if he shook hands and nodded and made grave noises over the state of Wall Street and the supply chain—then Oscar and his parents and everyone else would leave him alone.

Squire had elected not to tell Mr. Lawrence about the invitation to the aquarium. Now—nearing the entrance, scanning for familiar faces, whether friend or foe—he wondered if this had been a mistake. But besides the inevitable loss of trust and esteem after the revelation of

Mr. Lawrence's conspiracy with Squire's parents (which might, Squire suspected, continue even now), there was the fact that the better Mr. Lawrence became acquainted with Squire, the more his advice tended to favor caution and abstention—especially on the question of Squire's engagement with colleagues (to say nothing of rivals). Mr. Lawrence would certainly have advised him to decline the invitation—especially coming so soon before their business meeting.

And the fact was that deeper than any anxiety, personal or professional, ran this bedrock: Squire wanted to see the walruses.

HE PINPOINTED THEM almost immediately upon entering the greenish, salt-funked hall—not the animals precisely, but the crowd of jostling bodies surrounding their central pool. There was a distant splash; a hooting bellow that echoed off the tile; a ripple of answering, almost fearful amusement from the audience. Squire joined a queue for admission—an attendant sat behind a screen of plate glass and brass lattice, almost indistinguishable from the fish on display—and checked his watch. There would be a formal exhibition in half an hour, with a feeding demonstration and a zoological lecture on the animals' habitat and behavior.

The line shuffled forward. Squire checked his watch again.

More even than the special event and the socially confounding invitation, Squire was preoccupied with interest in the aquarium's inner workings, the aerating compressors and water pumps and steamer tanks hidden in the bowels of the building. He hoped that there might be special privileges afforded to Zoological Society members (and, by extension, their guests). He'd read there were separate taps of fresh, salty, and brackish water—how Squire's hands itched to work the levers!

"May I help you, sir?" asked the attendant.

Interrupted midstream, Squire had to bite his tongue to stop himself inquiring about the air compressors. Instead he gave his name—and, in a halting voice, Oscar's. Upside down and backward he watched the attendant run a finger down his column of entitled guests until he found *Mr. & Mrs. Oscar Schmidt*—and, appended in a hasty script, *Mr. S. Clancey.* (This, of course, was Vivian's work: with a murmured aside upon their arrival, a half hour earlier, she had made an unwitting accomplice of the attendant.) Squire's presence was confirmed with a check mark; there was no need, he was told, to pay an admission fee.

Seeing Squire's distress at this news, the attendant offered him the optional purchase of a program, featuring professional illustrations and educational captions. Relieved, Squire bought a copy and tipped handsomely. The financial exchange settled his nerves, somewhat. The more openly transactional a social situation, the higher were Squire's chances of success.

He paused in the grand hall's entrance, watching with undisguised envy as a member of the aquarium's staff slipped through a door marked EMPLOYEES ONLY—gateway to the specimen reserves, hatchery tanks, and laboratory for instruction in marine biology. Recovering from this distraction, Squire finally glimpsed Oscar and Vivian on the far side of the hall—though he thought of them still, at this point, as Schmidt and his young wife. They were examining the aquarium's display on the life cycle of the mosquito, Vivian leaning with apparent feminine affection on her husband's arm.

In fact, though the effect was not precisely feigned, Vivian's posture had the double function of making it easier to steer Oscar. Upon arrival she had subtly tacked him toward the mosquito display, as it was among both the least popular and the most thoroughly captioned exhibits and so provided an ideal situation for surreptitiously awaiting Squire's entrance. Oscar was not particularly interested in mosquitos, but he was almost as vulnerable to suggestion from educational museum placards as from his wife. With the two working in collaboration, he was lost. Dutifully he leaned close (he was slightly nearsighted, though yet undiagnosed) to read each label and inspect each terrarium of larval and pupal specimens.

"Mosquitos lay their eggs," Oscar read aloud (unconsciously—before his marriage he had never been made aware of his own inability to read silently, and Vivian had not enlightened him, loath to encourage any habit of increased obscurity). "Mosquitos lay their eggs," Oscar continued, "in clusters on the surface of still water such as is found in rain barrels, cisterns, ditches, stagnant ponds, undrained swamps, and marshes. Each female mosquito lays from 150 to 400 eggs"—absently Oscar scratched at his collar; Vivian quirked a smile but did not interrupt—"which in about a week hatch into larvae or wrigglers." He wrinkled his nose, leaning in to inspect the exhibition's illustrative jar of larvae.

Oscar was not, you must remember, squeamish—however nervous and self-loathing from boyhood, he had unflinchingly waded through offal and rendered slaughterhouse fat. But he remained in maturity a pathologically fearful man at heart, and a faithful cataloger of new dangers and anxieties. These numbers—one mosquito begetting four hundred offspring—appealed to his instinctive expectation of exponential disaster. "The mosquito is the only known source," he continued, "of malaria and yellow fever"—and broke off again, squinting once more at the aquarium tank and its stagnant stew of wriggling larvae. "Then why *breed* the things?" he muttered.

Vivian was on the point of answering when she saw Squire, crossing the damp tile in their direction. Smiling brightly, she tightened her grip on Oscar's arm. He jumped at the sudden pressure. "What on earth is—"

"Mr. Clancey!" Vivian sang out. With one hand she beckoned Squire welcome; with the other she clutched Oscar close enough that to escape he would have had to make a scene. (She had a surprisingly strong grip.) She felt him tense and pull like a shying horse, but he stopped short of actual flight.

Squire joined this odd couple, who were nearly embracing by the mosquito larvae. He drew breath to greet Oscar as his host, but Vivian anticipated him. "You're here to see the walruses," she said, a remark calculated to pass to both deceived parties as the kind of vapid comment they considered typical of feminine conversation.

"Yes," Squire said. And, with a stilted and careful nod to Oscar: "Thank you for thinking of me."

". . . Yes," Oscar finally wheezed, sounding like an accordion with a punctured bellows. He thought, of course, that Squire referred nonsensically to their business meeting, scheduled for the following week—the oft-imagined scene of Oscar's future professional triumph, so thoroughly rehearsed. (And now, he thought bitterly, as thoroughly spoiled—his adversary having surprised him *looking at fish* in the middle of a workday.)

"Have you been here before?" Vivian asked Squire. She was hoping to trigger one of his impromptu speeches, as with the detailed review of the mastodon skeleton he'd furnished at their last meeting. As long as someone was talking, Vivian reasoned, they were making progress. At the very least, she knew Oscar was too faithful a servant of propriety (at least in his daylit life) to leave a public conversation midsentence.

But Squire still had himself in rein. "Never for an exhibition" was his only comment, as he looked with poorly concealed longing at the crowd by the celebrated walruses' central pool. As with the subway's opening day, it was the validation of communal excitement that attracted him almost more than the object itself. Mr. and Mrs. Clancey's efforts to raise their son in existential quarantine had had many effects—among them, that he found even mild shared enthusiasm to be a rare and miraculous ecstasy.

"Shall we?" Vivian suggested.

THEY STROLLED A circuitous path toward the walruses, leaving visiting cards at sundry creatures' tanks en route: trout; pike; a bouquet of tropical tangs; a scrum of crabs and one grandfather lobster with a plaque designating it the donation of a generous benefactor; a sandy-bottomed pool skimmed by a pair of well-camouflaged, long-tailed skates.

Squire kept an uneven pace between the exhibits. Sometimes he strode ahead with an almost professional purpose, as if employed by the aquarium to assess the quality of its displays; at other moments he would suddenly remember his vow to behave unremarkably and come almost jogging back to join the Schmidts. He studied them sidelong at the rock penguin enclosure, tried to mimic their aloof distance and placid expressions. Tried to pass for a man who understood both why a sworn enemy had invited him to the aquarium and how to behave now that he had arrived.

In fact Oscar's seeming ease was only the tranquility of a blown fuse. With unseeing eyes he let Vivian herd him across the floor, from tank to rockery to imitation tidal pool. In his shock he had lost all sense of the world around him, or indeed of his own person.

This did not scuttle Vivian's plan—in fact, she endeavored only to strike before Oscar thawed enough to act for himself. A man catatonic with astonishment or shame, she had already had reason to observe, was all the easier to manipulate.

"How have you been keeping busy, Mr. Clancey, since last we met?"

She felt Oscar give a warning twitch, at this reference to an earlier interview with his nemesis. She held her breath.

Squire blinked. There were too many answers to Vivian's question— he'd been busy inventing and discovering and developing, weathering failure and betrayal and disappointment. After all his recent reversals of fortune, there was only one answer that still sparked any real happiness. Instinctively he followed the spark: "I've been riding the train," he said.

"The subway?" Vivian disguised her relief as mild curiosity. Of course, she scolded herself—she should have guessed. The feat of technological innovation; the eccentric and bottomless well of trivia; the marvel of speed and convenience executed at gargantuan expense. Of course, Vivian thought, this devotee of articulated mastodon skeletons and bespoke cocktails was smitten with the underground train.

"How have you found the tunnels?" she began. A sufficiently openended question, she hoped, to prime the pump. "Is the trip quite safe?"

She had, of course, ridden the train herself on several occasions—but it was in her best interest, as it still so often was, to feign ignorance.

It was lucky for Squire that Vivian's trap was not a more directly sinister one, for he surrendered to it completely. His defense of the Interborough Rapid Transit Company's latest venture—his insistence on the journey's safety and comfort, his enumeration of the stations' amenities and the scientific wonders of the tunnels themselves—could hardly have been more passionate had he been employed as an official spokesman.

With feeble desperation Squire fought against the flow of his own enthusiasm and tried, as at his parents' Christmas party five years before, to bridle himself. To steer things back to respectable conversation, or else to flee.

But there were essential differences: he *wanted* to be here (the celebrated walruses were yet unglimpsed!); he was wanted here himself (he had been invited by hand!); and Vivian Schmidt had asked him, directly *solicited* him, to tell her about the trains.

Besides, Squire was a more experienced and even, by some measures, a more self-possessed man now than he had been five years before. The underground world that then he'd only dreamed of visiting he now toured at least once daily, as a matter of habit. Indeed, he felt almost responsible for the subway—as though obligated to defend and explain a system that was as much a part of himself as, if not a limb, then one of his more mysterious yet essential organs. His liver, his kidney, his spleen.

"Quite the testimonial," Vivian said diplomatically. She tugged lightly on Oscar's leaden arm, to remind them all (not excluding Oscar himself) of his presence. Calculating another suggestion, she continued. "I'll have to see if I can tear Mr. Schmidt away from his soap long enough to—"

"Oh!" Squire cried.

The ejaculation was loud enough that several passersby turned in the direction of their party. Oscar, who at last snapped to full attention, was one of those startled.

"But you should—your company should contract with the subway!" Squire said. His hands spasmed, as though trying to physically transfer the substance of the idea.

Oscar flinched.

Besides being transported as usual by the suddenness of his notion, Squire had the unfamiliar feeling of striving to fulfill a social contract. He had been invited here for an unknown reason, by a businessman; here, against all odds, was a business proposition rushing to the surface of his mind. To communicate it seemed a matter of life or death. "The comfort stations," Squire said, by way of desperate clarification.

Oscar paled; he wavered on his feet. All his senses but smell, the must and ammonia heavy in the aquarium's damp air, faded from his awareness.

For Oscar was no stranger to the subway system himself—but he turned to it for rather a different species of relief than Squire. On the occasions that Oscar had invested in a five-cent ticket, he had been principally concerned with admission to the comfort stations that Squire now referenced: exquisite, almost supernatural blends of the public and private worlds, where he could make glancing eye contact with each man passing through in succession as he stood before the glass, feigning to settle the knot in his tie. Eventually would come the returning glance that caught his like flint to tinder, the rake of some man's eyes over Oscar's person—the bare suggestion of a beckoning nod into the stall.

As a trysting place the subway restroom was a luxury Oscar would not have dared dream of in his youth: inherently transitory and impersonal; suspended in both time and place; a cubby too small to conceal hidden dangers, with a door that locked.

With the torturous egotism of a guilty conscience Oscar thought at first that Squire was blackmailing him—that he'd been observed in one, or several, of these liminal encounters.

Ah, but what had *Clancey* been doing there? A smarming second voice objected in Oscar's mind. Was his rival a fairy too?

Involuntarily Oscar swept Squire from head to foot—a sack suit, well fitted but carelessly worn (he had missed a button on his waistcoat); one lip slightly fuller than the other, giving him a pouting expression; that uncanny silver hair escaping his hat as if the man's brain were on fire. Usually these things were all in the eyes, subtle and pointed—but Squire stared at him directly, his gaze crackling lightning. (Oscar was not, at this point, familiar enough to realize that Squire's expressions of interest were rarely bound by convention.)

Still, Oscar was disarmed. He found himself (oh, sabotage!) in the state of partial arousal that the piecemeal consideration of nearly any man's figure inspired in him. But—he checked again—no, there was no sign of proposition he found legible. They were in separate cells. If he was caught, he thought, he was alone. Mutely he turned to Vivian, though in panicked appeal or apology or even anger he could not have said. He'd been increasingly careless, he knew, since their marriage. In the previous seasons of his life, self-loathing and fear had kept him sharp. (Could he truly blame Vivian, for the unmasking of his own private shame? This reflexive impulse informed him that he would try.)

But: "The soap is terrible!" Squire was saying, laving his hands in the empty air as if to demonstrate.

Oscar thought at first the man was, in a general way, insulting his business. But then, finally, he understood.

(Let us count backward, like archaeologists labeling strata of sediment: it was Oscar's *fifth* instinct that penetrated obfuscating fear and loathing and reached as far as basic comprehension. Such are the impediments of wretchedness.)

Squire was enumerating the subway soap's flaws with the thoroughness of a prosecutor—venting, perhaps, his otherwise inaccessible disappointments with the beloved rail system that, despite its wonders, had not preserved the private playground of his new life as an entrepreneur, nor emancipated him from his family's disapproval. The soap, he explained, was dense—a fingernail would hardly dent the cake. (Oscar noted against his will the freshness of the other man's manicure—a habit Squire maintained not out of vanity but because he found the procedure almost primally soothing.)

Squire gained traction as he spoke—here it was, the miraculously compounding confidence of having found a subject of mutual interest with Oscar. To be in conversation with him, holding his attention. (He saw Oscar's eyes flick to his hands; a tremble passed through his suddenly self-conscious fingers.) To be doing him a favor, even! It was a fitting reciprocation, Squire hoped, for the still-incomprehensible—the now almost thrilling—olive branch of the aquarium invitation. A man was as likely, he continued, to tear his skin on the texture of a bar of municipal soap as he was to raise a lather, and it evoked a scent akin to wet paper in the basin. Each sink held a two-inch cake of the stuff in a shallow depression beneath the faucet, so excess moisture continually flooded the well and eroded the soap to a paradoxically abrasive mush over the course of the morning rush hour.

"You should draw up a contract with the IRT," Squire repeated. Too inexperienced in Personal Care to suggest any particulars, he turned to volume: "There are twenty-eight stops on the line." He began a mental multiplication by comfort stations and washbasins, but his enthusiasm trumped his patience. "It's a lot of soap," he said.

"Hmm," Oscar said, at some length. He was flushed with embarrassment and confusion, unable to process the fact that his most devastating competitor had just pitched him, if not a bona fide business opportunity, at least a promising lead worth further investigation.

Vivian, too, could barely believe her luck—but she knew better than her husband what to do with it. "Of course," she said, "we'd have to sort out the snags in the supply line first." She amended: "I mean, you gentlemen would, of course." A tactful air obscured the indelicacy of her actual comments—with men as with horses, she'd found, tone of voice was more consciously comprehended than substance of meaning.

Squire and Oscar blinked at each other in the green glow of the dimly undulating gallery. Once again, and for the first time since her parents had torn her down to her foundation in Utica, Vivian made the rigid shape of the world malleable simply by confusing the right people at the right moment. She felt her lungs draw deeper than they had in months, as though the bones of her corset had loosened. A welcome, returning flux of agency.

At this moment the clang of a bell arrested them. An attendant mounted a wooden platform to translate the signal into human speech: the official exhibition of the walruses was about to begin.

THROUGH A COMBINATION of Vivian's shrewd maneuvering, Squire's bald enthusiasm, and the involuntary breadth of Oscar's shoulders, our trio of latecomers ended up in the first ranks of the assembled crowd, pressing directly against the iron railing that ringed the central lagoon at waist height. The pool below them was sunken, extravagantly large, with artificial rock outcroppings jutting above the surface. Chunks of unformed ice, cloudy and brownish, bobbed in the fish-smelling water.

Oscar was distracted at first, still caught fast in the grip of social embarrassment, and obscurely desperate to discharge his debt of professional interest even to a former—a current?—enemy. "And your, ah—your business is good?" he managed.

Squire made a vague noise. He was preoccupied with the ice, aching to know the process by which the aquarium manufactured and replaced each fast-melting berg.

The habitat was dwarfed by the walruses themselves—twin behemoths of muscle and fat upholstered in rubbery, wrinkled skin, each many times larger than a man. They lolled indifferently before their spectators, with the sedentary, dull-eyed look of all captive animals. One rolled idly in the shallow water; the other lay heaped on the false land, rear flippers trailing like an unfortunate mermaid's. They were both tusked, ivory spars jutting violently down from their whiskered muzzles.

The attendant, again mounting his platform—which seemed more for the purpose of elevating him above the crowd than that of giving him any special access to the animals below—began to educate his audience. The Atlantic walrus, he explained, was a marine mammal principally endemic to the far northern sea ice of the Arctic region. Its skin grew up to four inches thick, beneath which it wrapped itself in over a foot of insulating blubber.

"Imagine the tallow," Vivian murmured, leaning to an ambiguous distance so that the comment might have been meant for either gentleman. Oscar began almost compulsory calculations of lye and oil, portioning each animal into a fantastic chimera composed of cakes of laundry and toilet soap; Squire felt another flickering of the candlelit curiosity that had been snuffed in his heart ever since his father's ambush in Mr. Lawrence's office. Both men turned to glance at Vivian—but having made her whispered comment, she had withdrawn. They caught only each other's eyes, and turned their attention again to the pool, embarrassed.

The educational lecture continued: the walrus's tusks, three feet long in the case of the largest animals, were present in both males and females. ("That's a new one on me!" interjected a nearby Zoological Society member. Sighting Vivian, he colored slightly and touched his hat in vague, self-condemning apology.) Both of the aquarium's specimens, the attendant amended, were female.

"Then there's no chance of a breeding program?" Squire asked—prompting a general wince, at the attention drawn to the impracticality of housing even two such enormous animals indoors on Manhattan. Even before their unveiling to the general public, the walruses' inevitable demise was the third elephantine beast gamboling in the pool.

The attendant went on, describing the use of the tusks—in combat and social dominance, in punching holes in the ice and hauling the animals' great bulk out of the sea.

It was difficult, watching the immobile hulks in the pool, to imagine such feats of athleticism—still, there was an inherent thrill in the intelligence that such power was coiled dormant within such enormous creatures. Oscar relinked his arm with Vivian's, by some vestigial chivalrous instinct interposing himself between her and the beasts. She patted his hand.

The attendant retrieved a metal pail from the floor by his feet and began passing it from hand to hand as he spoke. Throughout the encircling crowd spines straightened, gazes became more alert—as though the pile of gut-slick herring within were designated for the spectators rather than the walruses themselves. Even for this ivory-tower audience, purely theoretical facts were of comparatively limited interest.

"In nature," the attendant smarmed—savoring his power to delay the demonstration's climax—"walruses use their whiskers to feel for clams and other creatures buried in the muddy seafloor." Dutifully his listeners examined the animals, noted their bristling beards of—fascinating horror!—tactilely sensitive hair.

An idea caught Squire and pinned him. With his typical helpless candor he turned from the walruses to Oscar and back again, making several rounds of comparative study between their whiskers. Finally he caught Vivian's eye with an arch glance that made her burst into surprised laughter.

"What?" Oscar said, not quite daring to turn his back on the animals.

"Nothing," she said—resisting the image of his well-moisturized muttonchops snuffling over the Arctic seafloor in search of hidden shell-fish. She felt toward Squire, for making the joke, the same unexpected thrill of affection that had ambushed her when Oscar crept across her parents' woodlot to plan the escape from Utica. There was more to each of these men, she was confident, than they were capable of accessing on purpose. Vivian renewed her hopes for what she might use them to accomplish.

At last, the attendant hoisted the bucket. The walruses seemed to grasp the meaning of this gesture as well as their spectators—both animals raised their heads, blinking tiny eyes. The crowd gave a general shiver of antic-ipation as the beached walrus slid into the pool to join her sister, creating a wave of displaced water that slapped the tile.

Squire leaned over the railing to watch the animals swim, impressively sinuous for all their bulk.

"Careful," Oscar said nervously.

The audience, which had cleared a skittish space around the keeper's platform, took an additional involuntary step back as the walruses lazily crowded that end of the pool.

The keeper tossed herring one at a time into the water or even, some-times, directly into the animals' mouths. An adult walrus, he was explaining, might eat one hundred pounds of fish in a day.

"Not at that rate they won't," Vivian observed. It was true that disap-pearing into the walruses' gullets, the herring looked like minnows. If not for the keeper's pageantry—if, through mercy or lack of imagination, someone had simply upended the bucket into the pool—the whole feast could have been over in an instant. "Though I suppose—"

But Vivian was interrupted by a rippling gasp, as the larger of the two walruses heaved like a rearing horse to—almost daintily!—snatch a limp herring as it dangled from the keeper's hand.

While the crowd focused on the animal, Vivian watched the man flinch—saw the fear dancing in his eyes even as he bowed in response to the applause ringing the pool. Trying to regain his composure, the keeper passed his bucket from hand to hand again and swiped one wrist across his brow, leaving a slick of bloody fish grease.

A murmur of embarrassed distaste trod on the ovation's coattails, cutting it short.

Vivian clucked at the keeper, losing his audience just when he had them eating from his palm. He had most of what it took, she thought. But what good was that if he couldn't close the deal?

Having seized its prize, the walrus fell heavily back into the pool—fish-smelling spray splashed at the spectators' gloves and trouser legs; displaced waves slapped violently at the concrete walls. A short scream of indeterminate sex was quickly stifled. Squire jackknifed over the railing, ignoring its sharp press at his hip, the better to observe the commotion. His walking stick clattered on the mosaic, rolling underfoot.

"*Careful*," Oscar said again—to Squire in particular or to the room at large, it was difficult to say. Oscar tried to shrink away, tugging at Vivian's right arm. On her left, the unheeding Squire leaned as if pulling at a leash, as contrary and enraptured as ever. The keeper's narration was entirely lost, now—Squire had eyes only for the walruses themselves, their slapping flippers and musty saline exhalations, the fish they sucked down like greasy macaroni. He rocked forward, leaning on tiptoe. Oscar yanked with increasing desperation on Vivian's sleeve.

She could feel things deteriorating. This was her own unexpected setback, triggered by the aquarium keeper's. A walrus had lunged, and the keeper had bungled it—shown his hand, lost control of the situation. Now her own charges were threatening to stampede in response.

Well, Vivian thought, she would refuse to allow it. This was her only chance—if the afternoon fell apart, she would never get them back. The inevitable implosion at the office next week would be all the worse for the embarrassment of this memory. She could not—she scanned the room, blocking out the keeper's patter and Squire's delighted laughter and Oscar's insistent whisper in her ear—she *could not* let these two men recede back into separate corners. The one so focused on the show he'd forgotten the rest of the world; the other about to break for the exit.

The situation may seem impossible. If so, dear reader, we can only hope you never face Vivian Schmidt (née Lesperance) as a tactician.

She had a split second, a literal tipping point. Under cover of the crowd's confused excitement and a bellowing splash from the walruses and the rustling skirt of a dress that obscured all sins, she jabbed a swift unbalancing kick at the nerveless heel of Squire's right shoe—the toe of which, at that moment, was his sole point of contact with the slick mosaic floor.

TO SQUIRE, IT seemed as though he were the steady center of a gyroscope and the whole raucous world was pivoting around him. He felt gravity flip and tumble—the hard slice of the iron railing first digging sharply into his abdomen, then not at all. Instinctively he grasped for the bars, but too late—his fingers closed on empty air. The surface of the pool tilted and rose to fill his vision—gray water, a froth of foul-smelling bubbles, some piece of unidentifiable, vaguely organic flotsam. His half-somersault was checked just above the surface by the pool's concrete wall—his nose bashed, his cheek scraped like laundry against a washboard.

He hit the water in a tangle of confused limbs—knocked windless, he immediately swallowed a spluttering lungful. (A rancid and oversalted broth, cold enough that he ceased to wonder at the miniature icebergs' longevity.) Blood trickling from his smashed nose thinned in the water to a great hemorrhaging cloud, and he heard the first muffled screams of those onlookers who thought he'd somehow already been gored. (Squire could locate no sign, in the turbid subaquatic chaos, of the walruses themselves.)

His head broke the surface, and he kicked blindly for the bottom—expecting, from what he'd observed above, to be able to stand flatfooted with his chin above water. But as he coughed out a hacking lungful of old air and savory meltwater, first Squire's right, then his left, foot failed to make contact with the floor of the pool. His arms spasmed, his lungs seized—though he was not at the moment in an analytic or reflective

mood, his body itself seemed to have a thorough, even businesslike awareness that to sink again without taking a breath would be disastrous.

In an instant, a collage of impressions flashed through Squire's mind:
the heavy drag of his soaked clothes; the sting of his scraped face; the
claggy aristocratic blood stopping his nostrils. An inexplicable tightness
at his throat and band of sharp resistance across his chest. And the
walruses, twin brown islands at eye level, spouting volcanic spumes of
agitated vapor. (He had no sense of distance or direction—whether the
animals were at indifferent rest, or fleeing his intrusion into their habitat,
or charging at him where he floundered, tired of begging for piecemeal
herring and ready to get their entire daily serving of marine prey in one
sitting.)

A chaos of disembodied exclamations of mortification from the crowd
seemed to echo the reactions to Squire's entire abbreviated lifetime of
misadventure—the wine-cellar punch; the hummingbird fire screen; the
Christmas night spent wrestling with a manhole cover. An Arctic sea, a
flooded Manhattan storm drain rushing into a sewer culvert, a mythical
underwater cave draining Lake Ronkonkoma into the Sound. It seemed,
for one terrifying and thrill-spangled moment, as if all Squire's life had
been leading to this inevitable conclusion.

Before he could struggle again, he felt a painful tightening of that
strange resistance at his throat and chest, a sharp tug under his arms. He
twisted—and discovered that his feet would not reach the pool's floor for
the simple fact that Oscar Schmidt had vaulted the railing and was hoisting
him by the back of his coat.

Oscar wore a somewhat stupefied expression, as though he were as
surprised as Squire to find himself on the wrong side of the protective
railing, clinging with one arm to the ironworks and using the other to
haul his rival out of the artificial sea.

Squire—still three-quarters resigned to death, with no breath to spare
in his lungs, and unaccustomed to finding himself on the inside of any
joke—could not help but spasm with an involuntary gesture toward
laughter. It jostled them both, and Oscar nearly lost his tentative footing
on the concrete. "Steady!" cried an onlooker, unhelpfully.

With a heave that wrenched Squire's arms in their sockets, Oscar
hoisted him up high enough to catch him again, more securely—holding

him across the chest, under both arms. (This somewhat violent movement, unfortunately, knocked yet another nascent inhale from Squire's lungs.) Squire was a small man, but the saturating seawater had them punching almost the same weight—Oscar yawed again over the walrus pool, dithering slightly. His anchoring hand stung where the iron railing bit into his palm and the pads of his fingers. He was dimly conscious of other people attempting to intervene—nervous hands that flitted in and out of view, or else patted and tugged ineffectually at his own collar, as if afraid to spoil the rescue by becoming too involved.

Squire's face was turned away, but Oscar felt his chest shudder against him as, at last, he took a breath.

With a monumental heave, Oscar flung both himself and Squire back over the railing to safety. It was an awkward movement, rather the violent and ungainly reverse of Squire's tumble into the pool than any grand deliverance. The two men landed in a shuddering heap and a puddle of blood-stained meltwater—Squire immobilized by his still-winded lungs; Oscar by shock (at his own actions as much as anyone's). Gradually, their senses returned—a general alarm of horrified shrieks and dismayed laughter; the uniformed aquarium keepers struggling to keep order and establish fault; the apparently undisturbed splashing of the walruses. The chill and stink of the water that soaked them; the unforgiving grit of the mosaic tile beneath their heads; the fluttering pulse of the other man, still entangled.

The aquarium—its concrete, mosaic, fortified walls and decorative cupola—absorbed the incident as it had absorbed so much, over the course of its many lifetimes. Overhead, an incandescent corona blurred and starburst as Squire and Oscar blinked water from their eyes. A shape appeared, resolved with its approach. Vivian. She was exclaiming something they could not yet hear over the ringing in their ears, her cheeks flushed with an excitement that could have been anything—fear, adrenaline, triumph.

TEN

There was a brief, dissociated chaos. Calls for a nurse, for a doctor, for a veterinarian. (This last was alarmist: the walruses seemed to have taken no more notice of the commotion than of any of the other indignities of captivity.) The walrus keeper, appealed to first as the reigning figure of authority, could only gape in stupefaction; the crowd mutinied almost immediately. Variously hysterical runners dispatched themselves to fetch the ticket agent; the aquarium director (or at least his secretary); the in-house counsel.

Before any of these absent officials could be reached, however, Vivian had risen to fill the vacuum.

She whirled through the mob, catching everyone in her wake. She requisitioned handkerchiefs to stop the blood flowing from Squire's nose, palpated it with her own ungloved hand and pronounced it unbroken. (There would be time, in the years to come, for Squire to examine its somewhat jauntier angle in the looking glass and wonder if Vivian's diagnosis had been one of convenience.)

She identified her rivals for control of the situation—a pair of unaffiliated yet indistinguishable Wall Street bloviators—and entangled them in piecemeal errands, fetching towels and blankets from the aquarium's secret closets of terrestrial practicality.

Seeing that any litigation of fault and responsibility would burn all the momentum she'd gambled to gain, Vivian loudly implicated Squire's walking stick—still rolling blamelessly on the mosaic by his head—as the cause of his fall. This had the force of an incantation in speeding their exit: legal secretaries and insurance agents and aquarium administrators all melted away like so much smoke.

The aftermath was in some ways an echo of Squire's misadventure with the manhole cover, years before—though this time with the inexpressibly welcome addition of allies. An employee-washroom rinse to take care of the worst of the smell; a borrowed suit of rustic and ill-fitting but dry clothes. Finally, Vivian suggested they find a private place to regroup—and, as if by a snap of her fingers, spirited them to Squire's apartment.

SQUIRE'S ROOMS, WHICH Vivian and Oscar were left to inspect while Squire changed into his own clothes, were a reflection of the man himself: disconcertingly spartan in some corners, intimidatingly cerebral in others, with startling flashes of both eccentricity and opulence throughout. Books lay open on nearly every stable surface (and several more than a little precarious)—but a wide niche that could have served as a true library shelf held instead what appeared (to Oscar's unconvincingly surreptitious stare) to be a real Sèvres vase, holding a spray of live orchids.

The Schmidts were, in theory, present to help "get Squire settled" after his ordeal. In the service of this smoke screen Vivian deputized Oscar—still half-paralyzed with shock—to resuscitate the banked fire in the kitchen and put a kettle on to boil.

She mixed toddies, wafting the whiskey as she poured—as different from Ruf Thomas's baptismal moonshine as chalk from cheese. She fingered Squire's cut-glass bar set, another cast-off from the Clancey vault. Each tumbler felt solid enough to dent a cobblestone.

But for all these luxurious accoutrements, she found she could not safely rest the finished cocktails on the nearest table—Squire had designated it as his laboratory, and besides byzantine piles of half-assembled candle molds and riots of crumpled newsprint, paraffin wax pooled as much as a quarter-inch thick in places. (His long-suffering housekeeper, though she visited twice a week and did her best to keep Squire out of any real hygienic danger, had learned to fight the bulk of both her instincts and her training in "the Clancey maniac's" case.)

In the Clancey maniac's sitting room, Oscar and Vivian sat, respectively, on a giltwood armchair with scorched upholstery and a mismatched but clearly ancestral Queen Anne, its taloned feet eviscerating wooden spheres.

Oscar, as usual venting what discomfiture he could in occupation, set about coaxing this room's languishing fire back to life as well. A length of what looked like *point de Venise* lace, draped over an andiron and toasted golden-brown at one end, appeared to have also been recently used as both an ink blotter and a coffee napkin. "Jesus wept," Oscar muttered, rescuing it.

A traitorous blush invaded Vivian's cheek. She had not encountered a scene of such intimate and carless luxury since Sofia's hotel suite, where champagne had been left overnight to lose its sparkle and strings of Tahitian pearls had crunched underfoot. She felt a pang of regret over the loss of such casual opulence—and then, inevitably, over the relationship it had accompanied. The reminder was all the more painful for being unexpected.

As is so often the case, one vulnerability begat others. Vivian was suddenly sharply conscious of her life's lost glamour, its scrimping and scrabbling, its pleasures even more pathetic than its hardships—for goodness' sake, her husband had built an aesthetic religion around the worship of a single hatpin—and the desperate and irrational plan for recovery she clung to only by her fingertips. (How distant, suddenly, was her triumph at the aquarium barely an hour before!)

Entropy threatened, pricking at Vivian's eyes and shallowing her breath. Squire's treasures, like Sofia's, were part of his origin. One's origins, Vivian thought, were inescapable. Inevitable, destined. Ashes to ashes; dust to dust; nouveau riche to ruination. Utica would always be waiting.

Even worse, now Meg Booth's voice crowded into the chorus in Vivian's head—advocating for redistribution of wealth; avenging anarchic chaos; the mindful, purposeful, brick-by-brick destruction of everything Squire and his ilk squandered without noticing.

Enough, Vivian thought firmly, and took a punishing gulp of her scalding cocktail.

It was only furniture, she insisted. It was no different from the ladder-back chairs and tripod stools her father sold to farmers and their wives, for not-quite-enough money to support his own family. Someone had simply bought these armchairs, once upon a time, from someone else who had simply hammered two sticks together. What did it signify to anyone, what did it *matter*, if the money that had changed hands and the hammer and the sticks themselves had all been older than the American colonies? Regally crumbling antiquity, Vivian had long since decided, was a swindle that had run the table long enough.

Still, her saucer shook in her hand in the face of even these dregs of Squire's inheritance. (And can we blame her? She was reckoning with accumulation, awful and sublime, the pressure that builds infinitesimally to cataclysm. In geology, in metaphysics, in furniture—everything is a reliquary until it becomes an explosive.)

Squire himself rejoined them then, not only dressed but shrouded in a boutis quilt that trailed behind him like a cathedral veil. He was scrubbed more thoroughly clean, his nose still swollen, his silver hair a whorl of competing cowlicks. Despite his odd costume, and though Oscar still struggled to meet his eye after the embarrassment of the rescue, there was a palpable relief in his reappearance—the man himself no less strange, but so much less intimidating, than his societal trappings.

He accepted his mug from Vivian and settled himself on the carpet like a cat, apparently at ease and taking the fire's miraculous recovery for granted.

In fact, Squire was entirely overwhelmed by the novelty of visitors—Vivian and Oscar were the first of his life. He would have been surprised to learn that he had carried the quilt in from the bedroom; he could not have testified with any certainty as to whether he possessed a third chair. Once seated, he found himself incapable of more than the simplest rote comments—it was too wonderfully distracting, watching Vivian sip from a cup his own lips had touched. Watching Oscar sit, fidgeting with his trouser leg, in a chair where Squire had stroked himself to climax the evening before.

"Goodness," Squire said. His smile was still tinged slightly bloody. "What a day."

Vivian was impressed with Squire's apparent resilience, as with the performance of an investment. Oscar felt a somewhat parallel sense of awe—in his case, that any man could survive such public embarrassment without subsequently committing suicide.

Vivian proposed a toast: "To happy endings."

The men echoed her with uncertainty but drank with confidence.

"You have a lovely home, Mr. Clancey," Vivian said, after a mildly intoxicating pause.

Squire, who cherished his space but was long accustomed to making do without validation, reacted with visible surprise. "I do?"

"Certainly," Vivian said—covering her hesitation with perhaps an excess of enthusiasm. She was still casting about for the right piece of lapidary trash to compliment—the muddied swirls of oil paint drying on his encyclopedia endpapers? The antique portmanteau, its wardrobe compartment inexplicably containing a potted palm?—when Squire caught Oscar's involuntary glance toward the spray of pink orchids in their Sèvres.

"Oh, those," Squire said. "Those are from my mother."

"Well," he corrected himself, with the force of an interruption from a second person. "A man delivers them, every second Monday. But she hasn't canceled the order."

"How wonderful," Vivian said. "And is your family local?" (She knew, of course, both the strict facts and the interstitial society gossip about the Clancey clan and its divided households. But there would be much to glean from the tenor and pacing of Squire's own version of his biography.)

"Oh," Squire said. "Well—we—they—"

The answer spread in a strangling web: his parents were everywhere and nowhere, a separate yet united front. Madison Avenue, Lake Ronkonkoma, the Hudson Valley, sanitorium-bright St. Augustine. Even here, now—creeping out of this apartment's woodwork, coalescing in the crackling heart of the hearth fire, infecting the conversation.

By this point the day had stampeded well clear of propriety's paddock, and—with the smell of blood in his smashed nose; the chill of captive Arctic ice in his bones; the dislocating wrench of Oscar's rescue still an aching memory in his shoulders; the sugared whiskey coursing through his veins; and above all the *excitement*—Squire could not even feel blindly for social mores. "The thing is," he began, and told his story—as completely as he could (which was not very, but Vivian could bridge the gaps), from his childhood wreaking havoc up and down Millionaire's Row, to his present bachelor's purgatory.

There were some elements Vivian recognized, with a sympathetic chime: the parents with their strange mix of overbearance and indifference, unendurable at close range but (apparently) easy to vanquish via the tenuous yet simple method of physical avoidance. There were other elements she could only (and hungrily) imagine: the bottomless well of familial resources, tantalizingly close yet gatekept by a thorny hedge of cosignatories and conditionally promised inheritances.

She sliced into the conversation at precise angles, cutting with false innocuity against the grain: How had he found the summer crowds, in Lake Ronkonkoma? Which River Town was it, in which his family held their famous Christmas party? How had Mrs. Clancey found her florist—and my goodness, was it really still the same shop, after all these years?

Vivian calculated her questions to tame both Squire's social discomfort and her own feral jealously, which knocked constantly against the inside of her skull to remind her of the divine injustice that sorted some souls into gilded masculine cradles of power and others into country-girls' apple crates clumsily repurposed as bassinets. (It is not in the nature of such myopic jealousies to examine the continued spectrum of humanity *below* one's own station—to consider one's equally unearned *good* fortune, the privileges of health and race and advantageous friendships, the luck of having been placed by fate on Patience Stone's magnanimous bicycle in 1898 and not on Mount Tambora's rumbling summit in 1815.)

Vivian shook her angry thoughts away. She had repurposing of her own to do; new advantageous friendships to cement and manipulate.

Meanwhile, Squire continued to labor under the impression that he was answering a question about his mother's florist.

It was true that Squire had not yet found the impropriety or embarrassment grave enough to interrupt the tireless assault of his mother's orchids. (Whatever her son's supposed sins, it would have struck Mrs. Clancey as uncouth beyond imagining for even the rottenest egg in the Squire-Sacerdote basket to be caught without an arrangement in his vestibule.)

However—the thought occurred to Squire now with some alarm—a swan dive into a walrus pool, when word of it inevitably reached her ears, would be as strong a contender as any he'd yet produced.

In such an eventuality, Squire would not ordinarily have minded the loss of the orchids (to which he was habituated and indifferent) so much as the stormy familial weather it portended. One more strike against him; one step closer to the official confiscation of his allowance and his apartment, the return to a more supervised prison. He had, in all likelihood, just wasted his last chance for freedom.

But now, as he struggled to attend to Vivian's apparently polite inquiries as to his parents' situations and health, Squire found himself for the first time invested in his orchids—or at least in a bit of drama with the flowers at its center. He watched with fascination as Oscar Schmidt crossed the room—with a ridiculous stealth to his gait, as if he were trying to hide under cover of a nonexistent crowd—to examine them.

OSCAR WAS (OF course) embarrassed, but helpless as a pollinator. Earlier, there had been no time for hothouse tourism—he'd been preoccupied with chores to be done, and with all the lavish scraps of aristocratic rubble, and with his own agitation after the drama at the aquarium.

Now, though, with the lubricating whiskey and the blaze roaring in the hearth (given a well-maintained chimney, Oscar could compete with any chambermaid in the stoking of efficient, smokeless fires); and with Vivian and Squire occupied in small talk, leaving Oscar therefore (he presumed) safely unobserved in this comforting, even cozy set of rooms so removed from the morning's chaos . . .

The orchids grew on four spiked stems, one arranged at each of the Sèvres's cardinal points, cascading with between nine and twelve blooms apiece. Each bilateral flower was just the size to cup in a palm, star-shaped, with interlocking triads of rich pink petals—one set in blades that tapered to sharp points; the other set rounded, with a shaggy, vaguely obscene beard at the base of the star.

Oscar closed his eyes and inhaled.

Vivian followed Squire's spellbound gaze. "Oscar," she said sharply. He startled. "Yes?"

"What are you doing?" Vivian's voice lost some of its edge, as she realized her husband had stumbled into a better plan than her own.

"Nothing." Oscar's ears pinked.

"What do they smell of?"

"Nothing," Oscar said again, deepening to a shade that nearly matched the orchids.

"Don't be silly," Vivian said. Oscar made a helpless gesture.

And then, inevitable orchestration: all three noses pressed to the blooms.

Vivian did not have much of a palate for scents herself, and in Squire's case—with his nose numb and nostrils thick with dried blood—it was almost pure theater. Still, Vivian led a vocal appreciation for the scent, and prodded Oscar into a dissection of its elements.

He began reluctantly, but warmed to his subject with a professional's dry enthusiasm, encouraged by performative questions from Vivian whenever he attempted with awkward politeness to taper off. Rose, he thought, but more diluted than extract—more fresh than rich.

And what else?

Something spiced, almost candied. Vanilla; cinnamon.

And what else?

A whiff of rot at the edges—perfectly natural, he hastened to add, what with next Monday being the second—and besides, such a base bound and supported the other notes, deepened the complexity of the scent. He trailed to a flushed silence, perhaps insecure as to the object of all these apologetic reassurances. He occupied himself with the underside of a petal, and Squire was struck by the day's physical contrasts—felt again the shocking jolt and tumble of his rescue by these same, now exceedingly gentle, hands.

And what else?

Well, Oscar coughed. The remaining elements were not exactly—they were more precisely defined by their absence. But to complete the accord, he thought, it needed only something green or citrus, and a woody note to prolong—

At this point, Squire broke ranks. The fascination had become too much to bear, with this heady concept of phantom scents defined by their absence. He rushed from the room, toppling a stack of newspapers, and returned in a moment with his breathless arms full of half-burned candles.

"Oh," Oscar said.

"Yes," Vivian said, and passed Squire a fusee from the vase on the mantle.

As Squire lit the candles—which numbered seven, in the end—scents of floral extracts began to fill the room: lavender from one taper; rose from another; violet from a third. All highly—it might be said *extremely* highly—concentrated.

Oscar took a tactful step back, his eyes watering. Vivian, somewhat protected by her hardy constitution and her layman's palate, squeezed his hand.

Squire lit the last of the candles and extinguished the fusee with a slightly alarming flourish. "Well?" he asked.

"Um," Oscar said.

"What's the—" Squire waved his hands vaguely, encompassing the sickly-sweet orchestra of his candelabra. "What's the bouquet?"

Oscar trembled slightly. He lingered, dangerously, on the thought that *this* had been the fate of his lost supplies. *This* was why his career had no future.

"They're fascinating," Vivian anticipated him. "Will you and your partner, your"—she affected to search for the name—"Mr. Lawrence, will you put them on the market?"

Squire flinched. "Mr. Lawrence has not . . ." he began. "He does not precisely support the . . ."

Squire was at pains to avoid any discussion of his business—the discouragement and redirection he'd received every time he'd pitched his scent tapers; the large and increasing number of decisions on which Mr. Lawrence declined to solicit Squire's opinion; the generally diminishing returns on their entire venture. (To say nothing of the catastrophic revelation of Lawrence's smiling double-agency, the fact that it all might come tumbling down at any moment.)

Squire decided on something simpler. "The candles are disgusting," he said. "I want to know why."

The comfort Squire habitually took in bluntness seemed, for once, to be contagious. There was some relief simply in the open acknowledgment of their situation, the liberation from tactful tiptoeing.

Oscar took as deep a breath as he could without retching. "Too much fragrance," he said. "Far, far . . ."—he stopped, stammered, felt obligated to complete the sentence—"far too much."

"And what else?" Squire asked—his cadence a near perfect repetition of Vivian's at the orchid vase.

Oscar looked at Vivian. She nodded.

"They're—they're all floral," Oscar said. "They're all heart notes, they're—" He snarled his fingers into a violent knot.

Squire leapt into action again, this time hurrying to snuff out all but one of the candles he'd lit only minutes before. He licked his fingers and pinched each wick, moving quickly enough in his excitement that he burned himself only once. He flapped his arms over the table, attempting to clear the air of the warring scents.

"That . . ." Oscar nearly smiled, despite himself. "That isn't how it works."

Squire planted his palms on the table, leaned forward so intently the furniture creaked. "How does it work?"

"T-top notes evaporate in a few minutes," Oscar said. "These, maybe an hour. And, ah—" He swallowed. "Well, there is no base here."

"But if there were?"

"All night," Oscar said. He made a strange face. "Or day."

With both hands Squire pushed the lone remaining candle—one over-scented with violet oil—into the center of the table. Its flame wavered but did not go out. "How do I give this a base?" he asked.

Oscar blew out both cheeks—perhaps also, in defiance of nature, attempting to clear the air. "It's an ionone," he began, "so—"

"It isn't," Squire interrupted. "It's violet."

Oscar's eyebrows jumped. His patience with the situation wavered but did not go out. "There is," he managed after a moment, "chemistry for you to catch up on."

Squire was visibly delighted.

Oscar did his best to explain, interrupted frequently yet with greater attention than he'd perhaps ever commanded from a silent audience. (He was not a charismatic speaker, but much can be overcome by a sufficiently enthusiastic listener.) He began with the concept of synthetics, which Squire had been using in wasteful gouts without even being aware of their existence. Ionones that mimicked violet and rose; the toasted, mown-grass character of coumarin. ("Fougère," they called the scent family, or fern, though from boyhood Oscar associated ferns only with the briny smell they acquired when pickled for lean winter suppers.) He explained about soliflores, the three or five ingredients that went into a one-note scent like "lavender," and complex accords that might be made up of ten such simple scent compounds. (Though one didn't say "simple" in Personal Care, Oscar cautioned. One said "fastidious." They were in the business, after all, of describing ladies and gentlemen back to themselves.)

Then there was the fairly modern notion—one conceived, though Oscar did not speak in these terms, within the lifetimes of all three people present—of the fantasy scent. A product designed not to mimic any single flower or leaf or spice but to smell entirely of itself.

Such invention—such *creation*—took work. It also took a varied toolbox. There were animal smells, civet and musk and ambrette seed. Woody smells, patchouli and pine and sandalwood. Spicy, fresh, citrus, and of course—Oscar nodded pointedly at the wreckage of Squire's candles—floral. But very few of them worked alone. Violet needed something like anise, for spice, and bergamot, for a deepening lift. Orange blossom needed a dense amber blast of clove, incense, vanilla. Rose—

"What time is it?" Vivian broke in—and without waiting for an answer, she reached brusquely into Oscar's pocket, pulling his watch toward her by its chain. He bent to follow her movement, lest he lose a button—blinking rapidly, as though her presence in the room were a diverting surprise.

He was also attempting, Vivian noticed, to block the watch itself from Squire's heirloom-rich eyeline—having been obliged, in securing the lease on their apartment, to pawn his handsome gold timepiece for this cheap plate model. (Of course there had been no question of sacrificing his hatpin instead.) Vivian adjusted her hand to cup the watch more obscurely.

But Squire was oblivious to horological nosiness, startled instead by the absent-minded intimacy of Vivian's gesture. It roused in him not anger, precisely, or jealousy, but a covetous species of injustice.

Squire had never had occasion to envy a married person—on the contrary, he usually conceived of even life's most superficial social interactions as more than he could safely navigate. But perhaps, Squire thought now, matrimony was nothing but a legal loophole that excused all the so-called improprieties of basic human instinct. The right, Squire mused, to slot one's fingers into a fascinating person's waistcoat pocket and tug until he bent himself to face you—who *wouldn't* covet such a thing?

"We'd better let Mr. Clancey settle in," Vivian pronounced. She snapped the watch closed and returned it to Oscar's pocket. But rather than moving to gather her things, she clicked her heels and glanced at her husband expectantly.

Squire watched a silent conversation pass between the Schmidts. (Another, perhaps, of the paranormal gifts and curses bestowed by the City Clerk's Marriage Bureau.) Oscar seemed to lose the telepathic struggle—at any rate, he was the first to speak.

"Mr. Clancey," he began. "Have you ever considered . . ." He was at a loss, having over-rehearsed in anticipation of an entirely different situation. His hand drifted to his lapel. He scoffed, though at what it wasn't clear. "Would you ever consider . . ." He looked to Vivian for help, having forgotten—having willfully failed to absorb—the substance of her plan.

Vivian gestured to the scene of their impromptu workshop: innovation crossing theory; well-resourced experimentation crossing well-worn experience. Discomfiture and challenge, yes, but unexpectedly—even eerily—free of antagonism. And a rare chance for Squire to interact with New People, that scandalous race that—unlike Mr. Lawrence, a lifelong New Yorker—harbored no ominous loyalty to the world of Squire's parents.

"We think you should pool your business with Oscar's," Vivian said simply.

And Squire found—after a morning, a lifetime, of confusion as to other people's motives and expectations—that he did not need to ask why.

ELEVEN

Mr. Lawrence arrived at Oscar's office the following week already apprehensive, girded for what he expected to be a tense and antagonistic meeting. A meeting in which, Mr. Lawrence expected, he would have to somehow simultaneously squelch Squire's eccentricities and atone to him for conspiring with the elder Clanceys—all while protecting their so-called business from smiling assault by a *real* corporation, with clerks and middle management and paperwork copied in triplicate for filing at various regional offices.

Instead of this dreaded gauntlet, he found another.

Experience taught him to assume that the woman sitting—rather brazenly, he noted with some alarm—behind Oscar Schmidt's desk was his secretary. She was too old to be an employee's child, too well-dressed to be a charwoman. He interrupted her in the act of lighting a cigarette from the box on Oscar's desk. She finished the job in a smooth motion, glancing expectantly—even with annoyance—at Mr. Lawrence in the doorway. Her eyes and fingers were quick, but her posture relaxed—an unsettling combination. Mr. Lawrence scanned the room for assistance, but they were alone. (The clerk who had sent him in was loyal to Vivian, and had abandoned him.)

"I have an appointment with Mr. Schmidt?" Lawrence said, his briefcase slipping against his palm.

"You're in the right place," Vivian said, and gestured for him to take the seat opposite her. (She did not betray Oscar—or Squire, for that matter—by explaining that neither man had had the stomach for the conversation ahead. That she'd barely had to talk them into letting her handle it.)

Mr. Lawrence made an abortive move toward the chair, then stopped. He froze, waiting for the situation to transform into something he recognized. For Oscar to arrive, or Squire; for this strange woman to relocate to a less prominent place—or, better still, to leave the room entirely.

"Excuse me," he said. "But . . . Miss . . . ?"

It was, in a way, a complete question. A complete objection, even. And so Vivian resolved, with a smile, to allow herself a little Machiavellian joy in an execution that might otherwise have caused her some regret. For Mr. Lawrence reminded her, just a bit, of Oscar—or at least of where he might have ended up, without the benefit of her alliance. Too soft, too sentimental, too frightened of change; above all too *democratic* to be a successful capitalist. (Resources, talents, rewards—nothing, Vivian thought, was fairly apportioned. Not by God; not by man. Such gilded fictions were for the childish and the simple.)

"Sit," Vivian said, and Mr. Lawrence did.

What could a woman like Vivian do, in the world as it was, with a man like Mr. Lawrence? Inflexible, mealy-mouthed, his innate male chauvinism and his unquestioning respect for authority combining (in this case paradoxically) to make him a watchdog against progress. He was a skilled merchant, it was true, and an experienced one, with a sympathetic heart that was quick to bleed. In a way, these assets worked against him. *More* stupid, or helpless, or self-interested, and Vivian might have found a use for him. As it was, he was the thorn without the rose. There was nothing to do but prune him back.

She was not overly violent. She did not gloat. "Mr. Clancey has decided to end your partnership," she said. "He asked me to tell you."

And what else was there, really, that needed saying? There was no formal association to dissolve, no contracts, no board of investors—only one neat column of numbers in bottle-green ink, Squire's allowance flowing into Mr. Lawrence's accounts. The spigot had been diverted; that was that.

Mr. Lawrence even understood, or thought he did. The bookkeeper's allure of a better-established business, padded with cozy layers of bureaucracy. Or else a personal punishment, revenge for Mr. Lawrence's betrayal in spying for Squire's parents. He would regret the loss of regular new entries in his column of numbers, yes. But his arrangement with Squire had always been too whimsical and impractical for him to truly thrive, even when his table was laden and his creditors satisfied. There was some bedraggled relief, by Mr. Lawrence's internal reckoning, in suffering the inevitable return of a world that made sense. He took the news manfully.

Vivian, for her part, had had enough of men to see her through the end of the week.

SHE LEFT MR. LAWRENCE to his sweaty disappointment. Left Squire to settle in as a consultant: transferring his client accounts; organizing his portfolio of product concepts; and—most relished of all, after years without receiving this respect from Mr. Lawrence—seeing his own name stamped on letterhead and painted on frosted glass. She left Oscar to his clerks' and superiors' sighs of officious contentment, as once-loyal supply connections fastened—at last, after years of painful inefficiency and profit loss—into company pipelines once again. Vivian left her husband and Squire Clancey to get acquainted, to *consult*, to congratulate themselves on her victory. She had earned, she decided, a reprieve. A little intelligent conversation. A little amusement.

She met Meg at a Tiffany Girls' salon, held at someone or other's independent art studio in Greenwich Village. The walls were bare brick and plaster, the air fermented and thick with smoke, the art on display indistinguishable to Vivian from its by-products—smears of paint, twists of metal, shards of glass. An argument about Cuban politics and one about British poetry, both ill-informed but passionate, struggled to subsume each other. Laughter was everywhere—earnest and ironic, bitter and delighted.

"Are you alright?" Meg asked, slipping a hand between Vivian's shoulders. "You're quiet tonight."

"Mm," Vivian said.

The truth was, she had glimpsed the end of her situation—with Meg, and with the whole set. Strange to think she had outgrown them so quickly—she had fallen in with them less than a year ago, and was far from the oldest in the group. But things had changed; she did not belong here. She no longer saw herself reflected in the fear-tinged shine of the other women's eyes, their joy sharpened by the knowledge of its brevity. Vivian had found a way to make marriage work for her; she had won a game, she thought, that these girls were terrified to even play. She could feel herself being called elsewhere, to bigger and better and more difficult things. (These assertions, concerning both herself and others, we will have occasion to revisit in future chapters.)

Vivian's self-confidence and the weight of her thoughts held her apart, a sphinx and an observer now among these half-baked debaters and lovestruck favorites and traumatized confidants. Poor Meg, Vivian thought, half-earnestly: doomed to be the last of an era. Once upon a time, yes, there had been Patience, and Electra, and Sofia. But now that Vivian had found her footing, there would be no need—no *room*—for any friend in particular. Certainly not for one who asked "Are you alright?" whenever Vivian was quiet, and pried into her private thoughts, and ranted on the side of the worker against the capitalist machine.

No, Vivian thought. Her most difficult work was still ahead, and she would need to concentrate on it without humoring nosy New Englanders with ridiculous opinions. From now on she would require—she would *accept*—only a steady, novel infusion of safely anonymous women. Interesting, disinterested eyes and hands and laughing mouths. (If such a policy would also keep her insulated from another rejection as painful as Sofia's, and if it had only begun to seem possible now that Vivian had glimpsed a financial future stable enough to banish the threat of a return to Utica, she did not reflect on these facts.) Instead Vivian simply resolved, having reappraised her own value, to guard herself more jealously. She resolved never to allow another girl to take the liberty of assuming access.

All the same, Vivian reasoned, it was impossible—flush as she was with professional victory, starved as she was for opportunities to openly boast—to simply put on her coat and leave.

"I'm celebrating," she murmured, back in Meg's bedroom.

"Congratulations," Meg said. Vivian could feel her smile between kisses, pressing warm at the hollow of her throat. "And what is the occasion?"

"I'm going—into business," Vivian said, her voice catching slightly as Meg adjusted her position.

"*Oh?*" Meg's tone carried that kind of archness inspired only where skin meets skin. "Manufactory, or Wall Street?"

Vivian let herself smile. This was the scope of her achievement: so impressive, it could be taken only as a bedroom game. "Speculation," she said. "Investment."

"In*deed*," Meg said. "Quite the day on the floor, for your portfolio?" She was affecting herself, now. She melted a bit, shuddering, and laid her body flush along the length of Vivian's. "Did you have to discipline your secretary?"

Meg continued, a sort of melodic counterpoint to the rhythm of their bodies together. A capitalist fairy tale, Vivian in a walnut-paneled office with a rolltop desk. (We can forgive Meg this divergence of her daylit politics and her bedroom proclivities, having seen many a more dire case. And we must also forgive her for failing to understand the seriousness of Vivian's accomplishment, and the threat of her disappearance—for Meg was not a mind reader, and if Vivian hoarded her own counsel, that was not the fault of her paramour.) Meg added decor to her fantasy: a molded bronze Pallas Athene; an eleven-piece desk set of a style Meg herself had worked on for Tiffany, in etched metal and green glass. (This last, Vivian did have to admit, sounded attractive.) Meg swapped the cigarette case out for a humidor, slotted a cigar between Vivian's teeth. Cropped her hair and slicked it flat with oil. Dressed her in pince-nez, vicuña, a three-pocket cutaway suit in charcoal check—or midnight blue? Or—or—

Yes, Vivian said, to all of it. Yes, oh yes. She said yes so that Meg would not stop moving; so she would not look up from this strange dream of a person who was not Vivian but a blank-eyed hermaphroditic cipher. Vivian said yes so that Meg would not hear her aversion to the imagined scene and begin instead to ask kind questions, to guess at what Vivian was thinking or would prefer—to attempt an impossible connection and in so doing lose all the dumb, instinctual momentum that Vivian required from her.

It amused Vivian, even as she crested a trembling wave of pleasure, to think: women were, in the end, as simple as men; bohemian anarchists as simple as financiers. As easy to hold and manipulate by their fantasies.

IT WAS AN art that she would have many opportunities to perfect, in the months to come.

Like a hothouse seedling, Squire and Oscar's nascent partnership needed constant attentive care in the guise of natural serendipity. The still-tender scars of past injuries were everywhere, especially in the early days. A perfectly productive meeting might be ruined by an offhand comment—whether reminding Oscar of the years he'd spent profession-ally hamstrung, thinning his soup and pawning his accessories, because an aristocratic black sheep had taken an idle interest in chemistry; or reminding Squire of the controversy drummed up in the society pages that had made his parent-wardens reconsider his ability to govern himself. (The only time, in his invariably eccentric life, that *anyone* had tried to assassinate him in the press.) Vivian audited their meetings as often as possible, as much to keep the peace as to learn and influence the business.

But as one month stretched to two, then three, these pitfalls opened less and less frequently underfoot. Vivian was able to leave the men to their work, for the most part—to focus elsewhere, learning the webs of promissory notes and trades in kind, of clerks and counselors and middle managers like infinite and self-referential nesting dolls that made up a business. She became a familiar sight around the office: shadowing door-ways, scribbling notes, answering questions (whether they had been posed to her or not).

Of course, this arrangement could never have lasted indefinitely. But as it transpired, Oscar and Squire did not require any report on Vivian's behavior to get themselves into trouble with headquarters. Despite the financial and supply-chain relief of Squire's prodigal vendors, Oscar's superiors found themselves displeased by their representative's recent performance—both in the management of the New York office and in the tone of his communication.

From the first day of his apprenticeship, as an anxious and self-loathing farm boy violently transplanted to Cincinnati in a failed attempt to wither himself at the root, Oscar had always been dependently obedient (at least in his daylit life). Learning the way things had always been done; memorizing formulas and modes of address; writing slogans with an uncannily natural ear for the subcutaneous shame that was the surest method of advertising hygiene products.

Now, however, the company's steadfast tin soldier began to telegraph unsolicited and alarmingly unconventional proposals—for new scents; new textures; new business ventures (a contract with an underground train, for two-inch cakes of soap to be stolen and abused in public restrooms?); even entire new product lines. (Reinvesting their dearly won East Coast suppliers' materials in *candles*, of all things, when more American homes were electrified every day?)

And who was this other man, this consultant Schmidt had hired without the approval of his supervisor? (For the company did not, of course, recognize Vivian in this role.) Mutinous clerks wrote to the corporate headquarters to report on the controversy: a strange man in his thirties with a full head of gray hair, suddenly at Oscar's right hand in every meeting. Always taking zealous notes, unless delivering even more zealous remarks. At first Oscar had suffered this hovering presence, these interjections, with an appropriate expression of mortification. But lately, whispered the informants, he had begun to almost *welcome* them, to defer with a kind of interested, even affectionate anticipation when Squire spoke up in an all-staff meeting to propose a laundry soap and eau de cologne sold in a complimentary (but not matching!) set; or a triple-scented candle that burned in layers (floral to vegetal to musk, like descending from a forest canopy into the leaf litter); or lemon-flavored foaming tooth powder that might double as a kind of an effervescent and hygienic desert. (At this last suggestion, upper management heard with concern, Oscar—never known in the Cincinnati office to be a frivolous man—had actually *laughed*.)

The final nail, of course, was Vivian's presence in the office. The way she haunted and sometimes even spoke in meetings; the way she encouraged Oscar in his collaboration with the strange new gentleman; her unsettling questions and more unsettling silences.

After a certain period of shocked and bureaucratically inefficient silence of their own, followed by several semitactful hints either missed or willfully ignored, Oscar's superiors made themselves clear in writing: he was to terminate immediately any contract of employment or counsel with Squire Clancey, who had no résumé in Personal Care and whose engagement had not been approved by headquarters. Oscar was to retain relationships with those suppliers supposedly "brought in" by Clancey via traditional, straightforward management of his business dealings. (If such a task was beyond his abilities, this would be considered separately, as a performance issue.) Oscar was to submit all future personnel requests for approval by a committee of executives in Cincinnati as well as two of his own senior clerks (not coincidentally, the traitorous informants). And—here Cincinnati let cowardice drive it to euphemism, but it was a bridge too far to talk of *wives* on company letterhead—there was to be an immediate ban of any *nonemployees* on company property.

Oscar called Squire and Vivian into his office and locked the door. Together they leaned against the edge of the desk, trading the letter's pages. "What do we do?" Oscar asked.

Vivian maintained a calculated silence. For once, she didn't have to wait long.

"I have an idea," Squire said.

THEY WERE LUCKY: in a rare intersection of their complementary but largely separate orbits, Squire's parents were both in town.

With the company office now compromised, Oscar, Squire, and Vivian met at the Schmidts' apartment to plan their attack. It was a tripartite briefing, rehashed in urgent whispers from heads bent close in the landau heading downtown—the desperate pooling of their disparate expertise, as though attempting to form a single, perfectly equipped person. Oscar shared the principles of a solvent Personal Care concern, and the context of the New York market; Squire laid out both the plan of his parents' townhouse and—as best he could—the contours of their personalities.

And Vivian married the two pools of raw information, to catalyze a viable strategy.

THEY PAID THEIR call at Madison Avenue near the end of the visiting hour. Despite the stakes, despite the hearts fluttering in their throats, all three approached bravely: Oscar, if slightly out of practice, was no stranger to fine houses. And though she was more experienced now with foreigners and poets, do not forget that Vivian had started her career by acquitting herself preternaturally well in the airless drawing rooms of Patience Stone's aunt Daphne and her circle.

And Squire, of course, was arriving at home.

Let us take a moment here to acknowledge his courage, unprecedented in our story thus far: where Oscar had fled Ohio decades before without so much as a glance over his shoulder, and Vivian had been dragged back to Utica only under strong protest, Squire was striding purposefully toward the site of some of his deepest and oldest wounds. Indeed, he took the stairs two at a time, even shielding Oscar and Vivian as much as he could from the threshold judgment of a butler who'd known him since infancy (and disliked him almost as long—remember the braided rug tassels, the vintage wine and pedigreed dinner party both ruined in the name of scientific experiment).

To the others, the house was surprisingly less intimidating than Squire's half-feral bachelor's rooms downtown. Here, after all, were the fine furniture and liquid gilding and objets d'art arranged predictably, with "taste," as they were displayed in public tours of Stately Homes and in auction-house catalogs. There was nothing uncanny or unexpected, nothing to challenge Vivian's and Oscar's assumptions about how such privileges were enjoyed. There was only the conventional, rib-crushing, muffling weight of the money itself.

And, given their errand, Vivian was not disposed to find this unsettling.

There was a brief shared introduction. Vivian and Oscar were proper, more than proper—Mr. and Mrs. Clancey were frankly astonished, to see such a normal, even respectable, couple with an apparently genuine interest in their son. (Even if they *were* New People.)

At a certain point, past the teacup pleasantries, Vivian had to let Oscar and Squire represent themselves to Mr. Clancey alone, behind closed doors. The men filed into his office with facts and figures, a business plan, and a name: Clancey & Schmidt. (They were none of them so foolish as to give second billing to a desperately needed investor.) Meanwhile, Vivian stayed in the drawing room with Squire's mother—seated in a sage-green day dress beneath an enormous portrait of herself as a much younger woman, all dimples and organza on a garden swing—and set about brokering the deal.

"Your son is a brilliant young man," she began, accurately enough.

"Oh!" Mrs. Clancey gasped—an interruption that, though benign (even positive!) nearly capsized Vivian before she began.

It was one thing to prepare in theory to encounter a mother's love for her child (however smothering and misguided); to study the concept and develop a plan to manipulate it. But it was quite another, Vivian found, to face such a battle in person.

Mrs. Clancey did not know how to love her son; her attempts had done real and lasting damage. But there had *been* attempts, public and obvious, swathed in luxury and requiring what she at least perceived as great self-sacrifice. (She had spent nine New York seasons exiled to Lake Ronkonkoma!) There was insult now, yes, in Mrs. Clancey's stupefied delight at Vivian's praise of her son. But it was still delight.

Vivian was a brilliant woman—but in almost all cases it is an art of practice, not intuition, to fully recognize the shortcomings of other people's parents. (Even Oscar, in Utica, had required the better part of a day to get his bearings.) Vivian was not yet well enough acquainted with Squire to parse his mother's poisonous delight for what it was. Instead, her jealous child's heart turned traitor, resentful at never having been loved enough to inspire an exclamation of maternal delight. It filled her throat, chilled her fingers. She fought to master it.

"He's been with my husband's company three months," she continued, "and he's already *revolutionized* its reputation." (This was, in a certain sense, accurate.) "I've never seen Oscar so pleased." (This, too, was, in a certain sense, accurate.) "I'm sure that Squire—that Mr. Clancey has a wonderful career ahead of him," she said, "provided he finds the time and inclination." She was warming to her purpose now, back in the rhythm of her plan. She lifted a punctuating teacup. "I know handsome young men have competing responsibilities," she said, with an apparently easy laugh.

Mrs. Clancey was, or at least considered herself, a long-suffering woman. At the idea of her son being received as competent, effective, even *marriageable*—for surely this was the wink behind the comment on "the responsibilities of handsome young men," was it not?!—the very idea of

Squire being smiled upon by such American gods as commercial industry and societal convention . . . it was the hopeless dream of Mrs. Clancey's middle age. The culmination, she even credited herself, of all her labors. She felt almost faint.

"You're so kind to say so," she managed, her eyes dewy with self-reflection. "What a—my, what a darling girl you are."

It was empty pap. But this did not preclude it also being the distilled essence of nursery-rhyme maternity. For a moment—just a moment—the blood sang in Vivian's veins. Something began to rush rumbling toward the surface—an inexpressibly powerful feeling of no moral alignment, long-denied joy mixing badly with a directionless rage and resentment.

This feeling was familiar to Vivian, of course—but it was usually localized, its epicenter in suburban Utica. Seldom had it afflicted her so completely in the metropolis—such had been her success, unconscious but thorough, in associating with orphans and adventuresses.

Still, despite the sudden affliction, it was the well-practiced work of a moment for Vivian to cut off the spigot entirely. To snuff the eruption and redirect its focus.

"I hope this isn't speaking out of turn," she said mildly, "but I'm so looking forward to seeing what your son and my husband have in mind for their next venture."

OSCAR AND SQUIRE were, to their credit, holding their own in the next room. Squire had opened the conversation with a simple, well-reasoned, disarmingly confident request: for the investment of what amounted to a substantial percentage of Squire's eventual inheritance, to allow himself and Oscar to found a Personal Care concern. His dealings with Mr. Lawrence, he explained, had been on a different scale entirely—there, the infusion of his (more than generous) monthly allowance had been enough to finance their modest ambitions. Clancey & Schmidt, Squire emphasized with practiced style, would be different. Clancey & Schmidt would be revolutionary. And revolutions demanded revolutionary investment.

With convincing dryness and jargon Oscar had then explained the processes by which their independent business would operate; the scientific and fiduciary principles that would govern their choices and, Lord willing—ha ha!—profit their investors. (Rarely in daylight was Oscar in finer form than when annotating a column of backend figures—and we have discussed already his deep-held and orphaned drive to seek parental approval from miscellaneous sources.)

But even more striking to Mr. Clancey was the simple sight of his own son: attentive and relaxed, a neat and moderate custodian of his cigarette, asking point-blank for something Mr. Clancey understood to be desirable, and punctuating Oscar's narration at largely appropriate intervals and with largely relevant comments.

(It was not, of course, that any material change had come over Squire. It was simply that in Vivian and Oscar he had found people who understood him, and who could make themselves understood in turn—and in their afternoon's shared object, he had found a social pageant whose purpose he grasped and valued enough to put himself through the performance. In another world—in quite another world, with different geologic faults entirely—Mr. and Mrs. Clancey might have been well acquainted with this bright and charming young man, if only they'd troubled to find a lingua franca.)

Clancey & Schmidt, Oscar finished with his best approximation of a flourish, would manufacture scented soaps, talcs, salves, unguents, all manner of cosmetics and items de toilette—and, (ahem) yes, candles. Their existing assets were Oscar's three decades of experience in the field, coupled with Squire's (more or less) instant success as a consultant, and his excellent connections to—Oscar inclined his head tactfully—the best of New York. They lacked only a primary investor. They were, Oscar hoped Mr. Clancey would understand, keeping their proposal discreet for the time being—their plans being ambitious, and (they flattered themselves) so well conceived that if their current employers were to catch wind of the operation, they would take some considerable pains to sabotage it.

Mr. Clancey was impressed by the plan—or he was at least confused by its thoroughness and flattered by its exclusivity, which amounted to as much. He was all the more impressed, however, by the notion that Squire had apparently *already* made himself a success in this, in any, business—for Mr. Clancey read his son's story thus far as one not of creative innovation and autodidacticism but of failure and rejection. (Squire's strange and costly playacting with that fussy little Mr. Lawrence; his boarding-school expulsions; his utter disinclination to ever before display a conventional aptitude or enthusiasm.)

But most of all, if most obliquely, Mr. Clancey considered this: here were two people offering to . . . not *adopt* Squire, no, of course not—for goodness' sake, he thought, the wife out in the drawing room was younger than Squire himself. But, still . . .

Mr. Clancey was well accustomed to this kind of dubiously freeing transaction. In his youth, a substitute had been hired in his name to defend the Union against the Confederacy. (And, as it transpired, to die in that defense at Antietam.) No experience of Mr. Clancey's privileged youth, or of his purchased adulthood, had taught him to regret or question this exchange.

Now, as Mr. Clancey saw it, he was being offered the chance to hire another substitute—a pair of substitutes—to manage his offspring. And at no cost at all, really. Just the reallocation of some funds in trust, the premature delivery of what would always eventually have been Squire's due inheritance.

Mr. Clancey, he reflected, did not have so many summers left. Why not let himself spend them at ease, knowing the boy was being kept in hand?

"It's a very interesting proposal," he said. He shook Oscar's hand, and—with some self-conscious amusement—his son's. "I'll think on it." A wink and a roll of the eyes to Oscar, his fellow married man. "Talk it over with Mary."

Though it had been years since Oscar had thrived in society as a single man and survived by masculine posturing, the body never forgets a successful defense. A momentary transformation to lubricate their exit: his laugh deeper; his bearing straighter; his head-shaking expression mirroring Mr. Clancey's vague, sarcastic allusion to a ball and chain.

Squire's jaw dropped, as he realized by the sudden intrusion of this false Oscar—the brief reemergence of the Mr. Schmidt who'd haunted him in the public imagination, before the aquarium—how long it had been since Squire had been subjected to this callous character. And how different he had discovered the "real" Oscar to be, in recent months. How remarkably—how very remarkably, compared with Squire's past attempts at such connections—easy to know.

EVEN IN AMERICA, a country that has been obliged to manufacture a mold-cast imitation of a sceptered class, there exists a species of person best able—perhaps *only* able—to process strong emotion behind a placid facade. Mr. and Mrs. Clancey had both been born and bred to this group, and so neither betrayed their excitement. Even in the privacy of their conference after "the young people" had departed, their manner was reserved. But still they came from oppositional anxious fantasies—the thrill of imagining Squire somehow accepted by "normal" people; the thrill of imagining him simply taken off their hands—to the same conclusion.

TWELVE

In the first weeks of the fledgling company's notional existence, Clancey & Schmidt's headquarters floated in a liminal chaos between the founders' apartments. Drifts of paper covered the puddles of wax in Squire's home laboratory; corporate filing cabinets disgorged their contents into the study where once Oscar had rehearsed his clumsy denunciation of the candle industry.

The men's business, in those very early days, was subterfuge: escaping their previous employer with as many contracts, sources, vendors, and product formulas as possible. (There would be no use, Vivian continuously reminded them, in cutting themselves loose and leaving all their hard-won resources behind.) Oscar, preparing to give Cincinnati notice of his resignation as soon as possible, focused first on the smiling theft of the fruits of his career thus far. And Squire's early efforts were primarily secretarial, as he recopied a savvy and tactful letter (composed with Vivian's significant input) to each of his supplier contacts, expressing a hope that, having followed him to one new situation, they would repeat the move once more for the opportunity to collaborate on an even more exciting venture.

Since Vivian and Oscar had already arranged the unconventional amenity of a home study with room enough for two, their apartment quickly emerged as the locus of Clancey & Schmidt's secret development.

Squire became a regular, then frequent, finally almost constant presence, turning up each day with fresh supplies of both boundless energy and conceptual paperwork.

Their syndicate's early experiments in creating sample products were, while not entirely discouraging, amateur and chaotic at best. The men were limited, of course, by what they could produce in a home laboratory. Their fingerprints were everywhere, in wax and fat and glycerin: hand-dipped tapers, hand-mixed unguents, hand-poured cakes of soap. This last they set and cut into two-inch sample bars. Oscar suffered at first from a tragic focus on uniformity—an impossible quest, given their rudimentary equipment—until Squire observed that the cakes had the dimension and heft of business cards. They would deliver, they decided, only a single specimen of each product to each potential client and distributor. They would win business with the impression of bespoke exclusivity, rather than machine precision. ("For now," Oscar added, with a nervous glance at their irregular merchandise.)

Then there were the scents and flavorings. Their palette was limited. ("For now," Squire echoed, a reassuring hand faltering just short of Oscar's shoulder.) The cheapest and most bluntly aromatic ingredients they could distill themselves, at least in minuscule quantities—they rigged a simple still for peppermint leaves, steam condensing to capture oil and hydrosol (and make the Schmidts' apartment reek of Christmas and tooth powder). Squire purchased their soon-to-be rivals' bottled rose water, to incorporate back into new products—an inefficiency that rent Oscar's bookkeeper's heart, though he bowed to the necessity.

Certain rare and expensive ingredients could not easily be independently sourced. When Oscar bemoaned their lack of sandalwood oil, Vivian suggested he steal a vial from his employer while he still could. His refusal—the risk was impossible! He was on thin enough ice as it was!—was almost hysterical. But when Squire voiced support for the same idea, Oscar returned a few days later with the precious bottle clutched in triumphant, trembling fingers. Vivian could only roll her eyes.

The smells of boiled fat and concentrated essence were nostalgic for Oscar, who hadn't done work this tactile in years. The same scene was a frontier of excitement for Squire, who had never been so included (nor so well-informed). For her part, Vivian weathered these side effects of success—the stink of progress and the doubling of the men in her living space—and edged patiently along the crowded margins. Until, finally, the first seed check from Mr. and Mrs. Clancey was safely deposited, and the trigger pulled that ended the fiction of Oscar's loyalty to his former employer. At almost the moment that Clancey & Schmidt's nascent existence was finally admitted publicly, she set about negotiating the lease of an office and manufactory.

TO MANAGE LOGISTICS with a full purse was thrillingly, almost frighteningly easy—like navigating the sudden loss of gravity. Landlords and bank tellers and office supply salesmen all attended to Vivian without the need for any dazzling charm or misdirection, without any of the thousand invisible and exhausting steps that went into living on someone else's credit. For the first time, Vivian could almost empathize with the resentful paralysis of her parents' worldview—were things truly this easy, she wondered with a spike of jealous anger, for the independently wealthy? *Every day?*

But she thought of Mr. and Mrs. Lesperance, resigned and sedentary, pickling in self-pity until even their child became their enemy, and pushed her sympathy aside. So, Vivian thought, the rich have it easier. This was no great surprise, and need be no great tragedy. The solution was simply to become, and to remain, rich. The method was not so complex. It was simpler and simpler, she'd found, the farther one progressed.

She secured a small space to begin. One suite in a shared manufactory, a warehouse space with room for both a volcanic boiling kettle to do the dirty work and all its sundry aestheticizing accessories—molds, presses, cooling racks. Two private offices (for appearances—she would make the men share, when necessary) and space for a few clerks.

This was just the start, she thought. They would grow.

She was frugal in her choice of furnishings, modest (even stingy) in her advertised salaries, practical in her investment in supplies. At the end of her preparations she was surprised to find herself, for the first time in her life, under budget.

Well, she thought. Hadn't she earned a reward?

The Tiffany Studios showroom carried itself with dignity approaching haughtiness. Staggeringly expensive works of glass and metal—candlesticks and fingerbowls; letter trays and picture frames; waterfall mosaic lamp-shades with silver pedestals—were arranged dynamically on heavy, gleaming desks in tableaux complete with pens and blotters, as if their owners had just stepped away.

Yet Vivian found there was an overstuffed, silly quality to the display. This fantasy study implied an occupant of ridiculous mania, with fifteen lamps burning bright on fifteen writing desks; candelabras blazing in support; ornamental medallions like clusters of overripe grapes crowding shoulder to shoulder on every wall. Even Oscar would call it overprepa-ration, Vivian thought. Even Squire would wonder if it wasn't a bit impractical.

At first Vivian amused herself by wondering which of Meg's colleagues, over the many months she had danced and sipped and tumbled with them over chaise lounges in Village coffeehouses, had worked uncredited on which pieces.

But then, Vivian thought, most of the girls who had cut and shaped these items would be gone already. Rotated out of their industry, and out of the plush pleasures of the midnight salon, by the conventional knell of conventional wedding bells.

Not everyone, she considered with some regret, could be as savvy as herself.

ACROSS TOWN, SQUIRE was ringing into the overburdened study to make his daily contribution to the development of the Clancey & Schmidt business plan.

He had not, these past few sessions, felt of much practical use. Oscar had been drafting a bid for a contract with the IRT—a moderated version of Squire's proposal to supply the subway comfort stations with soap, scaled to a level appropriate for a fledgling syndicate still finding its feet. With the early securement of a high-volume client in the public sector, Oscar had enthused, and for such a simple, easily manufactured product—the two-inch cake of utilitarian soap—they'd be starting with a level of stability unheard of for such a new concern. And the IRT's clerical staff would remember Oscar, would have his correspondence on file from his first preliminary inquiry only a month before—when he'd written under the letterhead of one of the country's most established Personal Care companies. They only had to explain the change of address, and the fact that some *old establishments* were—regrettable only for their own sake!—*too* old to adapt.

"It really . . ." Oscar had paused, dripping ink onto his blotter, and looked at Squire. "It really was a very good idea."

"Thank you," Squire had remembered to say, after a moment. But a new worry had bloomed: that, having translated Squire's concept into an actionable business plan, Oscar might feel he had worked through any need for a partner. For Squire's partnership, specifically.

Squire had spent three anxious afternoons this week occupying the second chair (in fact Vivian's chair) in Oscar Schmidt's study (in fact Vivian's study), watching his own innovations being alchemically converted to practical terms.

Executing the visions of others had long been one of Oscar's greatest professional talents (perhaps personal as well, depending on how one categorized Vivian's influence). And if anything, he found Squire to be an ideal, even a supernaturally well-fitted collaborator—the implementation of the other man's ideas coming almost unsettlingly naturally to him.

But Oscar's anxiety and superstition (and Grandmother Hester's ghost) prevented him from naming this sense of ease, let alone commenting on it aloud—lest the punishing universe whisk it away. Lest Squire realize he'd been saddled with a brainless bureaucrat and begin to wish for a true creative partner.

And in the absence of encouragement, given Squire's own painful past experience, it was difficult for him to trust his own sudden happiness. Difficult not to fear the early stages of the same blight that had infected his venture with Mr. Lawrence, and every cautious happiness preceding it: what had always been represented to him as his own congenital inability to think practically.

Squire found that this time, in this case, he could not stand the thought of failure. He would not be able to bear, he thought, to one day find himself excluded from Oscar's study. To find his chair occupied by another, more conventional man.

After a sleepless night he'd arrived for this session determined to contribute to "the practical side," having prepared a list of (as far as he could judge) useful and multipurpose phrases in capitalist communication. *To whom it may concern, pursuant to which intelligence, I have the honor of enclosing.* He drew it now, thoroughly creased and damp with sweat, from his best red-Morocco memorandum book.

But Oscar anticipated him, with a well-handled sheet of his own. "I have been thinking," he said—and stopped to negotiate some mental obstacle of apparently complicated dimensions. Struggling, in fact, with a parallel gesture: the attempt to prove himself creative.

Squire's anxiety, like most of his emotions, was soluble in curiosity. "Yes?" he asked.

VIVIAN RECOGNIZED IT the moment she saw it: the desk set from Meg's bedroom fantasy. A starburst pattern meant to look like pine needles, in acid-etched metal and blue-green glass. An inkwell, a tripartite paper tray, a rocking blotter. Utility boxes in several sizes. A letter opener and seal. An ashtray and memo pad. A postage scale so sensitive it seemed to waver under her breath. It was beautiful. Vivian imagined Meg working on it, perhaps even thinking of Vivian as she'd shaped and cut. Each lozenge of glass, perhaps, still remembering the stroke of her fingers.

Vivian flushed, on her feet in the showroom. A pleasant release of the triumphant feeling she otherwise had nowhere else to express in daylight.

She considered: Could she own this desk set, without wavering in her resolve to give Meg up? Could she see it every day, dip her pens and blot her letters and rest her cigarettes on the delicate lip of the tray, without collapsing into sentiment?

The two options might perhaps have coexisted. Vivian might have invited Meg into her plans, introduced her into the fledgling syndicate. Meg was a radical, but an intelligent and open-minded one. She had already met Oscar, and found him profoundly unthreatening. Against patrician Squire she would inevitably have been more prejudiced, for the crimes of his class—but his individual eccentricity might have won her over. Her anarchist sympathies would no doubt have compelled her to challenge the very concept of a capitalist empire, however aspirational. But whether she would have striven to scuttle Vivian's venture before it began or instead shaped it, and Vivian with it, for the better, we can never know.

Yes, Vivian thought. Yes, she would be able to use the executive desk set without compromising herself—provided she made sure never to see Meg again. Provided she gave up the salon, the coffeehouses, even the pretense of opening her heart to the women she slept with. Provided that she tied these beautiful objects not to any person, only to this autonomous and disembodied sense of triumph.

Vivian and Meg never saw each other again. It was not an acrimonious parting—they were not girls any longer; their lives were full and varied. And besides, there had not been sufficient intimacy for either of them to rip anything internal in the uncoupling. Even before her resolution, Vivian had seen to that.

"WE'LL NEED A logotype," Oscar said. "Something to"—he ground the knuckles of one hand against the other—"to stamp into the soap, so people will know whose to buy. Provided"—he cleared his throat—"provided they like it."

"That's practical," Squire noted, with some performative bravado.

Oscar, already battling considerable self-mockery over the many hours he'd wasted on the project, went slightly pink at this apparent sarcasm. But he was already holding the latest version, hovering between them, for Squire's consideration. It was too late to rip it up, too late to pretend to be anything other than himself.

The logo was baroque, festooned with a bouquet—what might even be called a joyful abundance—of curlicues and serifs. *C&S*, it read, the filigreed ampersand curling with a flourish into each letter's negative space until it was almost difficult to read them as separate characters.

It was not, rationally speaking, a good design. Oscar knew this. Far too detailed to stamp with any clarity into wax or soap (or even in ink), this latest clean draft of the calligraphy had taken him twenty minutes simply to ornament.

And yet he felt cosmically beholden to the logo, bound to share it—to confess it—by a kind of awe at his own capacity for such impracticality. And without regret! Even now, passing it shakily to Squire and considering it upside down in the other man's hands, he felt an intoxicating pride in the effort.

Still, old habits die hard (if ever), and Oscar's lips were forming a reflexive apology when Squire leaned forward, almost tipping out of his (out of Vivian's) chair, and hooked two proprietary fingers into the pocket of Oscar's waistcoat.

There was a moment of startled suspension, both men ajar, in which even the clock on the wall declined to tick.

Then Squire tugged.

Squire was a man of considerable and varied privilege. But he had not often—he had so rarely—he had almost never—partaken in a shared pleasure. To fall forward into the helpless gratification of a desire and to find himself caught, held, to find another person falling with him, to find an answering mind and mouth and hand and—

Oscar was a man of considerable and varied experience. But he had not often—he had so rarely—he had almost never—been kissed on the mouth. And in his private home, well-lit and comfortable, in his own chair with its intimate and familiar creak against the small of his back, as if the wood itself were gasping softly in surprise, whenever he—

VIVIAN COULD SEE what seemed to her to be the entire future, contained within the desk set. The letters she would use it to write and seal, the checks she would receive. The memoranda and press releases, the cigarettes proffered as sleight of hand distractions, the datebook lists of allies and clients and rivals to be outmaneuvered. The office she would outgrow, and then the next one, and then the next. Years of success, decades, a lifetime. They would conglomerate—take over Oscar's former employer, the island of Manhattan, the world. Independence, security—Vivian could feel it as solid as the silver cigarette case she'd pocketed in Sofia's hotel suite, once upon a time; the golden statuette she'd vied for so desperately in the archery tournament; the stolen dinner rolls she'd lived on between nights at Electra Blake's. Only this time it was *hers*, and it was permanent as mortared stone.

"Beautiful, isn't it?" a sales clerk interrupted at her elbow, nodding at the desk set. "For your husband?"

Vivian paid in cash.

INTERLUDE

Ten years later: Summer, 1915.

    The map bristles with pins, the whole world menaced and armored in spines. War is a global paradox: threatening on the horizon; already raging. Ships traverse what was once dry land: the Panama Canal is open to commercial traffic, having been excavated, garlanded with dams and locks, and flooded via an explosion telegraphed direct from Washington. (The canal's opening ceremonies were canceled due to the outbreak of what our players have, at present, no reason to refer to as anything other than the Great War.) Elsewhere, ships molder on the ocean floor, scuttled by dreadful chance or dreadful purpose: the *Titanic*, the *Lusitania*. Already their wrecks are being colonized by extremophiles; ghosts and opportunists; the slow benign-malignant mass of consequence.

Still, one day, those who take comfort in Capital Letters will call this the Progressive Era. Hurry: we have turned the page and missed a decade's worth of Progress.

When last we met, women held the right to vote in four states. Now the total is eleven. (New York is not one of them.) Meanwhile, America has seen the stewardship of three presidents: Roosevelt, Taft, Wilson. It has adapted to innovation: the Ford Model T, the film industry, the long-distance telephone. Governmental regulations, including the establishment of the Federal Trade Commission, have served in part to transfer capitalism from a private to a public pursuit. Last year, in 1914, the income of America's forty-four richest families was equal to that of its one hundred thousand poorest. Taylorism has taken hold in the workplace: the "scientific management" of interchangeable workers for maximum efficiency. The system has triggered responsive unionizations and strikes for better working conditions. The success of these efforts varies. Factory disasters are a fact of life. The Industrial Workers of the World advocate for "direct action," dream of socialist revolution via a general strike. There are riots, battles, songs, parades, mass meetings. There are exposés and coverups; tragedies and farces; two-reel comedies and epic melodramas. There is life and death. There is Progress.

There is nothing to do but turn the page.

PART II

ONE

O n this teeming map, this overstuffed summer of 1915, find our pin: the Clancey & Schmidt executive suite, a glass-walled gallery overlooking a cavernous five-kettle manufactory floor on the west flank of Manhattan.

Climb the stairs—past the iron boilers, at two and a half million pounds combined capacity, in which kerchiefed workers mix white tallow shipped from Texas with resin from the Carolinas, potash and lime, oils and extracts; past the singing wires carving cooled sheets of soap into five hundred bars with each slice; past the pneumatic hiss of the pressers embossing the C&S logo into each scented cake; past the flutter of labels folded and glued and the stamping of fresh-inked prices. Mount the landing. Step into Vivian's office.

It was, on paper and in the frosted letters etched into the door, Oscar's office. But in practice it was Vivian's. Her lipstick ringed the coffee cups. Her desk set—yes, the very one she purchased at our last meeting, a decade before—ranged across the blotter. The telephone sat within her comfortable arm's reach.

Vivian loved this office. She was at home in it, and never more so than during this, the first of her daily rituals: her morning meeting with Elias Knox, her—the company's—factory manager and executive assistant. A thrilling eagle-eye swoop over all C&S's business. Habitually she rushed

the domestic duty of giving the housekeeper and cook their daily instructions, or even (when he and Squire were in town) delegated the task to
Oscar, the sooner to reach this office and ring for Elias.

She did so now, and he appeared: stuffed portfolio case, overstarched
collar, smile like a freshly wound watch. "Good morning, ma'am."

Elias had been with them from almost the beginning, having started
as Vivian's secretary. (As Squire's, officially.) As Oscar's and Squire's professional interest had waned, Elias (who seemed to be composed of nothing
but professional interest) had quickly shown himself to be a worthy lieu-
tenant: obedient, competent, ambitious (but not overly so)—and highly
absorbent of Clancey & Schmidt's unusual management structure.

In fact Elias was well suited to his delicate work, and through longer
lineage than Vivian could have known: his grandfather had been a
harvester for the Knickerbocker Ice Company, each winter traveling up
the Hudson to slice Rockland Lake into translucent cubes, packing them
in sawdust to cheat the seasons' turn. Elias's father, the iceman's son, had
made his own living as a night watchman patrolling Staten Island oyster
beds. His duty had been to shoot at those philosophical poachers who
argued that no man could own the bottom of the sea—and to explain (if
there was time) that while perhaps a man could not own the bottom of
the sea, a man *could* rent it from the state, and hire private security to
protect his investment.

In short, Elias came from a long tradition of monetizing and policing
the ephemeral; he was raised to accept—and, if required, to enforce—
intangible, even nonsensical rules with the highest of stakes. Working for
Vivian was not unlike farming ice or guarding the bottom of the sea
against intruders: it sounded impossible only until one had made one's
living at it for a decade.

Elias opened his memorandum book with his customary smart *thwack*
and squared its edges with the desk. "First order of business," he said.
"Your figures on the glue, ma'am."

Vivian beckoned, and Elias turned the book to face her. He'd drawn
a diagram. His lines were very clean. "Seven drops of glue per packet,"
he annotated, pointing. "On the laundry cakes. Current practice."

Vivian pressed her finger to each of the marked Xs, mapping them
onto the bars of soap. Mentally folding and securing the paper wrapping.

"This one," she said, tapping the central of the three drops that sealed the label along the soap's length. "See if they'll hold without it."

"They might not," Elias said, with some excitement. "It's a large bar, the laundry."

Vivian pursed her lips. "Let's see, shall we?"

She always preferred to lower costs rather than chase profits. Costs she could control; costs were less mercurial. A tight rein on costs let her keep her prices down, which let her expand her market share, which gave her leverage to grind her heel on suppliers and distributors. Which, in turn, let her lower her costs.

"Six drops of glue per packet on the laundry cake," Elias recited, taking note. He glanced up, allowing himself a small smile. "Pending testing."

This was the one trouble, Vivian thought, with Elias: he was slightly in love with her. But it was only a cowardly and indirect love, one it suited them both to tactfully ignore. The kind of immature infatuation that disregarded eligible girls in favor of a married woman of middle age. (Vivian had turned thirty-four in April, on the centennial anniversary of Mount Tambora's eruption.) And Elias used his fondness to stoke his performance, which if anything was ideal. Indeed, he worked so hard—almost as hard as Vivian herself—that she thought he would soon burn himself out like a spent match.

But that, she thought, was his own affair. Elias was a rare find, but not—if it came to it—an irreplaceable one.

"And the matter with Mr. Green?" she asked.

Elias shook his head, made a dismissive moue. "Handled," he said. "And we addressed all shifts on the dangers of unionizing."

"Good."

In her workers Vivian looked for people fundamentally unlike herself, or even—in their own way—her husbands, filling her factory with young people who expected to grow old where they stood. She'd found that the city, for all its glitter and bluster and fortune seeking, was full of such useful people. (Ellis Island in particular provided a perennially refreshed surplus of easily manipulated labor, new Americans culturally displaced and willing to work for low wages. Vivian, like many managers convinced of their own virtue, congratulated herself on giving her newest countrymen the opportunity to succeed.) Still, occasionally there were rumblings of organization. Occasionally it became necessary, in Vivian's view, to right the ship.

The telephone interjected with its shrill tone. The use of the direct line meant there were only two possible callers—and both would only just have gotten in from Shenandoah on the morning train. Vivian gestured for Elias to answer it.

"Mr. Schmidt's office," he annunciated. Then, glancing at Vivian with a question encoded in his eyebrows: "Good morning, Mr. Clancey."

Vivian gestured for the receiver.

"Welcome back," she said.

"Good"—Squire interrupted himself with an enormous yawn—"morning. We missed you."

"Mm," Vivian said—mindful of the switchboard, and of Elias (who was tactfully studying the wainscoting, blank as any operator). "Was the hunt a success?" The men's trip to Virginia had been organized around the auction of a rare hatpin that Oscar had particularly coveted, a work of plique-à-jour enamel in the figure of a lily. There had been several rival collectors interested.

"He got it," Squire said. "And it only *briefly* looked as though I'd have to second him in a duel."

"Hatpins at dawn," Vivian said, and had to work not to smile at Squire's answering laugh. She *had* missed him. "And the cave?"

Almost more than Oscar's celebrated pin, the men had planned their holiday around this event: a charity benefit with the gimmick of being held in Luray Caverns. Music, dinner, even dancing (for those who could) on a wood floor laid over the cave's largest chamber.

"*Oh,*" Squire said, a universe of meaning crackling over the line. "It was absolutely—" He paused. Squire at this point in his life felt far less general pressure to police his enthusiasm than he once had, but he had also learned to appreciate the economics of paying by the minute to express it. "Too much for the telephone," he said. "I'll tell you at home. But listen, that's why I'm calling. It was an early morning, and we hardly slept—"

"Hmm," Vivian said.

"Stop," Squire said crisply, barely breaking stride. "I'm headed straight out to my mother's, and . . ."—implied in the gap, the supernaturally draining force of a visit to Mrs. Clancey—"I can already tell I'll be turning in early. So, no need to rush home to play cards, if you're busy there. Or—with someone."

"What makes you think I'd *rush*?" Vivian asked. Again the familiar laugh; again the struggle to remain impassive. "You're sure you're up to Madison Avenue?" she asked. Vivian lived in (slightly judgmental) awe of Squire's commitment to caring for his mother, his willingness to cultivate such close acquaintance with such a parent.

"It's already been a week," Squire said. "You know how she'll get."

"Tomorrow, then," Vivian said. "Gin rummy and the full report."

"Tomorrow."

Vivian replaced the receiver in its cradle and nodded to Elias, who reengaged his attention. "A few pieces of correspondence for you," he said, releasing his portfolio's clasp.

Vivian reviewed them quickly: first, a brief letter agreeing to the extension of terms of C&S's rebate with its Canadian shipper. It was a bulk discount always renegotiated discreetly, to the (somewhat illicit) advantage of both parties. Second, a request to a supplier for a quote on a larger than usual order of essential oils, particularly the floral scents. A few competitors had begun to copy C&S's innovations in scented candles—Vivian intended to achieve by design what Squire had once achieved accidentally, and engineer a shortage of raw materials that reestablished her monopoly. The scent oils—in combination with their uncooked cousins, the solvent-extracted absolutes—were the keystone of the supply chain, its Achilles' heel, the ingredient easiest for her to hoard and store and hardest for vendors to mass-produce to meet a subsequent urgent demand. (There was, after all, no way to go back in time and plant more cabbage roses once all the petals had been macerated and expressed. As Oscar had learned long ago, there would be nothing for their rivals to do but wait for next year's harvest.)

Vivian preferred to speculate this way, with goods and people, rather than on Wall Street. She was not afraid of the market, exactly—promissory notes were in some ways *more* tangible than the tools she did manipulate—but it was more important to her to be in control, to observe her power's direct practical effects on products and markets and the actions of others, than to court the fantastic specter of unlimited capital.

In short, Vivian was no longer a long-shot gambler. She didn't have to be—she had already won.

The telephone rang again, and again Elias answered: "Mr. Schmidt's office." Again, he glanced at Vivian, "Good morning, Mr. Schmidt."

Vivian shook her head. Squire she could count on to be sensible, to have news worth reporting: their safe arrival at home; the final outcome of the auction; the fact that she could stay late at the office (or elsewhere) tonight without sacrifice. But this call, Vivian thought, meant one of two things: either Oscar wanted to subject her to an exhaustive history of their holiday—breakfasts eaten, trains missed, every melodramatic round of bidding on the hatpin—or else he was still caught in his spiral over Mrs. Clancey's ridiculous scheme to saddle Squire with a widow.

Either way, Vivian did not have time to humor him.

"I'm sorry, sir," Elias said into the telephone. "Mrs. Schmidt isn't in at the moment. Certainly. Certainly. I'll give her the message. Thank you, sir, and welcome back."

"Where were we?" Vivian asked.

She signed both documents before her—one with Oscar's slender loops and floating serifs; the other with Squire's abundant signature, the letters almost tumbling into a central heap. Elias received the pages with a nod. "And as it's the first of the month next week," he said with well-trained impassivity, "we'll send a check to Utica." He slid her a sheet of half-size statement letterhead.

Elias's forgery of Vivian's penmanship was barely competent—but, she supposed, at this point it *was* her penmanship, to her parents. If she ever had to fire Elias while they were still living, she thought, she would have to learn to counterfeit his counterfeit script.

He'd written the customary few lines about the weather, and best wishes as to her parents' health. (They were both declining, her father slightly faster than her mother. Senility had a defanging effect, but there was in its place a new disquiet, the uncanny responsibility of looking after the monster under the bed. Vivian's strategy was, as ever, to keep her distance. She paid a nurse to keep her informed.)

The letter included, Vivian noted, an unsanctioned reference to the latest of President Wilson's ultimatums on the sinking of the *Lusitania*—but it wasn't worth waiting for Elias to copy out another sheet. "Less blood and thunder, next time," she said, tapping at the offending line.

Elias nodded—pen scratching self-censure in his memorandum book, blush creeping faintly from his collar.

Vivian considered apologizing, given the stakes, but decided against it. (Is it stranger to ignore geopolitical tragedies in professional correspondence, or to acknowledge them? Is it stranger to designate a letter to one's parents as "professional correspondence," or to deny oneself such a boundary? How many separate chambers should a healthy human mind contain?)

Elias had closed, *With Love.* Vivian affixed her signature. "Next," she said.

"The anniversary celebration," Elias said. "You asked me to raise the matter with four months' notice."

"I did," Vivian said. She considered for a moment. "Raise it again in the fall," she said.

The pressure from their board of investors to observe the tenth anniversary of Clancey & Schmidt's founding with some sort of commemorative event, a gala for clients and partners and a holiday for the workers, was one she found disturbing. To Vivian the company *was* the monument; the daily hum of its success the celebration. She disliked the thought of reducing it to a party, which might go well or badly, at which people would waste a day and drink too much and say nothing, repeatedly. (If it entered her calculations that at public functions she was by necessity sidelined—denied any connection but a dewy-eyed wife's to the company she ran; whispered about for any "irregular" behavior no matter how small—these were feelings Vivian did not examine beyond a superficial annoyance.)

And, she thought, besides performing her own role at such a function, she would have to train Oscar and Squire to perform theirs. Coach them on the state of the business, help them memorize the names and faces of men they were supposed to know. Then there would be the anxiety of processing the milestone itself: Squire's bewilderment to realize that he had, for the first time in his life, spent a decade devoted to the same obsession; Oscar's particular brand of happiness, heavily seasoned with terror at the thought of its loss.

And all of this was before she would have to write their speeches.

"If we only set a date?" Elias suggested, his pen hovering. "Perhaps around Christmas? I could handle the—"

"Anything but Christmas," Vivian said. "It's booked."

In the five years since Squire's father's death, Mrs. Clancey had continued—even intensified—the family tradition of hosting grand Christmas parties on the Hudson. The entire Clancey-Schmidt house-hold's attendance was mandatory; any scheduling conflict would certainly be taken personally. Vivian was already going to have to disappoint Mrs. Clancey once this year, she thought, by ruining her plans for Squire and the widow. She couldn't make a *complete* enemy of the woman.

"Raise it with three months' notice," she said.

Elias, who enjoyed pomp and hors d'oeuvres and had been looking forward to the party that he was now confident—having seen Vivian triumph often and subtly enough over the expectations of the board—would never happen, subdued a tetchy nod and made a note.

"Next?"

Elias stalled for a moment—then covered the rest of his agenda with his hand, as if doing so would pause time. "Something we might try, ma'am," he said, "instead of the party."

"Don't tempt me, Mr. Knox," said Vivian. (There was a slight guilt associated with the way such comments clearly affected him, but she needed to rescue his mood before his workday began in earnest. Vivian had found that people were most useful when euphoric, and for people of Elias's constitution infatuation sang like cocaine in the bloodstream.)

"We might observe the anniversary," Elias reached slowly for the innermost pocket of his portfolio, "by announcing an intent to expand."

Vivian's gaze shuttered. "Not this again," she said.

"If you'd only look over the options," Elias said, creasing the packet of papers in his haste. "The site outside North Bergen is only nine miles from—"

"From my existing, extremely productive manufactory?"

Elias smiled carefully. This was his pet project, one Vivian might have had to discipline him for if he hadn't worked on it exclusively on his own time: a scheme to incorporate C&S as a company town, somewhere among the refineries and swamps of New Jersey.

There were things about the idea that made sense to Vivian: cheap land and unlimited space; the opportunity to be landlord and grocer to each employee, not to mention puppet master to the town council. She liked low overheads and control; Elias was offering her a terrarium. Vivian knew that it was a sensible idea, objectively at least worth investigation— and so it was with a secondary flush of embarrassed anger that she absolutely refused to consider it.

The truth was that she could not tolerate the thought of moving back onto the mainland of North America, even a single mile back in the direction of Utica. This deeply personal prejudice could not, of course, be explained to poor Elias, who—like everyone—saw only Vivian's public presentation: the entrepreneur who should have leapt at the idea.

"Manhattan has been a *company town* for three hundred years," she said now, a sneer at the provinces being a cheap but effective armor in most moments of weakness.

"Yes, ma'am," Elias said. He pressed at his notes, trying to smooth away the creases of his eagerness.

"Leave those with me," Vivian said finally, to keep him hoping. But she didn't reach for the packet, nodding instead to her green glass tray on the desk. Hope had to be rationed, dispensed in manageable crumbs: she could leave Elias in anticipation that she might *read* his notes—provided her schedule allowed—but not that she might approve of them.

"Thank you, ma'am," he said.

As he drew breath to return to his agenda, the telephone sounded again. This time Vivian used the opportunity to escape. "I have an appointment," she said, rising. "We'll finish this later."

As the door closed behind her, she heard Elias answer: "I'm sorry, Mr. Schmidt, you've just missed her."

VIVIAN'S APPOINTMENT WAS unofficial, but urgent all the same: she was midway through a time-sensitive, even perishable, acquisition.

Outside the Childs restaurant on Cortlandt Street, Vivian paused on the pavement to watch her latest girl—Sarah—flip pancakes in the window.

Vivian respected the Childs brothers for this advertising technique: locations spread over the city, each with arresting young women in hospital-white uniforms expertly manning hot griddles behind plate glass.

She allowed herself a few moments' spectatorship: Sarah's movements fluid and apparently casual, a studied effortlessness. Muscles moving under the starched sleeve of her uniform. The black cross tie—part service, part whimsy—slightly askew under her collar. She was a marvel of timing and instinct: pouring uniform pools of batter, every time; appearing to forget about each one as it began to bubble and shine in the heat; swooping in to flip at the perfect golden-brown peak, giving each just enough time on the second side to puff into fluffed crispness. Vivian watched Sarah through the ghost of her own reflection—a bit more gray dusting her mane now; a bit more weary wisdom in her eyes; the thickened strength of a body that no longer remembered scrounging crackers for supper—as short and tall stacks piled steaming on the counter. Maple syrup, melting butter, jam.

After a few minutes, Sarah shivered slightly and looked up from her work—the unsettled feeling of being watched yielding to a bright, even unprofessional smile as she caught Vivian's eye. She waved her in.

Vivian took a table by the window, ordered coffee and pancakes from one of Sarah's colleagues. (A perfectly nice girl, Vivian thought, striking in her own right—but fate had not seen fit to put her in Vivian's path, on her first visit to the restaurant.)

This was her fourth meal here, and would—with any luck—be the second consummation of her affair with Sarah. ("Visits," the girl called them.) Vivian calculated perhaps as many as two additional "visits" before the liaison ran its course. The lifespans of such arrangements were necessarily limited, both to allow Vivian to reasonably decline to provide any details of her identity or personal life and—crucially—to prevent the girls from getting attached.

Sarah brought Vivian's pancakes herself—leaving the smoking griddle unattended, radiant with danger at the unsanctioned disruption of a fine-tuned cycle. "Nice to see you again," she said, slightly breathless. "I'm through in twenty minutes."

"Then back to your post, soldier," Vivian said. They passed a wink. Then Sarah was gone, tightening her apron strings as she went.

It was long and delicate work, the cultivation of a liaison. They were like rare flowers that bloomed only briefly, in twilight, before withering. Today would be the peak of this one, Vivian thought. The single day on which she could enjoy equilibrium, both the certainty of successful conquest and the comfort of anonymity. If she visited again, dropped in toward the end of one more of Sarah's shifts, the girl might begin to feel secure and emboldened enough to ask questions—about Vivian's origins, her occupation, the provenance of the spare apartment two blocks away she used for these encounters. (When obliged to give a surname, Vivian introduced herself as Miss or even Mrs. Bianchi—taking Sofia's name a choice she examined no more than Oscar had his use of "Hester" at the Slide, a lifetime before. The alias left Vivian safely untraceable, but open to innocent questions that she did not relish.)

Vivian cut a careful wedge of pancake and dipped it in syrup, sponging off the excess before bringing it to her lips.

The girl really was very talented.

The first and most delicate step, of course, was determining the amenability of a conquest. There were, Vivian knew, Sapphic bars and teahouses a few minutes north that sought to remove the mystery and danger from this gamble. But besides the physical and reputational carelessness of frequenting such establishments, which the Committee of Fourteen might raid at any moment, Vivian found that the relative guarantee of success rather took the thrill out of the hunt. (On this subject, her philosophy and Oscar's former habits diverged sharply.)

Today's young people, Vivian thought, wanted everything to come to them too easily.

Her plate was nearly clean, just a smear of syrup and a few wet crumbs, when Sarah reappeared in street clothes. A blue linen day dress, a string of artificial pearls. Cheap and cheerful. "How was everything?" she asked, clearing Vivian's tray with one practiced hand.

"Delicious," Vivian said, and stood.

Her spare apartment was tiny, since she rarely required it for more than an evening's entertainment. (Or, as now, the day shift.) But still: a pied-à-terre! Where Oscar had once labored vainly to deny his loneliness in a crowd, Vivian converted hers to desirable (and expensive) privacy. The flat's size and simplicity made it Vivian's accomplice in anonymity—such a set of rooms, glimpsed only once or twice, might easily be the full-time residence of a widow on a modest fixed income, or an eccentric spinster waiting on a long-delayed inheritance. The apartment was spare and neat, though furnished with concessions to the varying personalities of its visitors: a velvet-upholstered lit de repos, for the dramatic. A firm bed with a frame of bird's-eye maple, for the practical. A wet bar, for those women who required such encouragement to come loose.

Sarah did not require encouragement; she was dramatic and practical by turns. They spent a pleasant hour "visiting," exploring the space's decor and its uses.

Afterward, Sarah helped Vivian relace her corset. The assistance was unnecessary—Vivian slept and dressed alone and did not keep a lady's maid, nor Oscar and Squire valets. (There was no question of it, from a privacy perspective: their house had servants; its occupants did not.) Instead, Vivian had a complex and well-practiced system involving bespoke tailoring for the independent woman; long-handled button-hooks; one corset lace left trailing as a pullstring (she instructed Sarah in this method, now); and the reading of her own dresses' fastenings like braille, with dexterous fingers and a double-jointed left arm. But on this subject Vivian was not irrational: when more convenient tools presented themselves, she took advantage.

"It *is* a torture device, you know," Sarah said, returning to a conversation of the previous week as she knotted Vivian's laces. "The way you wear them."

"Well," Vivian said archly. "Maybe someday you can vote them out of office."

It was a cheap retort—but then, Vivian thought, it had been a cheap critique. Anyway, she had never tight-laced her corsets—she needed flexibility, stamina, capacity. She needed to perform. (Only imagine, if she had been too wasp-waisted and delicate to climb aboard Patience's bicycle, or to cross the room to Sofia's piano!) Few real women had ever put themselves through the complicated ordeals illustrated in fashion plates.

That was one true rejoinder, and she might have made it. But it would have obscured a deeper truth. Because what girls like this Sarah did not appreciate, Vivian thought, was the value of certain limitations that gave a person shape and support; of posture ingrained until it was second nature; of a garment engineered to train the wearer in self-discipline. To keep one from coming undone.

Vivian had entertained many suffragists in this apartment—mixed them gin and tonics, unrolled their stockings, kissed the ink from their fingers. This madness for the vote struck Vivian as one more whining demand for things to be too easy, like the Sapphic teahouses and the abandonment of corsets—a bizarre need to ape men in all their clumsy, wasteful, unobservant ease.

After all, Vivian hadn't needed suffrage to scale to her present height. When she had been Sarah's age, Vivian thought, on Sarah's rung of the social ladder, she had been scrappy, canny, her opportunism sharpened by her hunger. She would, she could not help but think, have known how to *use* her own modern self. If the teenaged Vivian had met the matron, monied and powerful and with a spare set of rooms downtown, an icon of connection and access—well. She would have charmed herself, Vivian thought. Dazzled herself; wrapped herself around her little finger until the older woman's resources were her own.

As it was, success had made Vivian aware of her own exceptionalism. Because she had long been on guard for, even (after years of such waiting) thrilled to anticipate, such an opportunistic assault from someone as hungry as she had once been. Someone covetous and deserving, a match (or even more than a match) for her own ambitions and talents. Someone who knew how to maneuver against powerful limitations, to use her enemies' own weight against them to achieve the impossible.

But no such person had presented herself. These girls only wanted wide, visible, impotent, and state-sanctioned paths: the vote and loose laces, the right to slouch, to argue out loud on men's terms and lose.

And they all let Vivian abandon them after two or three encounters, without even the passion, or intelligence, or anger to hunt her down.

"Come by the restaurant on Wednesday," Sarah said now, reapplying her lipstick. "I'm off at four."

Vivian found her keys. "We'll see," she said. She was due back at the office.

∾

THERE WAS ANOTHER message from Oscar, when she arrived—just another request that she call him. He'd stopped in, as well, Elias said. Vivian scanned the office, looking for clues to her husband's anxiety du jour. If he'd moved any of her things, he'd replaced them before he left. There were possibly one or two fewer cigarettes in her case. Good, she thought. He could use them.

The rest of the day passed in its usual flow of productivity and crisis, the exhausting euphoria that animated Vivian like an electric current. Correspondence either promptly answered or strategically ignored; raw materials received and finished products distributed; profits and losses dutifully accounted for in an endlessly counterbalancing ledger. Oscar buzzed once more, giving up after the fourteenth ring. (Calling from his club, Vivian guessed—there was a telephone there he sometimes requisitioned when under the influence of port or gossip, feeling particularly maudlin or boisterous. Either way, she thought, it could wait.)

Elias flitted in and out with messages. Vivian gave notes on an early treatment for a filmed industrial short, to be screened with a two-reel comedy in movie houses—it was a thin but clear narrative about an average husband and wife somewhere in the vague middle of the country, pleasant misadventures solved by C&S products (clearly identified by name on interstitial title cards). They'd intercut with scenes of the factory floor, Oscar and Squire miming executive function behind glass doors.

People liked, Vivian thought, to know how things were made. At least they liked to think so.

Elias knocked again. The laundry cakes, it transpired, would hold their seal with only six drops of glue.

To celebrate this victory, Vivian followed Squire's suggestion and stayed late at her desk, long into the purple summer twilight. She ate dinner alone in a ladies' restaurant—three brisk blocks in the opposite direction from Sarah's pancake window—and, when at last she hazarded that Oscar would have joined Squire in retiring early to recover from their trip, she headed home.

They'd bought the house two years into their syndicate's official partnership, when their previous improvised lifestyle—Squire now a permanent fixture; Vivian renting rooms east of the park whenever she needed to flee the twin oppressive atmospheres of first love and experimental perfume—became financially, logistically, and reputationally impractical.

People might have talked, but once again the trio had made creative use of Squire's slippery, contradictory reputation as an alarmingly eccentric invalid of impeccable social pedigree: in appearing to take him on as a kind of dependent confirmed-bachelor companion, the Schmidts had garnered their own misguided reputation among New York society for performing the kind of charitable and selfless acts the gossips would themselves have taken significant pains to avoid. The glittering rabble's guilty consciences had stilled their tongues.

Vivian let herself in, her heels clicking on the tile of the vestibule.

It was a brownstone mansion, built early in the previous century by a tinpot tycoon with a large and varied family—the Clancey-Schmidts had found it already equipped with such a capacious and unconventional floorplan that very little architectural customization had been required to fit it to their purposes. It was of such a size, they might have remodeled it with gala rooms in which to throw grand parties, even balls—if, that is, entertaining outsiders had been their syndicate's priority. As it was, they'd sacrificed society to their private arrangement.

The entrance hall forked; Vivian mounted the left staircase.

The house was arranged in separate residential wings—one theoretically Vivian and Oscar's; the other theoretically Squire's—served by a single kitchen downstairs and overlapping in shared sitting and dining rooms. (Squire had referred to the latter as a "breakfast room" the first time he saw it, assuming that there would be a grander hall elsewhere in the house for larger dinner parties. Oscar and Vivian still mocked him for it occasionally, in put-on patrician accents.)

Throughout the renovation Vivian had repeatedly stressed to the architect and decorator the importance of privacy, the ministry of different rooms to different wants—as if her concern were the fussy decorative differentiation of drawing room from library, and not that of Sodom from Gomorrah.

It was largely a question of doors—locking, never sliding, since the latter were inevitably left open. Always hinged such that, when opened, the door would for a few protective moments conceal the occupants from the entrant. Never—not *ever*—portieres.

In the end they had had to install only one secret passage, concealed doors that swung on a pivot in the paneling connecting Oscar's den and Squire's bedroom. (A defunct servant's passage, they were ready to explain if asked—originally installed so as not to disturb the equilibrium of the decor, and to which the key, lost during the remodeling, remained unrecovered.)

Now Vivian crept past this weak point in their dividing wall, stepping carefully on the thickest pieces of carpet and the firmest floorboards. She paused to listen; hearing nothing, satisfied herself that both men were asleep.

Once the doors and passageways were settled, they'd furnished the house piece by piece, one room at a time—willow chairs and stained deal tables standing in until they could be replaced with better. Home improvement: it was the overwhelming but not unhappy work of a lifetime. Even Vivian had learned almost to enjoy herself.

Their wings, inevitably, reflected their characters. The men, Vivian knew, had furnished theirs with a loud and comfortable enthusiasm—despite his overlying chaos, Squire had an aristocrat's ingrained sense of proportion, the developed instinct to lend a room repose and distinction before he let himself explode over it. To this inborn privilege Oscar had married his practicality and his quadruply considered plans for the arrangement of furniture; the fruits of his endless self-debate concerning the placement of each piece of bric-a-brac; his productive inability to relax in a room that was not fulfilling its purpose.

It was a happy coincidence that Oscar's nominally dedicated room in Vivian's wing, his master's den, had found its "purpose" as a display for his hatpin collection (which ran at present to just shy of three hundred pieces, mostly early Victorian, sourced from eleven states and three European countries). The pins were arranged on specialized stands and dusted daily. Vivian wore them—at least those Oscar would allow to be exposed to the elements—on special occasions, in order to lend the collection a utilitarian legitimacy (and Oscar himself a reputation as a devoted husband, given to extravagant presents). But most days, she still preferred plain enamel.

Without his pin collection, Oscar's den would have gone unused—
except, as noted, as a passageway to Squire's wing. In that case, the trio
thought, the housekeeper and her assistants might have begun to suspect
something of an unusual arrangement—for only in this room were the
windows always obscured with decorative muslin, the chairs arranged in
poor light and at odd angles to the neglected fireplace. It required the
maintenance of a closed house, while Squire's rooms required the attention elsewhere occasioned by a robust and active family. But the display
of the hatpin collection had been calculated to forgive all sins—to render
the room eccentric, but not suspicious. It had the character of a museum
exhibit; an atmosphere of musty disuse, then, was only natural. (Whether
this plan gave due credit to the household staff's powers of observation
was not a question that occurred to our protagonists, the arrangement
having succeeded so long without incident.)

Vivian herself was still learning to use space, to be "practical" in the
manner of tasteful wealth rather than rural necessity. Even after eight years
of occupancy, her rooms were still spare. Spending lavishly was one thing;
it came less naturally to her to take up space, to be at ease. She was a
creature of clever and manipulative marginality, not one who had ever
yearned to learn the difference between a drawing room, living room,
and morning room (and to furnish all three appropriately).

She did, however, enjoy the library. The wide desk she had cleared of
knick-knacks so both elbows could swing free, and the built-in bookcases—
she favored surprising history, unsurprising poetry, and novels about people
with jobs—that padded the walls.

She entered the bedroom suite now. There was an animal comfort to
this too: the chain of simple chambers, each a reassuring buffer between
herself and the rest of the world (the rest of the house, even), allowing
her to unspool in stages as she moved through. First an antechamber;
then the boudoir with its writing table and straight-backed armchairs,
where she endured the strange daily meeting with the household staff.
And then, just before her bath, the bedroom itself. An enormous
master bed, for appearances—though she would never have invited one
of her anonymous liaisons to her home, and Oscar of course had never
touched it.

Vivian looked forward to it now, kicking off her shoes, reaching to unpin her hair—gloriously spent at the end of a long and bustling day; the comforting dimness and silence of a solitary—

"Vivian."

"*Jesus*," she hissed—still in an instinctive half-whisper, though it was too late now for secrecy.

Oscar flicked on the tasseled lamp on her side table and hoisted himself from the armchair in the corner.

He *was* tired after the morning's journey, Vivian saw—hair untrammeled, movements lagging, eyelids at half-mast. He'd kept himself up.

"What are you doing here?" she asked, one hand still paused in its quest for her hairpins.

Oscar gave a sleepy and (though Vivian tried to hide it) contagious chuckle at the question, posed as it was in his own nominal bedroom. He spun his wrist and clicked his heels, a self-presentation something between a military salute and a curtsy. "I've been trying to reach you," he said.

Vivian threw up her free hand. "Well," she said. "Congratulations." After a moment she added, "and welcome back." She stepped forward to greet him: a handshake, an avuncular kiss on the cheek. She regathered her hair, turned to offer him the back of her dress. "Undo me," she said. "Since you're here."

After ten years of marriage, and almost as long as the founding members of their syndicate with Squire, there was for both of them an inevitable comfort in this ritual. An alien familiarity. Oscar stepped in close enough to smell Vivian's perfume. Mystic Zephyr. He and Squire had designed it for her in 1906, as an attempt to express their gratitude—lemon and bergamot; rose, iris, and jasmine; civet, vanilla, and musk. They had put it on the market too, of course, and it was one of C&S's most popular scents. (It had, in no small part, paid for the house they stood in.) Still, whenever he smelled it in the wider world, Oscar found himself with almost a real husband's jealousy—territorial, offended that some other woman was wearing his wife's perfume.

For her part, Vivian appreciated Oscar's comfort with her clothes. He had a practiced familiarity with her buttons, her hooks, her laces that none of her rotating fresh-picked girls would ever be able to boast. He was the only attendant to whom she never had to explain her sartorial system—the custom configuration of her plackets, her inverted eyelets, the single pull-string corset lace left trailing.

"Who did this?" he muttered now, bending to pick at a knot in Sarah's lacing. "She's even worse than you."

"A suffragette," Vivian said.

"Ah." Oscar's laugh was a puff of warm air on her shoulder, his fingers light against her spine. A final loosening, and everything fell away. "You're done," he said, and gathered her things onto their hangers.

"Thank you." Vivian shook out her chemise, her hair. Scrunched her toes into the carpet. Took a breath. "How was your trip?"

She received, albeit in a mercifully abridged form, the itinerary she'd been dodging all day—starting, of course, with the successful purchase of the elusive hatpin. Oscar went on to give an exhaustive explanation of train timetables; menus for both rustic breakfasts and full-course dinners; a testimonial in favor of a humane tourist trap of an inn outside Luray, Virginia, that had every night served whiskey on a screened porch overlooking the Blue Ridge Mountains in the distance, across a valley meadow so full of fireflies it was as if gravity had drawn them there against their will.

Vivian listened gamely, tying off her braid for sleep. "And the professor enjoyed himself," she said—this in reference to Squire, the moniker coined by their housekeeper due to Squire's ever-growing list of scientific society memberships (and the associated newsletters that accumulated in drifts on every sideboard).

"Oh," Oscar smiled, a watery inhale interrupted by the shake of his head. "You have to ask him, in the morning—there was a party, down in the cave," he said.

"I know," Vivian said, as patiently as she could manage.

"He—" Oscar pressed the heel of one hand to his forehead. "He loved it." A wondering exhale, something—and yet nothing— like a scoff.

Vivian had by now seen this many times: Oscar overwhelmed, even frightened, by his own capacity for happiness. Even without details she could imagine his mounting euphoric panic, over the course of the holiday.

The details, for those of us who require them:

Squire whiskey-drunk in the evenings, attempting to transcribe the fire-flies' flashing into Morse code, drumming his fingers on the porch railing. ("It's gibberish," he'd concluded with a broad smile.) Squire triumphant in the collectors' showroom with a gold-and-amethyst snuffbox, holding it to his ear to hear the satisfying click of its sealing lid. (Neither man took snuff, but both were happy to make the purchase; this joy in expensive and useless souvenirs, if illegible to you, cannot be made otherwise.) Squire's gasps each night in bed, their tenor almost wondering—as if every encounter were a pleasant surprise, no matter how many times repeated. Squire doctoring Oscar's coffee perfectly each morning, taking a single sip like a poison-taster to test his work before handing it over, all without looking up from *The Scarecrow of Oz*.

And, most of all, Squire in the Luray Caverns ballroom. A careful quarter-mile trek beneath the surface of the earth in eveningwear, an endless warren of limestone chambers and formations massive yet still growing—stalactites as big as buildings, perfectly mirrored in crystalline lakes; towering columns that almost seemed to have grown complete with mineral foliage at their crowns; flowstone draperies of living rock as translucent as linen; bottomless abysses barely guarded by flimsy plywood rails. Electric lights glittered over everything, a miraculous and unnatural invasion keeping the clammy dark at bay. The tour ending in the "Ballroom," a grand and stalagmite-columned hall that geology had labored 450 millennia to clear, for the express purpose (or so it seemed to Oscar, who for his own part ran slightly claustrophobic and chilly and wary of collapse) that Squire Clancey might stand in it, in a white tie and tailcoat, with a string quartet echoing off the stalactites above him, and finally enjoy himself at a party.

Who is a cave for? Those who seek shelter in it from the elements, building fires and marking their stories on its walls? Those who tumble in through sinkholes and perish broken in the dark? The cows who find relief from the midday sun near the hidden fissures exhaling cool, moist air from deep beneath the surface?

Or does a cave form for its own unfathomable reasons, the slow and sacred accumulation of absence? Erosion and deposit, a trickling pressure equal and opposite to the fiery work of volcanic eruption? Are all humanity's subsequent uses, its hundreds of millions of moments open and secret, no more than accidental side effects?

At one point, late in the evening, the gala's host had with great fanfare (and a final appeal for donations) cut the electric chandeliers for sixty mind-wiping seconds. A blackness darker than pitch had somehow smothered every sense, even the sounds of the other revelers' champagne-fizzing exclamations. Hands had groped blindly, closed on empty air. And when—the grand finale!—they'd at last been snapped back into the light, Oscar had so thrilled at the restored sight of his husband—laughing with the delight that can only come from the unlikely, even the almost impossible, granting of a lifetime's wish, and immediately finding Oscar's eye to share in it—that even now, safe at home in New York with Squire waiting for him asleep in their wing and Vivian looking at him expectantly, Oscar felt at moments as though he were still fighting to regain his breath.

"Well," Vivian said. "I'm glad you had fun." She would remind herself, again, to put a hard stop to this ridiculous business with the widow. Before Oscar lost his mind. (The circles under his eyes, she thought, were from more than just the lateness of the evening. He was fifty-four now, yes; he looked fifty-four and fallen down a flight of stairs. And this after a week's vacation.) She would move it up on her to-do list. She would try to get to it before they began production on the industrial short. "What did you need, today?" she prompted, pointedly turning back her bedspread.

"Yes," Oscar nodded. "Right. I was wondering . . ." He floundered, then steeled himself. He'd lain in wait, after all; this was his wife. "I was wondering," he began again, "if we—if we might—have a child."

Vivian stared at him, one hand on her pillow. Eiderdown compressed slowly into a brick.

"Not tonight," he hastened to add. "I just wanted to . . ." He gestured obscurely. "Broach the subject."

"A subject you haven't broached," Vivian said at a simmer, "since our wedding night."

"Well, I—"

"And even *then*—"

"It's Squire," Oscar blurted. "It's—we—it's—he and I. Who want one." He knit his fingers. "A child," he clarified.

"*Do* you," Vivian said.

Acid against her teeth: violation, labor, a ruined body, and a permanently altered life. Bones warped, career derailed into a new role she could not escape. (And one at which, she stamped the thought like an errant spark, she was bound to fail.) Her legacy burned to fuel another. And she would be cut off from her life, her liaisons, her apartment near the office—for a year, for many years, forever. Oscar was proposing, for her at least, the end of everything.

She confined these visceral objections to an inner chamber. She stepped closer to Oscar, until her chest brushed his. "*Do* you?"

"Um," Oscar said. "Yes."

"And does Squire?"

"Yes."

"He said this?"

"Yes?"

"He said," Vivian said, "*specifically*, this." She grabbed a fistful of her chemise, brandishing her body at him.

"Well, not—*ah!*" Oscar yelped as she reached a hand between his legs, jumping back and cracking his head against her bedpost. "Not specifically," he said, wincing.

"You alright?" she asked, after a moment.

He wiped the back of his head, examined his palm. "Yes."

"You don't want a *child*," Vivian said.

"He does," Oscar said, uncertainly. "We do."

"Why?"

"Because," Oscar said. He appeared to struggle with something either too unclear or too obvious to articulate. He looked into the middle distance, as if waiting for a cue. "B-because . . ."

Besides the insult to her personally, the autonomy of her body and her mind, Vivian felt a rush of anger—confusingly outsized—at the concept of such ambivalent procreation. No child, she thought, deserved an indifferent parent. One of the greatest privileges of their syndicate lifestyle, in Vivian's opinion, was the freedom from such mutually damaging genealogical prisons. The freedom to author their own legacies.

There was no sense in this request that Vivian could see; no sense whatsoever.

In truth, it frightened her. She saw Oscar see it, momentarily, the responding fear in his own eyes at the rare show of weakness—cursed him for having learned to read her face as well as he read her buttons.

She buried her bewilderment in a sneer. "You had all day to polish this pitch," she said. "*Why* do you want to have a child?"

Oscar dithered.

Vivian leaned close. Mystic Zephyr filled Oscar's nose. "Take a piece of professional advice," she said. It was a tacit reminder of her first act of grace, preparing him to survive the encounter with his manager all those years ago. And—inevitably—a reminder of everything else he owed to her, in the years since. This house. C&S. Squire. Through all of it, her hand on the reins.

"Never make an ask," Vivian said, "without a reason."

She kissed him goodnight and locked the door behind him.

TWO

The reason for Oscar's proposition, indirectly but definitely, had
been plaque in the aorta of Luther Van Beek—undistinguished
lawyer, scion of old New York, and the three-years-deceased husband of
Rebecca Van Beek.

The widow Van Beek, according to the self-appointed authority of
Squire's mother, was: forty years old; still pretty; not "excessively sad" to
find herself widowed; a lady of leisure; an artist (primarily in oils and charcoal, not without charm but only middlingly talented, and perhaps
slightly gauche in her enthusiasm for her own work); an awkward but
generous hostess; heiress to a respectable real-estate fortune (the family
having purchased then-worthless lots far uptown in the 1820s, and the
city having subsequently grown to meet them); and the mother of two
children under the age of ten.

She was also the woman Mrs. Clancey had chosen—as if from a green-
grocer's cart, in Oscar's view—to put forward as a wife for Squire.

Oscar tried not to think about it now, waiting at their usual table at
Sherry's for Squire to arrive from his mother's. A half-dozen Buzzard's
Bay oysters commiserated with him—shucked of years of accumulated
armor and destined for annihilation, their confusing little hearts still
working. His first glass of Moët fizzled.

Mrs. Clancey had a certain inevitable sway over the entire Clancey-Schmidt syndicate, a center of power both as a mother and as a founding investor. In the years since Mr. Clancey's death—in her profound grief and loneliness; in her contradictory but undeniably coexistent flourishing as a widow no longer forced to negotiate with a contrary spouse; in her pride at Squire's conventional success, long despaired of—she had learned to love her son better, to welcome, often even to insist on, his company. This conditional affection was insulting to Squire, yes. But he was discovering, as Vivian had before him, the painful, paradoxical truth that insult and cruelty do not negate the power of parental approval long withheld. He was dutiful in his visits, sometimes several times a week, and Oscar accompanied him not infrequently. (Even Vivian had been known to make an appearance.) Mrs. Clancey liked Oscar—liked him very much, in fact—all the more for what she misread as his role in civilizing her son into a marriageable prospect.

Which made the whole torturous plot more unbearable, as early on she had tried to recruit him as an accomplice.

Over the last six months Oscar had on several occasions sat white-knuckled over tea and petit fours, alone in the wilderness of Mrs. Clancey's drawing room (the lady having manufactured some errand on which to dispatch Squire), while his unwitting mother-in-law thanked him for his service and tried to relieve him of his commission.

He had nervously agreed with insultingly phrased assessments of Squire's "progress": competent, even functional; capable of living in a household, in mixed company! He had weathered gratitude for his own supposed contributions to all this "improvement"—really, Mrs. Clancey stressed kindly, he and Vivian had done more than enough for her son. And their efforts had succeeded! He was ready (didn't Oscar think?) to strike out on his own; maybe even (she alluded tactfully) to continue the Clancey and Squire-Sacerdote lines.

Oscar had given tight-lipped and noncommittal nods to a series of candidates' profiles. It couldn't be just any girl, of course, Mrs. Clancey had allowed. They needed someone who was slightly *odd* herself—a widow, or an eccentric, or an old maid with not much to inherit. Not a divorcée, of course, or a woman who had to work for her living. But it had to be someone—not that Mrs. Clancey would have put it in these terms; not consciously—without confidence enough in her own prospects to turn Squire away.

Oscar ate two joyless oysters, sea-salt liquor and lemon tang, and drank half his champagne in one swallow. He checked his watch.

Things had reached a true crisis only in recent weeks, just before their trip to the Shenandoah Valley, with the presentation of Rebecca Van Beek.

Mrs. Van Beek was, by Mrs. Clancey's assessment (Oscar had still not met her; he hoped with any luck never to do so), kind and sweet and amiable. She reportedly had a graceful and feminine beauty, dimmed but not snuffed out by middle age and childbirth. She was unapologetically artistic, cheerfully eccentric in conversation, graceful at leisure. And she was of Old New York, her fortune springing literally from the bedrock of Manhattan, a prize for having gotten here—by their society's extremely selective measure—first.

In short, Mrs. Van Beek's biography seemed engineered specifically to drive Oscar dyspeptic with insecurity.

And then, press-ganged into an introductory visit (chaperoned, of course, by Mrs. Clancey), Squire had met the widow's children. It seemed, from Oscar's warped perspective, that for the last two weeks he had talked of little else.

Squire had enjoyed Mrs. Van Beek's company well enough—as well as he ever enjoyed anyone's, outside the syndicate—but he had *adored* her children. They were a girl and boy, eight and six years old. Perhaps shaped by his own deprivation, Squire had an excellent talent for speaking to children without condescending to them. He had submitted with unflagging patience to a tour of their nursery—games of imagination, whole empires rising and falling over bedspreads; schools of modern art evolving in hours and forgotten just as quickly; pseudoscientific hypotheses that could not be tested for at least another millennium, if ever. And the glowing assessment had been mutual, the Van Beek children not being accustomed to receiving from adults such positive and sustained attention on their own terms.

Squire had not previously expressed the slightest enthusiasm for his mother's attempted matchmaking beyond a regretful insistence that they "had to let her have her fun." (This was more than enough cause for concern, in Oscar's view—after all, though the comparison was awkward to say the least, who knew better than he the power of a Clancey "having fun" to ruin the plans of mere mortals?) But now things were different: on three separate occasions during the trip to Virginia, Squire had spontaneously recounted charming anecdotes about the Van Beek children. Leaving town, he had wanted to buy them souvenirs. (Oscar had pled an unforgiving train schedule and rushed him out of the shop.)

The fact was, of course, that Oscar worried the scales were tipping against him. Staid, old, unimaginative. (How the world shifts around us, or we around the world—fifteen years before, Oscar had been desperate to avoid any hint of unconventionality. Now, he feared being too ordinary to retain his husband.) But the idea had come to him, on the journey home: if it was only the woman's *children* Squire liked, and if he wasn't picky about where they came from—that is, Oscar caught himself, if he didn't share Mrs. Clancey's preoccupation with genealogy . . . well, couldn't an ambiguously intimate uncle be as tempting a role as a stepfather?

A waiter stopped to refill his glass. His reverie broken, Oscar ate three more oysters.

It was not, he would admit, the most thoroughly developed plan. But the vehemence of Vivian's reaction had surprised him. His plans, after all, were *never* thoroughly developed. Usually, it was more in her nature to correct and polish than to condemn.

There were things that Oscar could not alter or deny: his age, his provenance, his personality, his sex. The inescapable and repressive secrecy of their relationship, where Squire might instead enjoy a family made up of Mrs. Van Beek and her children in plain sight. (Shame had not been a significant part of Oscar's life in many years—the respite, he'd found in recent weeks, had only left him out of practice at withstanding its assault.)

There was just the one thing, really, that he had imagined he could counteroffer. And Vivian had said no.

"Oscar!"

Squire swept in, rattling the flatware. Oscar stood to shake his hand— returned the hidden, tickling caress of a fingertip on his palm.

"Nice to see you," Oscar said, with quiet desperation.

"Likewise," Squire said.

He had a talent—Oscar was fairly certain he was not imagining it—for infusing an extrasensory twinkle into certain words.

Squire sat. "Finally," he sighed, surveying the menu. (Much conversational fodder had been made, in their final days in Virginia, of the superiority of New York restaurants. A mean-spirited anticipation at the prospect of returning home after an adventure abroad.)

At Sherry's, Squire always ordered in French. Oscar didn't trust his own accent—instead he used the translations on the menu's facing side, which he suspected were intended only for surreptitious reference by those diners who trusted their accent more than their comprehension. And so they spoke in bilingual alternation: another dozen Buzzard's Bays, please. *Filet de boeuf aux champignons frais.* Canvasback croquettes. And their favorite, a dish of apples baked with raisins, dark rum, and honeyed apricot: *pommes surprises.* Squire had a ridiculous bit of eyebrow choreography that accompanied this particular order, each time. Tonight, it brought a pang to Oscar's chest.

Still, it was difficult to summon worry in the face of Squire himself, so at ease and in such a familiar setting. Sherry's had been their place for years—its leafy palms, its gilded sconces, their regular table in the corner of the dining room with its round-backed chairs and a crisp white tablecloth long enough for them to bump knees (provided they were smart about it). They chatted, with breaks to attend to each course as it arrived—apportioning shared plates, refilling glasses. Chewing. Slowly, Oscar's shoulders loosened. This was their life, he thought. Squire's face was his first sight each morning; Squire's voice the last thing he heard at night. He could have mapped the entire city using only their outings—theaters in which they'd nudged each other awake, collectors' galleries in which they'd discovered unexpected treasures, blocks of icy pavement they'd steadied each other to cross. And after dinner tonight they would go home to the secret passage, impenetrable to others—even to Vivian—that they both knew how to trigger silently in the dark.

They'd spent a decade wearing this track together, Oscar thought. It was not such an easy thing to interrupt.

"And how was your mother?" he asked, as dessert arrived.

Squire sighed. He had not wanted to keep it a secret, exactly, but he knew enough to predict it would not go over well. "She's fine," he said.

"We . . ." He rested his fork and knife on his plate. "We went again to Mrs. Van Beek's."

Oscar rattled his *pomme surprise*. "Oh?" he said. "You didn't—" A mirthless laugh. "That wasn't planned, was it?"

"I think perhaps my mother—"

"Ah!" Oscar set to, sawing his apple in half. "How lovely."

Under the table, Squire swung his knee until it bumped against Oscar's.

Oscar sighed, an abortive eye roll. Forked a mouthful of steaming fruit, blinking stoic through the pain as it scalded the roof of his mouth.

Squire watched him, eyebrows raised.

Oscar swallowed, stubbornly.

(All couples are at least partially accustomed to such subverbal conversations. Some, of social necessity, are more fluent than others.)

"How was it?" Oscar asked finally, inhaling cool air across his injury.

Squire smiled. "Honestly?"

"Yes," Oscar said, without confidence.

"*Fascinating.*" This was one of Squire's favorite benefits of marriage, even more so after marinating in it for a decade: a relationship in which his own enthusiasm was always relevant. (And in Oscar's defense, his distaste for this subject was an outlier.) "We hadn't seen them last month," Squire said, "but Mrs. Van Beek paints *frescoes*."

"Mm!" Oscar said.

"Right in her house," Squire said. "Right on the *walls!*"

Oscar need not have shriveled at the awe in his husband's voice. Though Squire would have been politely admiring of Rebecca Van Beek's frescoes (which were not particularly original or well done) as a learned social grace, he was *fixated* on them only as they affected his own understanding of the wider world. It was the same approving envy that had once affected Squire in trying to parse the sharp disparity between the public receptions of his own respective interests in candles and in sewer infrastructure: Why had his adolescent annotation of his mother's hummingbird fire screen been received as a federal crime, when Mrs. Van Beek was allowed to cover her walls with barely competent paintings of pastoral scenes, and show them off to visitors as though they were at the Metropolitan Museum?

The answer, of course, was simply that Rebecca Van Beek owned her own walls and had no disapproving guardians to convince before doing as she pleased. If Squire had examined his own modern situation, as an independent man of forty-one, he might have noticed similar developments. (Was taking Oscar to bed in Shenandoah, leaving Vivian to sign business correspondence in his name, not a rather more daring lifestyle than painting a Hudson Valley landscape on a piece of library paneling?)

If the amateur decoration of fire screens had truly been Squire's long-frustrated life's passion, nothing and no one would have stopped him now from procuring ten such screens and customizing them to his heart's content. But we are all of us perpetually caught, aren't we, in the grip of our first childhood injustices. Volcanoes growing in layers around the same fissures to our cores; caverns ever widening the same hollow spaces.

"She said she wants to paint her drawing-room ceiling next," Squire said now, "but she can't work out the proportions of the"—he craned up, studying the ornamental plaster design of Sherry's ceiling; Oscar watched his throat move as he swallowed—"of the people."

"Well," Oscar said. "What an interesting idea." He spoke with some difficulty, through a thickening haze: Rebecca Van Beek was *fascinating, artistic, unconventional*. She wanted to paint *people* on the *ceiling*.

"Really," Squire said. "I wish you'd—"

"*Would* you marry her?" Oscar asked abruptly, the question escaping him like a cat through a window. Belatedly, he checked their surroundings for eavesdroppers. (Though what, he thought bitterly, was he afraid of? It was a *perfectly normal* question.)

Squire's face could, at times, even now, be difficult for Oscar to read. Was he disgusted? Was he struggling to choose the right words to break his heart?

In fact, Squire was negotiating a confusing rhetorical thicket at the heart of Oscar's distress, one at which our more observant readers may already have arrived independently. ". . . *You're* married," he finally said, his tone somewhere between query and accusation.

"Don't change the subject," Oscar hissed.

Some lovers' quarrels end not in détente or disaster but in a kind of spontaneous alchemical puff of smoke, with one or both parties reaching a sudden awareness of their own ridiculousness. This was characteristic of many of Oscar and Squire's disagreements, though the roles were variable: one man spinning his wheels; the other thrusting a stick in the spokes; a statement of such plain stupidity that the argument could only collapse, unresolved yet dissipated.

Still: "It *is* different," Oscar insisted, when their laughter had subsided. By which he meant, Vivian was different. They *knew* Vivian.

If it had been pointed out to him that Rebecca Van Beek was a person in her own right, one who might in time also become *known,* Oscar would only have vehemently hoped not. But in truth, traitorous compassion urged him to concede: If Squire truly wanted a family, a daylight marriage, *couldn't* Oscar let him go, at least on the surface? Let him live his own version of the doubled fiction Oscar enjoyed, and let them continue on in the margins?

In *which* margins, quavered another, more selfish voice. Married men with children did not spend nights in one another's townhouses! They would have to see each other *at work*! Panic resumed its tingling creep across the back of Oscar's skull: he would be back to expressing himself clandestinely via advertisements for soap flakes, while Squire splashed frescoes across Rebecca Van Beek's mansion and taught her children to explore caves and collect snuffboxes and play peculiar instruments. Squire's abrupt laugh echoing in someone else's house. Squire's correspondence on the organization of the periodic table obscuring someone else's breakfast table; Squire's games of gin rummy in someone else's sitting room. Squire's somnolent exhalations on someone else's pillow.

Across the table Squire himself shrugged, forfeiting the point. Vivian *was* different. His *pomme surprise* was getting cold.

As reassurances went, it left something to be desired. And besides, the mention of Vivian had raised another guilty anxiety.

At times Oscar felt a particular squeeze of pressure as the hinge of their arrangement—whereas Squire and Vivian, he imagined, had only to pursue their separate lives and be polite to one another at the breakfast table, Oscar was a mechanism that might fail in the performance of its function. Might come apart and derail the entire syndicate. (Of course it was not such a simple arrangement as that, on any level. Squire and Vivian were partners, too—appreciative of each other's brilliance; frustrated by each other's flaws; accustomed to their many shared routines. But Oscar had at this point half a century's obsessive practice at imagining himself solely responsible for the maintenance, or failure, of complex systems. He was still, at his core, the boy Grandmother Hester had blamed for unseasonable weather.) "I believe I upset her," he confessed, now. "Last night."

Squire drew back. "Vivian?"

They were not accustomed to upsetting Vivian. Annoying her, yes, frequently—she did not take any great pains to hide it. Without hesitation or regret she would deny their requests, turn down their invitations, run her pen through their admittedly indifferent business plans. (As Vivian's résumé in Personal Care had grown longer, and Squire and Oscar's shared personal life more fulfilling, the men's interest in the day-to-day running of C&S had waned almost entirely.) She might dodge their calls and messages, or even disappear without notice for several days at a time, living between the office and the pied-à-terre at which she entertained her ladies. But one could not, in any of these regular situations, describe Vivian as "upset."

"What happened?" Squire asked. A natural enough question; an inevitable one, even.

"I—" Oscar stopped. Damn him, he thought. He'd strolled into it like a tree branch. "Never mind."

But Squire was still constitutionally incapable of dropping a question that had caught his interest, and Oscar's face—he could feel it—was turning telltale pink.

If it had to happen, he thought, perhaps it was better here than at home. (He checked more thoroughly, this time, for passersby.) Here, Oscar thought, it could be an embarrassing story that had happened to someone else, an imaginary person who happened to look just like him, rather than a confession of a failure of their own future. "I asked her," Oscar said with difficulty, "whether she, whether we might . . ."

Here he stalled long enough that Squire returned to his dinner. A decade of partnership with Oscar Schmidt had taught him a certain surface-level patience.

"Have a child," Oscar finished finally.

Squire choked, aspirating champagne.

"For us," Oscar said in a low voice. An addendum vague to the point of meaninglessness to any eavesdroppers, but of adamantine importance to those at the table.

When Squire subdued the last of his cough, his expression took on a dismayed delight. And thus Oscar was made conscious of his own wish: that Squire might have expressed a laughing indifference to this notion; might have teased him for indulging his anxiety that Mrs. Van Beek and her children were any temptation whatsoever; might have reassured him that a conventional life of open doors and open embraces held no interest for him, and Squire's only ambition was for him and Oscar to continue as they had been, for the rest of their lives.

All these secret hopes revealed themselves to Oscar only in the moment of their disappointment.

"*Really?*" Squire said. He knew how much the idea of change—any change—frightened Oscar. He knew the enormous significance of such a gesture on his part, a voluntary attempt to step into the infinite unknown from a man too scared to order from the French side of the menu. Squire ached for a public mode of expression for his appreciation of such bravery. Settled, finally, for raising his glass and bumping Oscar's knee again under the table. "I mean—*really?*"

"Yes," Oscar said. He submitted dutifully to the toast. "Well. But—no."

Squire recalled himself. "She didn't like the idea?"

This much, at least, was not unusual—nor even as disappointing as it might have been, in earlier days when their syndicate had been less experienced. Their arrangement's success, after all, depended on compromise. And though the wider world still taught both men chauvinism (and rewarded them for it), to live with Vivian was to cultivate a counterbalancing daily practice in masculine humility. In short, Oscar and Squire were more proficient than many of their peers at being told no.

"It was more than that, though," Oscar said. "She was . . . offended, I think. Hurt."

In truth, he hadn't seen that look in her eyes since their trip to Utica, shortly before their marriage. It had been the kind of wounded fear that explained a lifetime's efforts to escape it. It was not a feeling that Oscar had thought himself capable of inspiring.

"I shouldn't have asked," he said.

"She'll be alright," Squire said, if with some uneasiness. "It's . . . it's a perfectly natural question."

They sat for a moment in discomfited silence. It was an unsettling idea: that they had the power to wound Vivian, even (perhaps especially) accidentally. Oscar and Squire were not precisely accustomed to thinking of Vivian as a human being, with human weaknesses. She was more of a geological formation, a scientific law. A demigod. Not without feelings, certainly, but too powerful to ever be hurt by the likes of *them*. Never mercurial or sensitive. There was a subtle sense, now, clouding the atmosphere at Sherry's, that something in the order of the universe had slipped.

"Well," Squire said, signaling for the bill. "*I'm* glad you asked."

Oscar, mistaking pride for resignation, forced himself to smile.

THREE

Somewhat contrary to her husbands' ultimately solipsistic concerns about their own abilities to hurt her feelings, as summer waned, Vivian in fact had too much else on her plate to pay attention to their domestic dramas. From time to time, usually nearing sleep or with her hands full of something (or someone) else, she would remember that she needed to defuse the situation with Squire's mother and the young widow. Tomorrow, she continually reminded herself. Or else the day after.

But there was always something more urgent, more important, a real fire with real consequences that had to be put out. (In one case this was nearly literal, a chemical spill on the factory floor that might have ended in disaster had it not been for Elias's well-drilled response.) Then there was a silly yet sensitive bit of business with a group of labor organizers, who held a demonstration outside the C&S offices in protest of the successful outmaneuvering of the recently fired Joe Green and his union cards.

The organizers themselves Vivian might have handled, dispatching Elias as her avatar to the picket line—they were few, tired, hollow-eyed behind their homespun signs. She might even have made converts of them, had them mixing lye or pressing logos on her floor, advising their brothers in the movement that low wages were better than none.

But, through what seemed to Vivian to be a secret network of shiftless complaint, the demonstration transmuted into a general protest of all industry—full of anarchists and agrarian radicals, people with little in common beyond an obsession with turning Manhattan into (so she complained to Elias) something completely other than it was: Kansas or Sweden or the Moon. C&S—with its two large smokestacks, its brick facade, its broad freight lot on the waterfront—was a picturesque backdrop for any rant against success and industry.

In the end, the police broke up the rally without incident. But still, Vivian could hardly have ducked out in the middle of the day to pay a call on a grand dame of the nineties to discuss her son's marital prospects.

And there was this: Vivian and Squire played gin rummy in their shared sitting room most evenings after dinner (and after Oscar had either formally retired or fallen asleep in his armchair, his latest collector's catalog open on his chest). During these games Vivian would update Squire on business at the office, particularly any correspondence she had signed his name to. But for the most part, she let him run the conversation. Over the years she had absorbed a veritable encyclopedia of facts, and abridged versions of L. Frank Baum's entire oeuvre. She had received with a reserved but attentive sympathy many reports of Squire's visits with his mother—the cocktail of guilt and love and wounding habit they were continually remixing and passing back and forth for taste-testing, developing the recipe. Vivian had offered, once between hands, to help him invent an excuse to avoid Mrs. Clancey's visiting hours. Some urgent project at the office; a new account that couldn't do without him. "Oh, don't worry," he'd said, counting up his deadwood. "I'm elastic."

He was a middling player, but he shuffled with panache.

During recent installments of this standing card game Vivian had, yes, heard about the charms of the Van Beek children, and about their mother's fascinating frescoes. (She had interjected to make it clear their shared rooms were off-limits for redecorating.)

But all these subjects combined, in Vivian's estimation, would hardly have balanced the scale against Squire's mentions of Oscar. Oscar's reaction to every book or museum exhibit or amusingly proportioned dog they'd encountered that day; every allegedly fascinating thing that Oscar had done or said or ordered at a cafeteria. And, tellingly, it was only when

Squire spoke on the subject of his husband that he lost the ability to concentrate on the game in front of him—turns missed, suits mixed, cards drawn from the discard pile. The same thoroughly bewildered deck shuffled and reshuffled in expert but absent-minded hands, Squire turning to gaze moonily as Oscar muttered in his sleep and stained the upholstery with his hair oil.

In short, in Vivian's view, Mrs. Clancey was trying to squeeze blood from a stone. It would be only humane to stop her, before it ended in embarrassment and bruised knuckles—but Vivian did not see any real stakes to the plot. Soon enough it would be time for Mrs. Clancey to plan her Christmas party, and all this nonsense would fall by the wayside.

And besides, Vivian had amorous distractions of her own.

Alongside the perpetual hunt for new conquests, and the perpetually frustrated half-hope that she might meet someone compelling yet unconquerable (this being the closest Vivian came to the conscious experience of loneliness), there was in the early autumn of 1915 a rare—even an unprecedented—whisper from Vivian's romantic past: Sofia Bianchi was in America.

Sofia would give a series of eight concerts in September, in Los Angeles, in a grand old hall with a gilded ceiling. The kind of venue she might only have dreamed of filling, in the old days. In part the difference was that her career had risen, especially in those first years after she and Vivian had parted ways—but also, fashions had changed. Those few cavernous theaters that had not converted to install projection booths, declining to welcome at least the hybrid possibility of screening movies between live shows, were easier now to book. Indeed, the notices of Sofia's recent concerts in Europe and Canada—Vivian had read them all—had included effusive but almost eulogizing praise of her status as a one-time light of a waning age, a stage star still stubbornly twinkling in the face of cinema's dawn.

But these same pieces reviewed Sofia's latest performances with (in Vivian's admittedly biased interpretation) almost titillating adulation. Her graceful spine unbent, her throaty voice seeming to resonate anew with all the poignancy of the eras (both personal and geopolitical) that had intervened since last she had graced American soil.

Several of Manhattan's cultural reporters, their egos bruised, speculated that Miss Bianchi had bypassed New York in favor of a longer residency on the West Coast as part of a strategic move, to take advantage of the cultural revolution. An attempt at a professional sensory transition, as it were—from sound to image, chanteuse to screen actress.

Vivian, in a simultaneous act of self-congratulation and self-torment, had a different explanation for Sofia's refusal to alight in New York.

The two women had not spoken since 1904. Vivian did not regret this, of course; not precisely. She had needed to be on her own in order to build her empire—acquiring Oscar, then Squire, then the business and everything since. With Sofia, she would have remained an audience, a good luck charm. A hanger-on. Perpetually uneasy, dependent not just on her own charms but on another person's capricious taste for them.

To stay with Sofia, Vivian reminded herself, would have been to deny her own ambitions. To cede control. (So distasteful was the notion today, she was very nearly successful in forgetting that it had been Sofia, not Vivian herself, who had ended their association.)

Still, despite Vivian's determined satisfaction with her life and her choices, despite her pride in the trail she had blazed to her current summit, she could not help but compare those days of luxurious and self-sharpening companionship favorably against her current revolving carousel of paramours—these new girls with their high demands yet modest ambitions; their bland acquiescence to Vivian's terms (even when unfavorable); their absolute failure to surprise her.

In fact, of course, the young women Vivian wooed were accomplished, and ambitious, and surprising. They did challenge her, often openly. (Already in these pages we have seen it done.) The fact of the matter was simply that Vivian, without observing the change in herself, had amassed sufficient power and resources to ignore such challenges without facing measurable consequences or disappointment.

Do we celebrate this milestone, or mourn it? What is the ideal allotment of success, of power, for an individual human being? How does one measure the moment such an upper limit has been reached, and arrest the process?

Vivian was a reasonable person. She prided herself on it, even considered it the single major point of difference between herself and the rest of the world. Still, it was difficult to keep herself from reveries of a return to past glory. The years falling away as she knocked, once more, on Sofia's dressing-room door. Played a few familiar yet thrilling notes on a piano still miraculously in tune. (Vivian's youth, it must be remembered, had been austere. Nostalgia is all the more potent an intoxicant for those who rarely have the opportunity to indulge.)

Vivian suspected that Sofia had, in planning her American tour, conducted a kind of parallel sidelong inquiry into Vivian's own progress since their parting. Had found her, as she was on paper, Mrs. Oscar Schmidt—eleven years married to a Personal Care magnate; tradition-mired mistress of a brownstone mausoleum. (Might Sofia even remember Oscar, from her glimpse of him across the casino floor all those years ago? Drunk, vamping, at moments nearly tearful in his distress—at a distance, he might have been taken for a lothario. An audacious hand on Vivian's arm, stumbling against her as he spoke.)

In short, Vivian suspected that her cover was too impenetrable. That Sofia had, in a gallant and tragic act of self-denial, left her the island of Manhattan in an imagined divorce. Exiled herself to California in search of consolation, both professional and personal.

AS LUCK WOULD have it, Vivian had at her disposal the tools to correct this misunderstanding.

Parnacott Productions, the independent studio that Vivian had hired to film C&S's industrial short, had made much during the contract bidding process of its ability to complete all principal photography on location in New York. Parnacott's satellite facility in Queens, it stressed, was as well equipped as any Hollywood stage. The dynamic footage of the factory floor and offices could be captured by the same crew that would film the narrative scenes. It made excellent financial and logistical sense, compared with the alternative.

Now, Vivian affected to change her mind. She did not, she decided, trust the Parnacott facilities in Queens. She wanted the best. The shots of the factory, of course, would have to be filmed on location. But for the storyline, the narrative sections, she wanted Hollywood. She wanted any outdoor sequences lit by a summer sunlight currently out of season on the East Coast. She wanted experienced studio actors.

Most important, she wanted to supervise the shoot. Not as the director, of course—more a corporate consultant. Someone with the authority to answer questions about C&S's products and marketing philosophy immediately on set, and so avoid any production delays.

The crux of it was, she stressed, that she needed to be in Los Angeles in September.

Elias Knox, who was familiar with both Vivian's characteristic priorities and the terms of the film studio's contract, had some concerns about the sudden change of plan. But—and this, of course, was chief among his assets in Vivian's view—he was not confident enough to voice them.

Besides, in her absence he would have acting control of the day-to-day business. It was a heady distraction.

There were other, equally rare delegations of responsibility. Vivian left Oscar and Squire in charge of the house, and of Mrs. Clancey. She instructed them to do their best, if Elias had any questions about the administration of C&S's affairs. To call or cable her only if absolutely necessary—but not, by the same token, to overestimate their own faculties.

The men were more confident than they might have been, having just finished filming their footage for the industrial short. It had been a kind of cross-dressing performance: businessman impersonators. They'd sat behind their desks in their respective offices, pretending to know where things were; inspected the soap cutters and candle molds on the factory floor, as if this were an oft-repeated formality and not in many respects a genuinely novel tour; conferred nonsensically over a sheet of blank paper, a visibly uncomfortable Elias—by far the most knowledgeable industry man, but the worst performer—between them.

Vivian gave everyone their assignments and went to California.

The short would take only two days to film, barring disaster. Traveling so far for such a brief responsibility put Vivian in a decadent mood already, even if the trip was—nominally—on business. She and Sofia, Vivian mused on the train, could toast each other on these grounds: two successful women, in California on business. (And the happy discovery of something more, after hours.)

She arrived in town on the morning of Sofia's first show in the concert series, and a day before filming was scheduled—rescheduled, more precisely—to begin. Not knowing where Sofia was staying in town, she sent a note via messenger to the concert hall. The return address was a challenge—she settled on "Vivian Schmidt (Lesperance)," taking only partial satisfaction in the parenthetical past. She was appropriately cryptic, of course, both for reputational safety and for self-respect. She claimed to have just seen a notice about Sofia's show; to be happy to discover a dear old friend in town; to hope there would be time to visit and acquaint each other with the events of the years since their last meeting. (This was an investment in the future—Vivian had no expectation of being able to travel from such feigned serendipity to Sofia's dressing room in a single day. She was well accustomed, as we have already seen, to patience on the hunt.)

Her own hotel concierge reported that her message had been delivered successfully into the hands of a theater attendant, who had in turn promised to pass it along to "Miss Bianchi's people." Less direct than Vivian would have liked, but she had faith that if her name—or even her penmanship—could only make it within reach of Sofia's glance, all subsequent hurdles would fall.

She would have plenty to do, she thought, while she waited. There was, after all, a picture to make.

THE FIRST DAY on set at Parnacott Productions was like stepping through the looking glass. Vivian was startled—in some ways happily so—to learn by shocking contrast how comfortable she had become in the rhythms of both New York industry in general and Personal Care in particular. They made sense to her: soap, candles, and perfume had, in some form, been manufactured and sold since antiquity; Manhattan had been a center of international trade since what Vivian regarded as the beginning of its existence. There was, for her, an intuitive structure to these worlds, time-honored and perfected over centuries. (A common error: to transpose our own personal comfort into a sense of objective "correctness," even safety.)

In Hollywood, on the other hand, Vivian was witnessing the violent birth of a new industry. Here capitalism and art were more visibly entangled, both red in tooth and claw. Even in the peripheral subgenre of the industrial short, chaos reigned on set by default. There was little administrative oversight—no sign whatsoever of the eponymous Mr. Parnacott. The day's notional shooting schedule quickly became a rough guideline, and then a useless joke.

And yet progress was not only possible but reliably made—and through the alarming collaborative effort of dozens of people, milling through one cavernous room. (Had Vivian expected an executive suite, a gallery from which she and the director would watch the action behind protective glass? It appeared, judging by her alarm at the chaos jostling her on all sides, that she had.)

The director seemed to see himself as the star of something in his own right—a stocky man with the treble first-name moniker of Robert Thomas Wallace, he sat in a canvas-backed chair emblazoned with all three names (and never answered to less than two, though as a time-saver he suffered the abbreviation R. T.). He wore jodhpurs and spoke stubbornly into a bullhorn that didn't seem strictly necessary, given the modest size of the stage.

An iron fist and a male ego: these elements, at least, Vivian understood, even if R. T. Wallace was rather shockingly willing to rub elbows with his lowest-level employees—and to be seen puzzling out the raw, unflattering work of crisis management, shouting his unfiltered thoughts into his bullhorn.

"Don't light the candles yet, you maniacs," he was exclaiming when Vivian arrived on set. "We've got all the laundry to shoot first. I've still got breakfast in my teeth. You want wax puddles on camera?"

Turning at his assistant's tap on his shoulder, he seemed about to pose this question to Vivian—including her as one of "you maniacs"—or else to order her to fetch another box of candles. (Still a niche product for C&S but a reliable seller, available in four sizes and six scent profiles.)

"This is Mrs. Schmidt, R. T.," said the assistant director. "From the company."

"Thank God," R. T. said, without ceremony. "Now, how new do you want the candles to look?" He held a flat palm at chest height, raised and lowered it demonstratively. "Because if this is supposed to be, say, something this couple does every night, not a fresh set of tapers, we can get one of the kids working on burnin' 'em down for ya."

"Well, I . . . whatever you'd—" Vivian began, before catching herself. These were the questions she was here to answer. This was her chance to establish authority. "Habitual, but novel," she said—quantifying it with her finger and thumb, held about an inch apart. "If you can manage it."

It was unsettling, at first, to be asked so openly for direction—and given the opportunity to undermine R. T.'s shouted order of moments before. (In front of everyone!) But then Vivian began to notice: for the first time in her life, she was not the only woman in "the office." Mixed in among the teeming men on set were secretaries and script girls, hair-dressers and cosmeticians, even a matronly wrangler for the child actors.

Vivian did not particularly enjoy this sign of progress. Her hackles raised in imagined competition, despite her acknowledged (if purchased) authority in the room. And, paradoxically but simultaneously, it was depressing to watch all these professional women interrupt themselves midtask to obey the barked commands of R. T. Wallace's bullhorn. At C&S Vivian may have been singular and invisible, but she bowed to no one.

Most prominent of all these women—quite literally spotlit when Vivian arrived, during a lighting test—was the star of the short: Anna-belle Trask, an actress who took even this part as seriously as Shakespeare, nurturing as she did the hope to make it into "real" pictures. Runaway success was an unlikely prospect, unfortunately—Annabelle had neither the face for melodrama, nor the timing for comedy, nor the endurance to battle or bribe the men who kept the gates to either field. But she was talented enough, and uncomplaining, and always hit her marks—and not every girl who wanted to be "in pictures" would stoop to do industrial shorts.

As with so many innovations in art and technology, it had taken barely a heartbeat for advertising to bridle the nascent medium of cinema. Spon-sored one- and two-reel film shorts were by this point increasingly commonplace, played in movie theaters alongside cartoons, newsreels, comedies, and full-length epics. Vivian had seen enough to grasp their import: the chance to tell a story, ideally indistinguishable to the viewer from the narrative films they'd paid to see, that would convincingly "educate" them on the usefulness and thrift of a certain company's products.

The C&S short, tentatively titled "A Busy Day," would in twelve condensed minutes follow a hectic young family from sunup to sundown, rarely without at least one Clancey & Schmidt product on-screen. Interstitial cards, Vivian had made clear, should be as few and simple as possible. If she wanted the audience to read about her products, she could have taken out a magazine ad and saved herself the expense.

The short would open with a morning toilette—Mr. Smith washing with C&S toilet soap, shaving with C&S aftershave, brushing with C&S tooth powder. Mrs. Smith would be mysteriously fully made up and ready for the day without any of these ablutions, but the moviegoer would see her dabbing scent—Mystic Zephyr, of course—onto her pulse points. A deep, satisfied inhale; an exhale with a smile. A close-up shot of the bottle.

Next, the kitchen: dish soap, borax, baking soda. The Smiths would have a maid, but Mrs. Smith would work ambiguously alongside her—an attempt to appeal to as many families as possible. (C&S products were a luxury line for some, but Vivian hoped to convince thrifty housewives—or even those who simply harbored aspirations beyond their budgets—that they deserved the extravagance.)

The viewer would meet the Smith children, Betty and Jimmy. Jimmy would trip carrying his plate to the dinner table, spilling gravy down his shirtfront—straight into the wash, with C&S Laundry Soap! While the maid tackled this chore (the ruined shirt swapped out for a fresh one when the camera wasn't looking), the audience would watch Mrs. Smith preparing the children for bed. Bath soap on the edge of the sink; talcum powder shaken onto cheerfully outstretched limbs. Mrs. Smith would embrace her children, burying her nose in their fragrant hair.

An interlude, the camera close on Mrs. Smith's writing table as she composed a letter: *Dear Mother, Jimmy and Betty are well. Thank you for sending us the package of household conveniences and cosmetics from Clancey & Schmidt. We owe them a great deal.* The inherent satisfaction of watching the words spool out in a confident hand.

Finally, Mr. Smith would reappear at the end of (it would be implied) a long workday. Mrs. Smith, or perhaps the maid, would have dinner on the table—and C&S scented tapers burning. Again, it would be a challenge to render scent via movie screen. Vivian had scripted another exaggerated inhale, a visibly satisfied exhale. "Lavender," Mrs. Smith would say, captioned by a title card. (It was the most popular.) The narrative section would end on another card: *Clancey and Schmidt household essentials assist us in our labor and add charm to our relaxation.* And a third: *But how do these modern miracles reach Mr. Smith's door?*

From there—for the mechanically minded, those who cringed to spend money on cosmetics, but might be convinced if they knew that hydraulic presses and iron boiling kettles had been involved—the short would conclude with the filmed tour of the factory, the reassuring masculine fiction of Squire and Oscar at the helm.

In the treatment Vivian had requested that they put Mrs. Smith— Annabelle the actress—in a day dress, something a few shades too formal for her character's supposed activities of homemaking, cooking for her husband, and mothering two mischievous children. (Aspiration, after all, was the atmosphere of the piece. They were there to cultivate the sensation that the viewer's life could—even *should*—be elevated, to keep pace with her imagined peers'.) It was disconcerting, now, greeting Annabelle on set: shaking hands and trading pleasantries with a young woman more or less created by mail order to Vivian's specifications. As an experiment, Vivian requested a darker shade of lipstick. Annabelle disappeared for five minutes, and returned with her smile repainted.

It was a restabilizing comfort to exercise some power—and undeniably exhilarating, given the context. But Vivian trusted her instincts, even when they portended disappointment: there were no doubled meanings in Annabelle's glance, in her handshake, in her polite conversation. It was no surprise, a few minutes later, to hear her mention a fiancé in glowing tones.

The day did, however, hold other surprises.

PERHAPS IT WAS the unfamiliar and uncanny atmosphere; the heat and light and recycled air; the windowless stage echoing with bullhorn commands; the set, eerily familiar (and Vivian might in fact have seen it before, in a dozen other shorts produced by Parnacott): a false modest single-family home, the roof and front wall ripped away, all decor ending abruptly just outside the camera's frame. Perhaps it was the perpetually dangling thought of Sofia, somewhere in Los Angeles, possibly even now finally reading yesterday's letter. (There had been no answer, yet. As of this morning.)

Or perhaps Vivian had been right to resist Elias Knox's persistent suggestions that C&S move its base of operations to New Jersey—perhaps she really did draw some kind of arcane strength from the island of Manhattan, and in traveling to California she had broken a protective spell.

Whatever its causes, the uneasy feeling with which Vivian began the day only grew as it wore on. R. T.'s manner toward her, during setups and between takes, became harder and harder to parse—half deferential, half brusque. Was she his superior, or his subordinate? It frustrated her, after ten years at the helm of a thriving company, to doubt the answer. The feeling curdled under the hot lights.

Worse, the short itself began to turn on her—her own film treatment taking on a leering and upsetting aspect even as she watched. In take after take a perfectly made-up Mrs. Smith wished a freshly shaved Mr. Smith a good day at the office. Over and over again the Kewpie-doll children were smilingly forgiven for spilling their dinner, dusted with talcum powder and kissed goodnight. The best-selling lavender-scented candles burned down to stubs (R. T., it transpired, had been right to be concerned) as the loving couple greeted each other across an infinite series of dinner tables. Throughout the shoot, the actors' ad-libs—close enough to pass the test of any lip-readers in the audience, but ultimately just a pantomime of conversation—looped back on themselves nonsensically. "Isn't that lovely?" "Don't you smell nice?" "Have a pleasant day." "Don't worry, darling." "Let me help." "Here, use this." "There you are." "Isn't this delicious?"

Vivian watched this quintessential happy family of her own design, playacting according to her explicit directions, and didn't recognize a thing. Had she really written this? Beyond alien, it felt almost *mocking*—and Vivian, marooned across the country from everything she had built to counterargue and drown out such conventional and treacly expectations, found herself fighting to calm a racing heart. Resentment bloomed toward her own parents, who would never have shown her the tender care Vivian had scripted here—and, now, for eluding blame in an escape into senility that Vivian had tried but failed not to take personally. Watching the fictional Smith children receive their umpteenth good-night kisses, Vivian felt a spike of annoyance at her own younger self, for failing to be the kind of child who might have inspired better treatment. During the dinner scene she even found a sneer for Squire and Oscar, for demonstrating that there *was* such a thing as a matched suit, lifelong doe-eyed adoration, endlessly repeated declarations of love across endlessly repeated dinner tables.

To withstand all this self-inflicted offense, Vivian found herself drifting, daydreaming of the moment they would wrap for the day, when she would return to the hotel and find an answering note from Sofia. (She would recognize at once that sweetly spidery script, an anomalous calling card in such a confident woman.) Tucked into the envelope would be a ticket to tonight's show, or directions to a backstage entrance so that Vivian might watch from the wings. And then a tour of whatever nightlife Los Angeles had to offer—fecund wherever New York was seamy, Vivian imagined; bright wherever it was dusky; everywhere sunbaked palms rustling, denying the concept of autumn. Eventually: a nightcap. (Though it was over a decade since she had called upon the skill, Vivian still remembered how to mix a Brandy Crusta to Sofia's personal specifications.) They might retire to Sofia's hotel—Vivian imagined her familiar scent and wardrobe and luggage set, the same watered silk and seed pearls, the same arrangements of lilies (provided, Vivian supposed, they grew in California) that Sofia had always ordered to her suite at the Fifth Avenue Hotel. They would turn back the clock to the dawn of the century, let the years melt away, fall into the easy muscle memory of their youthful association.

Or perhaps, this time—how life had blossomed! How she had grown since her days as audience, as ornament, as good luck charm!—perhaps this time they would use Vivian's own suite instead.

Vivian knew this kind of anticipation was childish. But again and again throughout that first and deeply draining day on set, watching her own contrived scenes and characters take inexplicable arms against her, she returned to the refuge.

Another contrived scene, perhaps; another fiction.

There are some forms of comfort that intoxicate us and then turn traitor, having only robbed us of our resilience. This rare self-indulgence—or, perhaps more precisely, this rare *manifestation* of self-indulgence—left Vivian ill-prepared for the eventual realities of her evening.

THERE WAS NO message waiting for her at the hotel. The concierge double-checked at her request. (He was a seasoned professional—if he noted the desperate tenor to Vivian's voice as she asked again, or her nerveless fingers trembling on the countertop, he betrayed his awareness neither in pity nor in scorn.)

Alone in her room, Vivian weighed her options. She would not be a stage-door Johnny, she decided. She would not attend the concert uninvited, wait in line at the box office and purchase the right to ogle her onetime lover from the audience, rubbing elbows with strangers who had done the same. She would retain her self-respect.

But oh, the ache! The unbearable injustice of it all, the anger at whatever peon—whether in the theater's employ or in Sofia's—had failed to deliver Vivian's message in time! And she with only one day remaining that would excuse her presence in Los Angeles, gild her with the intriguing glamour of corporate and cinematic success. In two days' time, Vivian thought, the shoot would end. And with the suddenness of Cinderella's midnight, she would become a hanger-on. A pathetic castoff who had stalked Sofia to the other side of the country.

So, she thought, bridling herself. It would have to be tomorrow. That was all.

Had the events of the day left Vivian less dizzy and unbalanced; had she spent less time imagining every baroque and lascivious detail of a very different evening, one she now found herself cheated of by cold and capricious reality; had she been at home, in New York, in the innermost chamber of the bedroom suite she had personally refurbished from the walls in over the slow span of years, able to look about herself and recognize more than the contents of her disemboweled suitcases; had Oscar and Squire been with her, to lose happily to her at gin rummy and chat with pathetic domesticity about the quotidian details of the day and generally to annoy her to welcome, familiar distraction; had she been calm enough to remember she had not eaten since her cold luncheon at the studio, become conscious of her ravenous appetite and descended to the hotel restaurant before it closed—perhaps, in any of these different worlds, Vivian would have acted differently.

As it was, she wrote another letter.

In this second message Vivian was rather more open with Sofia—about her hopes for a reunion, and about her memories of the past. That imagined third party who had read her first note over her shoulder as she composed it, moving her to restrict herself to only the most oblique references to her and Sofia's relationship, was no longer on duty. She reminisced about favorite Village haunts, about idiosyncrasies in the hotel rooms in which they had cohabitated—living lightly, traveling often in a nomadic tour of summer-home salons. Their suite's temperamental steam heat and inconsistent turndown service. She recalled the night they met, in the first unformed and cacophonous hours of a new century. "The Sidewalks of New York"; Sofia's drunk accompanist slipping off the end of the piano bench to make room for Vivian. *Viva*, she interjected in closing, stamping her signature with a lipstick kiss.

Such radical openness was a strange tactic, perhaps, given Vivian's confidence that her first and more subtly encoded message had not made it into Sofia's hands at all. Why risk greater vulnerability, when simple repetition might have served as effectively? It was not like her—not like the version of her we have come to know. But the reasons behind Sofia's answering silence had paled in importance, for Vivian, beside the urgency of making herself as clear as possible, as quickly as possible.

She caught the concierge just in time. She paid extra, tipped extravagantly—a transaction that blurred the line between gratuity and bribe—for delivery at once, that very evening.

This was the method, Vivian thought: to intercept Sofia at the concert hall, rather than letting her message sink beneath a drift of lesser correspondence on some dressing-room side table. "See to it"—she said this as clearly as she could, speaking slowly to keep her voice from shaking—"that this ends in Miss Bianchi's hands."

A bicycle messenger was dispatched. That was, Vivian thought, as it should be. There was almost a kind of grand romance to the thought of a gangly adolescent pedaling furiously across town with Vivian's letter buttoned into his shirt, thrilling with the thought of where he might spend the quadrupled wage the errand was earning him.

Yes, Vivian thought. This was a message that should be delivered in such an attitude of spontaneous euphoria.

Sofia would be performing, when it arrived. There was, after all, work to be done—diadems settled onto waves of auburn hair, ballads crooned over swelling string crescendos; torches hoisted high in honor of an infinite songbook full of bygone loves. Applause. Encore.

But then—as she had so many times before, so many years ago—Sofia would return to her dressing room and find Vivian waiting for her, after a fashion: a bicycle messenger, green behind the ears, heart still racing and with a sweat-limp declaration of feeling in hand. Viva!

This was the vision that Vivian rode to oblivion that night. When she woke, it was to a different world entirely—as if Earth had shifted its orbit beneath her as she slept.

REGRET, OF COURSE, was thick and copper-tasting on her tongue. Her stomach was hollowed by the kind of spine-crimping hunger she hadn't felt since the nineteenth century. Breakfast arrived with an apologetic note from the concierge: the messenger last night had been denied entrance to the concert hall, on management's suspicion that he was simply angling for a free show. But he had given Mrs. Schmidt's name—the concierge, Vivian saw with fresh embarrassment, had even copied out her winking "(Lesperance)"—and been assured that Miss Bianchi's staff would deliver her message.

It had been a mistake, she saw now. A foolish act. But there was no way to undo it. She could only move forward: return to the studio stage for a second day of obscure torture, all the more painful on nerves still ragged and frayed from yesterday's trial; await Sofia's answer, or her answering silence; decide, no matter what transpired, whether to swallow her pride and attend tonight's concert before she fled back to the East Coast.

Vivian wolfed her food grimly, fueling herself for whatever challenges lay ahead—eating with her hands, sucking extra sauce from her fingers.

FOUR

Preoccupied as she was with her own misadventures, Vivian was not as focused as she might have been on how Clancey & Schmidt—referring both to the manufacturing conglomerate and to the life partners—fared in her absence.

As it happened, she missed a rather dramatic few days.

Perhaps there is a metaphysical explanation for this phenomenon; perhaps their syndicate had grown so thoroughly entwined that Vivian's elaborate, even unhinged gesture on the West Coast required an equal and opposite reaction back in New York.

Or perhaps Oscar simply recognized that if he was ever going to act, it would have to be while the cat was away.

Elias Knox arrived at C&S on what he expected to be his second day of interim control of the company—fresh from the barber's chair, in his favorite necktie (four-in-hand, in a pattern of narrow green and gold stripes; smart but not flashy) and a suit he considered lucky, despite claiming to repudiate superstition in all its forms—and was startled to find Oscar Schmidt in his own office, sitting behind his own desk.

"Good morning," Elias said, uncertainly. "Mr. Schmidt."

Oscar, hands folded awkwardly on the desktop, gave him a tight smile. He looked as if he'd been sitting there, motionless, since the evening before.

Elias was embarrassed, now, by how confidently he had swung open the door. How obviously he'd been expecting to have the run of the place, in Vivian's absence. He felt the nonsensical urge to lay his hand over his green-and-gold necktie, as if Oscar would be able to tell by the sight of it that it was Elias's favorite. Would be able to tell that he'd been imagining the figure he would cut, behind this very desk.

But Elias was also, of course, feeling the venomous urge to defend his imagined territory. "Can I . . . help you with anything?" he asked.

"No, thank you," Oscar said. Then he seemed to realize that this was not the correct way to answer a man who was ostensibly employed full-time as his assistant. "Well . . ." he said, and searched for the right words to explain what he needed.

Oscar, we should perhaps state for the record—his reputation having weathered challenges enough, in his lifetime—had not stepped back from the management of C&S due to any flagging of his talent in the field of Personal Care. On the contrary, especially in the early days, his experience in the industry and with C&S's network of partners and rivals had been extremely useful both in glad-handing and in the subtle manipulation of weaknesses. Early on Oscar had known, for instance, which regional distributors were most likely to negotiate alliances under the table—and which competitors would need to be intimidated out of striking their own underhanded deals. (The Clancey-Schmidts steered clear of outright blackmail, for obvious reasons.) Oscar's remarkably decreased involvement, after spending the first act of his life with his nose perpetually to the grindstone, had a simple explanation: simultaneous with the founding of C&S, Squire had also (and quite suddenly) brought Oscar both personal fulfillment in something outside his profession, and release from the shame that had driven his productivity throughout his youth. Squire was a fascinating person who made fascinating plans. Nearly every morning he proposed some more tempting way to spend the day than burying themselves in paperwork: attending expedition lectures at the Museum of Natural History, where (after sustained exposure to Squire's contagious enthusiasm) Oscar now found himself enraptured by tales of snakebite and leeches and birds previously unknown to science; picking through antique dealers', nabbing treasures for a song and overpaying for trash; tasting each other's sweat in bed. And all this quiet ecstasy—all this *now threatened* ecstasy, Oscar might even have said—had begun at almost the very moment that Vivian had wanted, for reasons Oscar could no longer fathom, to take the reins anyway.

It had not been a difficult decision, nor was it one Oscar had ever regretted. But it did leave him an uncomfortable and alien presence in an office in which he might, in another (if less happy) life, have labored in apparent contentment for eighteen-hour days.

"Shall we . . . go over the morning meeting?" Elias suggested, reaching for his memorandum book. His cheeks heated slightly—he would never have opened this conversation, with Vivian. He would have waited, in his own modest adjoining office, for her to summon him. Now he found himself with the sudden additional dread that Oscar would accept this presumptuous invitation, and Elias would have to sit in his usual chair across the desk and force Oscar to pass judgment on matters on which he had no context and no opinion.

"No, thank you, no need for that this morning," Oscar said quickly, to their mutual relief. "But—there is something."

"Yes, sir?" Elias stood a little straighter.

As a legend in Personal Care, and (not less significantly) as Vivian's husband, Oscar held a kind of godlike position in Elias's private cosmology. But he was also the man Elias lied to and hung up on, sometimes several times a day, while Vivian rolled her eyes from across the desk. Besides which, it was hard not to feel a certain resentment toward a man who had been granted all of Elias's wildest dreams and was doing with them exactly the opposite of what Elias would: neglecting both the extraordinary company he had the right to helm and the extraordinary woman he'd married, just to go to dinner at Sherry's and take extended rail holidays with his strange friend.

Still, Elias was a professional. He readied himself to take a note, to execute whatever factory management or executive assistance that Oscar might require. (Vivian would be back, he reminded himself, by the end of the week.)

"I've come in this morning," Oscar said, "for an appointment. Well—an interview, really."

"Oh?" Elias could not keep the surprise from his voice.

Oscar nodded, not looking entirely convinced himself. "At eleven." Automatically both men consulted the clock on the wall: he was hours

early. "If you'd escort the, the young lady in," Oscar said. "When she—"
He made legs of his first and second fingers, moved them demonstratively
through the air.

Elias kept his face carefully blank. "Certainly, sir," he said, and began
to back out of the room.

"Oh, and!" Oscar said, something evidently heartening occurring to
him. "In fact, if you'd join us, Mr. Knox, for the latter phase of the interview. When I—when I ring." He surveyed the intercom box on Vivian's
desk, as if trying to work out how it functioned. (The principles of Personal
Care may have been unchanged, but workplace communication technology
had come a long way since Oscar's last serious involvement with an office.)

Elias, in an uncharacteristic fit of distraction, percolated on this development for the next several hours. His initial chivalric outrage at the idea
that Oscar Schmidt might be entertaining a mistress—at all, let alone in
the sacred halls of the C&S executive suite—subsided somewhat as the
idea, obsessed over at length, seemed less and less likely. A factory office
was—Elias blushed again at the very thought—an impractical place for a
tryst under any circumstances; besides, Vivian was all the way in California. Why not simply entertain this strange lady at home, if it was truly
Oscar's intention to—Elias had to manually arrest the thought, collaring
it like an alley thug. It made him feel heroic, if nonsensically so: the idea
of himself, rescuing his idea of Vivian from the idea of such an insult to
her honor. An entire three-act melodrama of the mind, with even less
basis in reality than Elias knew.

And besides the many-layered impracticalities of an office rendezvous,
Elias flattered himself that his own loyalty to Vivian was well-established.
If Oscar Schmidt had been determined to make a cad of himself, this—
enlisting Elias as witness and accomplice—would be a glaringly obvious
act of self-sabotage.

No, Elias thought. Oscar was not here on the business of adultery.
Something else, something odder, was afoot.

THE ODDER THING was, of course, this:

Oscar had, in a fit of manic pique, written to Rebecca Van Beek (in his
capacity as "Mr. Clancey's business partner") to express the company's

professional interest in her artistic work, and to request an interview—
to which he hoped Mrs. Van Beek would be so good as to bring a portfolio
of her sketches and such finished pieces as could be readily transported.
(Oscar had heard, he emphasized with more punctuation than made
him appear strictly sane, that the lady *worked primarily in frescoes!!!*)

This was the kind of mood that ordinarily Vivian would have bullied
him out of, or else Squire eased him down from. But Vivian was out of
town, and Squire—well. Oscar had kept it from Squire. Purposefully.
(This was easily done. Squire had learned much in the preceding decade,
about both the world in general and his husband in particular—but he
was only human. It was still quite possible, whether by accident or by
intention, to disappear into his blind spots.)

Oscar felt strongly that he had had enough of being gentled and petted
and reassured, only to turn around and find things as close again to disaster
as they had ever seemed. It was time, he had decided, to take matters into
his own hands.

Here was the full extent of Oscar's plan: to somehow manage to engage
Rebecca Van Beek on the C&S payroll, thereby making her too unconventional for Mrs. Clancey to consider suitable as a bride for Squire.

This was not in itself a *wholly* ridiculous idea—Mrs. Clancey had, on
several occasions (far too numerous, in Oscar's opinion!), numbered among
Mrs. Van Beek's charms the fact that she had both the means and the
constitutional inclination to avoid employment.

Still, now that Mrs. Van Beek—only ever previously perceived as a
shadowy, villainous presence stalking the margins of Oscar's life—had
sent a warm but perfunctory acceptance; now that he was waiting for her
in his wife's office, his own name in inverted liquid gilding on the door;
now that everything was coming to a head, it seemed to Oscar rather a
thinner plan than a true tactician might have advised.

Oh well, he thought, with resignation that was a subspecies of bravery
(if a poorly developed one). If it was a mistake, there was nothing to be
done about it now—Vivian was in California, too far away to come to
his rescue in time. And he could not, of course, appeal to Squire to solve
this particular problem.

He had not, in his letter, forbade Mrs. Van Beek from mentioning the
matter to Mrs. Clancey, or to Squire himself. Even Oscar knew that such

a comment would have sounded a warning bell, and his plan would have been scuttled at once. But consequently he was at fate's mercy, now, waiting in miserable suspense to learn whether Mrs. Van Beek's instincts would tend toward the adventurous or the cautious—whether she would come at all, perhaps having consulted with Squire or his mother and brought the whole subterfuge crashing down, brought Oscar's happiness crashing down along with it, brought—

Elias Knox watched with morbid, wary fascination throughout the morning as Oscar, a dim shadow behind frosted glass, sat entirely motionless at the desk. So absorbing, in fact, was Elias's vigil that when the receptionist rang for him, he jumped in his seat.

WE HAVE DELAYED long enough, reader: it is time to meet Rebecca Van Beek.

Elias, despite the hours of uncertain anticipation, had not been well armed by Oscar with expectations. He was certainly not prepared for what he found: a woman a little older than Vivian, grayer at the temples, softer in the eyes, surveying the stucco ceiling of the reception area with what appeared to be deep interest. The receptionist had to call her name twice, before she came to herself enough to return to ground level and meet Elias. "We match!" she greeted him with apparent delight, and reached for his hand.

"Ma'am?" he asked. She had a strong grip.

She gestured from her dress (which, he noted, buttoned asymmetrically across the bodice) to his throat, his four-in-hand. Elias felt that urge, again, to cover himself. Then he realized: she was in green and gold, the same shades as his necktie.

Elias laughed more often than his colleagues and especially his subordinates might have assumed, but rarely—very rarely—in the office. The receptionist was frankly startled by the sound of it.

"Let me show you to Mr. Schmidt's office," Elias said. "And may—may I take that for you?"

He had nearly stumbled midsentence: Rebecca carried a large Morocco leather portfolio with a reinforced handle and a cunning set of snap closures. It was as beautiful a piece of organizational technology as Elias had ever seen. It was with a sense of almost personal disappointment that he heard her say, with a good-natured smile, "Oh, I can manage the old thing, but thank you."

"Mr. Schmidt?" Elias said with a simultaneous knock.

Poor Oscar: of all of us, now, the last to meet Rebecca.

In the spirit of honesty we must recall here that Oscar was a man of some considerable experience when it came to being unkind to women. In another season of his life, remember, he had consciously fostered the skill, as protection against the twin threats of matrimony and female friendship. He had been at pains, then, to avoid the recognition of a kindred spark between himself and the women of his set—as well as the damning tableau he might carelessly have made of himself, seen laughing at his ease among a bouquet of femininity when the men (the *real* men) came in from shooting. Selectively boorish manners, affected hypermasculine interests, and a uniform cold indifference to women's affairs had functioned then as a multipurpose prophylactic, and had of course cost him no popularity among the husbands and brothers of these long-suffering ladies.

Oscar had now left that phase of life behind him in a hundred ways. But besides the universal constant of old habits dying hard (the world outside his own domicile, after all, being as eager as ever to reward male chauvinism), there was this: the disdain he had once carefully cultivated in the general, he now had the strong intuitive instinct to deploy in the particular. In short: he was *so ready* to hate Rebecca Van Beek. In fact, he hated her already. And, far from affording the lady the chance to redeem herself with charm, Oscar's reflex was to work backward and infect formerly blameless neutralities with disgust based on their new association with her. (He had always, he thought venomously in these first moments of their acquaintance, hated green dresses. He had always hated shaking hands. And idle pleasantries. And sitting.)

But, Oscar thought, he had gotten this far. Now there was only one way to be rid of her: he'd have to convince her, somehow, that she wanted work.

"Mrs. Van Beek," he said with an unfriendly smile. "Thank you so much for taking the time to come in."

"Not at all," she said.

"We'd like to talk with you about some artwork, for the building," Oscar said. Together they took in the office's bare walls, Vivian's austere decor. "So it's all a little less . . ." He bared his teeth in an expression of Spartan brutality.

Rebecca, inconveniently, laughed.

"So," Oscar said. "If you've—"

"Pardon me, Mr. Schmidt," Rebecca said. She laid her portfolio on the desk with a flat *thwack.*

Oscar jumped. He had always, he thought, hated interruptions.

"I'm terribly sorry, if what I'm about to say is at all awkward," Rebecca said.

Oscar had to admit that her attitude of demure kindness was a convincing act. Some people, he thought, had been blessed with naturally considerate eyebrows—no matter the nefariousness of their plots.

"But I truly believe," Rebecca was saying, "it's better out than in: if Mrs. Clancey has put you up to this, I hope you won't feel obligated."

". . . Mrs. Clancey?" Oscar asked faintly.

"I'm a bit of a project of hers, lately," Rebecca said. "I'm not—it's kind of her, of course, ever so kind." (There was, Oscar noted, a certain familiar weariness around Rebecca's eyes. She was a fellow veteran of Mrs. Clancey's drawing room.) "But I'm not entirely sure where it's all come from." Rebecca worried the clasp of her portfolio, snapping it open and closed as she spoke. "There's Luther, of course, but—"

"—I'm sorry for your loss," Oscar cut in, in an effort to maintain the chivalric upper hand.

Rebecca acknowledged the interjection with a graceful nod. "But that's three years ago, now. And we're fine, the children and I." She smiled and made a kind of sweeping gesture across her front, as if to demonstrate her fineness. "And we're quite well provided for, financially. So, there's really no need for Mrs. Clancey to worry herself."

Oscar made a noncommittal sound. Squire and this woman, he thought against his will, would raise the frankest children the world had ever seen. (For a horrible, conventional moment, the notion cast Oscar in his own mind as the villain of the piece—a mustachioed lech, keeping Father from the nursery.)

"At any rate," Rebecca was forging on. "Mrs. Clancey has me . . . well, she's made herself my advocate on a hundred fronts." She gave her fingers an industrious wriggle. "And I—well. I just do wish she wouldn't make people humor her on my account."

". . . Oh?" Oscar managed. He had always, he insisted, hated radical acts of candor that taught him to hope.

"So I just hope you'll tell me," Rebecca finished, with an unburdening sigh, "if this is coming from her. And that you won't feel obligated." But her hand rested again on the clasp of her portfolio.

At first Oscar could only shake his head. "This isn't," he said finally. "Coming from her. Mrs. Clancey. Not at all."

"Then from *Mr.* Clancey?"

There was, unless Oscar was imagining it, an affectionate warmth to her voice. He cleared his throat. "Squire—Mr. Clancey—he only mentioned that you were"—he moved his hands vaguely—"very talented."

Rebecca smiled. "Did he?" she said. "That was dear of him."

"Yes," Oscar said. "Well." He beckoned brusquely to her portfolio. "Let's see, shall we?"

"It's rather a motley crew," Rebecca said pleasantly (and not without pride), opening the portfolio at last. "I wasn't sure what you were interested in."

She'd brought a miscellany of works on paper—pastels, charcoals, pencil sketches, and a few watercolors. Oscar clasped his hands behind his back—whether to protect the artwork or himself remained unclear—while she provided verbal annotation.

Rebecca liked movement, Oscar noted: all her landscapes centered on waterfalls; all her pastorals featured distant figures pitching hay or hauling water. Even her still lifes tended to cheat, including in one corner or another a lively bird or chipmunk or the blurred brush of a spaniel's tail.

The pictures were not, Oscar was soothed to find, technically very good. There was an amateurish flatness to them, a strangely foreshortened perspective—the quality of an aerial-view map, not just to the watercolor scene of a craggy mountain pass but also to the pencil sketch of a bowl of fruit. As if Rebecca had been trying to describe to a weary traveler the most direct route from a bunch of grapes to a bruised apple. But—alas!—the style was unique, and dynamic, and charming. "These are interesting," Oscar admitted gruffly.

"I wasn't sure what you had in mind," Rebecca said again. And if Oscar had been better able to focus on anyone's feelings but his own, he might have noted the anxiety in her voice.

THE FACT OF the matter was that with the possible exception of her children—or, more properly, leaving aside such impossible comparisons—Rebecca Van Beek treasured her own artwork more than anything else on earth. She liked to work in oils best of all—had even, in a brief moment of either courage or weakness that morning, considered whether she might stuff one of her oil canvases into the slender portfolio Elias had so admired in the lobby.

In the end, milder strategy had prevailed. But despite her gallant speech releasing Oscar from any sense of obligation; despite her unquenchable enthusiasm for her practice, which no lost commission could steal from her; despite the half-finished pieces she had waiting to welcome her home, no matter the result of the interview—despite all this, Rebecca was still nervous.

It is a rare artistic soul, after all, that does not crave patronage or validation. Perhaps these impulses have always gone together—the desire to create, and the desire to be applauded for it.

Rebecca Van Beek was a kind and decent and empathetic person, and she did not have particularly outsized ambitions. (We could not with any real accuracy, for instance, compare her to Vivian.) But she was not, by the same token, a shrinking violet. She was tactful, not modest; resilient, not resigned. A great untapped spring of vanity bubbled in her, kept subterranean as a path to practical happiness, but ready with the faintest encouragement to become a joyously raging torrent.

Rebecca Van Beek loved her work. She did not *require* anyone else to love it, or even to sanction it. But she was only human, and an Important Person—the founder and CEO of a company! The co-creator of Mystic Zephyr, which Rebecca was presently sweating from her racing pulse points!—was considering commissioning her.

Oscar was blinded by his own preoccupations—what had she meant, that was *dear* of Squire? Which was the *project* to which she wished Mrs. Clancey would devote fewer resources? *Did she want to marry him or didn't she?*—and devastated further by the awful fact that this woman, strange and frank and sneaking mischievous creatures into the margins of her still lifes, was proving difficult, in practice, to hate.

Difficult, even, to consider incompatible with Squire.

Made stupid by distraction, Oscar managed to persist in holding the misconception he had received wholesale from Mrs. Clancey: that Rebecca Van Beek, jewel of Old New York, loved leisure; that she would power-fully resist any offer of employment.

"As it happens," Oscar began portentously, making an ineffective gesture toward squaring the edges of Rebecca's stack of drawings. "As it happens, we're not so interested—not *only* interested, that is," he amended quickly, "in purchasing pictures for . . ." He gave a vague wave: this office; Squire's across the hall (used principally for storage); Elias's next door; the clerks'; the conference rooms; the long and blank-walled hallways. None of it, as yet, adorned. (Vivian, after all, had always been in charge.) "We'd like," Oscar said, "to speak to you about the possibility of retaining you, as a—well, a company artist, for the consultancy and execution of a consis-tent decorative theme, which—"

"Oh, *absolutely*," Rebecca said.

Oscar—who had a great deal more scripted for himself, including several dramatic personal appeals to deploy if Rebecca tried to cut the interview short—choked. Abruptly he assumed the attitude of an angler with a catch hooked but not yet landed. "Elias!" he almost shouted—unfortunately, before pressing the button on the intercom system. But as it happened he was loud enough, and Elias trying desperately enough to eavesdrop from the other side of the frosted glass—where he had strained to overhear with interest the condolences for a lost husband, pleasantly accepted with no audible distress—that he entered regardless, and almost at a jog.

"Yes, sir?" he said, looking at Rebecca.

"This is Mrs. Van Beek," Oscar said, to his credit confining any hyster-ical panic to a strange gleam in his eyes. "I need—we'd like to engage her, as an artistic counsel."

"Phenomenal," Elias said.

"She does"—Oscar gestured to the array of drawings and watercolors still spread across the desk—"these."

"And oils," Rebecca cut in, unleashing her own eager advocate. "And frescoes or murals. Anything you'd like, really." (This bravado was perhaps pushing things a bit, Rebecca being unpracticed in several media and entirely untried as a sculptor—but she was an angler too; she and Oscar had hooked each other.)

Elias, ever practical-minded, had up to this point assumed they were discussing package design—the sweet illustrations of bow-lipped Gibson Girls printed on each sleeve of C&S soap. The company's aesthetic, in Elias's private opinion, *could* do with a refresh—though he never would have suggested such a thing to Vivian, he was already with some excitement imagining the new label design when he realized that Oscar and Rebecca referred instead to purely decorative art. Pictures on walls. The kind-eyed widow with the Morocco leather portfolio and the frock that matched Elias's tie might spend hours on a painting intended specifically to hang over his desk.

"Phenomenal," he said again.

"If you'd only let me know," Rebecca made a third valiant attempt to learn what exactly she was doing there, "what sort of scheme you gentlemen had in mind, I could make some sketches."

There was a moment of silence—Elias still finding his feet; Oscar not having anticipated getting this far.

"Perhaps," Rebecca suggested, "I could ask Mr. Clancey—"

"No!" Oscar said. "No," he repeated, his tone more measured. "No. Elias—Mr. Knox—can get you started, can't he?" He looked hopefully at Elias, who nodded. "He and I can work out a plan. Pending your approval, of course," Oscar hastened to add.

"That sounds lovely," Rebecca said—and it did, if vaguely so.

"The main thing," Oscar said, wiping his hands on his trouser legs. (An interview that goes better than expected brings its own species of stress.) "The main thing, the first thing, is to make sure we get you on the payroll."

"Oh," Rebecca said, with a tactful shake of her head. "There's no—"

"I insist," Oscar insisted. "The paperwork—" He beckoned to Elias, almost as if he might have a contract on him.

Elias made an apologetic gesture, as if he wished he had.

"We'll get it drawn up right away," Oscar said. It would do him no good, he knew, for Rebecca's artwork to be a donation. (On the contrary, Mrs. Clancey respected a lady who was moderately active in charity work.) He needed her *employed*.

They said their adieus, shook hands again. Elias escorted Rebecca back to the lobby, this time convincing her to let him carry her portfolio as far as the reception desk. He held it carefully, lest he leave sweaty thumbprints on the leather. "Lovely to make your acquaintance," he said.

"Until we meet again," Rebecca returned, smiling—and spun out through the revolving door, to float home in confused but happy anticipation.

Elias returned to the office at such a pace he almost slipped on the lobby's tile.

After hours of tight-wound anticipation, Oscar had let himself collapse somewhat in the lee of the interview—his tie was askew, his posture slumped, his breathing ragged. Had he space in his brain for such a thought, he might have reflected on the exhausting nature of Vivian's everyday work—not only the administration of C&S but also the manipulation of human souls, the permanent influence of another person's life in the service of one's own priorities. Oscar had ample experience with it, of course, but never from this side of the desk.

"Elias," he said hoarsely. "You've got to find that woman something to do, please." He gestured at the blank walls. "Anything, just make it—you know. Professional. A series."

"Yes, sir." Elias stepped toward the door, wheels already turning.

"And Elias," Oscar said.

"Sir?"

"Give her as much as possible," Oscar said. "No . . ." He waved his hand, encompassing all the usual inconveniences of budget and schedule and business sense. "No object. This can last . . . years." (It would *need* to last, he thought, at least for the remainder of Mrs. Clancey's life.) "So, really, man." Oscar tried not to sound desperate. "Think."

Elias Knox had, after his own fashion, a brilliant and forward-thinking mind. He was also almost a symbiotic organism with the Clancey & Schmidt manufactory—he knew its every nook and cranny; which office walls were most advantageously lit in the morning and which in the evening; which rooms might well receive a picturesque mural or mosaic, and which were too often scoured by steam or chemical residue to make such an installation practical.

And, as we have established, he found infatuation to be a potent motivator.

"Yes, *sir*," he said—with such relish Oscar almost grasped his hand in relief, despite the slightness of their acquaintance.

Elias paused in the doorway. "Only—" he said. Oscar looked up. "We'll have to ask Mrs. Schmidt," Elias said—a rare direct reference to the C&S pecking order.

Oscar nodded. "We'll tell her it's important," he said. "She'll understand."

Elias found himself host to a curious mélange of novel feelings: a collaborative respect for Oscar; a distant, almost condescending confidence that Vivian would see things their way. "I'm sure she will," he said—and left at speed, to begin drawing up plans for a gargantuan lobby mosaic impractical as a valentine.

FIVE

On the same morning of Oscar's interview with Rebecca Van Beek, a superficially similar scene played out across the country: R. T. Wallace met with Vivian in a cramped office at Parnacott Productions, before the day's shooting schedule began.

They had made less progress than they'd hoped, R. T. explained, the day before. "We'll have to really light a fire under it today," he said. "Unless you could stand it to lose anything?"

Vivian wavered. Ruthlessness with her bottom line notwithstanding, she did not cut corners without a reason—nor did she tolerate the behavior from anyone on her payroll. There was no point in the effort and expense of producing an industrial short if the results were sloppy, or amateurish, or rushed. Worse than no point: such a film would only tar C&S products with the same brush.

But on the other hand, Vivian was already doubtful of her ability to withstand one more day of filming. If they were to delay until tomorrow, or the next day—it was hard for her to imagine herself emerging in one piece.

Besides which, there was the fluttering alien feeling of embarrassment whenever she thought of her careless, openhearted note to Sofia the night before. Los Angeles felt, this morning, like the scene of an obscure crime. Not necessarily a crime Vivian had committed, but one for which she had motive and no alibi. Her every instinct was screaming at her to run, while she still could. Back to where things made sense; back to where she belonged.

"It has to be finished today," she said to R. T. "That's . . . that's the company's position."

"Let's see how far we get," he replied, clapping his hands as he rose.

Vivian's spirits staggered—already, again, that strange mix of deference and refusal. Hadn't he begun by asking her a question? How was the conversation ending with him delivering a verdict?

At first, as they entered the windowless stage, Vivian thought that filming had already begun. Lights shone, a camera turned, figures whirled between the Smith household set's open rooms. But there was something off-kilter: the crew was hardly a fraction of the crowd from the day before, and Vivian didn't recognize any of them. Their clothes were shabbier, their shaves less fresh.

And in front of the camera, in place of the phlegmatic Mr. and Mrs. Smith performing their daily domestic ablutions and writing letters home about them, there were—

"*Get off my goddamn set!*" R. T. bellowed—only remembering to raise his bullhorn halfway through the exclamation. "You *clowns!*" he shouted, so loud and close that Vivian's eardrum rang.

They were not clowns, exactly, but there *was* something inherently farcical in the tableau: a gangly young man, his sad eyes emphasized in pencil, was splashing fully clothed in the cutaway house's bathtub. His face was impassive, dead-affect, making it unclear at first glance whether the scene was one of distress or recreation. His hat was sodden and squashed, streaming water from its shapeless brim. As Vivian stared, as R. T. drew breath to continue his diatribe, the man idly—almost coquettishly—raised one leg over the lip of the tub. Water poured from his shoe and splattered onto the floor of the set.

(Vivian wondered how the interlopers had managed to fill the bathtub—and hoped it could safely hold the water. There were electrical cables snaking everywhere across the studio floor.)

The man in the tub mimed soaping under one arm, then the other. His dreamy gaze wandered the room, passing directly across Vivian and the apoplectic R. T. Film, after all, was burning—to react to them would have been to ruin the shot.

Simultaneous with this scene came a chaotic, even violent movement from the other side of the house set: a second man, stockier than the first, wearing a jacket two sizes too small for him and trousers three sizes too large. A battle-worn stovepipe hat sat at a nervous-rakish angle on the back of his head, looking slightly dismayed to find itself there.

The man himself, though, spared not a moment for any dismay of his own at R. T.'s attempted interruption. He was midway through a confusing but impressive bit of slapstick: careening from room to room with great physical effort and continuous movement, yet making relatively slow progress through the false house. The man in the bathtub was his obvious goal, though whether to attack or assist him was still unclear.

And above them both teetered a figure who seemed more athlete than comedienne, even to the point of recklessness: a girl of perhaps eighteen or twenty, wearing gymnasium bloomers under a gingham dress, balanced on tiptoe atop one of the set's cutaway walls. Had it been a real house, she would have been walking on the ceiling. As Vivian's gaze found her, she was sighting a leap, swinging her arms to work up some momentum.

Despite herself, and for the first time in years, Vivian screamed. But the girl made the jump: across from the outer wall of the not-house to the interior wall of its not-bathroom, where she balanced for a moment before bending at the waist to grip the plywood with her hands. Her feet rose overhead, her skirt falling over her like an inverted bell. Working blind—or so Vivian could only imagine—she somersaulted down from this acrobatic pose.

For a moment, it looked inevitable that she would land in the bathtub, knocking the wind from the sad-eyed man still splashing with apparent cluelessness, and possibly injuring them both (to say nothing of flooding the studio).

But she aimed a precise kick against the wall as she flipped, ricocheting, to ultimately land as if planned—of course, Vivian realized abruptly, it *had* been planned—directly on top of the stockier man in the ill-fitting suit just as he, at long last and with perfect timing, staggered through the door.

It was virtuosic. The urge to applaud had to be physically repressed.

The three performers gave this climax a beat to breathe: the acrobatic girl and the man in the too-small top hat affecting to struggle to disentangle themselves from each other; the man in the bathtub standing in a startled cascade of water, covering his clothed chest like Botticelli's Venus.

R. T. screamed again into his bullhorn, wordlessly.

A door slammed. Assistants with clipboards rushed in from opposite sides of the stage, a pincer formation. But it was too late—the crew of set-crashers was clearly well practiced at this species of guerrilla filmmaking.

The actors sprinted wildly through and away from the set in a strange combination of getaway and interference, avoiding R. T.'s lieutenants while distracting them from the necessarily slower escape of the camera operator and skeleton crew. The larger of the two male actors was surprisingly balletic in his evasive maneuvers; the smaller one more confusing and dangerous, particularly since with every step he mopped the floor behind him in a slick of bathwater. (One of R. T.'s assistants took a daring but ill-advised shortcut through one of these puddles, slipping and falling hard onto the linoleum floor of the false house's cutaway kitchen.)

The girl, the acrobat, was difficult for Vivian to keep in her eyeline—it was like tracking a bird in flight. Instead of using her agility to make a quick getaway, she doubled and tripled back, zigging and zagging, luring their pursuers first one way and then the other. Giving her slower comrades time to make their escape.

Key among these, of course, was the cameraman—Vivian looked again—camera*woman*, pocketing the fruits of the troupe's effort. Working as tirelessly behind the scenes as when she'd kept the camera turning moments before, cranking with a quick yet steady hand, subdividing (even, at this point, when not on duty) each second of her mortal life into sixteen even frames.

Now, she disengaged the film magazine—removing the spring that attached it to its take-up spindle and to the body of the camera; lifting off the entire two-bulbed case with its precious four hundred feet of stolen story. She hugged it to her chest, in the manner of all things precious and under threat.

"*You*—" R. T. swore, and threw his bullhorn at her. But it was too late; it clattered ridiculously against the studio floor, as the camera operator made her escape—the rest of the cast and crew of this insane pageant acting now as her defensive line, screening her and the captured film from attack.

It was all over in a flurry of moments, perhaps not even a minute altogether. Last of the group to flee the studio was the acrobat, the girl who had run on tiptoe across the phantom ceiling of the half-real house and dodged disaster at the last moment. She wheeled back just as the door closed behind her—a move at least as risky as it was prudent; since Orpheus, every fugitive pausing at the edge of safety has been as likely to meet disaster as to confirm victory—and caught Vivian's eye.

It was not quite a wink, the expression she offered. But her smirk knew things it was not saying out loud.

The door closed with a heavy clang.

"I'll *kill* them," R. T. was ranting, snapping his fingers as if ordering his assistant to add the massacre to his calendar. "She's gone too far."

"Who was—who were they?" Vivian asked. Her professional mask was slipping, a little—it is difficult to conceal genuine breathlessness, the thrill of recognition of something long sought, especially when it finally arrives unlooked for in a moment of despair.

Luckily for Vivian, R. T. was entirely focused on his own grievances.

She got it out of him: Sybil Parnacott was a former junior athlete; a part-time secretarial student nearing expulsion; an aspiring comedienne and stuntwoman; and—most germanely—the niece of John Parnacott, the head of the studio and R. T.'s boss.

Mr. Parnacott had been instructed by his brother and sister-in-law not to support Sybil in her artistic pursuits, or her associations with unsettling performers and shiftless technicians of cinematic equipment. (Under no circumstances, for instance, was John to offer her an apprenticeship at the studio as an opportunity to explore her interest in the industry.)

But by the same token, Mr. Parnacott had also been prevailed upon to go easy on Sybil, whenever she took matters into her own hands and poached his studio's resources.

Of course there was never any question of pressing *charges*—not against a (more or less) beloved niece, one who didn't even cause much of an inconvenience. (At least not in John Parnacott's view, as an absentee studio head who had gotten into the industrial-short business from the industrial side of the equation, with little exposure to the day-to-day operation of a company he viewed more as a financial investment than an artistic concern.) But beyond her legal immunity, Sybil rarely endured even so much as a stern talking-to—only in those rare cases when her troupe caused what her uncle called "real damage," breaking equipment or so altering a set that it had to be rebuilt before it was usable.

"Please, Johnny, let her get it out of her system," Sybil's parents had pleaded. "If we forbid it, it will only encourage her."

Sybil Parnacott was, as it happened, a brilliant young woman. But it should be noted that she would not have needed to be more than middlingly intelligent to take advantage of such an obviously advantageous situation.

And so poor R. T. Wallace found himself in a position as impossible as it is timeless: the middle manager caught between his boss's conflicting practical expectations and nepotistic demands. And with nothing but a bullhorn with which to defend himself.

This was the first time that Sybil and her crew of "goddamn anarchist buffoons" (R. T. was on his way to calming down, but it was a long and circuitous process) had ever interrupted a live shoot. Usually she confined herself to disused stages, sets about to be struck or due to start filming the following Monday. These violations were still infuriating; they still caused inconvenience and expense. But they at least did not leave an active production, already behind schedule, short a camera magazine and covered in bathwater. (The magazine, R. T. knew from experience, would be returned in a day or two, emptied of its stolen and since-developed film. The equipment, he stressed, was not the *point*.)

"Excuse me," Vivian said, starting for the stage door. "I'll just be a minute."

R. T.'s face lit up. "You could make a complaint," he said.

"Excuse me?"

"You're the client." R. T. was full of manic, joyless euphoria. His bullhorn would have been more extraneous than ever. "You're upset." He gestured at her, as if presenting to an unseen jury Exhibit A: Vivian fleeing the studio, presumably to compose herself. To take deep, steadying breaths in the looking-glass of a ladies' powder room. A Woman, Upset.

"You can let Mr. Parnacott know," R. T. said, "that this was—" He flailed, putting his whole body into the attempt to convey the scope of Sybil's unacceptability. The extent of everything that had Gone On Long Enough, that he himself was powerless to protest. "You can tell Mr. Parnacott," he said again, with desperate hope for this own peace.

It was a kind of a plea for mercy. Finally, a clear establishment of Vivian's authority.

"Tell him," he said, "that you—that you won't pay, unless she—"

"I'll consider it," Vivian said, and pushed through door.

THE PARKING LOT was an expanse of sun-bleached pavement, the studio's windowless bulk marooned in its center with the incongruity of a glacial boulder. Vivian hurried through the last set of double doors just as a flatbed truck swerved out of the lot. The passengers were, for the most part, crammed too close together to distinguish as individuals—just a cacophony of young and flexible limbs, some jutting improbably from surprising windows. She thought she recognized at least the two male actors, tangled in the flatbed, bracing themselves against their comrades so as not to tumble out during the sharper turns. A human sound, something between a shriek and a laugh, faded in the distance.

The door closed with a *clunk* behind her.

But before disappointment could rush in—and behind it the fresh awareness of every unpleasant and mortifying shadow the guerrilla comedians had driven from Vivian's mind—came a scraping sound and a soft peal of laughter. Vivian whirled to face it.

Leaning against a dilapidated Ford were the camera operator—one foot up on the running board, the stolen film magazine still cradled in both hands, proffering a cigarette between her painted lips—and Sybil Parnacott, unfolding herself gracefully, having just struck a match against the sole of her own shoe.

Vivian was not conscious of making any sound or movement, but she supposed afterward that she must have: the girls turned at the same moment.

The camera operator gave a startled squeak, her first puff of smoke clouding her face as if she were trying to use it as cover to escape. Her hands tightened on the magazine.

"Hang on a second, Bea," Sybil said. With deliberate languor she shook out the match and flicked it away. As she moved to approach Vivian, she gave the other girl's—Bea's—arm a comforting squeeze.

Bea did not look comforted. She stood at attention, took her foot off the running board. Firmly planted and ready for flight.

Vivian thrilled at her own ability to inspire such fear. It was as R. T. had said: she was a corporate client, not part of the studio. She had a power, a ruinous potential, that lay outside the Parnacotts' sphere of influence—meaning both the industrial production company, formally licensed in the states of California and New York, and the troupe of trespassing clowns stuffed into a flatbed track.

On closer inspection, Sybil Parnacott was dusted all over with freckles. She also had a faint scar running across her forehead and bisecting one eyebrow. A souvenir, Vivian assumed, of some daredevil stunt. (In fact, she had tumbled at age four into the edge of a side table. Even the most accomplished performers have childhoods.)

"Look," Sybil said. Standing toe to toe with Vivian, she had to jut her chin to meet her eye. "We didn't break anything. R. T.'s a diva, but a little water won't melt him."

Her voice was surprisingly resonant for so compact a person, especially one so invested in a career where (Vivian thought, with confidence) such a voice was destined to remain a secret. She had a dry-vermouth rasp to her. It made you thirsty just to listen.

"But if you really want to get into it," Sybil was saying, "you'll have to contact our lawyer."

"Sybil," Bea the camerawoman said, faintly.

Vivian felt herself smile. It was, gloriously, involuntary. "You can afford a lawyer," she said, savoring the words, "but not a camera?" She jerked her chin, gesturing to the studio behind them. "Not a bathtub?"

Sybil held Vivian's eye, her gaze steady. "That's correct," she said. "Miss."

The last frantic suggestion that perhaps Vivian should spend her last evening in town attending Sofia's concert—buying a general-admission ticket and hoping, mentally prostrate, for the best—dissipated in a cloud of Bea's secondhand smoke.

"Buy me a drink," Vivian said. "And we'll call it even."

It was, at this point, early enough that most luncheonettes would still be serving eggs.

"Bea," Sybil said, after a moment. "Get that developed, would you?" She half-turned, as if she didn't trust Vivian enough to take her eyes off her. "We'll go over it tomorrow."

Bea—either long-suffering, or privy to an otherwise undetectable code, or both—crushed out her cigarette and started the car. "See ya," she said. "Don't do anything I wouldn't do."

This comment, from such a source—all tightly sewn buttons and meticulously maintained frame rates and whispered pleas not to say anything dangerous—amused Vivian. But Sybil smiled and promised obedience—"See ya, kid," is what she actually said, slapping the fender, but among close compatriots such phrases may resonate with cathedral acoustics—knowing as she did that when we disregard the Beas of the world, it is at our peril.

"You're lucky," she said, turning back to Vivian. "My doctor just told me I need to replace lost gin." She scanned the lot. "Where'd you come from?"

THE RESTAURANT SYBIL directed them to was perhaps not exactly, not *officially*, a gathering place for women of their type. But it was at least *artistic*. People with unusual haircuts huddled close together, in booths and on barstools—laughing, or arguing in hushed and violent delight, or collaborating in the review of mysterious paperwork. It seemed to be a different time of day, inside—vining plants in decorative window boxes had mutinied, or else been animated by a kind of protective instinct, and grown in trailing mats over the windows. Everywhere the light was muffled, close, tinted jungle-green.

They took a booth. Sybil ordered two gin rickeys, somehow, though she seemed to utter fewer words than the transaction ought to have required.

Vivian's conscience did not raise any of its usual objections to venues like this: that they were too embarrassing, too easy, too eagerly and openly mimicking the kind of masculine dive that Vivian found fundamentally unwelcoming to women—and not unpleasantly so, necessarily; as we have well established, attempts to impose limits on Vivian Schmidt could provoke miracles.

But now, on the contrary, she was at home in such a place. She was finally meeting someone she considered worth listening to, worth getting to know.

Was this rare respect intrinsically bound up in the fact that in the extraordinary figure of Sybil Parnacott, Vivian imagined she saw an echo of her own younger self? It was. Do we begrudge her this? She had been bleeding out on the studio floor, and Sybil's sudden appearance had saved her. That her wounds had been largely self-inflicted; that she had come to California under her own steam and on false pretenses; that she had paid quadruple to make sure that the second letter to Sofia, one of her stupidest mistakes in recent memory, was delivered promptly; that the letter in question was, even now, out in public and unaccounted for— these were matters of separate litigation. If, to borrow Sybil's phrase, she wanted to get into it.

Vivian did not want to get into it. She wanted to drink gin at lunchtime, with possibly the most arresting girl she'd ever seen, and forget that California—just on the other side of these vine-screened walls—existed.

"So," Vivian said. "You make pictures."

"That's the idea," Sybil said. She plucked the wedge of lime impaled on the rim of her glass and snapped its spine, drowned it in her cocktail. "Someday."

Sybil's troupe called themselves the Parnacott Players. (Nobody would ever accuse her of modesty.) They filmed one- and two-reel comedies, mostly—not always funny, but always daring. The loose plots they blocked out in overcaffeinated meetings, along with any stunts too complicated to improvise safely, but for the most part they arrived during off-hours at the studio lot and scavenged, riffing on the props and sets available to them.

Sybil volunteered none of this information. She understood, already, how to guard what she valued. Even without knowing the particulars, Vivian recognized and respected this. (We can only extend to Sybil our apologies, for taking the liberty of exposition despite her shrewdness.)

Vivian flashed compliments like palmed aces—on Sybil's acrobatics, her flawless timing, her ambition. Her conversation skated the edge of propriety, in praise of well-muscled legs and quick fingers and a boldness that would, she was sure, take Sybil wherever she wanted to go.

Sybil's replies were monosyllables, half-swallowed between sips of gin. She was canny, Vivian thought. She was too smart to fall for flattery.

Or: too smart to show how much it affected her.

"And the other actors," Vivian said. Remembering the two clownish men who had shared the stage with Sybil, helped her escape once they'd cut the shot. "Are they . . . ?"

Sybil's face twisted wryly. "Are they what?"

"How do you know them?" Vivian asked. It was difficult, given her own situation, for Vivian to imagine that Sybil was not somehow entangled with at least one of her two costars. For some material advantage, if for nothing else.

In fact, Sybil had met the men (Jack, the one in the bathtub; Michael, the one she'd crashed into from above) when all three had been independently sniffing around the Keystone studio lot, looking for . . . they didn't know what, exactly. A job for the day, or a glimpse of something amazing, or a pie in the face.

Michael, who had come up in vaudeville and already had good timing and the ability to take a fall, had gotten both a job and a pie in the face. Jack, who had married into a performing family and caught the bug from his in-laws, lacked experience but fit into the costume of an extra who hadn't shown up to work—so he'd at least gotten a job, and he'd stolen any scene that wandered close enough.

Sybil, then, had been left with the glimpse of something amazing. She'd recruited them on the spot—while they were still unsuccessful enough to say yes.

Still, she didn't see them much outside the Players' filming. The men were both busy, both doing background work most days on other lots to pay the bills, both married.

And there was Bea, of course. She and Sybil had met in secretarial school. (Bea had actually graduated. She kept her certificate folded crisply inside her stenographer's notebook, as if someone might at any moment demand to see it.)

"We just do the scenes together," Sybil said, out loud.

"You're very good." Vivian took a sip of her rickey and found it nearly drained. Time seemed to be telescoping, every word of conversation containing a condensed but infinite universe. Sybil signaled for another round. "Where do you screen your pictures?" Vivian asked.

Sybil's eyes narrowed. Vivian grinned: a sore subject.

The Parnacott Players were, after all, in a wholly unique position: able to produce films without a studio, a backer, a distributor, or any kind of official sanction whatsoever, but without the resources to independently syndicate their work. Vivian had (yet another) soft spot for the idea: a smart young woman making space for herself without asking for it, wedging herself in sideways and digging out something big enough to live in. One step at a time, improvising as she went.

Vivian might even, she thought, help this girl. C&S could diversify, produce pictures. At least rework the industrial short, so Sybil could star. The everyman relatability would be lost—no one, Vivian felt qualified to assert, was like *this* girl. But still, it would work out. Everyone needed soap. (If any part of Vivian heard in this thought the echo of Oscar's mealy-mouthed pitch from their early association—"Sales may rise and fall, but hygiene is a constant necessity!"—her conscious mind did not remark on it.)

But no, Vivian thought. To pluck Sybil from obscurity like that wouldn't be as fun, as *satisfying*, as watching the girl find her way to success on her own. And she would find it. Of this, Vivian was sure.

"We're building a catalog," Sybil sniffed. "We're considering our options for syndication."

This statement was at least two-thirds bluff. But it was true that the Parnacott Players' reels were getting better, their improvisations developing a certain chemistry. It could, Sybil thought, lead somewhere.

And it would—though of course, one way or another, everything does.

"What about you?" Sybil asked now, rattling the ice in her glass.

Vivian drew breath to reveal, in humble tone but impressive detail, the scope of the Clancey & Schmidt syndicate. It would be an unprecedented thrill, to own her professional accomplishments during a romantic conquest. Finally, she'd found a girl who was worth the risk.

But Sybil continued: "Aren't you supposed to be on set?"

Vivian realized with a bump that she was right—she'd told R. T. she would be back shortly. The actors must have arrived by now, the crew mopped up the bathwater. They were surely filming without her, trying to make up time—guessing at all the C&S product placement; doing God knew what with her treatment.

But what a novel pleasure: to be so thoroughly distracted as to have forgotten—by this affectionate thorniness, this playacting antagonism. So much more interesting than the cloying compliance of Vivian's girls back home.

Was it too early—the thought intruded—to wonder if Sybil might move to New York? Her uncle, after all, had the satellite studio in Queens. Vivian had been assured, on several occasions, that its facilities were state of the art.

First things first: to finish here, and perform the most delicate part of the conquest: inviting the girl back to the hotel. In this, though, Vivian had almost never been surer of success—certainly not since those early, hungry days, when success was necessary for survival. (Not since—her mind, padded with gin, glanced off the thought of Sofia.) Vivian almost understood, after a fashion, the appeal of such easy hunting grounds as the Sapphic bars. If only every girl in them were a Sybil.

But of course, there *were* no others like her. That was the whole point.

"Oh, the short they're filming doesn't matter," Vivian said breezily. "It'll turn out fine. And if it doesn't . . ." She shrugged, moving to take a coy sip of her drink—but discovered her glass was empty again. "I think we can agree it was worth it."

"Swell," Sybil said, and signaled for the check. "Then we're done here."

An ice chip fell against Vivian's lip.

THERE IS, IN this universe, no such thing as a dead end. Everything leads somewhere.

In this case, Sybil and her crew would bang their heads against the industry for a few more years, finally breaking through in 1918 with a two-reel comedy about a newlywed couple (Sybil and Jake) menaced by a sinister romantic rival (Michael). Derivative, but well executed—and in times of global turmoil there is certain comfort for audiences in seeing what they expect to happen, faithfully implemented. Sybil would go on to star in twelve comedy shorts and one "epic" melodrama—and this last effort, rather than the conversion to sound a few years later, would be the death knell of her film career. People, she would find, were ecstatic to applaud her as an acrobatic comedienne; they were far less willing to take her seriously.

Still, she would find that several years as a guerrilla film star, half a secretarial degree, and Bea were more than enough to live on. She would retire having gotten what she wanted out of the situation. She was Sybil Parnacott; it was what she did.

In the short term, she paid for Vivian's drinks, gave her nerveless hand a perfunctory shake, and left her in the booth.

Vivian watched, gaze unfocused through the vines that screened the window, as Sybil appeared on the sidewalk and straightened her skirt. Refreshed her lipstick. Lit a cigarette. Shook off the interaction; prepared to move on with her day.

If only Vivian had been more conniving, she thought; if she had withheld her affirmation of the girl's antics a little longer, she might have gotten her back to the hotel.

This was not, in itself, a cheering thought.

Vivian might have recalled the casino night, all those years ago, when she and Oscar had first meaningfully crossed each other's paths. She had noticed a middle-aged sad sack embarrassing himself, three sheets to the wind, and calculated how best to turn the situation to her advantage. How best to use him to hoist herself out of danger.

In the end, she'd chosen something—she flattered herself—mutually advantageous. In the end, they had grown stoically into one another's lives, like adjacent trees in an impenetrable forest.

But if Vivian had pressed herself, she might also have recalled the other option she had considered—briefly but seriously—before yoking herself to Oscar Schmidt for life: to stand by, watching the pathetic faux-tycoon embarrass himself. To wrest from the interaction only a brief moment of mean-spirited distraction from her own troubles, a petty but satisfying revenge on a world that had rewarded others before herself.

Outside, Sybil Parnacott checked her watch, ashed her cigarette, and stepped briskly down the sidewalk without a backward glance. Moving on with her own carefully guarded story.

Inside, Vivian ordered another drink.

SIX

If we have been neglecting Squire in recent pages, we hope he has been enjoying the spoils of the reason: compared with his spouses, with all their private messy schemes and crises of secret vulnerability, Squire had passed a very pleasant summer and fall indeed.

Still, experience borne cheerfully and with optimism is neither cheap, nor simple, nor even necessarily harmless, and we must give our Mr. Clancey his due attention.

On a typical November day, several weeks subsequent to the eventful interviews we have just witnessed, Squire as usual slept so luxuriously late as to miss the morning almost entirely. (It was a rich man's habit, learned too early to break.) Still, there were half-conscious sunrise routines he relied upon absolutely: the soft golden jangle of Oscar, waking at dawn, retrieving his wedding ring from the dish on the nightstand; the babble of splashing water from the en suite; the single kiss pressed to Squire's drowsy temple. Finally, the click of the sunken door between their (properly Squire's) bedroom and Oscar's office, that they might begin their respective public days from separate wings of the manse.

By the time Squire had washed and dressed, he had the syndicate's joint dining room to himself. On days when the men had no shared engagements Oscar tended to take lunch at his club, in one of those peculiar combinations of routine and variety that is a balm to the anxious constitution. And Vivian, of course, had long since left for the office, and for any extracurricular liaisons the day might hold. (If Vivian had been cagier than usual, in the weeks since her return from California—if she had been leaving earlier, coming home later, reviewing each day's letters with what in another person might have been called agitated interest—Squire was not the type of man to draw inferences from such behavior.)

Over a meal of persistently indeterminate identity—some days eggs and toast at noon; on this occasion rewarmed roast at eleven-thirty—Squire sorted through the mail. Having finished his most recent reread of the Oz series, he now had renewed attention for the morning papers, and—with considerably more enthusiasm—for the weekly issue of *Puck*. But the bulk of his attention he reserved for his newsletters.

As already mentioned, over the years Squire had collected a complex (and costly) series of memberships in amateur scientific, technological, and historical clubs and lecture series. He was a devoted reader of each organization's print circular, no matter how variable the quality of the publication (and the sophistication of the information within). His omnivorous interest and his own innate intelligence synthesized him into a kind of human anthology, with an enthusiastic layman's understanding of astronomy, zoology, chemistry, and a dozen other specialties leading often to the zapping thrill of ingeniously, eccentrically crossed wires; as on the evening, a few months before, when Squire had abruptly switched on the bedside lamp and asked Oscar what—in his professional opinion—he supposed outer space smelled like.

"Nothing," Oscar had said without hesitation, turning to bury his face in the pillow. But a decade of partnership with Squire Clancey had taught him a certain involuntary curiosity. After a few minutes he'd resurfaced with a sigh: "What's it made of?"

They'd gone back and forth, as with the French and English sides of the menu. Hydrogen and helium—nothing and nothing, Oscar grumped, just as he'd said. Sulfur was self-explanatory, as were ammonia and iron. Ozone—burnt wire.

Squire, arriving at the limit of his remembered elements and pronunciations, had at this point retrieved the latest American Astronomical Association newsletter from under his pillow and begun reading out stellar chemical absorption lines and meteorite ingredients. Naphthalene and aldehydes: mothballs and green apple. Phenylacetic and propionic acids: almond and honey and vomit. Coronium, Oscar had finished, either wasn't real or else Squire would just have to go to space himself and stick his face in a pile of it to find out. Now shut up and let him sleep.

And Squire had, eventually—after administering a brief reward.

There were no personal letters for him this morning.

Squire corresponded with several gentlemen (and, he suspected, at least one lady—the letters in question being ambiguously signed "T. E. Doe") whose acquaintance he had made through these scientific clubs—a social circle more robust, if remote, than he could possibly have dreamed of in his youth. Doe, for example, a fellow member in good standing of the New York Seismological Society, had published in one issue of the society's quarterly newsletter such a compelling opinion column on the disappointment, as an earthquake enthusiast, of residing in a geologically stable part of the world that Squire had written immediately to request the author's address as a personal correspondent.

(T. E. Doe, we will note in passing for the shivering brush of the narrative near miss, was a devoted student of the Mount Tambora eruption of 1815, and the subsequent Year Without a Summer. This had not, as of our present action in the fall of 1915, come up in the amateur seismologist's correspondence with Squire—they were still too preoccupied in the basics of bedrock to have worked their way to volcanology.)

Squire took the disappointment of the empty mail tray in stride. Perhaps, he thought, there would be something by the evening post.

ON HIS WAY to his mother's, Squire stopped in at the office.

This was a recent habit, as up until about a month before, there had been relatively little at Clancey & Schmidt that was of any real interest to him—beyond the periodic examination of any new machinery, and the opportunity to suggest the occasional experimental product to Research and Development (and to Vivian).

But Squire had become a much more frequent presence at C&S in the weeks since Oscar and Elias Knox (Oscar, in his retelling, had given Elias the lion's share of the credit) had engaged Rebecca Van Beek as the C&S

company artist. Squire had tried, at first, to restrain himself—he knew that his mother was devoting all her considerable social influence to weaving a connection between himself and Rebecca in the public imagination (to say nothing of Oscar's), and that every interaction between the two of them further entangled the whole mess. But self-restraint, we must remember, had never been Squire's specialty—and Rebecca was painting a mural in his lobby.

She had begun work at once, blocking out a two-story backdrop for the wall opposite the reception desk. It would, eventually, be a kind of hybrid wilderness scene and pastoral: a cascading woodland waterfall with figures at work and at leisure in every bosky corner, washing clothes or spreading them to dry; swimming in deep green pools; basking on flat, sun-warmed rocks. As an exemplification of Clancey & Schmidt it would be more evocative than representational—though there would, Rebecca's sketches and studies assured them, be telltale billows of pink-tinged suds around the laundresses, and tiny bars of C&S soap stacked close to hand. But she had rejected (with a kindness that only entangled him further) all of Elias's early suggestions that she depict a more literal advertisement for the company—a lady at her vanity, spritzing Mystic Zephyr; a collage of C&S's most iconic products, arranged in a line like a gallery of presidents; a burning candle ringed by a gilded halo.

This mural, Rebecca had insisted, was not an advertisement. Anyone who stood before it would already have passed through the doors of Clancey & Schmidt; there would be nowhere left to lure them. On the contrary, the scene should be a promise of the feeling that awaited them in the offices and conference rooms beyond: peace, industry, common sense. A fastidiously well-run Utopia where everyone was content and efficient and clean behind the ears.

Elias, it perhaps goes without saying, was by this point drowning in affection for the woman.

Squire loved the mural, all the more for its being incomplete. His visits were daily because the work grew every time he turned his back; he already regretted the future day when it would be finished, frozen in time and presenting a henceforth unchanging face to the lobby. Over the last month he had watched Rebecca and her assistants rig scaffolding, lay drop cloths, and cover the wall in two coats of primer and a grid of squares like a transparent chessboard—these squares corresponding to counterparts on a much smaller-scale model of the scene in oils that Rebecca propped on an easel for reference throughout the installation.

Now the team had made several full passes over the wall from left to right and top to bottom, laying down organic color-block undercoats like base notes: a gray-blue deep enough to fall into in places; a blackish-green that felt, when Squire stared at it for too long, like being lost in a forest at dusk; shades of brown that ranged from muddy red to stony gray, each of which, when considered in isolation, seemed to Squire to change the entire temperature of the room.

The figures had, thus far, been left untouched—they were ghosts on the wall, now, blank human shapes caught in a variety of attitudes in the abstract wash of color. Those closest to the foreground were about three-quarters of life size, a concept that pleased Squire inordinately for no definite reason.

"When do you think you'll start on the people?" he asked, greeting Rebecca—and Elias, who thus far had been a rather more attentive supervisor of the mural's installation than was strictly required.

Rebecca flashed Squire a distracted smile and raised her palms, stained gunmetal-gray in patches, as explanation for forgoing a handshake. (She also had a stripe of green paint across her forehead, to which neither gentleman saw it necessary to draw her attention—due to lack of interest in Squire's case, and a surplus of the same in Elias's.) "First things first, Mr. Clancey," Rebecca said with a laugh. "Rocks, today. People come later."

Squire nodded, resigned to the answer. After all, there was a well-established order of operations to the creation of a world.

Rebecca watched him as he sized up one of the spectral figures, this one placed so immediately in the mural's foreground that it appeared almost to be standing on the lobby floor. "I'll model that one after you, if you like," she said.

"Really?" Squire's delight was infectious; Rebecca could not help but laugh.

"Was there something you needed, Mr. Clancey?" Elias interrupted. His smile was polite but his eyes were flinty, an ancestral Knox stare first developed to make a Staten Island oyster thief weigh anchor. For Elias, too, had heard the trickled-down rumors about Mrs. Clancey's son and the widow Van Beek. Squire's exclusive focus on the mural during his daily visits was no great comfort to Elias, the project also being his own primary vehicle for the expression of romantic interest. And besides, Elias had seen this before, in many contexts: how the sons of millionaires came by the greatest prizes without the appearance of effort or even interest. The power of public opinion to contour individual lives.

Thus fortified by the sight of mural—and the thought of himself, at three-quarter size, eternally exploring it—Squire found the courage to complete the journey to his mother's drawing room.

MRS. CLANCEY, AS WE have already noted, had come to depend upon her son enormously in the years since Mr. Clancey's death. Indeed, her fixation on Squire's matrimonial prospects was somewhat curious, as taking on the responsibilities of a husband and stepfather would surely have compromised Squire's availability as her own helpmate and moral support. But it is in the nature of constitutions like Mrs. Clancey's to credit all stability to their own efforts, and to only miss their supporting crutches after they are removed. Mrs. Clancey had long, long ago identified Squire as a dysfunctional and embarrassing burden, and herself as a noble martyr to his survival. That reality had blossomed into an entirely different set of circumstances was invisible to her, and during these regular visits she spoke to her son as if from the other side of a portal to a parallel world.

"*There* you are," she was already saying as Squire entered the room this afternoon. As often happened, they began their conversation in medias res. "I can't understand it at all," Mrs. Clancey continued. She was brandishing a letter; Squire managed to catch it on its third pass. It was a quote from a prospective decorative vendor for the legendary Clancey Christmas party on the Hudson—still weeks away, but already being heavily prepared for. "Nearly twice the cost of last year!" Mrs. Clancey narrated as Squire tried to read. "For *garlands!*"

"Well, mother," Squire said. "It does look as if the order is a bit larger." (It was, in truth, nearly twice the size—though in fairness to Mrs. Clancey we will record that prices had also risen three cents a yard.)

"I had to," Mrs. Clancey said. "You don't remember—you never notice anything—but the second balcony last year looked *naked*. It looked like we hadn't had anyone in at all."

Squire made a polite noise. In fact, the balcony garlands had been a casualty of the most recent iteration of a complex tournament that he, Vivian, and Oscar improvised at every year's Christmas party—an escalating series of social and athletic challenges that served an inexact but load-bearing purpose in their household's sanity.

The Clancey Christmas party was designed, if obliquely and without malice, to disempower and drive insane all three members of the Clancey-Schmidt syndicate. It was that rare thing: an evening on which Oscar, Squire, and Vivian all had to perform, together and in public, a false version of their shared lives.

The imposition was greatest on Squire, of course, who throughout the party each year was treated alternatingly as an auxiliary host and as an adolescent. This much is most likely familiar to our readers. Who among us has not soldiered on through festivities honoring, or critiques berating, an identity that no longer applies? Who among us has not weathered a prodigal holiday return to a place once familiar, now made ancient and strange by personal growth, and felt the vertiginous, regressive pull of outdated expectations?

The sympathetic pool among our readership is, perhaps, rather smaller when it comes to some additional layers: Oscar, each year, disqualified from showing Squire any particular attention or support in public; Vivian, confined to Oscar's arm all evening, silent and smiling and letting him accept congratulations for her own business acumen—even tacitly signaling to him the answers to questions posed by his supposed fellow magnates.

And both Oscar and Vivian, still society transplants at heart, fighting throughout the long and decadent evening the urge to point at their fellow guests and gape, or laugh, or howl with jealousy.

Small wonder, perhaps, that each year by the time the revelry reached its chaotic peak—usually an hour or two past midnight—all three Clancey-Schmidts would disappear to reclaim themselves in mischief.

Last year, as already mentioned, it had been a vanishingly complex game involving the balcony garlands—specifically their attendant decorative pine cones, which had been coated in a chemical residue approximating snow that had the side effect of causing the cones to flare bright green when thrown into the billiard-room fireplace. (Oscar had attempted to explain the science behind the phenomenon, but by that point he was even drunker than Squire and Vivian, who at any rate did not care whatsoever.) Their game had few rules and a scorekeeping system that was convoluted at best; it had ended not in any one player's clear victory but in the accidental ignition of a nearby curtain, which the trio had extinguished and hidden in one of the room's closets.

The billiard room had not seen much use, since Mr. Clancey's death. Squire wondered now if they might find the curtain at this year's party, stuffed into a ball and still smelling of 1914's ashes.

Other Christmas parties had inspired other games—always childish, varying widely between daring and tame: grapes tossed into the grand hall's chandeliers, or cacophonic discord struck on the music room's piano, with the Clancey-Schmidts sprinting from the room before another guest could arrive to investigate. (Squire in the lead, of course, it being his native terrain.)

For the most part these collaborative challenges were devised in the moment, at that imprecise tipping point of the evening when to behave as expected became suddenly more unbearable than to run wild. But the games were so cathartic, and the mutual affection that followed in their wake so heady, that over the years some anticipatory brainstorming had become inevitable.

Two years previously, there had been the most dramatic development of all: a few days before the party, Vivian—claiming not to believe the number of appellations for different rooms in the Clancey manse, and not even in the *existence* of such places as the "gun room," "plunge-bath dressing room," or (most especially) the "gentlemen's odd-room"—had challenged Oscar and Squire to know each other biblically in this last location before the end of the 1913 party.

"Then, at least," she'd said, shaking out her newspaper, "we'd finally know what it's for."

As an invigorating challenge, and a promise to distract and raise their spirits during the long preceding trial of the party's early hours, this assignment had proved unmatched.

In 1914, after and entirely separate from the pine cone firebombs in the billiard room, they had repeated this second "game"—this time, Vivian had assigned the men the conservatory. This had been a memorable novelty: the unseasonably humid and vegetal air; the fragrance of green things, bruised under knees and palms; their shadows moving in the glass, against the pitch-dark and glowing snow on the other side of its fog-glittered membrane. (They were daring, not reckless: on both occasions, Vivian had kept a dispassionate and respectfully distant watch.)

There had already been much speculation, in the privacy of Oscar and Squire's bedroom, as to the site of this year's challenge.

"I am sure," Squire said now, returning his mother's letter, "that the balcony garlands will be worth every penny."

MRS. CLANCEY HAD MUCH more to discuss (or, more accurately, to air) in this vein: a catalog of disappointments in the party vendors for being overpriced or unavailable; in the servants for being unresponsive or insubordinate; in Squire himself for not having somehow intercepted or countermanded these many inconveniences. There were barbed reminiscences of the days before Mr. Clancey's death, and vague references to the exhaustion of raising Squire, as though this were an ongoing responsibility. (On the contrary, Mrs. Clancey's founding investment in C&S now produced returns that added considerable annual sums to the family fortune.)

Almost more disconcerting than all this criticism was the alternating and confounding praise, which Mrs. Clancey lavished on Squire as though mistaking him for someone else: she was impressed that he had been managing his business so well (he had no idea which accomplishments Vivian had even credited him with, in the most recent quarterly report to the shareholders); she was relieved that he was still keeping himself occupied enough not to get bogged down in any nonsense about sewers or caves (he was desperately hopeful to find a new correspondence lesson in seismology awaiting him at home); she knew that Oscar Schmidt, though a generous mentor, had better things to do, and she was glad that Squire was seeing less of him (it would have been almost physically impossible for Squire to see more of him).

This was how Mrs. Clancey had found her way at last to loving her son: by imagining a version of him she considered ideal, and then squinting until he seemed to fit the description. If she was grateful to Squire—the real Squire—for anything, it was for, in recent years, finally nearly *enough* approximating her ideal that she could plausibly live inside her fiction. (Without, say, policemen or social reporters or aquarium directors calling to intrude with unpleasant contradictions.) And, of course, there was the superficial but crucial fact that he had at last begun to age into his looks—his silver hair no longer immediately remarkable; his eyebrows salted with enough gray to almost match.

This was an inherently injurious dynamic, of course. But, as we have already observed: once withheld, the love of a parent takes on an almost occult power—even when bestowed cringingly, or incompletely, or with unfavorable terms and conditions. Squire called on his mother devoutly, several times a week, to receive just this mixture of blows and embraces— and to look after her own comfort and contentment, an effort for which he was never appreciated (and one that, it must be noted, neither Oscar nor Vivian had been strong enough to perform for their own elders). To withstand the long gaps between flashes of happiness, Squire drifted internally throughout these visits—much as he always had, despite his mother's repeated congratulations on his having beaten the habit.

There *was* a difference, however, between Squire's current flights of fancy and those of his adolescence. Where once he had escaped mentally into sewer systems or subway tunnels or frontispiece maps or great impractical schemes for candlemaking, now in his mother's drawing room he found himself escaping into thoughts of his own evening ahead: dinner at Sherry's with Oscar, where he would give updates on the company mural and his reading into earthquakes and his mother's health, and receive in turn all the latest gossip from Oscar's club or from the cutthroat world of hatpin collecting (sometimes delivered with levity, sometimes with distress, always made diverting by the rigor of Oscar's analysis); then home for the evening mail (perhaps, yes, the next lesson from the seismologist!) and a glass of port; a few hands of gin rummy with Vivian, over another glass or two; and to bed, to make sure that no matter the tenor of the day's gossip, Oscar lost himself in earthshaking pleasure at least once before the night was out.

It is not a small thing, to find that one's comforting fantasies are of one's own immediate future—of the life one has arranged for oneself. It is, perhaps, the ultimate dream of every conscious soul. We can celebrate this for Squire, at least, even as we watch his mother squash him flat.

"And have you called on Mrs. Van Beek?" Mrs. Clancey asked, performing a complicated bit of choreography with her teacup.

Squire brightened, recalled to the present moment. "Yes," he said. "In fact, I've just come from—"

"At *home*?" Mrs. Clancey amended.

"Oh," Squire said with a bump. "No. Not recently." This he reported with some regret—he did think fondly of the Van Beek children, and would have welcomed an update on the games of imagination to which they had meticulously introduced him on his last visit. "But—the mural—"

Mrs. Clancey groaned, swatting at Squire as if trying to close a door on him. "I don't know why you had to come up with that mural scheme," she said. "It's your own happiness you're spoiling, you know, not just mine." (Squire had taken responsibility for hiring Rebecca, in breaking the news to his mother. Mrs. Clancey liked Oscar, very much, and Squire intended to keep it that way. Peacetime was difficult enough to manage; animosity between his husband and his mother was the last thing he needed.)

"Nothing's *ruined*," he said now, trying for reassurance rather than petulance.

His mother made a doubtful sound, but she rallied. "We can adjust to it," she said. "It's only an artistic commission, which isn't . . . well, it isn't *employment*, exactly, is it? It's a disappointment, but . . ." she inclined her head in Squire's direction, a tacit acknowledgment that beggars could not be choosers.

(Alas, alas, for Oscar! After all his machinations, Mrs. Clancey had found it in herself to see around her prejudice against women with occupations! He had made all Rebecca Van Beek's dreams come true for nothing!)

"You need to call on her at home, though," Mrs. Clancey was advising Squire. "If we're going to have you settled by Christmas . . ." Again she brandished the quote for the balcony garlands. Even Squire caught the ominous hint: that the double-lush evergreens would make a picturesque backdrop to announce an engagement. "I spoke to Mrs. Van Beek's brother," she said—an alarming announcement for Squire, who had not realized such a man existed, let alone that Mrs. Clancey had recruited him as an accomplice—"and we agreed that by now you ought to be . . ." She searched for the phrase. "Laying groundwork. And *not* at the *office*."

(Rebecca's brother, we will state for the record, was a bland and even-tempered man named Paul who lived conventionally in the house he'd inherited and who found it a satisfying idea that single people should marry one another, much in the same way he found it satisfying when performances began on schedule or when bills worked out to exact change. Under the circumstances, this was quite enough for Mrs. Clancey to count him as both a tool and an ally.)

"Mother," Squire said, with a patience so hollow and muzzled, so threatened by the turn the conversation was taking, that it was almost something else entirely. "This isn't necessary."

Mrs. Clancey sucked her teeth—an uncharacteristically unladylike gesture. "Isn't it?" she asked.

SQUIRE DEPARTED, AS usual, in a combination of relief and exhaustion. The butler's ambiguous "Are we to congratulate you, sir?" as Squire retrieved his hat did little to settle his nerves.

He had the worrying impression, whenever his mother mentioned Rebecca, that if he did not fulfill her wishes soon, she would take matters into her own hands—as though Squire might awake one morning at the altar, in a tailcoat and a stovepipe hat and with the Van Beek children variously strewing rose petals and holding golden bands aloft on satin pillows. (In fairness, Squire's first experience of falling in love had come as almost as much of a surprise to him—though with the significant difference of the hands on the tiller, or, more precisely, thrust into Oscar's waistcoat pocket, having been his own.)

Still, this fear always faded into the background once he had cleared a few steps of Mrs. Clancey's door. After all, it seemed to Squire, his mother was a citizen of her own alternate universe—another world entirely, one in which his marrying Rebecca made any sense at all. The notion could be almost darkly compelling, wherever her influence was potent: within the four walls of her drawing room; or in Rebecca's, when they called on her together. And it was unsettling, seeing this version of the world spread like bleeding ink—through the always whispering network of Mrs. Clancey's friends and associates; to Rebecca's possibly insidious brother (had she other secret siblings, Squire wondered, who might creep from the woodwork?); to the servants who sometimes seemed to Squire to have more influence than their employers.

But he could still take refuge, this evening, in his own version of reality: *pommes surprises* and the day's gossip at Sherry's; an earthquake arriving via the late mail; two glasses of port and three hands of cards and to bed.

SQUIRE *DID* GET his letter from the seismologist, that evening. We must resist the temptation to say he deserved it, after weathering the trial of Mrs. Clancey's drawing room—the universe does not dole out rewards and punishments with any such sense of balance or desert. But Oscar— reclining on the sofa with his feet in Squire's lap, watching his husband read and reread with tipsy relish T. E. Doe's explanation of continental drift—found it impossible, at least in his own case, to remain impartial.

There was also something in the mail tray for Vivian, which Squire managed to pass her without looking up from his own correspondence.

We must pause here to attend to this, a matter of no small importance— leaving Squire and Oscar, well enough occupied for the moment, on the outside of the huddle.

SEVEN

To catch us up: Vivian had received no direct response to either of her messages to Sofia. Not at the hotel in California, to which she had returned in thick-tongued and head-twinging disgrace after her disillusioning interview with Sybil Parnacott; and not since, back in New York.

For a few weeks fate had left her in total doubt, ricocheting between unbearable options: on the one hand, perhaps Sofia had never received the letters, and they were still at large somewhere in Los Angeles's seamy underbelly—Vivian's second message in particular being ripe for blackmail by some unscrupulous theater hand, or janitor, or even the very bicycle messenger she'd tipped so handsomely to deliver it.

Or else, worse, Sofia *had* received the messages—but with indifference, possibly even laughter.

It had been a matter of some significant private deliberation, since Vivian's humiliation and return, as to which of these two outcomes would be the least appealing.

Interception and blackmail would be the greater danger to her reputation, certainly—and it would threaten collateral damage, Oscar and Squire and the entire company, their whole fragile syndicate. A decade of careful empire building could all be undone—Vivian had almost marveled at the thought—if only some opportunistic stagehand were to unearth a forgotten envelope in the corner of Sofia's dressing room and be smart enough to think of a way to earn a little extra money.

Still, at moments during the intervening weeks, it had seemed to Vivian—and by this we may know the depth of her distress—that she would rather have lost it all than to know that Sofia Bianchi, her first true flame, was as coldly indifferent to her memory as that teenage celluloid acrobat who had treated Vivian to two cocktails and enough rope to hang herself.

She might, perhaps, have borne rationally one of the two blows—Sofia's inconclusive silence or Sybil's definite sneer. But both together were too much even for Vivian.

She had not involved Oscar and Squire in this private spiral, requesting from them neither comfort nor advice. This in itself was not unusual. It had never been a feature of their arrangement—largely, of course, because Vivian had never faltered so egregiously. *Heartbreak* was not in her vocabulary. But even in the case of lesser disappointments (and they had occurred—Vivian was not made of stone) it had never been her custom to invite a crowd. She withdrew; she solved or excised the issue, as though amputating a gangrenous limb; she recovered and returned to action. And her husbands had been well trained by this customary strength (which had the advantage, from their perspective, of never requiring them to provide her with any real support) not to notice in her any signs of secret distress.

A few weeks into Vivian's lonely, fearful embarrassment—only partially tempered by renewed industry at the office, and by romantic conquests across the Lower West Side, and by the impulsive purchase of three new shades of lipstick in a single outing—everything had changed. Vivian received a letter, the predecessor of the one we have just seen Squire hand her.

THE AUTHOR OF this first missive had taken pains to remain anonymous: the penmanship was disguised (or at least unfamiliar in Vivian's memory); the return address a post office box near the Flatiron Building; the note signed only *An Old Friend*. But the message itself was clear and definite: the author of the letter was, she claimed (in so many words), one of Vivian's former lovers. She wasted little time on pleasantries before making reference to "souvenirs of old exploits"—some unspecified proof of their liaison that she might, in the regrettable event of an unfriendly reception to her enclosed proposal, deliver to "the authorities."

The proposal in question: five hundred dollars, delivered by mail to the same post office box, or—if Vivian preferred—via an arranged drop-off at a modest hotel uptown.

This was, of course, concerning. Prosecutions of queers (and the businesses at which they gathered) were on the rise, and legislation lagged decreasingly far behind the evolving social concept of female inversion. All of Vivian's careful coverage—her public and respectable marriage; her anonymity in approaching and hosting women; her meticulous limitation of her conquests to a few encounters per girl—served her well enough in daily life, among a basically stupid populace. But even light scrutiny might uncover to common knowledge at least the extent of her professional involvement at C&S, which on its own would label her unnatural and degenerate. From there public opinion might move exponentially, and sentence her to anything it liked. She had seen it done—from high-profile cases of personal defamation like Elizabeth Trondle's to any number of Village saloons and tearooms catering to "bachelor girls," raided on technicalities and reestablished under new names, their bohemian whimsy more battle worn with each reincarnation, until there was too little left to rise from the ashes. (Vivian had even contributed to the atmosphere—though she would never have described her actions in this way—in self-protective asides distancing herself from the more openly "unusual.")

Alongside all this concern—it came, almost, as a species of relief—a guilty and paranoid chime had been well prepared to sound in Vivian's heart. Here, she thought, after weeks of anxious obsession, was at last her answer as to the fate of her second message to Sofia.

And yet. Vivian had reread, and reconsidered.

There was an element of theater to the thing, wasn't there? It wasn't particularly well done. The inanity, the almost *sweetness*, of the blackmailer inviting Vivian to choose the method of delivery of her own ransom—in person, or through the mail? And the New York postmark: this was no opportunistic Californian sweeper of concert-hall dressing rooms.

Addressing the letter to Vivian herself, rather than to Oscar, meant it was someone who knew her personally, knew in broad strokes the dynamics of her household. (Though not its every particular—otherwise, of course, there would have been much more to ransom.) Someone, in short, who knew that to contact Vivian's husband was emphatically *not* to go over her head.

And then there was the matter of the signature: *An Old Friend.* How many of these, after all, could Vivian boast? She had always been careful with her attachments, if liberal in her glancing encounters. She did not idly leave behind "souvenirs of old exploits." It had been years since Patience Stone had moved abroad—besides, this was not Patience's style. And it was too subtle to be Meg Booth, who—leaving aside the shallow nature of their association—had always been a creature of public performance. She might have demonstrated on a picket line or chained herself to a wheel; she would never have sent an anonymous threat.

It was Sofia, Vivian thought, or it was no one.

For additional evidence there was the address of the post office box: just a block away from the former site of the Fifth Avenue Hotel, where she and Sofia had lived together. Since demolished, but this was New York: there was always something new going up.

Vivian had combed newspapers and concert notices, looking for any reference to Sofia's current location—Paris, Venice . . . New York? Was she touring, still? Had she returned to Europe?

Vivian could find no public announcement of her presence. She might have been anywhere. Perhaps, even, in Manhattan: playing a titillating cat-and-mouse game with a lover she had just learned was married in name only, still cutthroat sharp and white-hot at her core, a rocketing success in her own field and faithful to the memory of the time they'd shared.

The letter, the whole game, a half-playful repayment for Sofia's first misunderstanding—Vivian's cover story, too convincingly enacted, which had led to Sofia's avoiding her on tour.

Vivian might, of course, have hired an investigator to confirm all this. To stake out the post office box across from the ghost of her love nest, track down for certain whether Sofia was staying in town (possibly under an assumed name), file a report with the police.

But besides drawing attention to the very accusation Vivian hoped to bury, involving any authorities would have let all the air out of the game. She preferred to trust her well-seasoned instincts, returned to her at last in a welcome rush of certainty. An unmatched thrill at the thought that she had erred only in assuming Sofia would have with age become as simple and dumb as the new girls, reduced to superficial solicitations delivered via the front door. Hadn't the two of them once lied their way into men's gambling palaces and caroused all night with polyglot troupes of foreign actors?

This pantomime of extortion, Vivian thought, this deliciously frightening anticipation, was the punishment and the reward that Sofia had arranged for Vivian's careless bravado with the letter in California. It was as much promise as chastisement: Vivian had been outmaneuvered at last.

Relief flooded her, and arousal, and terror, and joy. She'd been a fool, she thought, to think a snub-nosed girl turning backflips before a movie camera could do *this*.

The feeling, of course, depended in part on the thrill of the next move being hers.

She had debated, at first, how much money to send. None at all would be bravely defiant—but might read as antagonistic (or worse, imply that Vivian had no money *to* send). She considered sending a portion of the sum demanded—a hundred dollars, perhaps—with the promise of more if her "assailant" were to meet her in person. At the pokey hotel already named in their "negotiation," or at Vivian's pied-à-terre, or—depending on the naturally evolving tenor of the game—in some agreed-upon park or patch of riverfront or watering hole of (moderately) ill repute. But to submit partial payment and promise the rest upon fulfillment of a liaison smacked of prostitution, and even in roleplay Vivian had her pride.

She had settled on the full sum, five hundred dollars. In the surface-level terms of the game, she would be following the rules. If this were part of Sofia's pleasure—to imagine her quarry frightened and compliant— then she would have her wish. But Vivian would also, tacitly, be showing Sofia how much wealth she had accrued. How far her star had risen in the years since she had charged every poached egg to Sofia's room number.

Let her see, Vivian thought, how casually she could now sacrifice five hundred dollars to a bit of stone-faced foreplay.

But she had enclosed with the money a sheet of heavy-weight card-stock: an invitation to Mrs. Clancey's Christmas party. (Every year she and Oscar were allotted a certain number, to distribute among the C&S executives and upper management. Vivian had considered the fact that one or another senior clerk's life would change for the worse, as a side effect of this game she was playing with Sofia; efficiently she made her peace with it.) It may have been many years since Sofia had called New York home, but everyone knew this party, and the value of an invitation. By the reckoning of some perennially snubbed hopefuls, that sheet of cardstock was worth more than the other contents of the envelope. To bestow it was its own act of largesse—and a show of bravado, besides, that within the world of the game Vivian was so unafraid of scandal as to invite her blackmailer to a party.

And: it was a chance to see Sofia again, on the strangest night and longest trial of Vivian's year, when such a reappearance would be most welcome. They could start over again, Vivian thought. They already had.

To An Old Friend, Vivian had written, *with no hard feelings.*

THAT LETTER SHE had sent two days ago. Now—her face so carefully schooled that Oscar and Squire took no notice, except perhaps of her absorption—she slit open the reply and read.

It would be my Honour to accept with Pleasure your Kind Invitation.

That same penmanship: too careful, yet almost sloppy. Sofia, Vivian thought, must be holding the pen in her left hand. Yes—now that she was looking for it, there was an almost-familiar, tell-tale spidery quality to the upward strokes. And what a polite, even prim, even *simpering* response. The British spelling! As if copied out of a petit bourgeois etiquette guide. What a difference, compared with the saber-rattling of An Old Friend's first letter.

The game, Sofia seemed to signal, was in flux. Anything might happen. Vivian's smile broadened.

"What's that?" Oscar asked.

Squire, who had been reading aloud for the second time a paragraph describing (with more enthusiasm than accuracy) South America plowing through the earth's undersea crust as though tilling a furrow in the floor of the Atlantic, broke off midsentence and looked up. "What's what?"

"Vivian's got a letter," Oscar said, pointing. "And she's *smirking* at it."

Vivian bit her cheek. "I am not," she said, lightly. "I am reading. You should learn, sometime."

"What is it?"

"An acceptance," Vivian said, "for the Christmas party." She offered it casually to the men, dangling the sheet from one lackadaisical hand. (This kind of bluff, misdirection through apparent compliance, remained one of her great tactical strengths.)

Squire—having had more than enough of party logistics for the day— shook his head, attention already returning to his own correspondence. Oscar shrugged and resettled himself on the sofa.

This in itself was a crackling boost to Vivian's euphoria—under the circumstances, even the most minor manipulation of Squire and Oscar recalled echoes of past glories. She felt like herself, again—like the woman who had flicked these men over an aquarium railing and sent them tumbling into each other's arms, while she built an empire on their names. Like the omnipotent architect of entire human lives. Like she still held the reins. "Speaking of the party," she said mildly. She folded An Old Friend's letter with a sharp crease, tucked it back into its envelope. "I haven't set you two this year's challenge, yet."

Squire fumbled his letter, dropping two of its sheets: Australia and Antarctica sailed in opposite directions across the floor. Oscar reflexively lunged after one—missed—stopped with one hand planted on the rug, his feet still in a tangle on Squire's startled lap.

Neither man spoke. Vivian delayed a moment, savoring it. With careful focus she refilled her glass of port, wiped the lip of the decanter, stoppered it, and returned it to the tray. Sipped.

"Well?" she asked, finally. "What does the professor have to say for himself?"

"Me?" Squire asked.

Oscar, with some effort, hoisted himself from the floor back onto the sofa.

"What uncharted corners of the Clancey country manse still wait to be explored?" Vivian asked. She feigned surprise at their equally feigned incomprehension. "Don't tell me you haven't talked about it."

Squire, businesslike, gave up the act and laid aside his seismology.

Oscar—immediately, furiously—blushed. "You don't have to—" he began.

"The gallery," Squire began, counting on his fingers. "The morning room, the gun room, the smoking room, the library, the south parlor, the breakfast room." (He paused here to dutifully receive a general, affectionately mocking jeer—the usual reference to his initial use of this label for their own dining room, due to its diminutive size.) "The ballroom and salons and dining room will be taken up with party. But there's all the guest suites, of course," he said.

"Oh, of course," Vivian interjected. Oscar squirmed. She smiled at him, pleasantly.

"And the plunge-bath dressing rooms, and the attic." Squire folded his hands.

"That's all?"

Squire cleared his throat, and looked to Oscar.

"We're declaring some rooms off-limits," Oscar said. He sat up, planting his feet on the floor. This turn in the conversation seemed to settle his nerves, a bit—the litigation of terms being a soothing exercise for him in almost any circumstance.

"Oh?" Vivian sipped.

"The servant's quarters," Oscar said. "And the master and mistress suites, and—the nursery."

Vivian let this hang in silence for a long moment. "The servant's quarters, of course, granted," she said. "Now, as to—"

"Vivian," Oscar groaned. Squire, his own ears pinking slightly, retrieved his letter and performed a bit of blind administrative work, shuffling and reshuffling its pages.

"*As to the rest*," Vivian pushed. "Disqualified on what grounds?"

"Don't make him—"

"My parents' suites are in use," Squire said—with quiet finality that cleared a patch of silence in its wake. No distinction, in this group, needed to be made between the "use" of a room by a living parent and by the ghost of one. The rooms were, put simply, occupied.

"There," Vivian said, after a moment's recovery. She raised her glass in a kind of abbreviated toast to Squire's candor. "Granted. See, now, Oscar? I'm not an unreasonable person. All I ask from my gentlemen is that they be able to articulate their wishes."

Oscar harrumphed, loosening his collar.

". . . And the nursery?" Vivian asked.

"Jehoshaphat," Oscar said. "I'm going to bed."

Squire grabbed a fistful of Oscar's jacket as he tried to stand, tugging just hard enough to resettle him on the sofa.

"Cowards forfeit," Vivian said, with another appreciative nod in Squire's direction.

"I am *not*," Squire annunciated clearly, without loosening his grip on Oscar's coat, "going to fuck my husband in my own nursery."

Oscar, making a sound as if he were deflating, buried his face in his hands.

Vivian laughed so hard she almost upset her glass. "Granted, granted," she managed at last. She felt loose and languid at every joint, mental and physical. She and Sofia would have their own game to play, she thought, this year. Perhaps she could choose them a room of their own to conquer. "Too bad," she said—and stood, wiping tears of mirth from her eyes. "I thought for a moment you were going to ask for a baby, again."

It was, on every plane but audible sound, as if a shotgun had gone off in the room—the startled spasm; the sudden and complete rupture of the preceding atmosphere; the sense of danger narrowly escaped; the smell of something burning. A final sense of satisfied power clicked into place, and at last Vivian was through for the evening.

Squire and Oscar, caught between shock and mania, spoke haltingly over each other. "Is that—" "Do—" "Are you—"

"Good night," Vivian said mildly, draining her glass. "Sleep well. I'll let you know as soon as I've reached a decision." She tucked her letter into her décolletage and started for the door to her wing of the house. "Whichever of the guest rooms is the grandest, I should think." With that, she retired.

Oscar and Squire lingered for a long moment in stunned silence, on opposite ends of the sofa.

"Fuck me," Oscar said finally, with a ragged exhale.

"Good lord," Squire said, raking a hand through his hair. "Was that—"

They both dissolved into nervous laughter.

"Leave it," Squire said, swallowing. With a flat hand he gestured for caution. "Leave it, for now."

This much, preparing for bed, the men agreed upon: that there was no need for further stimulation, on this particular evening; and that the chaotic season of the holiday, of the Christmas party, was clearly already upon them. A little sooner this year, perhaps, than in the past. But then— Oscar kept this last thought to himself, still superstitiously wary of raising the topic of Mrs. Van Beek—they had more than usual, this year, from which to recover in catharsis.

EIGHT

S uch banner events are always upon us sooner than we anticipate; there is never, it seems, enough time to prepare: we have come to the night of the Clancey Christmas party.

Another pin in the map: Yonkers, midwinter, the Clancey country house ablaze like a torch signaling to some sentry keeping a lonely, frigid vigil atop the New Jersey palisades.

We have been here before—this house, this party, this protest against the darkest week of quite another year. Do you recall? It was the site of Squire's eruption and flight, at the turn of the century. Together we watched him, fifteen years earlier, run gasping down these wide stone steps and pause, wretched, before fleeing into the city and scrabbling for entrance to the sewer system. That desperate bid for catastrophic freedom had put him on the path to St. Augustine and *The Chemical History of a Candle*; to ruining Oscar's life and then saving it; to reaching out for what he wanted and for the first time finding his hand clasped in return; to being swept up into the sublime and terrifying cyclone of Vivian's influence.

Time and cause unravel in all directions, and our story has countless points of origin—Patience Stone's safety bicycle whipping downhill outside Utica; Hiram Ainsley's proffered ladle of lemonade at an Ohio church picnic; Mount Tambora's pyroclastic blast blanketing the atmosphere—but this blue-blood cobblestone driveway, rimed in the punishing ice of the Hudson midwinter, is one of them.

What a time our trio has weathered, together, since last we graced this doorstep. Now, horse-drawn ghosts mingle with combustion engines at the curb. Electric bulbs burn incandescent in every window. Music blares from the open doorway, tangling with shrieks of laughter and the syncopated stomp of dancing feet. We are late; the party is already in full swing. Hurry, hurry!

WE JOIN THE scene as it begins to soar from revelry into bacchanalian chaos: arguments and intrigue; love affairs ended and begun; countless champagne cocktails splashed onto dresses and across carpets and, of course, down throats. Someone had found a piano and was taking requests, dueling with the strains of the live band in the ballroom; from yet another room, a Victrola insisted on last season's show tunes in a tinny whine.

It is always an overwhelming task, at such gatherings, to locate one's acquaintances among the swirling, brightly painted crowd. Mrs. Clancey's circle was no less exclusive than in years past—on the contrary, she was only becoming more devoted to her grudges as she aged—yet the house was fuller, this year, than it had ever been. Simply put, the New York elite were multiplying—each family tree branching into fractal patterns, variously diamond-encrusted or disgraced. A whole generation has risen almost to majority, since we began our tale. In Mrs. Clancey's white-and-gold ballroom the untitled princelings of ancient families, thin-voiced and freshly prepped for Harvard or Yale, bowed before their mothers' and grandmothers' purple-wigged contemporaries; girls just barely "out," still plump-cheeked and sweating nervously into their satin slippers, dodged these ancestresses' husbands and their too-friendly hands. Fir trees scraped the ceiling; the second balcony groaned under the weight of its garlands. Red velvet and evergreen; winterberry and holly; and over everything an even dusting of false snow. There was much talk of war, past and future; of politics and business; of pictures and books and dresses; and, always, of—was that a waiter?—a little more champagne.

There goes Squire! Catch him as he passes!

Squire was, already, run off his feet. He had never, when Mr. Clancey was alive, noticed his father being a particularly active host of each year's Christmas party. But in recent years his mother, her trust in paid employees eroding, had delegated to Squire a number of responsibilities—supervising the installation of the ice sculptures, the buffet of canapes, the program of musical performances—that Squire suspected might more properly have been assigned to a professional steward or housekeeper or social secretary.

And then there was the matter of Rebecca Van Beek. All evening, with almost clockwork regularity, Mrs. Clancey had sent Squire to refresh Mrs. Van Beek's glass, or to ask after her children's health, or to offer to find her a seat variously nearer to or farther from the musicians. (Elias Knox—devotee of pomp and hors d'oeuvres and now of Mrs. Van Beek, as resplendent as he could manage, approximately three-quarters full of champagne—had by Squire's fourth interruption of his attempted tête-à-tête with Rebecca given up on pretending not to look murderous.) And what was more, Mrs. Clancey was showing disturbing signs of a willingness—further lubricated by the wine—to escalate further, if necessary. With an unmistakably threatening air she had finally introduced Squire to Rebecca's brother (Paul had good-naturedly crushed the bones in Squire's hand) and suggested that they all "have a word" once Squire had seen to the last of the programming.

Still, Squire was enjoying himself as much as possible, given the fact that the evening was designed to pull him like taffy into shapes he hardly recognized. He was wearing a holly-sprig boutonniere that matched Oscar's; every time they caught a glimpse of each other across the room, the mirrored sight was a boost of courage.

"Mr. Clancey," said a red-faced stranger, with a tap on Squire's shoulder, "your mother was asking for you."

Squire flashed Oscar a distant, apologetic smile and vanished.

ON OSCAR'S ARM, Vivian was—of course—distracted. Already hours into the party, she had yet to see any sign of Sofia. This was not concerning, necessarily—in their youth, they had made it a habit to arrive almost in the final moments of a fete, to make a sport out of stoking its dying embers and bringing the celebration roaring back to life. The accompanying thrill of exercising power over lesser guests, scuttling others' plans for the rest of their evenings—their fogged heads and exhausted limbs crying out unheeded for sleep, their blind impulses toward pleasure so easily manipulated. By this method it had always been possible, no matter the initial purpose of a party, for Sofia and Vivian to end the night as its guests of honor.

And if anyone could steal the entirety of Christmas in this way, Vivian thought, it was Sofia. After all, on their first meeting, she had stolen New Year's Eve. She had stolen the entire twentieth century.

Still: times had changed, and Vivian was impatient. Continually she scanned the crowd, dragged Oscar from room to room, watched for signs of satin-draped movement in each doorway. She was on either her third or her fourth glass of champagne, she thought. Possibly her fifth. But equally possibly her second. (Times had changed, indeed: how far we have come, from Vivian's days of sober observation on the outskirts of the revelry.)

"Vivian," Oscar panted. "Vivian."

"Yes?"

Oscar was not counting his glasses of champagne. He was not having that sort of evening. He had noticed, better perhaps than Squire himself, what Mrs. Clancey was up to. He had caught the gossip, somewhere over his left shoulder, that their hostess was "giving the next generation one last chance to arrange its own affairs." With every lull in the music, every chime of silverware on crystal, Oscar half expected to hear the announcement that his husband was engaged.

Now he craned over his shoulder—Squire had been swept off, most recently, in the direction of the music room. "We're going the wrong way," he said, his voice slushy.

"There is no 'wrong way,'" Vivian said. "It's a party." Her patience with Oscar was wearing thin; he'd twice more brought up (or tried to—luckily his cowardice and discombobulation had outcompeted his recklessness) the idea of having a child.

It was Vivian's own fault, she thought, for reopening the subject even in jest a few weeks before. But back in their own house, marinating in their bespoke domesticity—Oscar's feet in Squire's lap; Sofia's letter warm against Vivian's décolletage—it had seemed a harmless, even a heady lever to pull.

Now, on the other hand—in rigidly heterosexual public, with Mrs. Clancey directing Squire every half hour to reaudition for the role of stepfather—settling once and for all the matter of whether they *could* perhaps counterpromise Squire a child had, by Oscar's reckoning, taken on a sudden dire urgency.

"This *is* the wrong way," Oscar muttered.

"Have a glass of water," Vivian said.

"I'm just . . ." Oscar took an unsuccessfully stealthy step back in the direction of the music room. "I'm just going to . . ."

Pink-gold silk flashed in Vivian's peripheral vision; she whirled to follow it. "Fine, I'll find you later," she said, and disappeared.

OSCAR HAD A doubled advantage over Vivian, in searching a raucous crowd for his beloved: his own size (he stood at least half a head taller than most of the other guests), and the silver flame of Squire's hair as an object to scan for. Still, it is difficult to overestimate the combined power of low-grade panic and a heavy pour to frustrate an otherwise straightforward task.

"Mr. Schmidt!" A delighted scold of a salutation accompanied a strong tug at his elbow—a swooping fall, a pillowed landing. Oscar found himself abruptly occupying one side of a tête-à-tête chair, the sinuous curve of rosewood and velvet nudging into conspiratorial embrace himself on one side, and on the other—in rich green velvet and yards of lace, glittering brightly but indistinctly at the earlobe and neckline—Squire's mother.

"*There* you are!" Mrs. Clancey said.

"Yes," Oscar managed.

"It's been too long."

Mrs. Clancey had a silk fan with a mother-of-pearl handle, painted with a scene of a youth playing the lute at the feet of a disinterested-looking girl. The tête-à-tête pushed the two so close that as she fanned herself, Oscar caught the breeze. Mystic Zephyr. He closed his eyes; opened them. His situation remained unchanged. "Hello," he said. "It's"—he gestured—"It's a lovely party. Have you seen—?"

"I wish you'd have a word with Squire," Mrs. Clancey said.

"Yes!" Oscar said. "Yes. Where is . . . ?"

"Now, you know as well as I do that he'll be a wonderful husband," Mrs. Clancey said.

Oscar began to have the impression that the tête-à-tête was, very slowly, revolving in the center of the room.

"You're all that's made him fit for it, practically," Mrs. Clancey was saying. "It's all your and Mrs. Schmidt's influence—and I can't thank you both enough." She gave Oscar's arm a grateful swat with her fan. "Lord knows I tried, for *years*, but you see where it gets me." She rolled her eyes.

Oscar found that the seat had picked up speed; he was beginning to list to the left from the strength of its spin.

"He just needs a little . . . push," Mrs. Clancey continued her diagnosis in a whisper, leaning even closer to Oscar's face. He could see where he might have better advised her maid in the application of her talcum powder. "There's the lady's brother," she said. "He understands the situation, more or less, and he's ready to step in if necessary—but I'd prefer it to come from someone Squire knows, someone who knows . . . how he is." Mrs. Clancey, still powerfully driven by fear of embarrassment, had never overcome the instinct to keep the inner circle of those who "handled" Squire—those who had to be fully briefed on his foibles—as small as possible. "*You* know how he is," she said again. And Oscar did, almost infinitely better than Mrs. Clancey herself. But his breath came with difficulty; he missed his chance to reply or refute. "He can't do anything on his own," Mrs. Clancey continued—somewhat ridiculously, given Squire's largely single-handed execution of the party whirling around her as she spoke. "But this is the one thing he really should. Well! Almost the one thing. Ha! Though even if that didn't—there are the other man's children already. And you should see, how he dotes on them! Anyone can see what's next, it's common sense, half of New York thinks they're engaged already. Wouldn't you think they're engaged already? Look at them! Oh, now where did they—well, never mind."

Oscar turned to follow her searching gaze—blindly, and several seconds late. He was by this point working hard to retain his seat on the tête-à-tête, holding fast to both his own dedicated armrest and the center bar. He was somewhat amazed that a woman as venerable as Mrs. Clancey was so at her ease, given the speed of the thing's rotation.

In another lifetime, Oscar had thought he knew fear. Fear of discovery, of unmasking, of punishments earthly and divine. Fear of police raids; charges of obscenity and sodomy; prison or worse. A shredded reputation, a ruined future. And fear of the judgment of Grandmother Hester—whose sneering ghost was also with them now on the tête-à-tête, subcutaneous but séance-clear. ("But he won't listen to *me*, of course," Mrs. Clancey was saying; "I'm only his *mother*.")

But this was different. This was not the crippling but generalized uneasiness that Oscar might—somehow, someday—be recognized by the wrong person. This was the specific, desperate fear of a specific, desperate loss. The loss of Squire. The loss of Squire.

"But you have such an influence over him." Mrs. Clancey was, somehow, still talking. "I'd hate to lean on the poor woman's brother more than necessary," she said, cringing at the potential embarrassment of forcing the matter. Whatever Oscar's face was doing, it seemed to pass to Mrs. Clancey's eye for a sympathetic wince. "I *know* if you'd only have a talk with him, man to man, about the thing," she said, "and explain how much he'll enjoy it. Marriage, I mean. And that there's no sense in cheating us all—himself included, I might add!—out of a little peace in our golden years."

Himself included, Oscar thought. The wallpaper blurred into a smear of fast-moving color. A little peace for Squire, himself, included.

"She's such a lovely girl, and she's well suited to him—well, as much as anyone *could* be, but you know what I mean, they won't upset each other—and besides that, there's—well—there's the continuation of two of New York's best families, if you don't mind me saying so, only I know the boy's father—God rest his soul—isn't here to say it. If you'd only make Squire see that it's just not worth the loss of *all that*, Mr. Schmidt, for the sake of avoiding *one* conversation he's just too stubborn and stupid to—"

A strong hand fell with a thump on Oscar's shoulder, and the tête-à-tête screeched to a halt.

"Excuse us, mother," Squire said. "But the arias have started, and in the meantime Mr. Schmidt had asked to see the Bouguereau in the Iris Room."

THE MAIN GUEST suite—the Iris Room—was made up as if for a visitor, but the offer seemed decidedly half-hearted. It was musty, smelling faintly of mothballs, and the fire was cold. "Whoever's drunkest may have to sleep up here, eventually," Squire said, shrugging off his jacket. "But that's ages away, even at the rate they're going." He retrieved a pot of Vaseline from his inner pocket. "I couldn't find Vivian, but you be arbiter; she'll believe you." He held out his hands for Oscar's coat. "Since you're such a terrible liar." (Squire himself, of course, was no better—but he could sometimes be obtuse enough to come across as disingenuous. As, for instance, when taking several minutes to notice his husband was having a nervous breakdown.)

"Oh, my God," Oscar said. He felt for the bedpost, missing it.

"What? What is it?"

"You're supposed to marry that woman," Oscar said.

"No, I'm not," Squire said, and reached for his jacket again.

"Your mother told me," Oscar said, slapping at his hands.

"Well, she doesn't—"

"She told me to *make you*," Oscar hissed, grabbing Squire's hands to stop a third attempt to unbutton him. "She told me to *explain* to you why you *should*."

"Oh?" Squire played it, we regret to report, a bit more arch than was perhaps strictly appropriate. "And why should I?"

"*Because!*"

This last was almost a shout. After a startled glance at the door, finally, Squire clicked into the correct groove. "Oscar?" he asked, dropping his hands. "Are you alright?"

Oscar made a helpless gesture. There were tears in his eyes, though of what complex accord of frustration, grief, and surplus champagne it would be difficult to define precisely. (Certainly the champagne was the top note; it was already evaporating.)

"I don't know what my mother told you," Squire said. "But I'm not getting married."

"Well, she didn't say *that*, did she?"

"I don't *know* what she said."

"Of *course* you don't!"

We here observe a moment of silence memorializing the countless victims of the alcohol-soaked argument of misunderstanding—an ancient ritual with many casualties and no victors.

Oscar, we must remember, had long been a scholar of worst-case scenarios large and small. We have seen him in these pages devote his scrupulously undivided attention to the complete text of a museum plaque on the life cycle of a mosquito, in order to be best prepared for where he might meet them (and how many of them, and to what dire end). With equal, if more consequential, devotion he had over the years read countless columns of newsprint and legal precedents breaking down men of his sort into subcategories, ascribing typical ages and physiques and personalities and entire new sexes on the basis of their carnal roles. (He knew, too, in the rational part of his mind, that he and Squire did not conform to even a meandering approximation of these rules' supposed sense.) But in this research he had also read about certain courtroom explanations of compulsive, coercing "congenital inverts," and the ill-fated, otherwise normal "acquired inverts" they waylaid—on nefarious purpose, went the legal defenses that invoked the concept.

Or perhaps, the thought had occurred in the whirling centrifuge of the tête-à-tête sofa, in other cases, entirely by accident.

But Oscar, not known for his oratory at the best of times, was not in anywhere near prime condition to express all this complexly repressed angst.

"I'm supposed to tell you that you're supposed to propose to her," he said. "And you are. Supposed to. Propose to her. Because she's—that's—" He gestured expansively at the world on the other side of the Iris Room door, as if the rest were obvious. "And this is just—because I made you," he said.

Squire actually gasped. "How dare you," he said.

And it is up to all of us, Squire himself included, to parse whether he meant this seriously, or in jest.

There is a natural disadvantage, in intimate arguments, for that partner less perpetually prepared for tragedy. Here, perhaps, is the doubled edge of Squire's optimism: all genuine disappointments occurred to him as ambushes, and so the river-smooth stone of Oscar's daily what-if worry struck him now as a knife in the gut. And though Oscar's concern was as to the acceptability his own behavior, it was a matter of no small pride and sensitivity to Squire, to hear the autonomy of his own decisions questioned once again.

"How dare you," he said again, still uncertain as to whether the matter—whether his own tone—was a playful or a serious one.

"Oh, darling, I'm sorry—" escaped Oscar instinctively.

Treading on the heels of his own challenge to their relationship's legitimacy, this was just ridiculous enough to tip the scales.

"You *made* me?" Squire asked in an aggravated whisper, thumping Oscar's chest hard enough to rock him backward. "Then I suppose you *make* me?"

"No," Oscar said. "Well—"

"I suppose it's *you* who fucks *me*?" Like a trained assassin, Squire targeted the most ticklish part of Oscar's side with a pincered hand.

"Stop it," Oscar said. "*Don't*, this is *serious*. *Stop* it. That's not even what I—"

"And I suppose," Squire slotted two fingers into Oscar's pocket and drew him closer, an echo of their first embrace. "You were the one to do this?"

"Well," Oscar said. "But—"

"You refused to even be in the same room with me," Squire said.

"That wasn't—" Oscar said. "That was different. I hated you. I mean—this isn't helping."

Oscar was so intent on his own shirtfront, Squire had to duck to meet his gaze. "I had to throw myself into a walrus pool to get you to touch me," he said.

Oscar had been for fifty-four years afraid of disaster in general, and for ten of those afraid of losing Squire in particular. This was a lifetime's practice, reinforced daily by the industrious Mrs. Clanceys and the blameless yet implicated Rebecca Van Beeks of the world, and was far too entrenched in him to be undone by one absurd and kittenish line. Still, a journey of a thousand miles begins with a single step.

He lost two buttons in the initial tumble.

"I HAD TO throw myself into a walrus pool." An interesting elision, there—understandably more noticeable to us than to Squire, who never saw Vivian kick him over the railing. But isn't it fascinating, how we tell and retell the stories that matter to us? How with repetition, chance is subsumed into inevitable fate, and accident into willful action? How, once we decide on our protagonists, the rest of the crowd fades to background?

Besides which, there is this: none of the events happening in the Iris Room this evening—the tears, the grief, the reassurance, the mock-wrestling, the gripping and stroking and half-stifled moans—would have happened without Vivian. And yet, did we miss her once, in all the preceding drama? Did we spare her a thought, now, when she needs it most, alone and unarmed behind enemy lines and still on the lookout for Sofia?

If only the happiness we brought to others (even in passing) was necessarily visited back upon us, according to the balance of some cosmic ledger. If only providing assistance was reliably more rewarding than visiting injury, that the universe might instinctively train toward not mere progress but improvement. If only fate were always reciprocal, and always linear, and always fair. If only all side effects were happy accidents, and all eruptions joyous. If only there were no years without summers.

AFTER SEPARATING FROM Oscar, Vivian had followed the champagne-colored silk phantom back to the ballroom—then promptly lost it in the crowd of dancers and spectators. Still, reason told her not to chase after the figure too desperately. That pinkish-gold, after all, had been the color of Sofia's dress on the night they'd met. Sixteen years ago, almost to the day. Of course she would not be wearing the same gown. Vivian was more reasonable than that, she scolded herself. She had to keep her wits about her. She had to be ready for anything.

She closed her eyes and took a deep breath, attempting to clear her mind of expectations.

"Vivian?" A light touch on her forearm.

Do *you* know, already, what to expect? Have you been reading with dread, peering between your fingers? Or have sixteen intervening years of success made you as forgetful as Vivian?

Electra Stevens (née Blake) was—as at their first meeting, when she'd been reporting as the Midtown Tattler on Patience Stone's debutante ball—wearing the shabbiest dress in the room. Back then, it was what had drawn Vivian to her in the first place. Now, it had made her invisible to Vivian as she scanned.

"I thought that was you," Electra said. A smile wavered on her face, flickering between warmth and uncertainty.

Electra was, to Vivian's eye, blowsy and disheveled with age. (In fact she was six months younger than Vivian and had redone her hair twice for the party.) It is true that life had not been overly generous to Electra—though we can at least report that the depletion of her parents' estate had not been hastened in any meaningful way by the parasitic months Vivian had spent with them in 1899, doctoring Electra's social columns heavily in her own favor (and eliding her homelessness by sleeping in Electra's bed each night), until the abrupt New Year's Eve on which she'd thrown her over for Sofia. The Blake family's ruin had been rather more quotidian: Electra's father had taken some bad advice on Wall Street; and then Electra herself had had the personally disadvantageous luck to marry, in Roger Stevens, that rare creature: a New York policeman who was wholly unskilled in attracting bribery. (Indeed, graft was such an accepted fact of the job that the salary, out of which Roger was expected to purchase his uniform and equipment, was kept low to compensate for it. The remainder had already strained to cover the couple's expenses before the birth of their second child, four years before.)

Vivian was, for a long and uncharacteristic moment, speechless. Even at an event built around glad-handing and social performance, there were certain circles she could not have anticipated combining.

Her first thought was that she had no interest in making small talk, in neglecting the search for Sofia in order to speak with Electra and ponder the ravages of time, wondering which of her own features—her creased forehead, her thickening waist—Sofia might remember differently, might regard with an echo of Vivian's own present shock.

At the same time, there was a harmonizing cringe of moral embarrassment. Vivian did not prefer to dwell on the particular segment of her girlish past that Electra represented. Vivian had *used* Electra—without delighting her, or furthering her interests alongside Vivian's own, or at least mixing her Brandy Crustas and letting her end their arrangement on her terms. Electra was an unwelcome visitor from an era in which Vivian had simply wrung people out and moved on.

(Perhaps you would argue that Vivian had never, in fact, left that era entirely behind. One step at a time; she has not even finished processing this first blow.)

"Electra Blake!" Vivian said finally, with a false laugh. She was still determined to hurdle over the distraction. "My goodness. What a—good evening. I'm sorry, I was just looking for—"

"I can't thank you enough, for the invitation," Electra said.

Vivian was a foolish person, but not a stupid one. When it finally came, the unraveling was complete and efficient. "It was you," she said. "You're An Old Friend."

"I'm sorry, if it wasn't the right thing, to come," Electra said. "I've never—I wouldn't have thought so, myself; not after . . ." With an oblique glance she made reference to the blackmail, to Vivian's five hundred dollars. "But then we've never—this was the first time we'd ever—we don't know, see, how it all works. And then you were so kind to send the invitation, and Roger was—he asked around the precinct, discreetly, and in the end he thought you might know better than us the rhythm of this kind of thing. And that we ought to accept." She glanced over her shoulder—to where Roger, an unremarkable and bulldoggish man of somehow intermediate height, was examining a leafy palm in the corner of the room and affecting to give the two women privacy.

Vivian followed Electra's gaze—but she would not have been able to pick Roger out of the crowd, even had she had the power to focus her vision.

"He thought perhaps you wanted to talk, more," Electra said. "Or arrange some kind of ongoing . . . arrangement. Which we—I should wait for him to talk about it, but if you—the money went quite a way to getting us clear, and we can't thank you enough, but you know how it is." Electra smiled apologetically: the embarrassment of poverty—of experiencing it, of acknowledging its very existence—at a bacchanal. "And Roger said that there wasn't much risk in coming tonight, since there isn't much you could do to us. I mean—" She blushed. "That's Roger's thinking, I mean. With him not knowing you, himself. He can only do his best, and it's hard for him, given—given my past. What we're having to discuss." She smiled, a shaky inhale. "But it *was* kind of you," she said, as if wiping the conversation clear again. "And I wanted to talk first, just the two of us. And make sure you know how dearly I mean that. You've done so well for yourself, and it's just—" Electra touched Vivian's wrist, again. "I know you didn't have to be so generous, after . . . everything."

Vivian smiled—unhinged, too broad, but quite genuine. Again, she thought, she had made the same mistake. Somehow, *again*.

And at least the first time a beautiful stranger with a husky voice had been turning backflips on the ceiling. Now it was only *this* ham-fisted plot that had outsmarted her. A moronic police officer, showing up to take formal credit for blackmail. And Electra, apologizing for the extortion as if she'd trodden on Vivian's foot at a garden party.

Sofia, Vivian thought, was not coming tonight. Sofia was, very probably, asleep—alone? Beside a partner?—on the other side of the Atlantic. Sofia did not care about Vivian whatsoever. Sofia had, perhaps, not spared Vivian a thought since she had collected the key to the hotel suite in 1904.

"What is it you have?" Vivian asked, grasping Electra's arm. She could hear that she sounded giddy. Perhaps, she thought, she was. Perhaps this was it, after all—hadn't she claimed to want to be outsmarted? Hadn't she wanted to meet her match? Why had she thought she would be able to dictate the terms of such a deception? The very idea was a paradox. This was—Electra inhaled sharply; Vivian was hurting her. Vivian tried to loosen her grip, but her fingers were nerveless. "What do you have?" she asked again. She leaned closer. Whatever familiar smell she might have recognized on Electra's skin had been overlain by Mystic Zephyr.

What had they done, together? What record of it had Vivian left? She couldn't remember anything, any notes or letters or receipts—but then, she hadn't remembered the godforsaken affair in the first place. She'd forgotten an entire woman; why would she remember every slip of paper or lipstick print?

"Because," Vivian said in a near whisper, "you can publish it, whatever it is." She could feel a laugh simmering in her chest. Whether she was trying to wrest control of the situation through intimidation, to find some titillation in the moment of downfall, or simply to destroy herself, she couldn't have said with any confidence.

"Publish it," she said again. "I. Don't. Care."

"O-oh," Electra said. "I—" With an abortive glance at Roger and a half-turn toward the wall, she reached furtively into her dress.

Distantly Vivian felt her breath disintegrate into quick pants; the trapped laughter was striking but would not catch. The amateurs had brought their weapon to the party. They were handing it over to her for inspection. A fire crackling not six paces away and Electra was leaning in to let her read—

It was a love letter, yes. But—Vivian's smile broadened, twitching—it was a note *from* Electra *to* Vivian. Left all those years ago on a pillow, no doubt, or clipped to the useless first draft of a Tattler column she'd handed Vivian to edit.

And how did Electra still have the letter? The question was answered even before it formed: because, of course, Vivian had not cared enough to pick it up. Indeed, it was possible that she scanned it now—*good morning, Angel—you were as soft as—lunch at my uncle's, but I shan't stop thinking of your—*for the first time.

Now Vivian did laugh. "I can't stand it," she muttered, feeling she spoke at random.

"What?" Electra asked at a whisper, bending close—as if they were conspirators, rather than antagonists. Getting this wrong, too, Vivian thought—and still holding the obviously unpublishable letter between them, this note that was at least twice the threat to her own reputation as it could ever have been to Vivian's. This utter failure of a blackmail.

Except it *had* worked, hadn't it? Vivian thought—and on even more pathetic grounds than intended. Because Vivian, it transpired, was more desperate for "souvenirs of old exploits" than anyone.

The depth of her disappointment at the threat's evaporation was unaccountable, staggering. "Enjoy the party," Vivian said. She raised her glass—high overhead, as though toasting to the entire ballroom and not to Electra alone. She waved it expansively in the general direction of the potted palm. "Enjoy the party, *Roger!*" she called.

"Wait," Electra said. "Are . . . are you alright?"

"Good-bye," Vivian said. She waved, already turning, her four fingers hinging as one at the knuckle.

HERE WE FIND ourselves, at the promised moment at which every Clancey Christmas party dissolves into chaos. But oh, for the innocence of years past, when the Clancey-Schmidts had stood together and vented their impulses by lobbing grapes into chandeliers and pine cones into fireplaces!

The entire party seemed somehow to have gotten louder, as if someone had raised the volume on a hidden speaker in every room of the house at once. As if Santa Claus had brought every guest the twin of R. T. Wallace's film-set bullhorn.

Electra was struggling to explain this new development to Roger, holding back tears of disappointment and also confusion—because *why* was she disappointed? What more than five hundred dollars and an invitation to a high-society party could she possibly have been expecting? But Vivian, of course, was not the only one shouldering the baggage of the past. There were souvenirs, after all, if only intangible and upsetting ones. "She just didn't—" Electra was saying, wiping at her eyes. "Oh, it's only just that she wasn't—"

"There, there, now," Roger said, patting her back. He resolved to give it another five minutes before he suggested they either leave for the train or find something to drink.

VIVIAN HERSELF WAS moving blindly but without pause, careening from room to room with as much apparent purpose as when she'd been following the woman she thought might be Sofia. Every corner was either too crowded or too empty, cacophonous or repressively hushed. Indeed, all any given room had to recommend it was a full tray of fresh champagne cocktails, so Vivian's hand was never empty for more than a few moments.

She hated Electra. For not being Sofia, of course; for her audacity and lack of embarrassment in being here; for her failure to even carry off the blackmail, when Vivian in her foolishness had done almost all the work for her.

And for her happiness, such as it was—whatever perverse satisfaction with her lot in life had enabled her to lay a kind hand on Vivian's wrist and thank her for her contribution to it.

Vivian was back in the ballroom, somehow. The house had turned on her. She left, determined this time, through a different door.

Roger the traffic cop, indistinguishable from the potted palm beside him. That was enough, Vivian thought, for some people. Oscar and Squire swooned watching each other floss. Elias Knox melted to the floor for any woman with a cross-indexed address book. Mrs. Clancey already spoke with apparent longing about joining her equally small-spirited husband under their doubled obelisk in Green-Wood Cemetery.

Every idiot, it seemed to Vivian as she exchanged her glass, could stumble into contentment. She downed her drink in two swallows and took another. Where had she gone wrong, that her only romantic loyalty was to a ghost both hateful and imaginary? What did all these stupid and happy people *get* from each other—and why was Vivian unable not only to get it but to want it at all?

Perhaps this—the fear rose unbidden, on a bubbling tide of champagne—was Vivian's family curse. Perhaps she was fated, like her parents, to be a faithful and fastidious curator of her own secret unhappiness, no matter her outward-facing situation.

It is a common enough ache: when some part of ourselves has lain too long fallow, to attempt its cultivation at last begins to feel impossible, even undesirable. To do so would be to admit to years, perhaps decades, of hurt. To *create* the hurt, almost, as if inflicting loneliness on oneself simply by admitting to it.

From the next table, Vivian seized a bottle by the neck. She dragged it behind her down a dark and depopulated hallway, bumping it against the wainscoting.

What, she asked herself furiously, did she *want*? She felt used up, or perhaps just the wild and raging opposite—as if she'd done everything she'd ever wanted to, everything there *was*, with still half her life ahead of her. Everything there was left to want—everything people were willing to give her, or even to let her ask for—was of no interest. An endless parade of girls who knew nothing about her and about whom she was not curious. The simpering sympathy and hollow extortion of Electra Blake. Her parents, haunting her at every turn no matter how many barriers she erected against them; Sofia, refusing to haunt her no matter how pathetically Vivian arranged the séance. There were dead ends everywhere she turned: according to Elias, there was nowhere left to take the company but to New Jersey. And according to Oscar and Squire, there was nowhere left to take their marriage but—

Vivian stopped. The bottle of champagne thumped against her leg, sloshing.

ALL THROUGHOUT THE house, things had reached a fever pitch. In the ballroom the dancing had taken on a careening and dangerous quality, with collapsed fans and broken-feathered aigrettes and diamond stickpins repurposed as physical hazards. Elsewhere, an alderman splashed vomit into an umbrella stand. A charades tournament of ambiguous organization had spontaneously combusted in the drawing room—Elias Knox was in the early stages of acting out the clue "octopus," Rebecca Van Beek already on the right track but laughing too hard to voice her guess, when Mrs. Clancey appeared at her shoulder and pulled her aside. "Mrs. Van Beek," she said. "Come with me, won't you?"

Mrs. Clancey was a bit unsteady on her feet, but her grip was surprisingly strong—and the crowd parted before their celebrated hostess at every turn, so the path, if circuitous, was at least of little resistance.

"Did you need something, Mrs. Clancey?" Rebecca asked, wiping tears of mirth from her eyes. "It's only, our team is—"

"Squire was looking for you," Mrs. Clancey said. "He wanted to ask—oh, damn the boy." She pulled up short, craning to see over the heads of the nearest guests. "Now where did he say he was going?" After a moment she set off again, tugging Rebecca with renewed purpose in her wake. "Don't worry," she said. "It'll come to me."

IN THE IRIS Room, things had progressed.

Oscar and Squire had tried, at first, to avoid the bed. It seemed too easy, not in the spirit of Vivian's challenge—the purpose of which, after all, was the novel conquest of unexpected locations. And it would make it harder, afterward, to erase the signs of their presence.

But after the drama of the preceding scene neither one was sober enough to compute the calculus of unusual positions, or cool-headed enough to delay gratification. They had decided, in the end, that they deserved softness and ease. Let Vivian play her own games.

They were in the full rocking rhythm of the thing—Oscar's grip on the bedpost so tight that its initial pulsing creak had been stifled into a shuddering stillness; Squire varying the speed of his thrusts with a well-practiced instinct that was almost a musical improvisation; tears and tender murmurs still salting their gasps—when the door flew open with a bang.

They tumbled immediately off the mattress—Squire wrapping his arms around Oscar and heaving them both to the floor with a thud. The quilt dragged after them, half-stripping the bed. Squire leapt up first—his hair in disarray; his hands clenched into ill-prepared but passionate fists.

"Idiots!" Vivian said. She closed the door behind her and locked it with enormous pedantic exaggeration, as if demonstrating the method. She removed the key and brandished it.

Oscar stood with difficulty, pressing one hand to his chest as if trying to physically subdue his heart. Squire took an unsteady step backward, his feet tangling in the puddled quilt. Oscar caught him at the waist.

"Idiots!" Vivian said again, pointing. "Let's make a baby."

"What?" said Squire.

Oscar tried to respond, but he'd had the wind knocked out of him. "*Now?*" he finally wheezed.

"Now," Vivian said. She toed the heels of her shoes as she advanced, wrenching them off her feet still laced. She swigged from the neck of her champagne bottle, took no notice as it fizzed across her front. "Before I change my mind." She dropped the bottle and reached for the back of her dress, then beneath her skirt. Bespoke tailoring for the independent woman.

"Wait," Oscar said. "Wait a minute."

"*You*," Vivian said, pointing an accusing finger at Squire. "Do you think you can bring yourself to touch me? Because I know he can't."

"I—" Squire looked at Oscar.

With impressive athleticism, given her state, Vivian vaulted across the bed and seized Squire by his lapels. Oscar in his surprise at this maneuver lost his grip on Squire's waist; Vivian half-spun, half-dragged him to flop onto the mattress on his back. Before he could get enough leverage to sit up, she straddled him.

"Vivian!" Oscar objected.

Squire had on many occasions been driven to or over the edge of climax by Vivian's influence, or comment, or indirect manipulation. But he had never in all their years together felt her body against his own, her breath hot on his face, her hands on his chest. It felt hugely powerful but incorrect—like seeing the sun approach too near in the sky. Like seeing smoke begin to rise from a long-familiar mountaintop.

"This is perfect," she said. A breathless giggle. "It'll look like you, and everyone will talk."

She kissed him, with more tenderness than her present attitude would have suggested her to be capable of. Her fingers, accustomed to tangling themselves in long tresses, trailed over his scalp and cupped his jaw.

Unlike either of his spouses, Squire was a sensualist first. His body and mind—those generous traitors—did not demand any certain configuration of anatomy in order for Squire to find himself suddenly voluptuous. He made a sound of helpless pleasure.

"Vivian!" Oscar said, pulling at her shoulder.

"Do you think you can work out what to do?" Vivian asked Squire. She pushed against his chest, sitting up. "Because I don't think either of us can tell you."

"Vivian, *stop*," Oscar said.

She twisted at the waist, finally considering Oscar. She hooked one arm around his neck and drew him in, tightening her legs around Squire's body to guard against Oscar pulling her off the mattress. Squire's hips bucked of their own accord. "It's now or never," Vivian said. Her nose brushed Oscar's. "It's this."

Oscar staggered a little on his feet—forward, then back.

Squire reached up, looped a gentle thumb and finger around Oscar's wrist. Squeezed once, then reached farther—cupping, stroking.

Vivian wrapped her other arm around Oscar's neck and, clasping her hands behind, used him to lift herself enough for Squire to maneuver beneath her.

Oscar dithered, his pulse racing under Squire's familiar caress, but he held her up. Trembling, his free hand found the curve of her waist.

Vivian kissed him, hard.

A confusion of gasps and hums, of grasping close and rocking closer.

It fell apart in minutes. There was not enough to hold it together— only alcohol and unstable inertia; only blind arousal and rage and grief.

It was unclear to all three of them, in the immediate aftermath, what exactly had happened. They were fucking, and then they were not. They were one tense circuit of friction and pleasure, and then they were collapsed and shaking on separate corners of the mattress.

Oscar and Squire saw to each other, first. There were hysterically comforting murmurs and crushingly fortifying embraces; light kisses spangled over cheeks and noses; hair pushed gently back from foreheads as if to ascertain whether there was any injury. Darling, darling, are you alright? Are you? And you?

They were alright.

They turned to Vivian with some still-palpitating fear. She was hunched with her back against a bedpost, face hidden against her knees, one fist beating at her temple. This was, in itself, frightening: Vivian in distress. But it was not menacing.

"Vivian," Squire said. He crossed the bed to her, unsteady on his knees. "It's alright. It's alright."

With a wordless protest, Vivian pushed him away. He fell back, catching himself with his hands on the mattress. "What do we do?" he asked Oscar in a half-whisper.

"Vivian," Oscar said, standing behind her. Hesitantly he laid a hand between her shoulders.

"Leave me alone," Vivian said, with a wet sniffle.

If only we could impart to Oscar the benefit of context on the events of Vivian's evening, her autumn, her life. Everything she had been through, both without him and in his distracted presence. And the compounding confusion and shame of watching the men comfort each other, moments before, in those first harrowing seconds after they had broken apart. The lonely terror of independence—and the horrific shock, one level removed, of that loneliness itself, which Vivian had never before allowed herself to recognize.

Oscar bent close to her face, still hidden in the folds of her disordered skirt. "What do you—?"

She meant only to push him away, the way she had Squire. But he had gotten closer than she realized. Her half-clenched first struck him in the eye, and he staggered backward.

Squire yelped.

"It's fine," Oscar said. He touched the skin under his eye; worked his face experimentally. "It's fine."

Vivian curled into a tighter ball, wrapping her arms around her knees. She did not look up. She did not weep, but her breath came thick and ragged.

Oscar wavered a moment. "Go back to the party," he said, finally. "Well"—he pushed Squire toward the en suite, searched the floor for the rest of his clothes—"clean up and go back. Your mother will be looking for you."

"But," Squire said, watching Vivian spiral. "But she's—"

"After," Oscar said. "After the party."

Squire washed and dressed. He finger-combed his hair, taming the worst of the cowlicks. His tie was hopeless—but by this point, he thought, so was everyone's. His face telescoped in the looking-glass; he gripped the porcelain to steady himself. He could pass for a reveler, he thought. He could get through the rest of the night. He had a lifetime's practice at aping social mores without genuine feeling.

He came back into the bedroom. Oscar was still hovering over Vivian, hesitating. Calculating angles of approach.

"Will you be alright?" Squire asked.

"Will you?"

To some questions there are no answers but unspooling time. They kissed, Squire's hand on the doorknob.

"I love you."

"Be careful."

He went out, slipping over the threshold, shutting the door quickly behind him.

Oscar turned the key and saw to Vivian.

His first attempt she parried, striking at him with an outburst of indistinct anger. He flinched, protecting his face this time. Held his breath and tried again.

Threading one arm around her back and the other beneath her knees, he half-lifted, half-dragged her from her hunched position at the foot of the bed. It was ungainly, but it worked—and she stood it, even curling to burrow a little into his chest.

"Oof," Oscar said. He staggered and dumped her back onto the mattress at the head of the bed—less gently than he meant to, but her head ended on the pillow. She lay on her side.

Tilting sideways Oscar undid the buttons along the spine of her dress, picked at the lacing on her corset to loosen it as best he could. She murmured something, the words blurred—but its tone, at least, was relatively peaceful.

Oscar retrieved the quilt from the floor and laid it over her, taking such care to tuck it around her shoulders and her feet that eventually he began to feel ridiculous. He looked for something more to do, but he had attended to everything he could. Vivian was snoring softly. There was nothing left but to face the rest of the night.

Beneath the champagne's numbing mist, his eye was beginning to throb. His head felt too heavy; it was a struggle to hold it up. He considered the bed, which was two-thirds empty—even began to climb into it, lifting one knee onto the mattress. But this alone triggered a crisis of fortitude, so instead he dragged a heavy armchair to Vivian's bedside and curled into it as best he could—legs trailing over the carpet, one knuckle brushing the floor.

≈

SQUIRE RETURNED AT dawn, haggard with the administration of merriment—shaking hands, applauding encores, mopping spills, and herding stragglers toward the door. With the dim, underwater quality of a dream he recalled that he had said something vague but horrible to his mother. (For the record: it was "Let me alone," repeated thrice, angrily and at close quarters, when Mrs. Clancey had finally tried to instigate a private interview with Mrs. Van Beek and her brother. A mild protest, by many standards—but unprecedented for this particular mother and son.) The episode would, Squire was certain, reverberate.

Still, exhausted now beyond dread or regret, Squire bent to wake his spouses: Oscar with a kiss on the cheek; Vivian with a hand on the ankle.

Oscar's eye had darkened overnight to a purplish bruise, but he claimed not to feel it. Once roused, Vivian did not speak—only surveyed the scene and set about cleaning herself up enough to respectably order a car back to the city. The sour smell of stale champagne they could do nothing about—but this was the Clancey Christmas party, after all. The funk of spoiled revelry was oozing from every southbound cab.

Vivian slept, or feigned to, the entire ride. Squire tried at first to stay awake—but after remaining vigilant through the party's tattered denouement, the hum and rock of the cab was too much for him.

Oscar folded his jacket and eased it between Squire's head and the window, so he wouldn't thump against the glass with every bend in the road. Vivian, he was allowed to cradle.

At home, they hesitated as one at the foot of the main hall's doubled stairway.

"Breakfast?" Squire suggested—puffy-eyed and heavy-limbed, but beckoning uncertainly toward their shared dining room. Oscar slumped gratefully toward him for this instinctive wisdom: the chance to reset something with ham and eggs and coffee taken three ways, overlapping but distinct; the chance to realign the universe before true, deep sleep in their own beds fixed the evening forever in their history.

Vivian shook her head and mounted the staircase. "No, thank you," she said—her first words to them since the night before. Without further pause she disappeared into the heart of her many-chambered boudoir, locking every door behind her as she went.

NINE

There is never enough opportunity for us to collect ourselves, after an upset—time does many things, but it does not pause. There is fallout and recovery, development and decay, but there is no rest.

Mrs. Clancey returned to town, directing (or at least criticizing) from afar the party's cleanup and the closing of the house in Yonkers.

There were the usual casualties: two vases had been broken (one more expensive, the other of greater sentimental value); someone—the hunt for the perpetrator was inconclusive—had urinated on a brocade ottoman in the library; an armchair in the Iris Room had for some reason been clumsily dragged across the Persian carpet, snagging one of its tassels and damaging the weaving. At least one engagement had been broken off, due to some controversy during the charades tournament—though there was a general hushed debate as to whether it had all been a misunderstanding, and the young couple in question might still make it up and proceed as planned.

Farther down the social news column, further ripples outward in the party's aftermath: early in the new year, Rebecca Van Beek and Elias Knox at last announced their engagement. Four months from first introductions to the exchange of a lifetime promise was unusual behavior for either of them, but then it had been an unusual acquaintance. The couple would marry after Easter and (though of course there was no newsprint mention of this detail) honeymoon at Niagara Falls.

(Mrs. Clancey took the news bravely, but it is difficult for any of us to fully recover when success slips so narrowly through our grasp—and through no fault of our own thankless effort or oft-repeated counsel.)

THE FOLLOWING WENT unannounced in any newspaper:

One morning in mid-January, Squire rose uncharacteristically early and left the house before Oscar for possibly the first time in the history of their partnership, pleading only "an appointment."

He did not have an appointment, exactly—the salesclerk at Black, Starr and Frost had messaged only that the order was ready for pickup at Squire's convenience—but in this case Squire's convenience was as soon as humanly possible.

They were matching signet rings, gold medallions engraved with what appeared to the untrained eye to be the Clancey & Schmidt company logo: a more practical simplification of the design Oscar had breathlessly handed over like a pen-and-ink bouquet all those years ago, the C and S curling into each other's negative space until they were each more ampersand than distinct characters.

"Tell me if it doesn't fit," Squire said, "and we'll get it resized."

He did not, he added in a low voice, intend this ring to spend half its life in a dish on the bedside table.

Oscar wept—it had, after all, been an extraordinarily emotional fall—but only briefly. The ring fit perfectly on the last finger of his left hand. In nervous moments—and there would be many more, throughout his life, though never again on the topic of his husband's devotion to their partnership—he developed a habit of tapping Squire's ring lightly against his wedding band, a gentle scuffing click of gold on gold. A reminder that not all unknowns were evil; that some yielded immeasurable happiness—if, occasionally, via circuitous routes.

BUT WHAT, YOU are no doubt asking, of Vivian?

With the same discipline and ferocity she had brought to most pursuits since leaving Utica, seventeen years before, Vivian dedicated those first few weeks of 1916 to her own dissociation from reality. It was not an entirely conscious effort, but then it didn't need to be: Vivian's instincts and her work ethic were too well developed to require self-awareness.

Oscar and Squire saw her even more rarely than usual, those first days. She ate at restaurants, or in her own rooms. She completely avoided their shared sitting room. She was like a ghost haunting the mansion—a blurred presence moving quickly past doorways; light footfalls and the rustle of skirts leaving every room just as another person entered. (They had, remember, remodeled the entire house with privacy in mind.) The eternal gin rummy tournament was suspended without ceremony or comment: after the second evening with no returning champion to challenge, Squire simply put the cards away and stopped his nightly vigil.

In another era—in remarkably, even achingly recent days—Oscar and Squire might have pressed Vivian for attention. Called her at the office; waited up for her in her wing. Even simply continued for a few more nights to sit in her habitual path with a deck of cards, ready to spring on her as she passed and suggest a game, a conversation. To ask that she take pity on them all and address the situation.

But under the circumstances—in the confusing mire of guilt and grievance and relief in which they found themselves floundering—both men felt that any such forced interaction was unconscionable. To lie in wait in Vivian's boudoir was a newly charged tactic; just to think of it triggered an embarrassed, confusing flip in Oscar and Squire's stomachs.

It could not last forever—this thought in itself was a stressor—but for now, by unspoken mutual agreement, they held each other off.

Vivian was more devoted to the C&S office than ever, but only for its physical properties: a space she utterly controlled, with no one to challenge or even approach her authority. A space in which, once she had locked a door, to knock upon it became a prosecutable offense. She spent almost all her time in the office—but she did not, notably, lose herself in work. Indeed, she did not even see to her regular duties.

Of course, the business suffered for it—doubly so due to the inconvenient coincidence of Elias Knox's sudden development of a personal life. In fact, Elias (operating, of course, without the benefit of context regarding the Clancey-Schmidts' experience of the Christmas party) found himself with a foreign feeling of annoyance, even resentment, toward Vivian. After a decade of fervent industry and insistence on complete oversight of the company, now—at the very moment when Elias wished to bask in his happiness, at least for a week or two—she malingered listlessly in her office, waving away the morning meeting and ignoring even his most urgent memoranda.

Aside from the usual management of manufacture and distribution, there were newly simmering issues of worker unrest and public relations. The labor activists held another demonstration outside the C&S offices, with the frustrated organizer Joe Green giving impassioned speeches before a rotating crowd. (Ironically to Elias, they seemed to take it in regular shifts.)

He did his best to defuse the situation without Vivian's oversight—but as ruthless as he could be with schedules and logistics, when it came to battling human beings, Elias was a clumsy tactician. He flinched from conflict; he let things simmer too long without choosing between diplomacy or force. Twice in one week the crowd grew large and vociferous enough that the police took it upon themselves to break it up. It became usual, peeking between the blinds in the C&S executive suite, to see at least a few figures at any given time milling in circuitous protest on the pavement below—a mix of anarchists and organizers and those miscellaneously radical young people who defined themselves not by their allegiance to any particular "-ism" but only with a sense of deep dissatisfaction with the system as it currently functioned.

This last philosophy—though she would never have submitted to the comparison—was a fair description of Vivian's own state of mind, in those first weeks after the Christmas party. All her former animating mania was gone, evaporated in the caustic instant that Electra had revealed herself and banished Sofia's enveloping ghost, shredding the false universe that Vivian had not been aware of meticulously weaving around herself. But in place of this stolen passion came neither anger, nor sadness, nor conscious shame for any of the events Vivian had precipitated and withstood at Mrs. Clancey's. She did not dwell on the feeling of Electra's hand on her forearm, neediness of a hundred types curdling in her gaze; or on the embarrassment of Vivian's own love for Sofia, so unrequited that at least one of them might as well have been fictional; or on her behavior in the Iris Room, manhandling Squire and punching Oscar in the eye.

Vivian thought of none of this; she was conscious only of the fact that life was unbearable.

She was empty, drifting slowly and without motivation through the world—though still with enough subconscious awareness to let her duck and weave to avoid Oscar and Squire and the servants at home; Elias and the anarchist protestors and her professional correspondence at the office; the eyes of beautiful women throughout the city. She *kept* herself empty—and though it felt protective, this in itself was difficult work.

VIVIAN'S SENSE OF the mechanics of reproduction was imprecise, as was her champagne-soaked memory of how far she, Squire, and Oscar had advanced—how far, a muffled voice amended, she had been able to force them—before everything had fallen to pieces. (She could not, of course, ask. She would rather have attended medical school and performed an exam on herself.) She did not realize what she was waiting for, indeed did not consider that her numb drift through the icy waters of early January might have any natural end at all, until finally she felt the familiar monthly ache, a tightening fist in her abdomen, and saw the first punctuating curl of blood in the toilet bowl.

She collapsed, sobbing—with relief, with shame, with fear. Gone was the practical dread of a practical crisis: the end to Vivian's life as she knew it, whatever its suddenly unbearable flaws; a real, whole child only patchily wanted by any of its parents, in moments of anxiety on Oscar's part and amusement at other people's children on Squire's and drunken chaos on Vivian's. Gone was the guilt of responsibility for an entire new human being's disappointing life. A child who would, Vivian was sure, have come to hate her the way she hated her own parents as soon as it was able to reason—and possibly before.

In the place of this dissolving concrete terror came only a greater portion of existential panic. Vivian, as we have observed at length, was a skilled and frequent manipulator of other people's lives. This was the first time, however, that she had been conscious of playing dice with her own. It was deeply unpleasant to have lost the reins of her own faculties, to have been buffeted by outside forces as disparate as her ancient (and perhaps entirely false) reminiscences of Sofia; Roger Stevens's shoddy traffic-cop bribery, its subtlety calculated for a target passing at forty miles per hour; Electra Blake's pathetic middle-aged smile, muddying the question of who owed whom forgiveness; Sybil Parnacott's dry-vermouth voice and fearless tumbling, bamboozling Vivian into making love to her own flawed, flattering memory, like Narcissus in a carnival funhouse mirror; and two cumulative bottles of traitorously fine champagne.

It should, Vivian thought with vehement, almost childish anger, be a more complicated and obvious process to lose control of one's life. It should take longer. The cliff edge should be clear enough for one to stop in time.

She had always assumed that the people she met, and used, and repositioned at (she liked to think) more advantageous angles for all concerned, differed from herself in some fundamental way. That they could not, as it were, feel the pain of the manipulation. (They had certainly, after all, always seemed unconscious of its workings.) She had considered herself vulnerable to practical challenges—lack of resources, unseasonable weather, the volatility of markets—but immune to emotional frailties. This had always been a hard line between herself and others—and not an entirely imaginary one, or else how could she account for the arc of her life so far?

And yet here she lay, weeping on her bathroom floor, after four months of increasingly senseless chaos—a lit fuse leading up to one explosive disaster. And all of it her own doing.

For most people, this lesson—that only luck, not any constitutional difference, distinguishes the master from the puppet; that natural disaster or misadventure may humble any one of us at any moment—comes either in childhood or not at all. To weather the epiphany at thirty-four is no small trial.

And Vivian did, to all outward appearances, weather it.

There are as many types of self-control as there are methods of controlling others: gentle, sustained habit; firm-handed discipline; mocking abuse; lackadaisical mismanagement; manipulation of a guilty conscience.

And, of course, white-knuckled denial.

When practiced by a person of exceptional will and intelligence, this technique can be enormously powerful in the short term—few forces are more remarkable than the human capacity for ignoring negative revelations. But there are always casualties. One cannot, in most cases, be selective in the emotions one declines to feel, or in the relationships one declines to nurture. And besides, this method of self-regulation is roughly the equivalent of plugging a volcano's caldera with an enormous stone. A hopeful enterprise, perhaps; certainly an industrious one. But in no way sensible. All one can reasonably expect, in such cases, is that eventually the repressed firestorm will express itself elsewhere.

THE CALL CAME on a Sunday morning. The housekeeper rushed the message to, of course, Oscar—thanks to Vivian's clever arrangement of doors and furniture, even entering at speed and with only the most perfunctory of knocks, Mrs. Banks found Mr. Schmidt at apparent ease on a sofa in the communal sitting room and Mr. Clancey perusing a bookshelf several feet away. (His breathing barely affected by the initial spring to his feet.)

The news was, finally, important enough to break the household ice. Still, it took some trembling hesitation and a reassuring squeeze of Squire's hand before Oscar could work up the courage to knock on Vivian's library door. To, in the absence of an answer, hammer on it. To try the knob—locked, of course. And, finally, rattling it desperately, to call: "Vivian, you've *got* to open it. There's been a bomb."

There is a certain perverse elation, when we are in private crisis, whenever outside reality finally reflects our inner state. Vivian burst from the room—cheeks feverish, hair coming loose to ring her face in a disarrayed halo.

Investigation was still unfolding, and when called to the telephone Oscar had not been calm enough under pressure to ask as many questions as Vivian would have, but this much the police and fire department's representatives had been able to communicate: it appeared that a person or persons unknown had planted an explosive at the C&S headquarters, the detonation of which earlier this morning had caused a partial collapse of the building's southwest corner.

Without looking at Oscar and Squire, Vivian forced them to deliver this news at a jog—moving quickly down the hallway to her suite. She laced on a pair of fleece-lined boots and dealt perfunctorily with her hair, excess pins bristling from her mouth.

Oscar continued his report, stammering a little through his panic: there had been, it appeared so far, no casualties. Given the timing of the explosion, early on a Sunday morning, there had most likely been none intended. An act of political terrorism only, likely by anarchists or labor organizers, the police representative had said over the telephone—with almost a hint of disappointment peppering his professionalism, as if he'd hoped to compete with the *Los Angeles Times* bombing for Crime of the Century and knew he needed bodies to do it. Investigation would continue, of course, throughout the day. The authorities would keep Mr. Schmidt and Mr. Clancey apprised of any updates, and any further details—or explosive devices—uncovered.

Vivian—still heading with blind, almost joyful dread toward the house's front door—brought herself up short at the top of her stairs. "Christ alive," she said—her first words to the men in several days—noticing for the first time that they were still dressed in their Sunday-morning loungewear. "Get a move on."

"What?" Squire said, in genuine confusion.

Vivian made an angry gesture, conveying the self-evident ridiculousness of wearing silk smoking jackets and velvet slippers through slush and icy winds to a bomb site.

"Vivian," Oscar said, in helpless comprehension. "We're not *going*."

"Of course we're going." Vivian pushed between them, forcing them to follow her toward their own wing, their own wardrobes.

"*I'm* not," Squire said, reaching as he jogged for Oscar's hand.

"We're not," Oscar said, reassuring.

Vivian, hearing this, whirled on them. They had made it as far as their shared sitting room. She had gotten them halfway there. "We have to go," she said. There was no small measure of desperation in her voice—her presence at the crime scene, she thought, would be considered inappropriate enough even *with* the company's supposed heads in attendance alongside her.

"There's nothing for us to do there," Oscar said. "The police will investigate, and there are"—he struggled to remember exactly what he'd been told on the telephone—"crews of people to assess the damage, and help make a claim for insurance." His voice was shaking. "And it's dangerous, besides. They don't know if anything more might go off—they don't know if it's organized. Someone with, you know. A manifesto. They might have meant the whole thing to come down."

"It's an interesting point, when you think about it," Squire said—ever devoted to new ideas; ever candidly forgetful of his own milieu.

Oscar shushed him, but Vivian was hardly listening—she had already rushed forward, grabbing fistfuls of both men's quilted lapels. "This company is *your* legacy too," she said. Not being close enough to shove Oscar and Squire into any walls, she knocked them against each other. "How much is that worth to you?"

There was a long, stammering pause.

Squire was the first to say it: "Nothing, really."

If it had not been for the lingering guilt of the Christmas party, Vivian might have slapped him. All three of them felt the wincing hypothetical.

"Look, he means, nothing is worth getting blown up for," Oscar said. "I mean, nothing is worth getting blown up for." He searched for an elaborating point, seemed on the verge of repeating himself a third time.

"It's only bricks," Squire supplied.

Oscar gestured to him gratefully. "It's only bricks," he said.

It is worth noting here that Vivian remained, even—perhaps especially—after the events of the preceding month, fundamentally a mystery to her husbands. Two savvier men might have been able to predict—precious as C&S was to her; volatile and vulnerable as the rest of the world had lately forced her to become—the effect these attempted comforts would have on her.

"Oh?" Vivian said. She scanned the room. "Well, if you really don't care."

With exaggerated precision she reached for the leftmost vase in the mantlepiece's garniture: an ormolu-mounted Meissen, with delicate floral motifs in both paint and porcelain, purchased by Oscar and Squire on their first holiday after C&S had become an unqualified success. (They had overpaid, but then they had still been under the influence of love's first euphoric lap around the psyche—and in France, besides.)

Vivian flipped the vase over as if appraising it for auction, studying the crossed swords marked on its base with brief and affected dispassion.

Oscar and Squire had bought this vase, she reflected, with money she had earned them. Her business sense, years of her life, sweat and blood and dirt under her fingernails, all so these men could call themselves immaterialistic while dining every night at Sherry's and building the finest hatpin collection in private hands in North America and bidding on antique vases with her money. Claiming that the company that made it all possible "didn't matter," because it only mattered to Vivian. *It's only bricks.*

"It's only clay," she said, and dashed the vase into the fireplace.

One of the men—without looking at them, Vivian could not tell which—yelped.

"Oops," she said. "Lucky thing, that none of it matters."

She reached for the second, central vase in the garniture, hefting it with a ready sneer. She turned to challenge Oscar and Squire. To threaten the souvenir—the first grand antique Oscar had ever purchased; the first "heirloom" Squire had been allowed to choose for himself rather than inherit against his will. To force them to credit her as the architect of all their happiness, lest she smash any more of it.

But when she turned, she caught them looking not at her but at each other—a split-second communion of reassurance, each man pausing to make sure the other had survived the first vase's destruction.

Quickly they faced Vivian again—one dithering, the other with cautious-pleading hands outstretched. They were still distraught, still grieving the broken porcelain like their own shattered bone.

Because Vivian had not been wrong, of course, in diagnosing their material hypocrisy. It was true that much of what Oscar and Squire took for granted in their lives—whatever appeared to them to be effortless windfall, a previously indifferent or even cruel universe suddenly acting in their favor—had in fact been charged to Vivian's account.

Things might have gone very differently, had she not seen that quick, reassuring glance pass between the men. She had nearly a decade's worth of fragile, flammable furniture and decor at her disposal, after all, and an almost inexhaustible, not unfounded rage.

But she looked up just in time to catch it, the echo of the moments after they had all broken apart in the Iris Room: Oscar and Squire comforting each other; Vivian, having thought she controlled them, standing by foolish and alone.

She tossed the vase onto the sofa—it bounced once, but rolled safely to rest on the cushion—and marched from the room.

"*Please*, don't go," Oscar called after her.

"I'm not," Vivian said. She readied the door to slam. "Leave me alone."

This last request Oscar and Squire found easy to obey—they were frightened after her outburst, wounded and resentful, and besides had plenty to attend to in picking shards of the damaged vase from the ashes in the hopes of repair—and so they missed the click of her library door a few minutes later, and her light, efficient steps on the main stairway.

FROM CERTAIN ANGLES of approach—from the east, especially—it was almost impossible to tell that any disaster had occurred. Both C&S smokestacks were intact, as was the building's northeastern flank. There was a caustic burnt smell to the air, yes; there was a brick-red haze that smarted in Vivian's eyes and set her nose running. But this was New York's industrial waterfront. All of this might have been business as usual.

Then she rounded the corner.

The southwest corner of the building had been blasted away, with much of the surrounding brickwork crumbling into the crater. This was the side fronting the river—it looked almost as if it had been attacked from the water, by pirates.

Fire had spread from the warehouse through much of the factory and offices, after the initial blast—fed by the ethyl alcohol and concentrated fragrance oils that Vivian had been stockpiling, with their varied but eager flash points; the reams of paper labels and vats of printing ink. Personal Care was an explosive business.

The fire department had been on the scene for hours—for the first-responding shift, this was a story already in its denouement. A three-story ladder leaned precariously against the side of the building; the soot shadows of extinguished flames scarred what was left of the walls. The air was still thick with smoke.

Police officers and firefighters and city officials of no coherent uniform, unidentifiable but confident, milled in the maimed building's shadow. They had already cut rough pathways through some of the rubble—barely navigable clearings in the thicket of smashed brick and twisted steel, splintered wood and pulverized plaster. Lakes of mud and cakes of sodden ashes formed at every low point, water pooling from the firemen's hoses and burst pipes alike. (It was becoming difficult, by this point, to pick apart the effects of the disaster and its response.) Amid the apocalyptic chaos these middlingly authoritative men stood in various precarious postures of industry and administration and idleness, with the most urgent activity appearing to be crowd control.

Vivian, it transpired, needn't have worried about the propriety of being a woman present at a bomb site: half of Lower Manhattan had turned out to gawk, shoving with horrified fascination against the hastily strung rope barriers (and the arms of the insistent, ineffective policemen) for a closer look. Young families dressed for church jostled elbows with red-eyed men and painted ladies not yet retired from the revelry of the night before. A gang of unattended children had already made a game of ducking under the rope and grabbing a chip of brick or twist of metal from the edge of the rubble's skirt, skipping back to safety before the policemen's notice swept their way again.

Vivian hated them all equally: the terrorists who had planted the bomb; the grubby-fingered daredevils snatching her crumbled bricks with shrieks of laughter; the dutifully offended rubberneckers, trading conspiracy theories and handkerchiefs against the soot. The police detectives conferring, gesturing at the open wound in the side of her building. And Oscar and Squire, who hadn't even cared to—

"Mrs. Schmidt!"

Vivian whipped to face the hail.

Like a fallen angel's recording secretary, brimstone-smelling soot smeared over his face and his overstarched collar, Elias Knox stumbled over a cobble of smashed concrete just on the other side of the cordoning rope—extending his hand to help her cross.

"Elias," she said, grasping.

He was already speaking, answering a question she hadn't asked about how he'd come to be there. The police had sent for him, he said, as the site manager. His name—this he reported with anguished, apologetic gratitude, with tears standing in his eyes—was listed in case of emergency.

In truth there had been no space in Vivian's mind for wonder at Elias's presence. Rather, it would not have surprised her to hear that he'd felt the impact, the crumbling brickwork like a bullet in his own chest.

She could count on Elias for that much, she thought, leaning with uncharacteristic frailty on his arm as he helped her under the police barrier. She could count on him to care, in his bones, about what happened to Clancey & Schmidt. Not like Oscar and Squire—who were accustomed to luxury, yes, and would cry out reflexively if it was taken from them, but who had shrugged at the news of the bombing. Ultimately, they would weather the loss together and move on. They would simply buy fewer vases. This, for them, was the sum total of their syndicate's shared legacy.

Vivian clung tighter to Elias's arm.

In a rasping voice he walked her through a tour of the crime scene, a summary of the investigation thus far. It was a new and horribly cock-eyed version of their usual morning meeting: he reported the exact, still-unfolding specifications of Vivian's ruin, pausing periodically to cough acrid smoke into the crook of his elbow.

A squad of specialists—or so they claimed, though Elias had his doubts—was in the midst of the slow, careful, terrifyingly anticlimactic process of sweeping the premises for further explosives. Elias had taken the liberty, he admitted, of supervising the unloading of lye from the warehouses—he'd realized quickly that it would react with its own caustic eruption to the touch of the fire brigade's hoses, and so would have to be safely cleared before the building could be fully extinguished.

Elias moved briskly past this admission of frankly outstanding bravery, continuing with the administration of his duties. The assistant-management of a blasted crater.

"They say it's too early to name suspects," he said.

"Joe Green," Vivian countered. "The union."

Elias shook his head. "Green's not the violent type," he said.

And Vivian found she couldn't argue—after all, she'd never even spoken to the man. Only surveyed the chessboard from her office and directed Elias's moves. Joe Green, in all likelihood, didn't know she existed—certainly not that she ran the company that had squashed his organizing. If Someone had a vendetta against her, she thought, it wasn't him.

"Then who?" she asked, her voice faint. Rubble shifted underfoot.

Elias gave a helpless, slightly hysterical shrug. (We must remember that it had been a long morning for him, already.) "Honestly," he said, "it could have been anyone."

Vivian felt this, the universality of the forces arrayed against her, like a nail splintering through plywood. Who had been willing to risk death, in order to kick away the last stable leg she had to stand on? *Honestly, it could have been anyone.*

"They said," Elias sniffed, rubbing at one eye with the sooty heel of his palm. "They said there's an anarchist group they'd been watching. So maybe . . ." He trailed off, as if listening to a silent partner; then suddenly rejoined: "But then *why*, why just *wait*, until they—"

Vivian followed Elias's gesture and saw, finally, the specific ruin that had webbed his voice with tears: the remains of Rebecca Van Beek's lobby mural, torn through the center where the wall had come down; fire-blackened and blasted by the engine's hoses. Punched through in places by splintered timbers.

"She'd only just finished it," he said, miserably.

So, Vivian thought. Elias too.

"What else, Mr. Knox?" she asked. "Any damage to the factory floor?"

She'd call it a kindness, distracting him from his private grief.

Or perhaps she wouldn't, she thought. Perhaps she'd call it a deliberate cruelty, for her own cold comfort. What difference did it make, either way? Who, in the end, cared?

Elias continued his faithful, thorough tour of her destruction. Beat cops and detectives blinked after them in confusion as they passed, but returned to their work without banishing her—with the same singular presence that had once earned her entry to bunting-swagged gambling palaces, Vivian now picked her way over the frozen wreckage of her livelihood.

Even in those sections of the building still mostly intact, all the windows had shattered in the blast. Broken glass slivered and cracked with every step. The front facade had been ripped away, leaving the overall effect of an enormous, derelict dollhouse—half the upper-floor offices had been completely destroyed; those remaining were open to the elements on at least one side. Furniture lingered—some splintered to sticks; some curiously whole, as if an individual clerk or secretary had simply stepped out for a moment (possibly into empty space, several stories above the ground). The main staircase still ran up from the ground floor, but now exposed like a theatrical set, coated with the morning's light accumulation of sleet, its railing blasted away. Toward the second floor, several steps had fallen in.

Back at ground level, Vivian craned to see farther into the broken shell of the lobby—at the foot of Rebecca's ruined mural, half of the marble-topped reception desk was still intact. Vivian thought she could even see the warped shell of the bell to call for service, blistered with heat and lying on its side in a cake of wet ash.

Vivian could not help but think—suddenly, finally—of Meg Booth. The anarchist with the apartment by the elevated train, and the strangely persistent coral lipstick. The Tiffany Girl who, during the brief window of their acquaintance, in the last days before success lifted Vivian high, had inspired the purchase of her desk set. Meg had railed in favor of socialism, anarchism, the assassination—or at least the embarrassment—of robber barons. That whole impractical sisterhood, Vivian thought, all those smirking, sighing, artistic young women with their Chianti and black coffee and cigarettes, their strong opinions never relinquished, had been radical. Anticapitalist, antimonopoly, antipower. (At least they had played at it, outside the bedroom.) Could they, could Meg, have . . . ?

The thought spiraled quickly. It was a strangely tempting vision: Meg at the head of a column of Tiffany Girls; Electra; the ghostly Sofia; every cagey suffragette and pancake waitress and aspiring film star that Vivian had ever seduced or wronged or embarrassed herself for, storming the factory with a lit fuse in her hand. All of them, unionizing against her.

But no, Vivian, thought. Those women were all married now, or pursuing their own professions, or sharing Village art studios with one another. Raising traffic cops' children and worrying about money, or else turning backflips while the cameras rolled. Ringing room service for the perfect Brandy Crusta. Moved on or moved away.

That they all might descend on her now, Vivian thought, ready for battle, was only her private nightmare. Or her fantasy. Either way: she was the only one here, crawling through the rubble.

Well, she amended. Her and Elias Knox.

She almost had to laugh: less than a year ago, he would have been fawning over her like a schoolboy, and she sneering at him for it. Less than a year ago, she had thought herself solid as brick and mortar.

A clot of broken-lathed ceiling tumbled from the third floor and thudded in a cloud of dust.

Tracing its path, Vivian gasped.

Elias followed her gaze. "Oh," he said.

Just visible, ripped open and half-collapsed at the new edge of the third floor, was Vivian's—nominally Oscar's—office. Beside it, Elias's cubby still huddled. The frosted glass between them had been blown out, creating one egalitarian ruin—its two halves, perhaps, still even connected by a fried intercom wire. Vivian, craning on tiptoe, could just barely glimpse the battered hulk of her desk—like a wounded animal, crouching in the back of its den.

"I need to get up there," she said.

At first, Elias did not dignify this with a response. Then, Vivian began to double back toward the staircase.

"Mrs. Schmidt," Elias said, stumbling after her.

"I—we need to see what we can salvage," Vivian said. Her desk set was acid-etched brass—the glass would be broken, of course, but maybe the skeleton of the thing had survived. She could have it repaired. Any damage would just be one more layer in its patina. One more hardship it had lived through; one more obstacle overcome.

"It's not safe," Elias said, jogging to outpace her. He turned to walk backward, watching his heels over his shoulder. "The stairs aren't—" He tripped, and, flailing, steadied himself against her. "Excuse me." He resettled his footing. "The staircase lost its supports, it's coming away from the—"

"Your plans," Vivian tried. "All your research is up there, for the move to New Jersey."

Elias hesitated for the briefest moment. (He was, after all, only human.) "It isn't safe," he said again, sorrowfully. "And they haven't cleared the area yet, there might be another—"

But Vivian had ceased to listen to him.

There had been no path cleared to the staircase—on the contrary, what rubble the first responders had been able to shift, they had heaved into relocated heaps between Vivian and her goal.

She hiked up her skirts and made a start.

Bricks slid treacherously under her feet as she climbed the first pile. She stumbled, catching herself on one hand. Her palm scraped, skin shredding.

Descending the other side of the pile was easier: she kept her footing but let herself fall, riding the bricks as they collapsed.

"Mrs. Schmidt!" A second avalanche, as Elias followed her over this first hill of refuse. "Please, it's not—"

Vivian tried to pick her way around a wide and turbid puddle, a manmade lake of hydrant runoff and burst sewer pipework and melted snow, mud and plaster and ten years of incinerated paperwork—but the rocky perimeter was too narrow, too steeply canted. She staggered and stepped heavily into the center of the lake, icy, foul-smelling water flooding her boots and soaking her skirt almost to the knee.

Oh, well, she thought. One less thing to dread might happen.

She pushed through the puddle in dogged, dragging strides, taking a straight path across. Something scraped her leg, insistent through the numbing cold. The ground was uneven under the surface. She stumbled again. Something clicked painfully in her ankle—she hopped twice on her other foot and pressed on.

Elias caught up with her on the far side of the puddle. "Mrs. Schmidt," he said breathlessly, touching her arm. She threw him off, more violently than his hesitant grip required. She hauled herself onto a great cobble of concrete, surveyed her next move. A blasted landscape of brick and stone and tile, raw and unstable, at once ravaged by the explosion and untouched by the work crews. She would have to step carefully, she thought—or else quickly enough that by the time something collapsed, she would already have moved on.

On the other side of this waste, perhaps another forty feet away: the staircase to her office. (What was left of the staircase. What was left of her office.)

She leaned back, sighting her trajectory. Planning her next step.

"*Mrs. Schmidt*," Elias said. From the ground he could reach as high as her waist; he seized her there with both hands. She wrenched against him with a yell.

"Vivian!" he pleaded, saying her Christian name aloud for the first time in his life.

Even with gravity on his side, he was struggling. Her dress, heavy as it was with mud and water, made her hard to get a hold of, and she had the high ground—her footing on her single, slightly canted block of concrete was more stable than his grappling stance in the loose bricks.

Finally he managed to lift her off her feet—but immediately this success overbalanced him; as Vivian kicked and twisted in his arms, he staggered backward and nearly fell.

He might have tipped into the virgin debris and broken his neck. Instead, he managed not even to drop Vivian—he lurched forward rather than back and set her roughly on her feet again, jarring them both.

Vivian gasped as the shock traveled up her leg. Then she wheeled on him.

"Help!" Elias shouted. Vivian shoved at him, scratching his face. "Somebody, help!"

Vivian turned back toward the building, the staircase, and readied herself to leap. There was a heap a few feet to her right that looked relatively solid, as a first foothold. She'd stay on her feet as long as she could, she thought. Then she'd crawl. She'd swim through the rubble, if she had to. They couldn't stop her if they were too scared to follow her.

There were more voices, variously counseling alarm and caution. The clatter of more displaced bricks. Someone blew a whistle, as if in general protest of the whole situation. Vivian teetered on her concrete diving board.

Elias was snatching at her dress, yanking at her arm. Calling for someone to fetch Oscar and Squire.

Good luck! Vivian thought—and lunged from the broken lip of the cliff, reaching for the first step on the staircase that still rose splintered from the wreckage. Ready to collapse, or explode, or do anything she had to in order to salvage something, anything.

TEN

Time and cause unravel in all directions, and without cease. Any attempt to arrest the process, to arrange the universe into a single linear narrative, is hopeless.

Still, we try to make sense of things. We draw the map; we mark it with pins. Mount Tambora's eruption, Hiram Ainsley's ladle of lemonade, Patience Stone's safety bicycle. "The Sidewalks of New York," a Manhattan manhole cover, *The Chemical History of a Candle*. An aquarium walrus pool with an irresponsibly shallow railing.

Now, add to this list: the medial and lateral malleoli of Vivian Schmidt (née Lesperance)'s right ankle.

Had she not sustained and ignored a hairline fracture in her initial scramble to the edge of safety; had she not further jarred her damaged tibia and fibula in her lashing struggle against Elias; had she not in her final self-destructive leap for freedom happened to come down punishingly and at an unnatural angle on the same foot, everything might have been different. She might have made it to the staircase; she might have climbed high enough to kill herself.

As it was, she crumpled within an arm's reach of her assailing saviors. She continued to struggle, to scream and kick and exacerbate her injury, right up until the moment they loaded her into the ambulance—but her snapped bones would not bear her weight, let alone navigate the unstable terrain of the factory's ruin.

In the end, she had no choice but to yield to rescue.

TRIAGE AND INVESTIGATION continued without her. The report, in summary:

No additional explosive devices were found on the Clancey & Schmidt property, or in its vicinity. Additionally, no significant evidence of the first device was recovered. As a result, the incident was never definitively declared a bombing. Rather, the leading theory posited a gas leak, igniting warehouse supplies—aldehydes and absolutes and concentrated oils. All the bulk raw components of Mystic Zephyr, transformed by a chance spark into its own explosive.

The case was never closed, though. The fact of the matter was that C&S was a ruthless, canny, powerful force with many victims among its competitors, its workers, and arguably even the customers it persuaded to spend beyond their means. Angry demonstrators had picketed at the very site of the explosion, barely two days before.

And we are all made so uneasy by the threat of chance disaster—or even chance success—that in most cases we refuse to accept its occurrence. If a lucrative canal bypasses our city; if we bump into a strong-willed acquaintance in the street outside our office; if we lose our balance at the edge of an aquarium pool; if a volcano erupts half the world away, and summer ice forms on the millpond: insistently we will read in these events the workings of destiny, or verdicts on the quality of our souls. There is no threat so unbearable as randomness.

For decades, long after the deaths of the company's founders, conspiracies would persist about the maybe-bombing of C&S. And Elias had been right: it could have been anyone.

But what *really* happened?

This is—if you can bear to hold such an incandescent thing in your bare hands—a question with no answer. Or else with too many answers for them to mean anything. We could dig forever; we would never hit bedrock.

Try to release such questions, now. What lies ahead will be easier for you, if you can.

ONE MORE REASON for the screws in Vivian's ankle to be pins in our map: her injury necessitated surgery, a thick plaster cast, months of painful convalescent recovery. Without these advantages, Oscar and Squire could never have persuaded her to sit still long enough for them to finally figure out what was going on.

There were weeks of bed rest, and strengthening exercises that made her feel like a child—rotating her ankles, balancing on one foot, standing on tiptoe—and hobbling, humbling laps around the second floor.

And for all of it, for every moment, asleep or awake, she needed help.

Squire took the first decisive action: on the second day after the accident, the men were called downtown to hear the police report and to meet with the insurance adjusters. Hanging up the telephone after receiving this summons, Oscar moved to update Vivian on the development; Squire stopped him, reaching for his hat. "Let her have a day off," he said. "We can manage."

And they did, barely—with any apparent confusion as to the operation of their business perhaps attributed to shock and grief.

"They asked about plans for rebuilding," Oscar said, that evening. He and Squire stood at the foot of Vivian's bed, almost at attention. Two Gentlemen of the Bedchamber, reporting on the events of the day. "We told them . . ." He cleared his throat.

"We thought we'd better let Elias decide," Squire said. "But we've just put them off for now, in case you . . . don't want him to. We said we needed time to think."

Vivian was small in her nightgown, sallow, the rest of her body dwarfed by the bulk of her cast under the blankets. She could not look at them, or else refused to. "Tell Elias to do whatever he wants," she said, surly with pain. "He knows both your signatures."

And in another life, having delivered her decision and twisted the knife, she might have sent the men out of the room and hardened herself against them.

But her vision was jumping—she was only one sleepless night on the other side of catastrophe. She had just been glibly forced to release control of her most precious accomplishment, because she was battling the same impossible disaster on too many fronts and losing. She had carefully arranged a life with as few intimates as possible, independent in everything from her business correspondence to her undergarments.

But she'd snapped her ankle into three pieces, and she needed to use the bathroom.

"Wait," she said, as they turned to go. She struggled to sit up, wincing. "Help me?"

OSCAR WAS HER crutch, they worked out quickly. She and Squire were too evenly matched in size; she was liable to capsize him. As directed by her doctors, twice a day—sometimes three times (Vivian was, of course, impatient)—she and Oscar made a stumping, painful promenade through both wings of the house. Their figure-eight route ended in the shared sitting room, where Squire (with the housekeeper's assistance) laid Vivian's meals out on a breakfast tray, and (under the housekeeper's protest) made her a nest of pillows and blankets on the room's largest sofa.

Their nightly gin rummy games resumed, in combination now with the physiotherapist's prescribed exercises. Squire studied the diagrams, and (though he tried not to show it) delighted in performing a kind of imaginary mental X-ray while manipulating Vivian's foot according to the instructions. Oscar kept things moving—either playing Squire's hand of cards for him or taking over the ankle rotation, depending on where his husband's attention was lagging.

Nothing smooths over pain and awkwardness, or distracts from worry, quite so well as a shared chore—something as crucial as it is straightforward. Such as, for instance, keeping weight off an injured limb.

In the early days of Vivian's recovery, her true invalidity, the Clancey-Schmidts could almost successfully forget about all the devils at the door. Elias was overseeing the demolition of the remainder of the building; he had paused the receipt of new orders, and of course the fulfillment of anything not already in the distribution pipeline. But to Vivian, Oscar, and Squire the loss of the factory, and the whole company's uncertain future, both felt strangely distant—like problems afflicting other people entirely.

Which, in a sense, they were. Elias's daily updates remained diplomatic, but with a marked and steady decrease in sycophancy as his responsibilities grew and Vivian's hand slackened on the reins. (This trend, too, the syndicate declined to notice.)

Perhaps most significantly, if least remarked upon, the shared project of Vivian's recuperation also drowned out all the tension there had been in the house in the weeks before the accident. There was no closure, no resolution. There was simply the apparent substitution of a new and different world, one with its own emergent concerns.

Slowly, Vivian began to recover.

Then, because she was Vivian, she pushed herself.

As the men escorted her to bed one night, all three of them laughing at some sweet nothing from one of Squire's radio telemetry newsletters, Vivian mistook Oscar and Squire's support (one at each elbow) for her own strength and stepped lightly out of their reach, as if to simply climb into bed. She had the muscle memory—but no longer bone or ligament.

As her ankle gave out she fell with a cry, grasping the first thing she laid hands on—which happened to be Squire.

He caught her as best he could, cracking his own kneecap on the floorboards, and hauled them both upright. He passed her to Oscar (who shrugged a shoulder under her arm) and flopped backward onto the bedspread—hugging his knee to his chest, rolling as it smarted, still half-laughing through the pain.

"Are you alright?" everyone asked at once.

With equal simultaneity, they caught the dreadful echo: Christmas in the Iris Room.

Squire struggled off the mattress, settling his jacket where it had ridden up.

Oscar, as quickly as could be done kindly, disengaged himself from Vivian and deposited her on the bed.

"Sorry—" "Sorry—" "I'm sorry—" They stepped on one another.

There was a horrible moment's silence.

"I really am," Vivian said finally. "I really am sorry." Her voice was small and waterlogged, almost unrecognizable. "That night, I—I was . . ."

She had the almost overpowering instinct to brush it aside, to misdirect and move on. To say something cutting about one or the other of their neckties and send them out of the room, feigning exhaustion.

They would let her, she knew, if she tried.

"I'd just been jilted," she forced herself to say.

But that wasn't it, either, she thought—she could see it in the misfit reactions on the men's faces, their simple, sympathetic shock.

"No," she said. "I . . ." She grabbed fistfuls of her skirt, squeezing until it hurt. "The truth is, I don't know what happened." (Someone gasped, softly.) "Maybe nothing happened, even," Vivian said. And with a sudden vehemence that startled all three of them: "But then, I don't know why I made such a fool of myself."

Squire reached slowly for the bedpost and hoisted himself onto the mattress. He took a few wobbling, wincing steps—catching his balance, favoring his bruised knee.

Automatically, Oscar extended a steadying hand. Squire took it and tugged—not hard enough to pull Oscar up beside him, but enough for him to get the idea.

They settled themselves cross-legged on the bedspread at her feet.

Vivian took a deep, shaky breath and tried to explain. About Electra's hapless blackmail, and Sofia's indifferent ghost, and Sybil Parnacott's laughing sneer. The story unraveled. She blew her nose on her sleeve and brought up, out of nowhere, Patience Stone's aunt Daphne and her habitual afternoon glass of lemon squash. Vivian tried in one gasp to explain herself in all the years before she'd known Oscar and Squire—and all the years since, kept almost as tangled and secret from them. She elided any mention of her parents, and so of course there was a yawning void in the explanation big enough to fall into. (And fall into it she did, repeatedly.) She hiccupped through tears, flushed in anger, buried her shamed face in her hands.

It was the bottomless lake of confusion underlying every straightforward declaration that Oscar and Squire ever heard from her. It was a looping, recursive history, with the past and future endlessly intruding upon each other. It was an unholy mess of an account.

But through the muddle shone the truth that it had not been a sudden unhappiness at all, these last few months. It had been the eruption of something that had been eating away at Vivian's insides for much longer—years; possibly forever.

It was difficult to follow, precisely, but Oscar and Squire did not require precision. Indeed, probably they would not have been prepared to withstand it.

Eventually Vivian exhausted herself to the point of nausea. By this metric, she determined the end of her story. Abruptly she realized that her apology, her excuse, had mutated into something else. Something she had no vocabulary to describe.

"So," she said, coolly. She smoothed her forehead with her palm, as if turning her mind to a blank page. "That's that."

If she had been able to walk under her own power, she would have left the room herself—never mind that it was her own bedroom. But she couldn't.

"I didn't know," Squire said.

Oscar reached out and squeezed her good ankle.

"I'll say good night," Vivian said.

"I'm so sorry," Oscar said. "We should have—"

"Oh, *don't*." Vivian's face twisted. "Not after I . . ." She kicked at them, as best she could. "Good *night*," she said, with an insistence that bordered on a warning.

The men didn't push her. But they conferred, and they came back in the morning.

OSCAR DID NOT come to breakfast with a formal proposal in writing, or with any tabulated supporting data—but he managed to convey the impression of them, somehow. Oscar Schmidt's method of negotiation would always be dry and evidence based. Even in retirement; even when the matter on the table was the path to existential peace.

They had agreed that Squire would give the signal—it was too big a thing for any one man to do alone. Halfway through his eggs, Squire cleared his throat.

"Vivian," Oscar said. He laid an officious piece of toast on his plate.

"Oscar," she said.

"You're thirty-four."

"Thirty-five in April," Squire interjected.

"In April, yes," Oscar allowed, with a polite nod.

For a long moment, this seemed to be the end of the interview. With two working ankles, and with a factory at her disposal that was more than a diminishing pile of loose bricks, and without the shaming memory of last night's outburst, Vivian might have already been on her way to the office, rolling her eyes.

As it was, she was forced to patience, ambiguously vulnerable and insulted, feigning occupation with her coffee cup.

"Neither of *us* . . ." Squire prompted, reaching for the butter.

"Neither of us," Oscar retrieved the thread, "guessed right the first time."

"About what?" Vivian asked, startled.

"I mean to say, at your age," Oscar blustered, "it can be difficult to guess what will make you happy."

"You were much older than she is, now, actually," Squire said. "When we—"

"Yes, thank you for keeping track!" Oscar said.

"Well, you're the one who brought it up," Squire muttered. "As if age has anything to do with anything."

(We must remember that it was earlier in the day than Squire preferred to be awake, and that the men had sat up late preparing for this conversation.)

Oscar, perhaps looking for a fresh start, flipped his toast to the other side. It was burnt. He flipped it back.

"It's invisible," he said. "Because you've made such a success of yourself. But, ah . . ." He hesitated.

"You're miserable," Squire said—in much the same matter-of-fact tone he had once declared his early attempts at scented candles "disgusting."

Oscar gave a regretful, abbreviated nod of agreement. "And to be miserable *is* to fail."

"That's not what he means," Squire said.

"That's not what I mean," Oscar said.

"You'd better say," Vivian said dangerously, "what you mean."

Would that any of them had the words for it. Oscar and Squire knew only, in their separate and overlapping ways, that they had once been burnt down to the very ends of their happiness, disillusioned and despairing and with no plans for the future but to either cling harder to their wretched known circumstances or go insane. (Or, very possibly, both.)

And then Vivian had arrived, and helped them push through the false wall at the back of their lives into something better.

It was a harder favor than it looked, to repay. After all, they had no suggested alternative into which to manipulate her—she had only just begun to admit the very existence of her feelings. They had only their own saccharine testimonials, and the suggestion to a devastated, heart-broken woman with one good leg that she should let go of her only func-tional definition—once-functional, at least—of happiness.

"You don't have to keep trying," Squire said. "You don't have to go back to work at the company, or to meet those women, that way, or . . ." Out of his depth—these were meant to have been Oscar's lines, but after his most recent failure he was catatonic—Squire reached for his husband's toast. "You don't have to keep doing anything, if it doesn't make you happy," he finished. "Or, if it doesn't anymore, I mean. If it's used up."

It is one of the most terrifying things we can ask of ourselves: to let go of one thing in order to reach for another.

"You're idiots," Vivian said. She was animated by the same angry, threatened impulse that had made her smash the vase, when Oscar and Squire had called the factory "only bricks." (Which, now, it truly was.) "I'm not—it's not *used up*," she snapped.

And it wasn't: the factory would be rebuilt; the company would reopen for orders; there was a sloe-eyed pancake waitress on every corner. Even the floating gin rummy tournament was back on schedule. There was nothing objective, no definitive reason why Vivian could not go on as she had been. Her cast was about to come off.

"It's just," she said. "It's only that . . ."

But she did not have the vocabulary to describe the uncharted, widening crevasse between success and privilege on one side, and happi-ness on the other.

Oscar and Squire had, in previous lives, plumbed its depths. They had adjusted to see in the dark, before Vivian hauled them to the surface.

Vivian stammered, grasping.

Oscar observed a brief, careful silence; gave an apologetic bow for what he was about to do. "When we were in Utica," he said, gently. He swept a demonstrative hand over Vivian, frayed and angry, braced against the table. "It was like this, for you. Being back."

Vivian did not trust herself to speak, or even to exhale with stability. Eventually, through resistance, she raised her chin in acknowledgment.

Oscar flipped his hand. "Imagine if you'd made yourself stay," he said. "Past what you could stand."

"I wouldn't have," Vivian said, vehemently.

"You are, though," Oscar said.

Vivian's throat stung. For a long moment she said nothing.

Utica had, it was true, once become too crowded with its confusion of ghosts and failures and expectations for Vivian to breathe its atmosphere. Had New York become too crowded now too?

And if such a thing was possible, was there any city in the world big enough to hold her?

"Wh-what about . . ." Her voice was full to the brim; she stopped before she spilled something. Instead she gestured silently to the three of them, the whole syndicate trembling at the breakfast table.

"My mother has dictated a thesis," Squire said, "on the hardships of being a bachelor cohabitating with a married couple. I just never thought to apply it to—*oh*, no, please."

Vivian was crying, through an expression of some dismay. The sting of this particular turn had taken her quite by surprise.

Squire reached across the table for her hand, smearing jam between her fingers. "You're not a bachelor," he said.

"But," Oscar said, "perhaps we should let you be one."

The thought of it intruded: Vivian in her own house. Not a bang-up apartment for one-night stands with no food in the cupboards; not a tripartite castle with secret passageways and a Spartan, many-chambered boudoir, a haunted house in which she'd gone so insane she'd ransomed herself to an imaginary lover for five hundred dollars.

Vivian tried to see herself in some entirely new place, one she could not yet even imagine with any specificity. Her bachelor flat. (Or, perhaps, not.)

It is one thing to remodel a mansion for privacy, and spare no expense on the project. It is quite another to feel at ease, to feel *oneself*, in one's home.

Still, the prospect of moving on was not entirely a happy one.

"Divorce?" she asked, looking at Oscar. The word was fragile.

Oscar struggled. "If you'd like," he swallowed. He clicked his rings against each other. "But I would miss it."

Squire, distraught, upset the sugar bowl. This kept all three of them gratefully occupied for some minutes.

"I'll think about it," Vivian said, and closed the subject.

WHATEVER HER THOUGHTS on the proposal, she kept them private during the final weeks of her recovery. She played gin rummy and listened to dispatches full of crackpot amateur seismology read aloud. She focused on small things—skating over the surface of conversations; politely ignoring Oscar and Squire's few tentative attempts to plumb deeper again. (A common reaction, to avoid the repetition of personal vulnerability: it is such a painful experience for the unpracticed, and its benefits so delayed and indirect when compared with its challenges. Many a reasonable person, handicapped by their own intellect, has weighed their options and mindfully chosen relapse.)

She received memoranda on the slow, painful recovery of Clancey & Schmidt. Elias had rented an interim space, to minimize the interruption to production in the short term. Vivian demurred on the central question of whether to rebuild on the site of the former factory—its foundation was still intact—or to look for a new location. Repeatedly, and with uncharacteristic vagueness, she begged more time to consider.

She had her cast removed; continued her strengthening exercises; submitted to the final postoperative examination of her ankle.

And then—overnight, without ceremony or announcement—she disappeared.

SHE LEFT NO forwarding address. Oscar and Squire found her apartment downtown back in the hands of the building manager. (It was soon back on the market; there was almost no wear and tear on the appliances. As if, the owner boasted to prospective tenants, it hadn't even been lived in.)

Oscar and Squire knew their wife well enough to not long indulge their search for sentimental messages left behind—not in her wing, or in their own, or in the shared sitting and dining rooms. They'd all but told her to go; she had gone. What else was there to say? (There was, of course, plenty; there would be enough to occupy the men, in melancholy moments, for the rest of their lives. But we are not all of us cut from the same cloth—and they had long since learned to distinguish their warp from Vivian's weft.)

In the end, they had to be satisfied with noting what she had taken with her: though she'd left behind all her furniture and most of her clothes and jewelry, her wedding band was missing. And of the set of worn and dog-eared cards they'd used for gin rummy, only Squire's deck remained.

Is it fair, to ask one's family to read the implied shape of one's affection in the empty spaces one leaves behind?

For better and for worse, we will all of us have many more opportunities to consider this question.

SOME QUESTIONS WERE easily and immediately decided. Oscar and Squire formally transferred executive control of C&S to Elias Knox, themselves retaining largely ceremonial (and lucrative) positions as board members.

Elias, of course, elected not to rebuild the factory in Manhattan but to move operations to a newly incorporated company town outside North Bergen, New Jersey. It was a success. (Indeed, the plans were so well prepared, and the move so financially advantageous, that the insurance company reopened investigation on the company's claim with additional scrutiny. No foul play was detected—some people, the adjustors concluded, were simply in the right line of work.)

THE NEWLY MINTED C&S buildings were adorned, inside and out, with the artwork of the newly minted Mrs. Rebecca Knox. (Despite the delay it caused, before breaking ground, Elias had the main lobby redesigned to accommodate her mural at an even grander scale than the destroyed original.)

Over the years—eventually decades—of the company's reestablishment and growth, each new building erected was capped by a unique decorative pediment of Rebecca's design. Even long after her death, C&S would continue the tradition, using an uncredited reproduction of her first relief. You can still see them, now, if you remember to look up.

BY THE TIME Oscar and Squire officially retired, they were so little involved with the workings of the company that the difference was largely rhetorical.

Shortly after Vivian's exit, the men gave up the Clancey-Schmidt mansion: it was no longer suited to their practical purposes, and too crowded with memories. For years they all but lived abroad, traveling almost constantly (as geopolitics allowed). After Mrs. Clancey's death, they moved into the Madison Avenue house—and set about reclaiming it, with new memories in every room.

They might, instead, have started over entirely, somewhere less expensive and easier to navigate. Somewhere unburdened by the past. But they were at the mercy of certain impractical attachments. To Manhattan itself, of course—and to the idea that if Vivian ever came back, they wanted her to know where she might find them.

THE CRASH IN 1929 was a blow to their personal finances, and Squire's family fortune was decimated. (They counted themselves lucky that Mrs. Clancey had not lived to see it; and, for their own sakes, that they had not had to attempt to persuade her to economize.) They compensated for the blow: they sold off the houses in Yonkers and Lake Ronkonkoma; they curtailed their travel. But Oscar had been mostly right, in his youthful, miserable, sweaty-palmed speech to Vivian: economies may rise and fall, but hygiene is a constant. The company, gentling to Elias's hand (by now eminent with experience), pivoted temporarily from indulgences like perfumed candles to simple, affordable necessities.

But Personal Care was, for the most part, a Depression-proof concern. (And Mystic Zephyr, for all its frivolous luxury, never entirely ceased to turn a profit.)

INVOLUNTARILY, OVER THE decades, Oscar and Squire became a minor New York institution. They were seen as harmless eccentrics, comically devoted friends and business partners, dining—when in town—every night at Sherry's. (This tradition they continued even after the restaurant moved to its new location in 1919, sliding fifteen blocks up Fifth Avenue to the corner of Fifty-ninth. The men were faithful to their established rituals, but flexible enough to change with the times.) They were not a tourist attraction, or a novelty—certainly people never sought them out—but there were elbows nudged into sides, smiles and whispers concealed behind hands, whenever this insistently matched set of increasingly outdated magnates happened to come strolling (or, later, shuffling) down the pavement. They became cultish figures, an obscure oddity worn the way New York wears all its oddities: with belligerent pride.

Around the middle of the twentieth century, it became an occasional source of fiery debate at Manhattanalia enthusiasts' dinner parties as to which founding partner of Clancey & Schmidt had been the first interred in their adjacent plots in Green-Wood Cemetery—and which had continued to sit vigil nightly at Sherry's for eight months longer, before joining his associate on the other side.

Eventually, it became possible to settle such questions with a few taps on a cracked and fingerprinted telephone screen. But we are practicing—we are drilling ourselves mercilessly in—nonattachment. We are learning to leave questions unsettled, that we might better weather the disappointment when the universe presents us no other option.

C&S, OF COURSE, has long outlived all three of its founders: in its product lines and its scholarship programs; in the sprawl of its company town, and the demographically uneven policing and protection of its residents; in the chemicals and petroleum its shipping containers have spilled into the

Gulf of Mexico; in its responsive environmental initiatives (and accompanying rebranding of certain products); in its relentless pursuit and advertisement of Fairtrade and B Corp certifications; in the minor Springsteen B side about life as a C&S man, still heard blasting from car windows and soundtracking bar fights—never a national hit, but with substantial and persistent play in the local radio market, and a cult favorite in tristate karaoke bars.

And in the temporary adoption, each June, of a rainbow version of its classic C&S logo on social media platforms. In the subsequent, eccentrically capitalized discourse about whether a company like Clancey & Schmidt has ever taken any actual pride in supporting the LGBTQIA+ community.

This question, like so many, remains undecided.

POSTLUDE

D id Vivian, or some version of her, watch any of this happen? Did she ever come back? Where did she *go*?

After her disappearance, speculation on her whereabouts evaporated from New York drawing rooms with equally disturbing speed. But, after all, she had always kept herself aloof.

She was generally understood to have hurt her leg, or possibly developed a respiratory complaint, and to have retired to the country for her health. (Some said Newport, others somewhere on Long Island; still others *Utica*, for some reason.)

She certainly did *not* go to Utica—this much we can say for certain, knowing as we do where and how to seek her there. (Though for the remainder of her parents' lives, checks arrived monthly for their care and nursing—accompanied, from spring 1916 onward, by notes written in a slightly altered hand. The nurse did not recognize it, but her charges seemed to.)

DOES IT SURPRISE you, that we cannot follow Vivian?

But, no—that does not precisely describe the situation.

The fact is that *this* story's Vivian, the Vivian born on a speeding bicycle in 1898, was finished. Once upon a time, she had built herself out of nothing; in the end, she vanished in a cloud of smoke. Transformed into something new, outside the scope of this story. Somewhere off the map.

We cannot know what future versions of her looked like—whether she moved abroad or retired to Florida; whether she became a mother; whether she fell in love, and with whom, and whether it ended happily or unhappily; whether she founded a new, even more successful company, or lived in the woods foraging mushrooms, consciously cultivating a lifestyle immune to capitalist manipulation.

We can't know how many of these Vivians there were, or how long any of them lasted. We might meet them, but would we recognize them? Or would we blink in confusion, unable to clear our vision of our own intervening ghosts?

Still, it is impossible not to see her in the enduring edifice of C&S. Look for her, too, in the people she propelled before her, or dragged in her wake. In spiraling progress and ruin. In the pins she left in the map; in the cascading, unraveling past and future. Feel her ripples; count her rings. This force is within you too. This force is within everyone. Try to keep your footing as the earth rumbles beneath you. You have no time to catch your breath! More is coming! More is already here!

ACKNOWLEDGMENTS

Thanks first and foremost to my agent, Danielle Bukowski, and my editor, Grace McNamee—for the fact that any of this exists, and for being so delightful to work with all along the way. Thanks to everyone at Bloomsbury who contributed to *Mutual Interest*, including Gleni Bartels, Marie Coolman, Paula Dragosh, Valerie Esposito, Emily Fishman, Callie Garnett, Suzanne Keller, Kenli Manning, Rosie Mahorter, Nancy Miller, Lauren Moseley, Jillian Ramirez, Valentina Rice, Olivia Treynor, and Lauren Wilson. Thanks to Brittani Hilles and Amelia Possanza at Lavender Public Relations for helping this book find its people, and to all those who have been generous with their time and with their words along the road to publication.

To write about New York City is always, in part, to mythologize. In many ways, the same is true of the personal care industry. All liberties taken, inconsistencies indulged, and errors made are my own. Among many other resources, I am indebted to the collections and exhibits of the Brooklyn Botanic Garden, the Metropolitan Museum of Art, Luray Caverns, the National Park Service, the New-York Historical Society, the New York Public Library, the New York Transit Museum, and the Preservation Society of Newport County. I'm grateful to Alison Brown for illuminating the art and science of soap production. Helpful and inspiring texts included *American Colossus* by H. W. Brands, *Utica: For a Century and a Half* by T. Wood Clarke, *Low Life* by Lucy Sante, *The Chemical History of a Candle* by Michael Faraday, *The Big Oyster* by Mark Kurlansky, *Annals of the Former World* by John McPhee, *Nose Dive* by Harold McGee (by which Oscar and Squire's conversation about the scent of outer space is particularly informed), *Perfume* by Lizzie Ostrom, *Scent* by Elise Vernon Pearlstine, *When Brooklyn Was Queer* by Hugh Ryan, *Camera Man* by Dana Stevens, and *The Decoration of Houses* by Edith Wharton and Ogden Codman Jr. I am especially delighted to acknowledge Blair Rainsford's *Scholastic News Grade 2* story "The Volcano That

Stopped Summer," which introduced me to Mount Tambora and its connection to the invention of the bicycle.

Squire's copy of *Les Misérables* is Charles E. Wilbour's translation.

Thanks to the Firefeet—Emily Alford, Charlie Beckerman, and CJ Hauser—for their gifts of accountability, feedback, and all varieties of support, large and small. And to Laura Steadham Smith, Leo Hunt, and Vanessa Saunders, both for their thoughtful notes and for the invaluable favor of asking me, early on, to articulate what I was trying to do.

This project, even more than most, kept me mindful of the many-faceted relationship between creativity and capitalism. I am grateful both for my day job and for my fellow members and organizers of the News-Guild of New York, which together allow me both to support myself and to protect my free time to write.

This is a book concerned with webs of influence. A profound thanks to everyone who has been a part of mine—the deep community of friends and family, teachers and classmates, acquaintances and strangers who have shaped and will continue to shape my life, through all of its seasons.

And thanks as always to Jude Wetherell, for everything.

A NOTE ON THE AUTHOR

OLIVIA WOLFGANG-SMITH is the author of *Glassworks*, which was long-listed for the Center for Fiction First Novel Prize. She holds an MFA in creative writing from Florida State University and lives in Brooklyn with her partner.